Praise for the novels of Patricia Rice

"Patricia Rice's historicals are deliciously fresh, sexy, and fun."
—Mary Jo Putney

Magic Man

"Never slows down until the final thread is magically resolved. Patricia Rice is clearly the Magic Woman with this superb tale and magnificent series."
—*Midwest Book Review*

Much Ado About Magic

"The magical Rice takes Trev and Lucinda, along with her readers, on a passionate, sensual, and romantic adventure in this fast-paced, witty, poignant, and magical tale of love."
—*Romantic Times* (Top Pick, 4½ stars)

This Magic Moment

"This charming and immensely entertaining tale . . . takes a smart, determined heroine who will accept nothing less than true love and an honorable hero who eventually realizes what love is and sets them on course to solve a mystery, save an entire estate, and find the magic of love."
—*Library Journal*

"Rice has a magical touch for creating fascinating plots, delicious romance, and delightful characters both flesh-and-blood and ectoplasmic. Readers new to her Magic series will be overjoyed to learn that she has told the stories of other Malcolm women and their loves in previous books."
—*Booklist*

"Another delightful, magical story brought to us by this talented author. It's a fun read, romantic and sexy with enchanting characters."
—*Rendezvous*

continued . . .

The Trouble with Magic

"Rice is a marvelously talented author who skillfully combines pathos with humor in a stirring, sensual romance that shows the power of love is the most wondrous gift of all. Think of this memorable story as a present you can open again and again." —*Romantic Times*

"Rice's third enchanting book about the Malcolm sisters is truly spellbinding." —*Booklist*

Must Be Magic

"Very sensual." —*The Romance Reader*

"Rice has created a mystical masterpiece full of enchanting characters, a spellbinding plot, and the sweetest of romances." —*Booklist* (starred review)

"An engaging historical romance that uses a pinch of witchcraft to spice up a tale with a rarely seen uniqueness. The story line mesmerizes. . . . Fans will believe that Patricia Rice must be magical as she spellbinds her audience with a one-sitting fun novel." —*Midwest Book Review*

"I love an impeccably researched, well-written tale, and *Must Be Magic*, which continues the saga of the Iveses and Malcolms, is about as good as it gets. I'm very pleased to give it a Perfect Ten, and I encourage everyone to pick up this terrific book. It will brighten your summer."

—Romance Reviews Today

Merely Magic

"Simply enchanting! Patricia Rice, a master storyteller, weaves a spellbinding tale that's passionate and powerful."

—Teresa Medeiros

"Like Julie Garwood, Patricia Rice employs wicked wit and sizzling sensuality to turn the battle of the sexes into a magical romp." —Mary Jo Putney

"*Merely Magic* is one of those tales that you pick up and can't put down. . . . She is a gifted master storyteller: with *Merely Magic* she doesn't disappoint. Brava!"

—*Midwest Book Review*

Other Historical Romances by Patricia Rice

The "Magic" Series

Merely Magic
Must Be Magic
The Trouble with Magic
This Magic Moment
Much Ado About Magic
Magic Man

Other Titles

All a Woman Wants

Mystic Guardian

Patricia Rice

A SIGNET ECLIPSE BOOK

SIGNET ECLIPSE
Published by New American Library, a division of
Penguin Group (USA) Inc., 375 Hudson Street,
New York, New York 10014, USA
Penguin Group (Canada), 90 Eglinton Avenue East, Suite 700, Toronto,
Ontario M4P 2Y3, Canada (a division of Pearson Penguin Canada Inc.)
Penguin Books Ltd., 80 Strand, London WC2R 0RL, England
Penguin Ireland, 25 St. Stephen's Green, Dublin 2,
Ireland (a division of Penguin Books Ltd.)
Penguin Group (Australia), 250 Camberwell Road, Camberwell, Victoria 3124,
Australia (a division of Pearson Australia Group Pty. Ltd.)
Penguin Books India Pvt. Ltd., 11 Community Centre, Panchsheel Park,
New Delhi - 110 017, India
Penguin Group (NZ), 67 Apollo Drive, Rosedale, North Shore 0745,
Auckland, New Zealand (a division of Pearson New Zealand Ltd.)
Penguin Books (South Africa) (Pty.) Ltd., 24 Sturdee Avenue,
Rosebank, Johannesburg 2196, South Africa

Penguin Books Ltd., Registered Offices:
80 Strand, London WC2R 0RL, England

First published by Signet Eclipse, an imprint of New American Library,
a division of Penguin Group (USA) Inc.

First Printing, July 2007
10 9 8 7 6 5 4 3 2 1

Printed in the United States of America

To my own mystical guardian, who stands between me and reality when my mind drifts into the ether in search of strange new worlds.

And for those who believe history repeats itself until we've learned our lessons, this one's for you.

Prologue

Brittany, June 1789

"I dreamed of bread last night," Franc[illegible] longingly, rubbing her pregnant [illegible] yeasty bread with a crisp crust fresh from [illegible]."

At these words, Mariel St. Just suffered [illegible] deep that even the cramping of hunger paled in comparison. How could they—daughters of a [illegible] mayor—come to such dire straits that she [illegible] even feed her sister's unborn child?

"You will have that bread, as soon as [illegible] turns," she said, hoping the lie might [illegible], although after the drought and hail last [illegible] and the extreme cold this past winter, wheat was [illegible] as gold, and the money to buy it was [illegible] scarce.

While her sister dreamed of bread, Mariel [illegible] sioned savory hares and bubbling stews [illegible] gravy. She had attempted to net fish [illegible] she'd walked home empty-handed and [illegible] ever from the exertion. Her stomach [illegible] painfully when she'd passed the castle [illegible]. The air had been redolent with the aroma [illegible] venison, because even if nobles didn't have [illegible] owned the land on which the game roamed.

No one in the village had had meat [illegible] since early this spring, when the starving [illegible]

Prologue

Brittany, June 1789

"I dreamed of bread last night," Francine murmured longingly, rubbing her pregnant belly. "Soft, yeasty bread with a crisp crust fresh from the oven."

At these words, Mariel St. Just suffered a pain so deep that even the cramping of hunger paled in comparison. How could they—daughters of a former mayor—come to such dire straits that they couldn't even feed her sister's unborn child?

"You will have that bread, as soon as Eduard returns," she said, hoping the lie might become truth, although after the drought and hail last summer, and the extreme cold this past winter, wheat was as costly as gold, and the money to buy it was even more scarce.

While her sister dreamed of bread, Mariel had envisioned savory hares and bubbling stews with rich gravy. She had attempted to net fish yesterday, but she'd walked home empty-handed and hungrier than ever from the exertion. Her stomach had clenched painfully when she'd passed the castle on the cliff. The air had been redolent with the aroma of roasting venison, because even if nobles didn't have a sou, they owned the land on which the game roamed.

No one in the village had had meat to fill their pot since early this spring, when the starving menfolk had defied the game laws and mowed down the vicomte's fields and clubbed the wild creatures hiding there. Since then, the vicomte had hired militia to protect his lands.

Mariel helped ease her sister into a rocking chair in the sunny front window of the cottage and gave thanks that they had a solid roof over their heads, courtesy of her brother-in-law, Eduard Rousseau. She prayed for his safe return from Paris, where he met with the other elected officials of the Assembly, intending to ask the king for reforms to repair the country's bankruptcy. If only he would return soon. Her sister desperately needed him.

"Tell me again about Maman's promise," Francine said wistfully, picking up her lace-making pillow. "I want to hear happy stories so the babe will be born sunny-natured."

As the eldest by four years, Mariel had memories of their mother that Francine did not. She shared as generously as she could, but Francine did not possess their mother's special gifts and could never understand her as Mariel did. Perhaps it was better that way. The baby would no doubt be as contented as Francine, never knowing the anguish that Mariel experienced because she was *special*. Maman's word for her eldest daughter's differences didn't ease the danger of her oddity, or the loneliness of not fitting in anywhere. Only her family knew and accepted what she was, and loved her anyway.

"Maman looked so beautiful that day," Mariel began the story. "Her ebony hair never had a thread of gray, and it was long, oh so long, down to her waist and past. Her eyes were lovely and tranquil."

"Was she sitting up?" Francine rocked gently, asking the questions she had as a nine-year-old child, after their mother's death.

"No, this was one of her last days, when she lay against the lace-trimmed pillow from her trousseau. She always worked the lace so beautifully. I could never learn lace making as you have."

Mariel couldn't sit still as she told the tale. Restlessness drove her to dust the shelf of precious possessions from their former home, avoiding the tomes of the rebellious Diderot and Voltaire that Eduard perused so often. She watched out the window for any sign of change in this miserable life to which all of France had been reduced. She saw one of the vicomte's soldiers idling in the narrow cobblestone street and felt a frisson of fear that the village had come to this state of neighbor armed against neighbor.

"You have Maman's forceful character, and I have her talent. That is fair," Francine said, as she always did. "Finish the story."

"Forceful character," Mariel said with a laugh. "You mean I am bossy and order people about."

"You get things done. People listen to you."

"I think I inherited our father's character, not Maman's," she teased. "I must do everything myself, while Maman promised us a golden god who would save us. A *god*, not a goddess, you'll notice. Like you, she awaited a man."

"Eduard cannot help it if the Assembly argues lengthily. He will return as quickly as he is able."

"Eduard is a good man," Mariel agreed, "but I cannot believe the Assembly can help if the king's ministers tell them that we must eat grass."

"The story, please," Francine murmured, rubbing her belly. "The babe is restless today, and I would calm him rather than raise a rebel."

Nine months pregnant, Francine sought comfort and reassurance for her child's future—a future that grew more grim with each passing day. These were uncertain times. On days like this, it seemed only a god *could* save them.

Mariel patted Francine's arm reassuringly, and she spoke the story in the singsong voice of their childhood. "You'll remember Maman's eyes, how they went all dreamy when she prophesied, as if she were seeing heaven?" At Francine's eager nod, she continued. "Well, she smiled as if seeing angels, and she sounded proud and strong, and oh, so certain. Just ask Agnes and Belle. They will tell you."

As the maids had told the entire village. The prophecy had become legend, and these days the villagers surreptitiously scoured the harbor, waiting for it to come true.

"Maman looked straight at me," Mariel continued, "and said, 'You have the eyes of the sea, Mariel.'" She rubbed away a tear, knowing Maman had been the last person to understand her daughter's odd proclivities. "Then she squeezed my hand and said, 'Watch for the golden god who will sail in on a ship from the past, lured by the Song of the Siren. He will bear a sword of justice to save all in our village in a time of great famine and danger. He will be stronger than Hercules, faster than an Arabian steed, and more beautiful than a sun-blessed day.'"

Even Mariel's stomach quit complaining as she repeated their mother's vow.

Francine smiled in satisfaction. "I like the part about the Siren. When we were little and lived in the big house by the sea, I used to imagine I heard the Siren sing from the legendary isle of Ys. Her song was my lullaby after Maman died."

It had been Mariel's song of loneliness and grief that Francine had heard, but she would not mar her sister's sweet memory. Since their mother's death, she had vowed to use her special abilities to protect her younger sister from all hurt.

In recent months she had been failing to keep that vow.

Outside, a shout drew her back to the window. Old Yanick was racing this way, his gray beard flying across his shoulder as his wooden sabots clumped the cobblestones. Yanick never ran anywhere. That he stirred himself in this manner foretold something momentous, and both hope and dread caught in Mariel's throat.

"The god, Mari, the god is here!" she thought he cried.

Had their hunger and longing and the oft-repeated story conjured the golden god Maman had promised? Or, driven by her own desire, had she misheard what he was really saying?

Mariel caught the wistful gleam in Francine's eyes, and without a second cynical thought she rushed out to meet the old fisherman, praying that dreams really could come true.

One

More beautiful than a sun-blessed day.

As promised, the god stood on the prow of the ship, his broad shoulders and golden hair outlined against the setting sun, the light capturing the sharp angle of his bronzed cheekbones.

Mariel gaped in awestruck shock and nearly stumbled to her knees in relief at first sight of Mama's promise. The filling sails accentuated the god's image of power and command as the sleek ship raced beneath his booted feet and the sun glinted off the jeweled scabbard at his side. In billowing [illegible] and gold-embroidered vest, he stood head and shoulders above all the common sailors rushing about [illegible] lines and raising sails. The strong brown column of his throat emerged from the open lacing of his shirt, and Mariel thrilled at the sight. He was golden [illegible]

If the god her mother had predicted truly existed, this giant of a man with his square jaw and air of confidence must be he. Seeing him from the top of the bluff, Mariel almost wept in gratitude that once more her mother's prophecies had come true. They were saved! Francine would eat again. [illegible] would be born healthy. All would be well.

And then, as she waved a greeting and [illegible] for the path leading down to the beach, he turned away.

One

More beautiful than a sun-blessed day . . .

As promised, the god stood on the deck of the ship, his broad shoulders and golden hair outlined against the setting sun, the light capturing the stark angle of his bronzed cheekbones.

Mariel gaped in awestruck shock and nearly stumbled to her knees in relief at first sight of Maman's promise. The filling sails accentuated the god's stance of power and command as the sleek ship rolled beneath his booted feet and the sun glinted off the jeweled scabbard at his side. In billowing shirtsleeves and gold-embroidered vest, he stood head and shoulders above all the common sailors rushing about, knotting lines and raising sails. The strong brown column of his throat emerged from the open lacing of his shirt, and Mariel thrilled at the sight. He was golden all over.

If the god her mother had predicted truly existed, this giant of a man with his square jaw and air of confidence must be he. Seeing him from the top of the bluff, Mariel almost wept in gratitude that once more her mother's prophecies had come true. They were saved! Francine would eat again. The babe would be born healthy. All would be well. . . .

And then, as she waved a greeting and raced for the path leading down to the beach, he turned away to watch more of the ship's sails unfurl in preparation for catching the outgoing tide.

Waves of despair and fury washed over her as cruelly as the ocean wore away the rock. The ship had weighed anchor and was ready to sail away! *He can't leave! The golden god is supposed to save Francine.*

Standing on the bluffs above the harbor, Mariel choked on a half sob and pressed her fist to her lips as the wind licked the canvas sails. Hunger brought her emotions too close to the surface these days, and she wrestled with her failure now.

The cries of the gulls wailed her dismay.

Maman's predictions were *never* wrong. She had promised a golden god would save the village from dire straits. Mariel didn't think a single person in the village would survive if their situation became any more desperate.

She was the only one who could act on Maman's predictions. It was her task to do so, as her father had before her. But she'd arrived too late.

No, she hadn't. She'd been here on time. The wretched man simply refused to wait! More must be required of her.

With the force of fear goading her, she scrambled down the rocks.

On this, his last journey into the world outside his own, Trystan l'Enforcer admired the cliffs of Brittany without a trace of regret. He was looking forward to what awaited him at home, the life for which he'd prepared these many years.

Behind him, the sails of his pride and joy, the *Sword of Destiny*, rose in preparation for catching the tide that once and for all would carry him back to Aelynn.

Odd that at this moment of rejoicing he heard a poignant cry of defeat echo over the wail of the wind, a cry that reached deep down inside, as if to draw him back to shore. With the strong breeze whipping his hair, he scanned the scene for the source of the sound and was arrested by the sight of a Breton maiden standing atop the bluff, waving her farewells. Tall and slender, her cap a lacy crown against her ebony hair, she wore the long black skirt and pristine white apron that identified her as a simple villager, unlike the richly dressed merchants with whom he often dealt. He had learned many things about modes of dress in countries other than his own, knowledge he must pass on to his nephew, who would sail the *Destiny* once Trystan married and took his place on the Council.

"Now there's a lass someone has made happy." Nevan l'Nauta, Trystan's Navigator and closest friend, watched the willowy girl shout and wave from the path. "Can you read lips in that language? What does she say?"

"She tells us to wait," Trystan replied, his gaze not wavering from the comely wench. "She needs to speak with us." He stood at the rail, boots spaced widely, adjusting to the rise and fall of the ship as a gust tugged his shirtsleeves and blew the maid's words away.

The tide was on the way out. This was the moment he reveled in—when ship, man, and sea became one, and home became more tangible than just a thought.

There was no chance of waiting, even for this comely miss.

But for some inexplicable reason, he could scarcely tear his gaze from her mouth, as if an invisible tether had bound his eyes to her lips. And to her nimble figure as she scrambled down the rocks, calling. . . .

Abruptly, the wind stilled, abandoning the sails with a single loud slap of the canvas, as if it, too, felt the tension of her call and dared not interfere.

"What is happening?" cried a crewman from the rigging, puzzled by the sudden calm.

With trepidation, Trystan wrenched his gaze from the vision on the cliff to search the sagging sails and the clouds above. Nothing marred the perfection of blue sky and calm wave. What sorcery was this?

The cries from shore merged with those of the gulls above and the sea creatures below, calling him to turn back. . . .

Nonsense. Trystan snarled in denial, setting his shoulders, resisting the call. His future lay ahead, on the beautiful isle he called home. The wind did not stop and the gulls did not cry for him, but for a caprice of nature. The woman was a mere distraction.

Without warning, the canvas again filled with a stiff breeze, seeming as eager as he to be off. Or more like the *Destiny*'s captain, Waylan Tempestium, had stirred the winds. Dismissing the maiden's futile cries, Trystan crossed his arms, leaned his hip against the rail, and forced his thoughts back to the future. "Despite the charm of Brittany's maidens, I'm eager to return to the black sand of Aelynn," he said with firm assurance.

"Are you missing the sand, or Lissandra?" Nevan responded with a laugh. "If absence makes the heart grow fonder, she should be on the beach, waving you home."

Trystan tried to picture cool, enigmatic Lissandra waving joyfully—or even furiously—like the maid on the bluff, and could not. "If she makes room for me at the dinner table, I will be grateful. We are of a like mind."

"You both love our island home and wish to guide its future," Nevan agreed.

Trystan caught another glimpse of the woman approaching the shore. She had lifted her skirts to scramble down the path, revealing fine ankles. He wished he had been the lucky man who'd wooed her during the brief hours they'd spent in this coastal village.

He shook his head to dislodge his whimsy. As a man driven by his sense of duty, he'd resisted the ladies on this short journey. Given her gift as a Seer, Lissandra was bound to know if another woman held his thoughts, and her stubborn nature would require that he pay—with great pain, no doubt. He grinned, imagining the form of his intended's revenge, even as he continued to watch the lass clamber expertly down the rocky path, shouting and gesturing.

The increasing wind blew the flaps of his vest, tugging his hair loose from its binding, and he swayed with the roll of the rising waves. "Maybe some other time, fair one," he shouted, although he knew she could not hear over the roar of the breakers.

"You don't think one of our men has made her promises?" Nevan asked with interest as the lithe dynamo recklessly grabbed boulders and slid on wooden sabots to the sandy shore, as if she would dive in after them.

Did he mistake, or had she just called him a rude name? Judging by the way she shook her fist, he assumed those weren't pleasantries she was hurling.

"It wouldn't be the first time, nor the last." Trystan sighed his regret as the beautiful creature ran down the beach through the foam, her skirts up to her knees, exposing shapely calves. "We all know we must choose carefully, but she seems hale and hearty enough, if a bit thin. Ask around, see if her suitor left sufficient coin to last her until next time. From all reports, they've had drought this past year, and the harsh winter has driven the fish away."

He watched as the lass caught the cap falling from her loosened hair, then flung it down and stomped it into the wet sand left by the receding tide. The wind captured long glossy curls and tossed them over her shoulder.

"Her hair is the black of Aelynn's sands." Trystan nodded at the furious female. Then, fighting a strange longing for what he could not have, he deliberately turned and walked away. He was going home. For him, that was freedom—freedom to finally begin his future as he had planned.

He had been groomed since birth for the privilege and power of a princedom that did not exist to the Outside World. For the good of all, it must remain that way. His home wasn't called Aelynn, the Mystic Isle, for naught.

Mariel's heart sank in despair as the ship caught the tide and rode it to the open sea. But she refused to spend another day watching the villagers die. Her mother's prophecy had to be true. If still more was required of her, then more she would do. She had never attempted such an impossible goal as the one before her now, but she could not let the ship escape without her.

She seldom dared indulge her rare gift in daylight, but she would risk discovery in order to fulfill the prophecy.

She stepped into a cavity in an outcropping of rock, kicked off her shoes, and ungartered her stockings. Coarse sand squeezed between her toes while she unfastened her skirt and bodice ties. The breeze pressed her linen chemise against her breasts and caught tendrils of her unbound hair as she stashed her clothes into a hole she'd often used for this purpose.

On land, she must conform to the ways of civilization, but she was never as comfortable on land as she was in water, and unlike her neighbors, the fish did not mind what she wore.

In only her thin chemise, she raced into the pounding surf. Filling her lungs with fresh salt air, Mariel dived into the icy pool just beyond the shoals where the dolphins swam. With a powerful surge of joy, she glided beneath the waves and darted under the surface like a minnow. The strength of a lifetime's practice took her out beyond the shoals in a few deft strokes.

Time lost its meaning as she swam, weaving in and out among the sea creatures, following the shadow of the retreating ship's hull, closing the distance between her and her mother's golden promise. Despite her rage at the retreating god, she shivered with delight to be at one with the sea again. Overhead, the sun sank toward the horizon, blurring the lines between light and dark.

Mariel had learned long ago that she might feel her way through water darkened by night, but she preferred the noontime waters, when the sun glittered like diamonds overhead and she could follow the sea bass as she pleased. Usually she herded schools of bass toward the fishing boats, but this winter the harsh cold had sent the fish to more southern climes, and the fishermen had retired to port.

Pleased that she had caught up with the ship, she surfaced just as a towrope dropped over the bow and dangled within reach. Now that night was upon her, she saw no sense in exhausting herself more than was necessary.

She knotted a loop into the rope and swung into the seat she'd created. The sky glimmered with constellations, though the morning star winked on the horizon. She'd never swum so long or so hard before. She'd never needed to. Despite her pumping lungs and failing strength, she was bursting with exhilaration. She wrapped her arm in the rope and sang a dolphin song while she untangled her hair with her fingers.

The golden god had led her to her natural element. Here, she was free from the burdens and limitations of home, and her heart soared with the melody that emerged from her lips. She swung gently in the cool night air, enjoying the salt scent and the rocking ship as it cut through the waves. She had never traveled so far in all her life. Even the stars above looked different.

There was so much she could do, so much she could learn, if only she could spend her time beneath the waves instead of tending her duties at home. Her soul longed for the freedom to frolic beneath the moonlit sky, to explore the mysteries of the sea bottom, to find a heart to match her own. . . .

But she was the only creature like herself that existed.

"The towrope has been thrown over the bow. Already the Sirens sing sweetly as they tug us home," Nevan said, entering the captain's cabin.

At his friend's words, Trystan's thoughts drifted to the lass on the beach, calling her siren song urging him to return.

Foolishness.

Waylan, who acted as captain on this voyage, jotted a note in his log. " 'Tis just the song of night and wind and sail. It's a silly superstition that our women will tow us home if we hang a rope over the side, but it convinces the crew we sail faster."

Despite his scarred visage, Waylan charmed the ladies with his enigmatic silences, but in private, he was a no-nonsense man who kept informative notes for the next generation of sailors. His mother had been from England, and he'd spent the better part of his youth compensating for his lowly breeding—until the full extent of his weathermaking ability had become known. It was an honor for him to be trusted with this mission to ensure Aelynn's security by confirming that their former friend Murdoch LeDroit had been rendered powerless in his banishment.

The ship belonged to Trystan. The son of a powerful Enforcer and a gifted Healer, he had known influence and prestige since birth. The sea voyages were merely a stepping-stone on the path to his destiny: marriage to Lissandra and assuming Council leadership. It was fitting that he should lead the expedition to confirm that Murdoch remained safely in exile and was no longer able to use his unpredictable powers to bring harm to Aelynners.

Knowing that Murdoch's banishment had opened his own path to marrying Lissandra and assuming Council leadership nagged at Trystan's conscience, but he had not been on the island when the Oracle made her decision. If the gods had so chosen, he must accept it, though the loss of the island's most promising talent worried him.

Still, he preferred the distraction of a solid political topic to the strange notions engendered by the call of a black-haired maiden running along the shore.

"I realize you are content in knowing Murdoch has employed his dangerous skills in the army of a king," Trystan said, continuing a conversation that had been interrupted by Nevan's entrance. "But I'm afraid that punishing him for a malicious prank that went awry has merely removed any control we once had over him."

"He killed a man with that prank!" Nevan objected. "Perhaps he only meant to celebrate Luther's birthday, as he claimed, but his use of explosives to do so was ill-advised."

Luther had been Council Leader, spouse of the Oracle—the island's highest authority—and Lissandra's father. Trystan still couldn't believe the powerful old man was dead.

"Especially when Murdoch let Lissandra anger him," Waylan agreed with a grunt. "He was never able to control his firepower when in a temper. He knew better."

Trystan had seen an infuriated Murdoch accidentally set dry leaves on fire and send rapiers flying from scabbards. As the baseborn child of a hearthwitch, Murdoch should have had no powers at all. Instead, he had been one of those rare Aelynners whose passionate emotions entangled with his talents until the two were not easily separated or controlled. But Murdoch had been a boy when the worst depredations had occurred. Surely by now he'd learned some way of commanding his strengths. He'd had plenty of teachers.

But he possessed a combination of abilities never before seen in any Aelynner. No one person possessed enough knowledge to teach him how to prevent destruction when he was unhappy or angry. And he was very often both, since, even on Aelynn, people feared and despised what they didn't understand. It would be enough to cause even the strongest of minds to run amok.

"The Oracle could have done nothing less than suppress him," Nevan said. "Luther's death seemed like an assassination to her. Even had the explosives not collapsed the platform, the noise and flame alone would have given him a failure of the heart that even Lissandra could not heal."

"The Oracle fears Murdoch for sound reason, I

grant that, but banishing him after having already reclaimed his powers . . ." Trystan shook his head. "I am relieved he's merely taken up soldiering and not decided to appoint himself dictator of France."

Nevan laughed. "France is full of petty dictators. He'll make himself king."

Given the weakness of France's Louis XVI, Trystan thought that Murdoch as ruler might be an improvement. Using their abilities to interfere in the events of other countries was forbidden for their kind but, since his banishment Murdoch need no longer heed the island's legal restraints.

Banishment had been a mistake, in Trystan's opinion. Even though the Oracle had suppressed Murdoch's troublesome talents, he was still an Aelynner with speed beyond that of mortal men and training in weaponry that could be put to good or evil.

Trystan prayed to Aelynn that Murdoch chose the path of good, but with an intellect far exceeding that of most humans, Murdoch was an unstable powder keg. Thank the gods that the ring of silence prevented his ever speaking of his home, or all would be lost of a certainty.

Rather than fret over issues he could not control, Trystan leaned back in his seat at the table, crossed his boots on a chair, and listened to the seductive song of the wind. A vision teased the back of his mind, of a slim figure racing toward him, her voice joining with the song of the sea. Loneliness and hunger for something he could not name seeped under his skin.

Trystan inhaled sharply at the treachery of his scrambled wits and slammed his boots back to the floor. "We've been too long at sea when we hear a woman's voice in the breeze," he growled. "It's the reason seafarers speak of mermaids and Sirens."

With a grunt, Waylan scooped a scrawny animal

from under his desk and shoved the creature across the polished floor with his foot, displaying a ragged hole chewed into his sailor's trousers. "You are fortunate we did not need to eat your scrawny beastie while we were away. I'm particularly fond of goat meat."

Unperturbed by the threat, Trystan rescued the kid, scooping it into his lap and scratching behind a silky ear to be rewarded with a butt on his chin from a bony head. Sprawling his long legs, he relaxed at this reminder that he was going home. "This beastie is a rare breed," he replied, stroking his pet's fine thick coat. "Her hair will spin like silk."

Nevan laughed. "It will take more than silk to win Lissandra's favor. You do not fear some other man has wooed and won her while you were gone?"

"Lissandra will do what is best for all. She and I agree that a man experienced in the Outside World is needed to guide us into the future. Her mother is too entrenched in the old ways to see that the world is changing, and we must change with it."

Waylan snorted. "The island never changes. The world has no effect on it. Lissy is simply feeding you what you want to hear so she can beat her brother to the Oracle's chair."

"That's unfair," Trystan corrected. "They both know their mother grows weaker without Luther's aid. They wish to take the heavy burden of power off her shoulders so she may rest and enjoy the remainder of her years."

Nevan refilled their glasses. "I, for one, believe it's superstition to think the Oracle must have a spouse in order to keep the island safe. Dylys acted swiftly enough to banish Murdoch when his power went to his head."

"I believe the Oracle should not have the power of a dictator," Waylan said. "She acted arbitrarily, without giving Murdoch a chance to argue his case. She could have *killed* the man by stripping him of his powers. I'm relieved to discover he survived the ordeal."

Trystan had occasionally questioned the authority of the Oracle and her spouse to rule with only the guidance of the Council, but if the gods chose the Oracle, then surely the gods chose the best person for the island. "Only time will tell if Dylys was right, so let us enjoy the good wine and not waste our last day aboard with unanswerable questions."

He swallowed his wine and wished he could follow his own advice, but the lady on the cliff had unsettled him. Perhaps Murdoch's banishment had shaken the island—and him—in some elemental way he did not fathom.

Outside the candlelit cabin, the Siren's voice harmonized with the wind in a melancholy verse that echoed Trystan's unease.

Two

"There she is," Trystan said quietly, respectfully, as the *Destiny* approached a fog bank in the midst of rocky shoals. No sign of land could be seen through the murk, but he sensed the isle's solid presence. Black boulders the size of brigantines loomed over them, casting the slim schooner in shadow, but Nevan's unerring senses would steer them safely through the narrow, winding passages.

In the centuries of Aelynn's history, no Outsider had ever navigated the island's formidable straits—no Outsider could and live to tell about it. The coral reefs below the surface were even more dangerous than the rocks that could be seen above it, and the defensive force field that the Guardian maintained around the island would allow none but an Aelynner to pass.

"The fog is a beautiful sight with dawn's light above her. Even the towline is taut with eagerness," Waylan remarked, speaking Trystan's thoughts.

Standing in the darkened bow, Trystan lifted his arms to the threatening fog, spreading his fingertips to catch the mist, then curling his hands into fists. His schooner had been empowered to pass the shield that he enforced, but he took pleasure in feeling Aelynn's energy surge through his body. He knew that once they penetrated the barrier and emerged from the cloud, he would glow with the strength of the sun, but for now he was content to feel the power that his absence had depleted.

Satisfied that all in his world was well and thriving, Trystan returned his hands to the rail and rolled his shoulders to relax them as the ship entered the final shrouded channel.

"The first time I saw you do that when we were but lads, I thought you were a sorcerer, and you terrified me," Waylan said, leaning against the rail, happy to let Nevan take the wheel at this stage of their journey.

"I was only practicing then. I could do nothing but feel the energy my father created. At the time, I thought you little better than a feral wolf who would drown us in your tears."

Waylan snorted. "It is hard to remember my days as a Crossbreed who never knew Aelynn's ways, and I'd prefer to keep it like that. The island is a paradise in comparison."

Even though the ship had yet to breech the barrier, a scent of citrus and gardenia permeated the moist air, and through the fog the sun shone golden beams. Even the water was of a crystalline clarity not found anywhere else on this earth. Although the island's volcano could not be seen past the high walls of the channel, Trystan knew the peak loomed protectively over them, ever watchful.

"I would have no child of mine grow up alone and misunderstood, far from these shores, as you were," Trystan said, remembering the wild creature Waylan had been when he'd first arrived. The previous Finder had rescued him from a flood in England that the untrained Weathermaker had brought on out of grief for the death of his parents. "It is another reason I prefer to remain on Aelynn, where my children will know only safety," he added.

Waylan laughed. "Children are as tough as your little

beasties." He shoved away the goat nibbling at his trousers. "They adapt. *You* grow soft with moonlove."

For a moment, Trystan let down his inner shield to consider the gifted orphans his fellow sailors often spawned and left behind, and an appalling thought occurred to him. Could *Murdoch* pass on his erratic traits to his children, even if he'd been stripped of his power? Waylan might joke about sorcerers, but Murdoch came as close to one as any mortal could imagine.

Trystan shook off his unease, and closed his mind again on what he could not change, choosing to revel in the future awaiting him, just moments away. Both he and Waylan had discarded their Other World clothes for more comfortable island ones, and the breeze blew with tropical warmth against their loose linen. Could they be seen by Outsiders now, they'd be labeled pirates. It wouldn't be the first time. Long hair, jeweled scabbards, and uncivilized clothing suited island life better than that of the Outside World.

Trystan rested his hand on the hilt of his sword and embraced the roll of waves beneath his feet. "I haven't grown soft," he told Waylan. "Just eager for the next phase of my life."

"Tupping Lissandra?" Waylan grinned as they passed a barnacle-covered boulder. "You may as well tup a fish. The two of you may be just cold enough to make good leaders. Your ambition hardens you."

Sensing that they were about to enter the force field, Trystan braced himself with feet wide apart, and wrapped his fingers on the rail on either side of the prow. The field didn't part so much as *yield* as the ship sliced through the first layer of energy. The power crackled up his arms and legs through the rail and deck, strong and thick as he'd designed it. The shield was still resilient. It wasn't time for him to renew it.

"I'm practical, not hard. Consider all the men suited for Lissandra's hand. Is there one besides me who could be her equal?" Since he had begun to glow with the first touch of the island's force field, Trystan was aware of his consequence. The gods touched few. He was fortunate to be one of them. Trystan hooked his fists in his trouser band and let the energy flow around him.

"Ambitious and arrogant." Waylan nodded in wry agreement. "Lissandra would eat her offspring alive without a strong spouse to temper her natural inclinations. There is still Iason to consider. Should he find a wife, the Oracle might more readily pass on her seat to her son. His nature is more amenable than his sister's."

"Iason cannot take his mother's place without a political spouse to balance him, and there is no other woman on the island strong enough to lead the Council," Trystan said without hostility, concentrating on the island's invisible protection. Had he just felt a ripple that had not been there before? Or had his earlier unease simply caused a refraction of energy? "Iason has the nature of a monk and will never marry."

Waylan laughed aloud—until a crack of thunder boomed.

That was more than a ripple in the force field.

Both men tensed. The schooner sailed through the drenching fog that shielded the translucent barrier. Water dripped from the ship's masts. Boulders mere feet from their faces were no more than dark shadows. Even the birds ceased to call in this thick porridge. The single unfurled sail caught the slight breeze that Waylan had set in motion when he'd handed the wheel to Nevan.

No lightning flashed. Silence reigned among the rocks as the boat glided through the passage, but the boom had shaken the shield—which meant it had disturbed Trystan to his core. He'd never been so unsettled, and his foreboding rose as the fog lifted. Anyone attempting to sail this passage who was not a ring-bearing Aelynner would hit the force field and his ship would sink—*without sound.*

Unable to discover any disturbance beyond that one slight shiver, Trystan asked Waylan, "You would know if a storm had moved in, wouldn't you?"

"That was no storm," Waylan said. He stalked off to examine the ship for damage, as a good captain should.

With his inner senses, Trystan searched the gray cloud that closed behind them, and still found no gap in his shield. As always, he glowed with the dawn lighting the other side of the fog, as if nothing singular had happened.

Aside from his gift with languages, he had no skill for weather or navigation or whatever was useful to his fellow sailors. His main contribution to the island was defense—a unique transmission between him and the island gods that ensured the safety of the precious chalice and sword the islanders had possessed since the beginnings of known time. Trystan could claim many admirable—and a few not so admirable—traits, but he had no explanation for the thunderous boom. It had almost sounded like a warning.

He glanced down past the ship's bow at the sparkling blue waters of the island's natural harbor.

The towline dangled loosely, no longer taut—as if last night's Siren had, indeed, tugged them home, only to be tumbled into the dangerous surf by the force of his shield.

While the others unloaded the ship, Trystan strode down the gangplank to the dock. Bitsy the goat scampered down the plank after him, her hooves clattering against the wood, her black nose sniffing for edibles.

The unnatural boom, which even now had Waylan scanning the masts, needed to be investigated before Trystan could call the voyage officially ended.

It wasn't as if Lissandra was on the beach—or anywhere else—waiting for him, even though she would know of his arrival. He might resent her aloofness, but he knew neither of them had time for sentiment. The safety and well-being of Aelynn always came first.

His short linen trousers and sleeveless tunic suited the warmth of this tropical dawn. His leather sandals sank in the black sand as he scanned the port side from stem to stern. He saw no gaping holes, no bubbling beneath the water. The crew had already tied the towrope to a pier. Trystan strode to the starboard side, examining the hull for damage.

Nothing. The schooner bobbed in the water as it should. Leaving his pet to nibble her way through the jungle foliage, he held still, searching his mental awareness of the island's thick gray barrier. As before, he sensed no weakening.

Trystan breathed in the lemon-scented air and tried to relax the knot of worry between his shoulders. He discarded his disquiet as a necessary adjustment from the Spartan confinement of a ship of men to the lush green jungle that was his home. Few Aelynners would have noticed the sails cutting through the fog at this early hour, so there was no crowd to greet them.

An odd bit of flotsam bobbing on the incoming tide caught his eye, and he strode toward it. He would have investigated even if he wasn't already uneasy. Little of the ocean's waste ever survived the shoals.

A bundle of white rags in a decidedly human form washed up at his feet.

No living being could survive the barrier he'd erected around his home.

Appalled that he'd actually *killed* an intruder, Trystan dropped to his knees beside the gossamer-clad female lying on the black sand. Her seaweed-entwined curls were a dark smudge against the sparkling crystals, and with grief, he tangled his fingers in their silken beauty. His purpose was to save lives, not take them. How could she have passed the reef to run afoul of his shield?

Waves lapped at her shapely limbs, tugging bits of cloth to reveal a glimpse of breasts as beautiful as the pearls from which Aelynn gained its wealth. To take such a life . . .

Gut clenching in denial, he leaned down to listen for her breathing. *Nothing.* He knew it was impossible to survive the barrier. With despair stinging his eyes, he caressed her cold, unresponsive skin, then tested the pulse in her neck.

Her blood beat weakly beneath his fingers. *She lived!* For whatever reason, the shield had rendered her unconscious but had not killed her.

A prayer of thanksgiving escaped his lips. Trystan didn't know what instinct he acted on when he scooped the female out of the sand as if she were one of his troublesome pets. His role as Guardian might be to keep invaders out, but he could not let this one die.

Disturbed by the physical awareness of her slender flesh in his arms and against his chest, he told himself it was her pale beauty that moved him. Besides, it was his duty to find out how she'd penetrated Aelynn's defenses. *His* defenses.

He knew without hesitation that she was an Outsider. Somehow, unbelievably, the *Destiny* had brought in a stranger. And not just any stranger, if his imagination did not play him tricks. Judging from the long glossy black curls, she was the maiden from the cliff.

She had been the source of the boom. She'd broken through his barrier. Yet no human could do that.

Despite her length, the lass weighed next to nothing. Trystan's hands brushed her ribs when he adjusted his grip. She was so thin, he had to be wary of his strength lest he crush her. Her breasts were almost unnoticeable against the breadth of his chest. How in Hades had she had the vigor to steal on board the ship?

He was grateful to feel her heart beating next to his as he carried her down the crystalline, palm-shaded path. The ship and the beach disappeared from view behind a thicket of foliage.

Waylan had once tried to explain that the fog surrounding Aelynn was a result of the island's volcanic warmth mixing with the icy waters of the sea, but Waylan was a man of science and sought physical explanations for a metaphysical phenomenon.

Since Trystan was the one who channeled the island's energy to form the foggy shield, he understood that there was far more at work than science. As the future spouse of an Oracle, he preferred to accept his faith in the island's power without question. He *felt* the force of the island. He felt its troubled shiver now.

The well-traveled path from the shore widened. Lined with camellias, gardenias, and other flowering shrubs garnered from distant shores over centuries of the islanders' explorations, the sandy crushed-shell path led to a temple and its healing altar. Trystan said his prayers to the gods as he hurried, but his mind was on the more human fate waiting at the end of the path.

The Oracle would not be pleased.

* * *

Lemons. She smelled the fragrance of a long-ago Christmas when Papa had bought lemons and oranges from a southern ship. That had been a magical holiday, and Mariel sank eagerly into the memory.

But instead of welcome laughter and familiar voices, angry words hissed nearby.

"By Hades, what have you *done*?" a furious female whispered.

"She followed me home," a male voice rumbled. "Shall I keep her?"

Oddly, the self-confident male teasing was comforting, but the woman's response was not.

"Are you serious? You know it is against every law of Aelynn to bring an Outsider here. Do you wish to be banished like Murdoch? Tie up your goat before it strips the gardenias. I'll fetch Mother."

Mariel sensed someone departing, and the lemon-scented memory returned. *Papa!*

But Papa was dead, struck down by an apoplexy in the middle of a confrontation with the Vicomte Rochefort. She would never have lemons again.

Her eyelids were heavy, and she wasn't certain she wished to wake. A worse memory hung on the edge of her consciousness, and she didn't want to name it. If she was dreaming, she could go back to sleep. She would just snuggle down into this . . .

This *what*? It wasn't a bed, although it was both soft and firm, like a sponge she'd once ripped from the bottom of the ocean. The pillow beneath her head smelled of the exotic spices in Maman's cabinet, rich and aromatic and tantalizing.

A breeze lifted her linen chemise from her thigh, and a strangled sound from somewhere in her vicinity shocked her into wakefulness. She was nearly nude and not alone. This wasn't a dream. Where was she?

Frantically, she tried to remember. Her aching muscles recalled her effort to swim after the prophesied savior. Had she died in the attempt, and he'd taken her to heaven?

Jarred fully awake by that thought, she grimaced at the dampness of her chemise against her salty skin. She lay on her back, so if she'd gone to heaven and wore an angel's wings, she was crushing them. Had she followed a devil and gone elsewhere?

Warily, her cheek resting against the soft pallet, Mariel lifted her salt-encrusted lashes just enough to see past her right shoulder. Her first sight was of a large flame on a squat marble column. She almost swallowed her tongue in instinctive fear.

But she had learned that fire had its purposes. This one remained at a safe distance. She took a deep breath and trained her thoughts elsewhere.

If this was a bed, it was high off the ground. She recognized the base of two enormous standing stones—menhirs—nearby, and a forest beyond them, much like the stones and forest of home. How could she have washed inland?

A scarlet flower dipped just beyond her nose, balanced on a long green stem covered in fine foliage. The aromatic air reminded her of the incense in church. A gentle breeze wafted over her near nakedness, tickling her in places the wind should never touch, raising goose bumps on her skin.

She reached to brush a wayward curl from her face. *Her hands wouldn't move.*

Panicking, Mariel sought the cause of her imprisonment. Her gaze swept downward to her wrists, where spongy straps bound her to the bed. She writhed to free them, then realized she could not move her ankles. Alarmed, she opened her eyes wide, turned her head to see what held her feet—and shrieked.

The golden god loomed at the foot of her tall bed.

He'd discarded the golden vest he'd worn when she'd last seen him. Massive shoulders filled a sleeveless linen tunic that barely covered a broad torso dusted with gilded brown curls. Copper bands on his upper arms emphasized the bulge of muscles there. Golden hair brushed his sun-burnished shoulders.

In her village, the people were small and dark, with glossy black hair like hers, although she resembled them in no other way. Sometimes, she had seen sailors whose muddy brown hair contained some strands lightened by the sun. But until this man, she had never seen such golden glory. No wonder Maman had called him a god.

Even his arms were a warm bronze. And his eyes! She shivered as he studied her, and she became more conscious of her position. She was held prisoner, unable to escape his scrutiny, forcefully aware of his smoldering gaze as it touched her face, her breasts, her . . .

She gasped when his eyes turned from a smoky gray to a warm gold and the place between her thighs turned liquid. He could see *all* of her.

And she couldn't move.

She was terrified. Sweat beaded her brow. Too frozen to fight her bonds, Mariel lay there like a sacrificial virgin beneath the regard of a man so powerful that he—

"I trust you like what you see." A dry, elderly female voice shattered the illusion of isolation. "For unless someone else speaks for her, the two of you must exchange rites."

She could see the shock hit him in the way his eyes sharpened to ebony and a ripple slid through his massive muscles and stiffened his wide jaw. But he didn't release her from his stare.

"I bow to your wisdom, my lady," he growled, looking as if he'd never bowed to anyone in his life. "But I merely placed her there so you might heal her."

If he would just look away, Mariel might recover her mind and protest, but his gaze had reduced her to trembling incoherence. Her breasts ached from the sheer linen blowing across their heavy weight. And her womb wept with a desire to be filled. What strange magic was this? She had no desire for men or children.

But the insistent throb between her legs swelled to a physical demand that lifted her hips off the bed. The god uttered a word from deep in his chest and stepped closer. The high bed still concealed his lower half, but primeval instinct and his flaming gaze warned of male arousal.

"She does not need healing. You placed her there because the gods know the two of you are ready," the unseen woman noted. "Does she bear the signs of an Aelynner?"

The intensity of the golden god's gaze faded into puzzlement. "None that I can see, but how else could she come here and still breathe?" He dragged a shaky hand through his hair and stepped backward again.

Mariel relaxed slightly, relieved to be freed of a force more potent than the bonds holding her. She still ached with the new and unwelcome knowledge of her body's needs—to the extent that she actually wondered what it would be like to have those needs fulfilled.

That thought should shock her, but she seemed to be beyond shock now, in a state of semiconsciousness that left her enervated and helpless as she listened to her future being discussed by strangers.

"No Outsider has ever breached the barrier without rites, so I do not understand the phenomenon," the elderly voice replied. "She seems to be awake. I assume we are speaking her language since you chose the words. Yet she does not respond. Her silence may be a protective defense of some sort. I would advise you to say the vows and take her as she is now, since the altar seems to have prepared her, but I'm not certain she's in a condition to repeat the words."

"Vows?" The god looked as if the world had exploded in his face. "Of *amacara* or marriage?"

"They both involve the ring of silence. I leave the choice to you, although it's unlikely you'll find another amacara now that Aelynn has chosen this one. Of course, there's always a third choice. You could kill her."

Confused by the earlier word that didn't translate into her language, Mariel wasn't certain she had heard right.

The god looked as if he hadn't either. He shook his head in obvious disagreement.

"Taking her now would be crude," he objected. "She deserves some say in her fate. Perhaps she would prefer Waylan or Nevan. They are equally responsible for bringing her here."

The old woman stepped closer, and Mariel stiffened with shock to see a woman who looked like her mother bending over her, her mother touched with the white hair and haggard wrinkles of an age that she had not lived to acquire.

Iridescent aqua eyes weary with the wisdom of the world had replaced the innocent blue of Maman's.

"You'd best think again," the old woman said dryly. "Look at her eyes. You may have found a mermaid."

Three

The primeval male instinct to claim his mate roared through Trystan with a brute force that stunned him. All the blood in his brain shot straight to his groin, leaving him dazed and dizzy. He knew absolutely nothing about the female held captive by the ritual altar except that she belonged to him. And he wanted her. Now.

The shock of finding an amacara—his perfect physical match—after all these years astounded him. Yet his reaction to her body upon the altar of life could mean nothing less. How could he be matched to a Crossbreed, a creature of mixed Aelynn and Other World descent, a *mermaid* with no value whatsoever to the island?

In the blink of an eye, his life had been hit broadside, overturned, and wiped out.

Amacaras were for bearing the hereditary traits Aelynn needed, children with the special abilities of their fathers and mothers. He had hoped Lissandra would be both legal wife and physical amacara to him so they could carry their traits into the future through their legitimate offspring. But until this revealing moment, he had underestimated the potent sexual ramifications of an amacara relationship. He lusted after Lissandra, as did every man on the island, but the

Oracle's daughter had never fired his imagination and held him enthralled as this stranger did.

As far as he was aware, Aelynn granted a man only one amacara at a time, and while they both lived, this—*mermaid?*—was his. A man with an amacara could take another woman as wife, and she *might* bear heirs with the required characteristics. But proud and possessive Lissandra would be furious, and might even refuse to become his wife, if he took an amacara before she had a chance to prove her ability to carry another Guardian.

Trystan knew himself to be an eminently practical man, yet he was aroused and ready to spill his seed into a seductive cleft at the mere flutter of the wisp of gossamer covering his rescued maiden. He wanted her long legs wrapped around him as he pumped into her, creating the child that would be his physical heir, if not his legitimate one. He clenched his teeth against an overpowering urge to taste rosy nipples practically pleading to be plucked. Her hips rose and circled and urged him on. The altar gave him permission. Heaven opened before him—or more likely, hell.

The gods had driven their spike into his soul, and after all these years of freedom, he was nailed firmly by their wishes.

But not here, not now, and not with any lifelong rites. He curled his fingers into fists of restraint. A concubine in the Outside World, yes. A man was allowed to have women outside of vows. Given their need to propagate their own kind, it was almost a necessity.

But the rites of amacara were for the propagation of specific talents, and the vows of marriage were reserved for power and prestige. A mate for life should be of equal lineage and status, or the relationship would be unbalanced. An unbalanced bond caused discord in every aspect of a man's life, and thus, to his children and all the inhabitants of the island, especially if he was to be Council Leader.

He could not let lust lead him astray. Perhaps this was a test of his worthiness.

"Mermaids are a sailor's superstition," he said with all the scorn he could muster for a creature so frivolous she had no purpose but to laze about the ocean. "May I release her? She does not appear to be in any danger of harming herself or others."

"Are you sure you would not prefer to settle this now?" Dylys asked, eyeing him with curiosity. "The altar accepts her, as you can plainly see. We've not had a mermaiden in decades. The gods must have brought her here for a reason."

"Get a mermaid with child? She could swim away and I'd never see my heir again," he scoffed. "Unless you See that reason, and me as her rightful mate, I don't think we ought to take away her right of choice."

"You are well aware that the future appears to me only if the impact affects many, unless I ask otherwise," the Oracle reprimanded him. "Envisioning your mate is not worth my energy, especially since you've already made up your mind."

Irritated by her tone, Trystan didn't wait for the Oracle to release their prisoner. He squeezed the ancient sponge that served as Healer's cot as well as ritual bed: the gateway to both life and death. Most of the inhabitants of the island had been conceived under the blessing of the gods here. Most of the ancients had been brought here to die. Their souls—and their powers—waited to enter the right child conceived under the proper conditions. Or so it was said. He'd heard similar legends elsewhere.

The sponge released the living bonds holding the

intruder. She didn't immediately understand. Her lowered lashes half concealed the shining green eyes that marked her as the descendant of some Aelynn seafarer. Trystan should have noticed that she was taller and paler than the other inhabitants of her village, but in his travels he was accustomed to seeing people of mixed race.

Gradually, she awakened from the dazed state of arousal the bed engendered in amacaras. Trystan tried not to think about that. He was a man of faith, not science. He fully believed the altar recognized mates who were meant to be joined. It had never occurred to him to question how that was possible. But he was questioning it now. An amacara was more than a reproductive vessel. The ritual pairing of souls was more sacred than the legal ties of marriage. Surely the gods did not intend him to spend eternity with a mere *mermaiden*.

He'd best not question with the Oracle present. Dylys was already furious with him. He could tell by the way the elder's eyes narrowed as he helped the intruder to sit up without her permission. He'd overstepped his authority—again.

"She cannot leave the island without rites. You know that as well as I do, Trystan. She must choose from among you, or she must die. Her life is in your hands."

Despite her age, the Oracle walked away with the straight-backed stride that reminded him of Lissandra—who had called him more names than a drunken sailor when he'd brought his unconscious mermaid here.

That the Oracle's angry daughter had not returned after fetching her mother boded ill.

"I don't suppose you are able to tell me how in Hades you came here, or even why?" he asked the intruder in a tone that was much calmer than he felt. His father had taught him that a wise leader did not reveal his thoughts.

Sitting on the edge of the altar, Trystan's stowaway—he would not think of her as his amacara—glanced at her unbound wrists with puzzlement, then leaned over to look at her feet. Long strands of drying black curls coiled around her breasts and shoulders, nearly concealing the breasts he wanted to claim, and dared not.

Cautiously, she eased off the high altar, touching her toes to the crystal sand and crushed shell that comprised much of the island's floor. Despite his fury, Trystan was fascinated with every aspect of her. She was tall enough to reach his shoulder, but she was little more than a thin waif next to his bulk. He had the urge to feed and shelter her like one of his stray pets, though her stiff avoidance of his person and his own common sense warned him off.

The oleander that had been dancing over her head seemed to follow her from the altar, and she gazed up at it in surprise. With a defiant glance in his direction, she plucked the flower from its stem.

The world didn't explode as she had so obviously expected. Hiding a smile at her boldness, Trystan plucked another flower and stuck it behind her ear. Then he crossed his arms and studied her linen-draped form. "You are as well dressed as any bride. Shall we take you to meet your suitors?"

She balled up her fingers and drove her fist into his midriff.

Mariel bruised her hand. And probably shattered her knuckles.

The golden god merely shook his head in amusement—as strong as Hercules, just as her mother had predicted. His golden mane wafted about him as if with a will of its own. With his massive build and mighty sword, accompanied by his stern jaw, he would appear a pirate were it not for his simple sandals and golden visage.

Had he and the strange woman actually been discussing *marriage*? What manner of madness had she fallen into?

The god had kept his hands off her until she'd foolishly broken that taboo. Now he gripped her upper arm and steered her down a path lined with glossy emerald foliage, more of the lovely red flowers, and some wonderful white ones that smelled of an exotic fragrance she did not recognize.

"You were obviously speaking when last I saw you on the bluff. Did the barrier take away your tongue when you broke through it?"

She hadn't a clue what he meant. Now that she was free of the dismaying lethargy caused by the bed, she realized he was not actually speaking words she knew, yet she understood him. Well, she recognized the words. They just didn't make sense.

"I can speak," she answered in her native tongue. "You do not want to hear what I have to say." Truth, she had no idea what to say. She walked as if in a dream. The man—if he was a man and not a god or a dream or a monster—was overwhelming. There were few men in the village as tall as she. He was not only taller, but twice her breadth. He strode with the muscular grace of an Olympian. It was a wonder the ground did not tremble beneath his feet.

The ground itself was strange, crunchy and yet resilient. And the vegetation . . . Mariel gazed in wonder at slender trees with fronds unlike any she had known and shrubs that bloomed in glorious colors. Were there no houses? Fields? *People?* Accustomed to the crowded stone village bustling with inhabitants that she'd known since birth, she could not help but be frightened by the isolation . . . and herself . . . and *him.*

She wore next to nothing, yet she was amazingly warm.

He wore little more than she did. In the strapped soles, his bronzed feet were as bare as the muscular calves revealed beneath short sailor's trousers. A ripple of what she'd felt on the altar returned, and she dragged her gaze away from his legs.

"On the contrary, I'm exceedingly interested in what you have to say," he corrected her. "Can you tell me how you arrived here?"

"Where is here?" she asked. "And what was that . . . that *thing* back there?"

"The altar? Or Dylys?" he asked, with a wry chuckle.

Before she could answer, they entered an area that almost reminded her of home except for the width of the road and the glowing white of the buildings lining it.

A herd of goats gamboled around a towering menhir on a patch of ordinary grass. The houses were constructed of what she assumed was the same crushed shell she walked upon. As at home, the two-story buildings shared side walls, although each door displayed the owner's individuality in its color, size, and shape. Sand crystals sparkled in the walls. Brightly painted storm shutters, many of them faded from the bright sun, adorned unglazed windows.

Smoke rose from a stone chimney in one of the wider houses, and the scent of roasting meat made Mariel's mouth water. If she was any judge of time, it had been noon yesterday since she'd eaten, and that had been the leftovers from the spring greens she'd given Francine.

Francine. She had to return to her sister. There was no one to look after her.

First, she must talk to the god and explain their problem. But how?

The formidable stranger led her into the house with the chimney and called out in a language that was both strange and familiar to her ears. A number of men almost as big as her companion sat at tables in the front room. They all stared frankly at her.

She tried to tug her chemise over her breasts, but it was little more than a tattered rag after its sojourn in the water. Not that it had been much more before then.

She stepped behind the god in his indecently thin linen and let his bulk conceal her until she heard a woman's voice and dared peer around his brawny shoulders.

A perfectly normal woman stared back. This woman was shorter than Mariel, pleasantly plump, and wearing little more than pearls and a piece of flowered cloth wrapped around her breasts and hips.

How did she keep the cloth on? It was the most immodest garment Mariel had ever seen, just barely concealing the swell of the woman's breasts, and showing almost all of her legs. One side of the cloth parted to reveal one plump, smooth thigh.

And still the men stared at Mariel.

At a brief explanation from her captor, the woman exclaimed, took another curious peek at Mariel, then hurried off.

"You'd think you'd never seen a woman before! Turn your gawking eyes back to your food and leave the lass alone," the golden pirate roared into the silence in that strange manner in which he made himself understood to her.

Most of the men obeyed. An elegantly lean gentleman with hair the color of sunset, the one Mariel thought had stood beside the golden god on the ship, rose and offered her his high-necked blue frock coat trimmed in gold braid. His handsome eyes danced with laughter.

She knew better than to trust laughing eyes. Turtlelike, she pulled her head behind the pirate god again.

"Laugh, if you will," the god growled, seizing the coat from his friend. "But the law says one of us must bond with her, and you look as likely a candidate as any."

Well, she'd thought she understood him, but she must be interpreting some word wrong. She certainly had no intention of *bonding* with anyone. She tried to guess what he really meant by judging the man's reactions.

No longer laughing, the auburn-haired man spoke hotly before returning to his seat. Once there, he exchanged words with a formidably scarred sailor, who tried to see her better.

When the god half turned to look for her, Mariel hastily grabbed the coat from his hand, pulled it on, and was immediately engulfed in masculine scents. The coat was wool, and much too warm, but she wrapped it tightly anyway. She noticed most of the men here wore garments similar to her captor's—sleeveless linen shirts and linen trousers or trews in varied colors, some embroidered, some trimmed in braid, a few pinned or belted. Their simplicity of dress emphasized their purely masculine muscles, and she desperately tried not to gape.

Her guide shoved her down on a bench at an empty table. If he meant to feed her, she wouldn't object. She was utterly famished and needed to build up her strength for the return trip home. Her undersea journeys burned the flesh off of her unless she replenished adequately. She had a suspicion the pirate wouldn't offer to sail her home.

The woman returned with a steaming bowl of fish stew in her hands and a lovely flowered fabric in reds and blues over her arm. Chattering, she set the bowl on the table in front of Mariel and held out the garment, gesturing for her to stand up.

Buttoned, the coat covered Mariel from neck to mid-thigh, but the scarf would be useful. She accepted it and wrapped it around her waist, forming a skirt that fell almost to her ankles, much to the surprise of her benefactor. Combined with the bulky coat, she was covered modestly enough. She returned to the table and her food.

Regarding her new garb with lifted eyebrow, the annoying god took a place across from her, blocking her view of the room—and her from their audience, she assumed. She had seen possessive men mark their women as their territory in such a way, but as the mayor's daughter, she'd never expected to be on the receiving end of such crude behavior.

Nevertheless, she actually seemed to be enjoying his medieval idea of protection. She'd read her father's history books of gallant knights and dazzling damsels. She'd always thought the knights had the more exciting life—until now. It seemed being a sheltered female had titillating rewards she hadn't recognized. She enjoyed this knight's surly regard and didn't want a roomful of giants gawking at her.

He waited politely, if impatiently, until she'd finished her first bowl of the delicious stew before he questioned her again.

"How did you come here?"

Mariel broke a loaf of freshly baked bread the hostess had produced, and she almost expired from happiness sniffing the yeasty aroma. How long had it been since she'd eaten fresh bread?

"I swam," she answered before delicately nibbling a warm morsel. She'd have liked to stuff the whole piece into her mouth, but she feared he would snatch the food away if she couldn't speak.

"You swam? From where?" He sounded perplexed. "The ship?"

She knew this was where the plow hit the manure. At home, they'd burn her for a witch if she spoke such heresy. But here . . . She already seemed to be under a sentence of a fate worse than death, and she had no better way to explain her presence. "From the bluffs. You would not wait to hear me out, so I dived in after you."

"The bluffs? From the village? In Brittany?"

He hadn't called her a liar, made a sign of the cross, or clapped her in irons yet. Mariel smiled gratefully as the woman placed another bowl of excellent stew in front of her. She ignored her hostess's anxious glance at the god's angry disbelief and remembered to say grace before she dug in this time.

"Yes," she finally said into the telling silence. "Had you waited, we could have saved ourselves a great deal of trouble, but I must admit, I have enjoyed this odd visit. I had no notion there existed such a lovely country so close or I might have tried this sooner."

She knew when she pushed a man's temper. She did it frequently, since men tended to push hers. Antagonizing a god was probably reckless, even for her. She was strong and could hold her own in a fight, but most men in the village didn't dare lay a hand on her. Her mother had been highly respected for her reliable forecasts, and her father had been a minor aristocrat as well as the mayor. Her brother-in-law was a lawyer who had been elected to the Assembly as deputy for the district. She was protected by all the powers of her small home.

She wasn't at home any longer, but she had never known fear and wouldn't start now.

The god curled his fingers into fists but kept them firmly on the table. "The island is not close by. It cannot be accessed by any man unless we allow it. You have done what no man has done before." His voice was taut with fury.

"That explains it, then." Mariel pushed back her bowl and sighed with satisfaction. "No *woman* has ever tried it."

She thought the blood vessel in his forehead would explode before he curbed his rage.

As her father had warned, sometimes she had a tendency to push too far, without thinking things through to their obvious conclusion.

Four

As the island's diplomat, Trystan could have sworn he didn't have a temper.

The urge to murder the slender woman across the table disproved that notion. She inspired a form of madness in *him*—a man known throughout Aelynn for his impeccable good sense.

And the Oracle thought he ought to couple with this madness-inspiring wench? If so, it really was time for the island's most powerful leader to step down and pass her duties on to someone more sensible.

Like the woman approaching. At a hasty scraping of benches, Trystan looked up to see Lissandra glide through the doorway. She nodded regally at the men standing to greet her, but she did not stop to welcome them home and ask the results of their search for Murdoch. Being Lissandra, with her gift of Sight, she no doubt already knew.

Garbed resplendently in a sky blue silk sari, her flowing white-blond hair wrapped in delicate circlets of silver, she immediately advanced on Trystan's table—with no delight in her eyes.

The Oracle's daughter seldom lost her temper. She was like him in that. But she had a way of cutting a man into pieces even so.

Trystan sighed and rose from his seat. His stowaway did not. Garbed in her ridiculous attire of oversized coat and ankle-length sarong, her jet-black curls drying into a luxurious mop, she remained seated while studying Lissandra, as if she were a curiosity in a museum, instead of the other way around.

He was torn between his duty to Lissandra and his fascination with what the mermaiden would do next.

"I am Lissandra, daughter of the Oracle." Adapting her language to Breton as Trystan had done, she held out her long, thin-boned hand for the traditional kiss.

"I am Mariel St. Just, daughter of the mayor of Pouchay," the black-haired wench replied, eyeing Lissandra's outstretched hand with skepticism. "Pleased to meet you. Does the god have a name?"

"The god?" Taken aback, Lissandra retrieved her hand and glanced around as if she expected the pantheon to step forward.

Trystan enjoyed her shock too much to acknowledge his own at this perception of him. He and Lissandra had grown up together, and were aware of each other's flaws. She had never looked at him as the man of accomplishment that he knew himself to be. It soothed his frayed temper to know that, for whatever inane reason, the mermaid considered him some form of god.

"The god beside you. I have never seen a man with such hair. The two of you almost look like brother and sister." Mariel, daughter of the mayor of Pouchay, returned to consuming her meal.

Trystan tried not to snicker, but the expression on Lissandra's face was priceless. The all-knowing woman was thunderstruck.

She shot him the malevolent glare he remembered from their childhood when she was about to pull a truly wicked stunt on him, and his grin grew wider in anticipation.

"The golden thug is far from a god. He is usually

called Trystan the Enforcer, but after this morning, perhaps he will be reduced to Trystan the Translator. Since he is to be your lover, you ought to know he spends only a day or two a month here and has a penchant for goats."

Trystan winced. Mariel, the mayor's daughter, spluttered in her soup.

Lissandra's eyes lit with malicious glee as she patted Trystan's arm. "Congratulations. A slippery mermaid is the perfect mate for a man who thinks he owns everything he sees. She even knows how to milk your goats."

She swept away, leaving stunned silence in her wake. Everyone knew they had teased each other unmercifully since childhood. Trystan prayed she was teasing now.

Still, the proud Lissandra he knew would never accept a husband who had an amacara.

Those who would compete with him for Lissandra's hand rose hastily from their seats, hoping her pronouncement was a prophecy and she had just rejected his suit. Trystan contemplated running after her and shaking her, or challenging the asses who followed her out, but he refused to encourage Lissandra's mercurial humors. He would defend his position later, when she could not gloat over the trouble she had caused. After all, he was the only one on the island who knew how to handle the haughty princess.

"How does she know I can milk a goat?" Mariel asked. "It's not a common skill."

Trystan sat down heavily. Lissandra was angry, yes, but that did not make their marriage an impossibility. He could still *kill* the mayor's daughter.

He glared at her. "Lissandra knows everything. That is why she's destined to be the next Oracle. I cannot begin to explain the extent of her abilities."

"My mother knew things. She knew of you." His stowaway studied him, tracing the line of his jaw with her gaze before brazenly dipping it to follow the breadth of his shoulders and chest.

Trystan shifted uncomfortably as his body responded to the almost physical touch of her stare, while puzzlement clogged his thoughts.

An Outsider should not know of the peculiar abilities of Aelynn's inhabitants. That was the reason for the vows of silence. The island hid many secrets, among them the Chalice of Plenty and the Sword of Justice, objects so powerful that the gods had seen fit to give the island's inhabitants skills and abilities beyond that of mere humans in order to protect them. Mariel was already in danger because she had learned of the island's existence, yet she showed little fear, much less surprise at what she saw. Still, he could not risk her learning more.

And he could not—would not—allow her to enchant him and relax his vigilance as Guardian.

"All you can do is speak my language?" she finally asked. "Lots of people can do that. Not many people can swim under the sea as I do."

She was teasing him, just as Lissandra did. It was evident in the way her eyes turned a laughing aqua, indicating her shifting mood, marking her indelibly as the descendant of an Aelynner. She usually hid the beauty of her changing eyes behind lowered lashes, probably a habit developed over a lifetime of disguising her nonhuman qualities.

Trystan tried to relax and put himself in her place, but it was impossible. Descendant or not, she didn't belong here. For the first time since he could remember, he had his purposes confused, and he replied with the first words to reach his tongue. "I can speak and understand any language, but that is a minor talent.

)o you turn into a fish when you swim under the ea?"

She had a captivating, wide-lipped smile.

"I don't think so, although I must have some simi-arity to a fish to allow me to breathe underwater. My 1other did not have sufficient knowledge to explain."

"You're a Crossbreed," he said with infinite weari-ess. "I assume one of your parents was a Crossbreed r from Aelynn. Did you know your parents?"

"That is insulting." She dipped her spoon to scrape he soup bowl clean. "My mother had the second ight. Are there more like her?"

"Not many, but that's not what I mean." He rubbed is hand over his brow and sought words to explain. 'or someone to whom words came easily, this was 1ore difficult than he had anticipated. "Perhaps we hould leave this to another time, when you are 1ore rested."

Swinging her spoon in the air, she considered that. 'We need to talk, but I suppose I should rest before oing back. The sea invigorates me, but it's a very ong swim."

"You will not be going back," he said firmly. "The)racle has decreed it. You will die here unless you xchange vows with me or with one of the other men n the island, promise never to speak of Aelynn again, nd wear the ring of silence." He brandished the ring e wore on his right hand.

"Very pretty. Black opal?" She set down her spoon nd stood up. "If it takes a ring for you to believe I'll emain silent about this place, I'll happily take one, ut I must go home. My sister is in her ninth month f pregnancy, and she'll starve without me."

Francine might starve in any case since the goats ad been sold last winter, the greens made her ill, and he fish had yet to return in any quantity.

With her belly pleasantly full, Mariel tried to ac nonchalant as she strode out of the dining area int the lane outside. At some other time, she might enjo exploring this incredible place, but not now, not wit her dangerous attraction to this man stringing he nerves taut, not while Francine needed her.

The god—Trystan—followed her. She had expecte nothing less.

"So you will take the vow and the ring of silence? he asked warily.

"I said as much," she snapped, more impatient wit her own responses to this man than with his barel concealed anger and frustration. Better to concentrat on the price the opal would bring. She could bu bread, even if the baker charged a hundred times wha it cost last year.

She had a feeling that this man's idea of vows ha much to do with the very odd bed, and the way he' looked at her, and little to do with promising to b silent. As curious as she might be about coupling an many other things, her responsibilities lay elsewhere and she would act cautiously until she could escape "Did you say there was somewhere I could res awhile?"

He appeared to struggle with himself, then reluctantl held out his arm for her to take. It was a gentlemanl gesture, and she appreciated his acknowledgment of he status, even if she looked like a derelict who ha crawled from the gutter.

His forearm was as hard and thick as an oak limb and touching his bare flesh caused an odd sensatio in a place deep within her belly. She wouldn't win i a fight with this pirate god. She had to use her wit to elude him, once she'd said her piece.

"This is the bachelor's village," he explained, lead ing her down still another shell path. "My town hous is over there." He nodded to a line of whitewashed houses with red shutters that were broader and less individual than the first ones. "Until you are bound by vows, it is not proper for you to stay there. I will take you to my sister's home. She is married and will have room for you. The children may drive you insane, but I'm sure she will see that you rest easy."

With a muttered curse of apology, he dropped her hand and hastily crossed the town square to a group of adolescents tying cans to the tail of a long-haired goat. With a speed that had Mariel blinking in astonishment, Trystan swung his powerful arm in a broad arc, causing the young men to dodge and tumble like bowling pins to escape a blow. They laughed, unhurt, but made no attempt to leap to their feet and take him on in combat. Instead, they hastily untied the cans and appeared to apologize while he castigated them. Appeased, the golden god hefted the kid under his arm, and scratching the animal beneath the chin, returned to her side.

Amazed that so large a man, one who apparently carried a heavy weight of responsibility, should care what happened to a small animal, Mariel almost regretted having to betray him. But god or man, he did not listen to her, and she could only give him this one last chance before making her escape. "I followed you for a reason," she reminded him.

"You followed *me*?" The goat nibbled blissfully at the shoulder of his shirt as Trystan appropriated Mariel's arm again and led her into the forest of exotic plants. Sunlight danced along water droplets on giant leaves that he impatiently shook from his hair, revealing bursts of bright color inside the wall of foliage. Life flourished here, as it did not at home.

Regarding the loveliness wistfully, Mariel continued. "Yes. Before she died, my mother had a vision of a golden god carrying a sword of justice. She said you would come at a time of deep despair, that you were the savior who would rescue us."

"A sword of *justice*?" he asked in disbelief. He hesitated, then shook his head firmly. "I am a peace-abiding man, and Aelynners are foresworn against interfering in your world."

She shrugged. "Visions are often metaphors. The sword could mean any weapon of strength. Or your ship." She'd noted its name—*Sword of Destiny.* Not the same as justice, but *sword* was close enough.

She wanted so badly for it to be enough.

She glanced at his taut square jaw, but his expression had closed up. She hoped he was still listening. "The last two wheat crops have failed and the one before that was poor. The price of bread has soared beyond the means of all but the wealthy. The rivers froze last winter, raising the cost of transporting coal, taking what was left of our coins. And still we are taxed until what little land we own is lost. My brother-in-law has been elected deputy to carry our complaints to the king, but I have yet to see politics feed the hungry. We need a miracle before we all die. I thought if you were our savior, you might see some way out of our difficulties."

"I am not a god or a savior," he said with derision. "The only purpose of our kind is to guard Aelynn and her treasures until the gods decree it otherwise."

Fury jammed her thinking. Mariel halted on a forest path that wasn't quite as exotic as the earlier one, only her interest wasn't on her surroundings, but on this stubborn man who cared more for goats than people. She removed her hand from his arm to clench the fingers into a fist.

"Then your gods are either dead or blind!" she

shouted at him. "People are *dying*, and you would simply shrug and walk away, even if you had a means to help them?"

"I cannot interfere in the affairs of Outsiders," he repeated. "It would bring disaster to our kind. Too often in the past we have been burned and stoned as witches and chased from your shores by primitive men with narrow minds. We cannot have them following us to the only place where we are safe. Even if Aelynn is well hidden, men have died trying to find her and the wealth they think we possess. Would you wish death on your friends?"

He talked nonsense. Mariel could accept that he was no god, but he was certainly a man with strength and possibly knowledge beyond her own. Strength and knowledge he would not share. She started to stalk away, but he grabbed her arm and pulled her back, gazing into her eyes with the intensity she'd noticed earlier. Only this time his irises had returned to a stormy gray, changing colors as hers did. She really had found the people from whom she sprang. Her stomach knotted in fear and anticipation, but she had nothing to say.

"You are a Crossbreed," he declared in a tone that implied she was a cockroach. "You are the best we can produce to help mankind. You have been raised among them, know their ways, and are accepted there. It is your duty to provide for your friends, not mine."

And she had failed that duty. Tears welled, but she would not let them fall. "And so I shall," she answered defiantly, tearing her arm from his grip. "As soon as I return home."

Trystan thought he should have promised the mermaid anything she wanted, if only she would take the vows so he did not have to kill her. But he still held some hope that Nevan or Waylan could be persuaded into taking her off his hands.

Except Nevan and Waylan would throw her back into the sea to die upon the rocky reefs. *He* was the one who had broken the law and brought her to land. He was beginning to think he'd been bewitched.

After leaving Mariel and his goat in his sister's capable hands, Trystan strode back through the forest to find his hard-hearted friends. Neither Nevan nor Waylan was truly interested in Lissandra or governing the island, nor was either particularly eligible, not as Trystan was. They carried out their duties to Aelynn by sailing to foreign shores to bring back news of the world and any necessary items that the island could not provide.

Trystan assumed that since neither man seemed interested, Mariel was not their destined mate—not as the altar had proved he was. But it wouldn't hurt either Waylan or Nevan to have a wife in the Outside World since neither of them spent much time on land. And since a man's wife was forbidden as a mistress, Mariel would be out of his reach.

Of course, given Mariel's plea to save her village, Trystan suspected she would nag her husband until he robbed a granary and dumped it on her family's doorstep, and that would be only the first of his many chores.

He didn't see the necessity of explaining that to his friends.

"Don't look to us for help," Waylan warned the instant Trystan strode into the tavern the crew favored. "You're the one who brought her to the Oracle."

"She's one of us, you simpleton." Feeling torn in so many ways that he couldn't fit the pieces of himself back together, Trystan ordered one of Aelynn's fine ales and sank down at the long table with the others. "She *swam* here. Dylys claims she is a mermaiden."

"I'd almost believe that," Kiernan the Finder mused.

Of them all, Kiernan was the next bachelor most eligible for Lissandra's hand. But he was honest to the point of bluntness, a bad trait in a leader who must exercise the fine art of compromise to keep the peace. Besides, his curiosity led him off the island with increasing regularity. Realizing he was looking for an excuse to foist the mermaid on another of his friends, Trystan returned his attention to the discussion.

"All that long black silky hair floating like seaweed on the waves . . . ," Kiernan mused. "I can see her as a mermaid. But I believe I distinctly saw toes."

Waylan leaned over and hit the heel of his hand to his friend's temple. "You're supposed to be seeking a mate for Iason, not looking for toes on mermaids."

Before Trystan could argue, Waylan turned his scarred cheek toward him again. "And don't go saddling me with a wife I'll never see. She may have the abilities of a Crossbreed, but she's also an Outsider. She'll want to be with her home and family, but my life is at sea. The same goes for Nevan. She has no place here, no family, no status, no ability from which we can benefit. If Oscar the Fisherman were about fifty years younger, she might suit him. Throw her back into the sea if you don't want her."

Trystan dug his fingers into his pewter mug and resisted using it to brain his selfish friend. "The Finder should have thrown *you* back in the sea, if that is your attitude toward all Crossbreeds but yourself. If I throw her into the sea, she will simply swim back the way she came and tell her people how to find us."

Waylan shrugged. "Then we hold her prisoner or

sacrifice her to the volcano. Shall we vote with our swords?"

"You'd reduce my life to a melee?" Trystan asked incredulously, but he was rising to his feet as he said it. Turning his back on any of his comrades would be a show of weakness. Besides, the physical release of action seemed preferable to stewing over his dilemma.

As was their custom, half the men in the room leapt to their feet, producing their swords with zeal at this chance to challenge Trystan's prowess. Defeating the acknowledged champion would put them in a position of leadership and give them a greater chance of winning the maidens of their choice.

"To arms!" Nevan cried. "I haven't had a proper fight in weeks. Let's say we sacrifice Trystan if he loses."

The men tumbled out of the inn into the grassy field, ready to cast their votes with the strength of their swords.

"He's a dead man no matter who wins," Waylan grumbled, clashing his blade against the sharp edge of a newcomer's, pushing the youngster backward and nipping his tunic belt in one swift movement.

"This is a damned childish manner of choosing leaders and making decisions," Trystan grumbled, placing both hands on the hilt of his sword and swinging it in an arc, preventing the approach of half the men in the field who were eager to gain points by besting him.

"What, you want women to cast a vote?" Raising his sword, Nevan deftly cut the ties securing Kiernan's breeches. "Or do you just want them to watch?"

Kiernan grabbed his trews, cursed, and swung wildly to defend the rest of his garments. "Since we only fight about women, that might make more sense."

Wielding his sword to fend off Trystan's thrust,

Nevan added, "Which is why the first man naked buys a round for all!"

"I, for one, am damned tired of ruining perfectly good cloth," Trystan said in resignation, slicing a belt here and a tunic there in one smooth arc of his weapon. "But if that is your wish, so be it. I'm still the best swordsman here." Shifting his sword from one hand to the next, he deftly caught the point on the gold braid on Nevan's shirt and ripped it off.

With the uncanny agility with which they were born, and the skill acquired during years of practice, Trystan's companions reduced their argument to a melee.

Five

Mariel waited until shadows lengthened between house and trees before slipping out of the bedchamber she'd been given.

Trystan's sister Erithea had hair as golden as his but had looked more harried than calm when he'd handed Mariel over to her. Erithea had given her brother a good scold in words Mariel couldn't understand, then sent the giant on his way with an angry push. But she'd been all smiles and hospitality when she'd turned to her guest. Mariel hoped that meant the lady's anger was reserved for her stubborn brother.

If she'd been told her brother had to marry a lost waif he'd dragged from the ocean rather than some rich woman who controlled the town, she supposed, she'd give him a tongue-lashing, too. But she'd solve her hostess's problem now.

She had a lifetime's experience in slipping from shadow to shadow to reach the sea. She always knew in which direction to find it.

She'd made her life seem simple to her captors, but it had never been any such thing. Had her odd ability to swim beneath the water with the fishes been discovered, only the village's isolation and her parents' place in society would have prevented her from being stoned or worse. And depending on the priest at the time, even her parents might not have been able to save her. If all the people on this island had her odd talent, she could understand their fear of outsiders. The church and those of her world were not kind to those who were different from themselves.

She had walked to the sea with her very first baby steps. She'd been secretly herding fish into nets since she was ten. Even as a child she'd known her strange skill had given her a duty to others, as her mother's second sight added to her responsibilities as mayor's wife. The ability to see visions was apparently acceptable—and even saintly—to the church, as long as the visions did not contradict church doctrine. Swimming underwater like a fish would invoke pagan legends and would not suit current church teachings.

With the onset of adolescence Mariel had eased her loneliness by learning to communicate with dolphins. Not that she'd found much use for her new knowledge of sea coral or sandbanks or the other things that dolphins knew—or the time to exploit the insight. Her mother had died the year she'd turned thirteen, and her land-bound tasks had multiplied.

Mariel reached the edge of the forest without being seen. As she'd left, she had heard her hostess scolding her children in the kitchen and assumed they'd sat down to dinner. Her belly was empty again, but she'd lived with that feeling for so long now, she scarcely noticed.

Her biggest challenge was avoiding the island's inhabitants. She was surrounded by the sea. All paths would ultimately lead to water, and the cloudy peak of the volcano gave her a sense of direction. She had to choose her way carefully if she didn't want to end up walking through the village. Or wind up at the temple with the old woman. She wasn't eager to repeat that terror-inducing experience.

She attuned her ears to the pounding of the incoming tide against the shore and sought the most direct path. How big could the island be?

The forest of ferns and broad-leafed trees ended abruptly, and she emerged into an open field where golden wheat rippled, ready for harvest. Potato vines circled among the rows of grain, and she wondered how the inhabitants harvested entwined crops. She would have liked to have asked. Two crops from one field would be beneficial to the farmers, but this field might be the result of a magic peculiar to the island.

She'd never thought of her ability to swim as magic. She still didn't. So why did the notion pop into her mind with regard to Trystan and his friends? His *kind*. Hadn't he said that earlier? As if the people on this island were different from the rest of mankind.

Her mother, Marie-Jeanne, had said Mariel's grandfather was a seafaring man who had married Mariel's grandmother and sailed away, returning once a year until Marie-Jeanne was nearly grown. Was this the land he'd sailed to? Her mysterious grandfather had left his small family wealthy enough to make her mother an eligible prospect for a nobleman's younger son.

If that was sorcery, the world could use a little more of it.

Leaving the field behind, Mariel entered the exotic forest she'd traipsed with Trystan to reach the bachelor village. She hoped to skirt past the populated area. Tucking a multipetaled white flower behind her ear just to have the scent with her, she turned toward the ocean again.

It was a pity her grandfather had never seen how his family fared after Marie-Jeanne married. Perhaps he could have helped them from these sad straits. If he was the source of Mariel's unusual ability, might he have lived here, on this island? The old woman and Trystan seemed to think her mother was related to their people. Would her grandfather have had the ability to swim like a fish? Or was he a Seer, like her mother? Or was he just a sailor whose ship had one day sunk in a distant sea, never to return again?

She'd like to ask a thousand questions, and knew that if she were to find the answers anywhere it must be here. She suspected that everyone on Aelynn was enchanted, yet she had no clear idea why she felt that way. Beyond the odd bed and her ability to understand their language, she had no tangible evidence that these people were extraordinary.

Despite the Breton legends of Sirens and other fey creatures, and her mother's oddities, Mariel had never met anyone else with strange abilities like hers. Had the inhabitants of the legendary city of Ys not drowned but been swept away to this perfect island?

As much as she wanted to know more, Mariel had to return to Pouchay. Maman had made her promise to look after her sister.

Maman had made a lot of promises in return, but they weren't being fulfilled. The golden god certainly had proved disappointing.

Mariel halted when she arrived at the edge of the clearing where she'd first awakened on the strange, spongy bed. The incense still called to her, allowing her to locate the altar even through the screen of flowering shrubbery. This was obviously not a public temple.

Standing stones formed a circular barrier around a narrow altar that she knew was made of some substance other than the granite surrounding it. The flame still burned—probably the source of the incense. She'd seen menhirs scattered through the fields of home and often wondered about the people who'd had the superhuman strength to place them there.

Maybe she'd just met some of those people. The belated realization that the man who held her captive might be superhuman in some manner finally frightened her. If he could lift those stones, there was no end to what he could do.

The intoxicating fragrances of the clearing reminded her too forcefully of unwanted physical desires. Her woman's place tingled and ached, and her womb tightened expectantly. She had never understood what drove women to procreate, until now. Since she could not swim if swollen with child, and had no intention of bearing a child who might be feared or despised by all she knew, she had always known she had no right to indulge in those feelings.

In fact, she must resist them.

Slipping back into the trees, Mariel worked her way around the glade, following the sound of the ocean, this time with regret. She would have liked to have explored this new world—and discovered what it meant to be touched by a man like Trystan.

But he would kill her if she stayed, so there wasn't much future in it.

Dripping with sweat and bleeding from shallow cuts, Trystan defended his position with all the frustration and rage of this day, until he finally caught his sword tip in the shoulder seam of Waylan's tunic, and reduced it to thread. Swinging his blade in a broad arc, he realized he was the last man standing, the one still clothed. A strip of his trousers clung to his hips.

They did not fight to the death but to the skin, although often the flesh was nicked in the heat of battle. Even with an Aelynner's natural swiftness, it took years of practice to fight with naked swords without causing lethal accidents.

Trystan's bare companions lolled in the grass, accepting his authority for any decision that must be made. As usual, his position as leader remained uncontested.

"So, how do you choose?" Waylan demanded, sheathing his weapon before picking up the remnants of his clothing.

Flinging his arm around Waylan's brawny shoulders, Trystan shoved his friend toward the tavern. "I choose for you to buy the next round."

"Bah, it's just your long arm that makes the difference." Waylan knotted the remains of his tunic around his hips, staggered to a seat, and circled his fingers at the serving maid. "I still know more moves than you."

Kiernan collapsed on the bench beside Trystan, and rather than swing to sit properly at the trestle table he leaned his back against it and stretched out his long legs. "Remind me again why we continue this primitive form of entertainment."

"Because it makes us good with a needle?" Trystan suggested. "Since there isn't a woman on the island who will repair our garments after a fight, we've all become skilled at repairing sail."

A feminine voice joined the argument: "To exhaust swaggering bachelors and keep them from rutting among the women and producing far more children than the island can bear." Unfazed by a room full of brawny masculine nakedness, Lissandra slapped a tumbler of mead upon the table. "I trust you are now enlightened as to how you will deal with your intruder."

"I won. I choose," Trystan replied gruffly. It had

taken hours to defeat his comrades. The sun was setting behind Aelynn, and he was no closer to a conclusion than he had been before.

"Then choose, and send the loser after her," Lissandra hissed. "While you've been playing your silly games, she has escaped."

Abruptly alert, Trystan swung his legs over the bench. "Which way did she go?"

She looked at him in disbelief. "Where do you think a mermaid would go? And I thought you the smart one."

So had he, but obviously they were both wrong. The mermaiden had truly addled his brainpan. What in the name of the gods had possessed him to bring Mariel ashore?

Possibly the gods.

Meeting Lissandra's gaze, Trystan felt his gut knot. Her eyes had turned the color of regret. What had she seen with her inner sight?

That Mariel could die upon the reefs?

"Who goes with me?" he shouted with controlled panic to the room at large. But without his direct command, his so-called friends merely lifted their tankards in surrender.

As Guardian and leader, he could not force his friends to accept what he would not.

Cursing the fates, Trystan raced for the door. There were several accessible beaches on the island, but if Lissandra had just "seen" the mermaid leave Erithea's home, his stowaway wouldn't have had time to reach any shore except the one she'd arrived on—the dock beach. The paths would lead her directly there, although if her descent of the bluffs of her home was any indication, she was capable of climbing rocks like a goat instead of following any path.

Not wanting to imagine her pitching off one of the

towering black cliffs that guarded the island, Trystan applied all the powerful speed within him and prayed Mariel did not possess the same swiftness.

He shouldn't have lingered, playing at games in hopes of finding someone to take her off his hands. He'd expected her to act like any Outsider woman and wait for him to choose a husband for her. In his observations of other lands, their womenfolk seemed submissive sorts who did as they were told and liked nothing better than to tend hearth and home.

But Mariel was a Crossbreed, not an Outsider. A woman with Aelynn blood would always be different. Judging from this incident, *submissive* was not in the mermaid's nature.

Even a mermaid could not survive the island's reef. And though his shield hadn't killed her earlier, it had knocked her unconscious. She might drown should she swim into it again.

Heart pounding in fear that he should so endanger an innocent creature who had done no more than foolishly believe him a god, Trystan raced to the top of the path where he could see the dark sea swirling across the darker sand in the early twilight.

He cursed at the sight of a white figure fleeing down the winding lower half of the path to the shore. She'd apparently left behind the coat and sarong she'd been given and was down to the rags in which she'd arrived. He should have provided her with proper garments.

Berating himself, wishing he had Iason's more useful trait of reading minds, Trystan took a shortcut—straight over the cliff boulders to the beach.

He didn't have the power of flight, but he had the agility of a goat and the experience of a boyhood spent on these rocks. He hit the black sand just as a splash that wasn't a wave sounded close by.

Curse Hades and thrice damnation! Kicking off his

sandals, grateful he wore little more than a loincloth, Trystan dove into the waves.

She swam like a fish, but he knew the undertow, and his strength was greater. He admired the supple way her limbs cut the dark water. Her long hair rippled to guide her, much as a cat's whiskers sensed its surroundings. She belonged in these waters, free as the porpoises. He would have loved to return her to that freedom, but he would not risk his home for a wild creature, no more than a man who admires lions would allow one to attack his village.

Especially not for a woman who did not keep her word.

She knew he was there. She cast a challenging glance over her shoulder before diving deep beneath the waves where he could not go for long. He followed her down and circled one slender, kicking ankle in his hand and held tight.

She swirled around to fight, swatting uselessly at him as the waves crashed over their heads. She could breathe down here. He could not. But his lungs held a large capacity of air, and he had experience in underwater fighting. She could not surpass his strength.

Taking advantage of her new position, he grasped her waist, kicked hard and hauled her upward. He found his footing on the sloping shore and gasped for breath as his head broke the surface. Before the slippery mermaiden could squirm away, he wrapped an arm around her throat and pulled her head back.

"I could snap your neck right now and no one would be the wiser," he growled against her ear. He struggled to keep her trapped while trying not to notice the enticing wiggle of her curvaceous buttocks against the wet linen covering his groin.

"Then snap it," she shouted. "Snap it and be done! You cannot hold me prisoner on this accursed island!"

"Why waste a sacrificial virgin?" he mocked. "Aelynn's volcano will be happy to take you. We haven't thrown a maiden into her fires in decades."

That shut her up. He knew his kind well. Their strengths all had natural weaknesses. Fire had to be a natural anathema to a sea maiden. Fire and water created steam, he conceded, and as Aelynn's conductor of heat, he was fire to her water. They were both nearly naked, pressed tight against each other's bodies, and despite the cold water, steam was definitely forming between them. If he weren't so infuriated by her senseless risk of life and limb, he'd have her here on the beach before either of them knew what they were doing.

"We have no other choice," he said implacably, forcing down the temperature between them. "If you would spend one moment thinking of someone other than yourself, you would realize the danger to my people if we let you go."

He clamped a hand over her mouth before she could argue.

"You would have to explain to your family where you've been," he continued. "Why should you lie for us? You've found a people much like yourself. When would it occur to you to come looking for us again? How would you keep from being followed? Wouldn't it be tempting to tell your sister or her child of the island, where you really belong? How do you think legends begin? There are already enough foolish tales out there to have idle men killing themselves on the shoals in search of a treasure that doesn't exist."

He swung her drenched form into his arms and carried her up the beach much as he had done earlier.

This time, he wouldn't make the mistake of letting her run free.

"I've found no one who wishes to take you off my hands, no easier person for you to get along with. We have no choice left. If you'll share the rites with me, wear the ring of silence, I will return you to your sister. If you won't take the vows, you've already proved you cannot keep your word, so I must fling you into the volcano. If the choice is between you and my home, my home and my people will come first every time."

He released her mouth now that he'd had his say. She could scream to her heart's content, and no one would sympathize. Even his sister had berated him for risking his chance to wed Lissandra and rule the island. The prestige did not interest Erithea so much as the security of knowing the island was safe in his hands.

He might salvage both their hopes by taking Mariel as amacara, praying that eventually Lissandra would have to see reason and become his wife. If Lissandra wanted to be Oracle, she had no other choice.

Mariel was not likely to understand the difference between physical amacara and legal wife, and he saw no reason to explain. Both were bonded for life.

"Fine, I'll say your vows, wear your ring, and then you will take me home, and I will never see your face again," she said, her scathing anger tinged with tears. "You hold me prisoner, refuse to help my family, treat me as a piece of poisonous trash you don't know how to be rid of, and you think *vows* will make it all better? You are crazier than people think me."

Satisfied he'd made her see reason, Trystan didn't try to argue with her. He didn't explain the nature of the vows—or their consequences—either. Amacara matches always created children. He had her agreement, and that was all that mattered for the moment.

Except that she'd agreed before and promptly attempted to escape.

He would make certain she could not run again.

"There are preparations to be made," he said calmly. "I'll leave you with Dylys. She will explain them to you. I will have to make my offerings and say my prayers, then we'll sail the day after next. Your impulsive pursuit of a foolish prophecy has caused no end of trouble for many people."

"My mother could see the future!" she cried. "Her promise was not foolish. I believed you to be the golden god she predicted. Times can be no more desperate, and there are no others like you. It should have been you she spoke of."

"It cannot be me. My place is here. You are welcome to stay as my . . . mate. Perhaps that is what she saw—that you lived safely here on Aelynn. If you insist on returning home, however, we will, after the ceremony." He already knew he wanted to keep her, but he couldn't for the life of him imagine how he could persuade her to it.

"I'll swim home," she replied sullenly.

Trystan still held the images of her bloody body caught on the reefs, and he shuddered. "The straits are guarded by coral that will scrape your hide raw should you try," he warned. "Take my word that I am a far preferable fate."

"You threaten me with torture and death, and you think I should take your word?" she asked in outrage.

"Every other man on this island would have thrown you into the volcano's maw. Even Dylys would have done the same. You will benefit from our vows far more than I shall."

She didn't have an answer for that.

As they traversed the path to the temple, her silence left Trystan free to contemplate his grim future. If Lissandra refused his offer of marriage after this, he might as well stay at sea and continue his duties as Translator.

They said Aelynn never gave a man burdens greater than he could carry. That didn't mean it was much of a life living beneath the weight of a mountain.

Six

"Where's Dylys?"

Soaked, defeated, chilled by the cold evening breeze, Mariel heard her captor's question with only half an ear as he lowered her to the ground. She wrapped her arms around herself, missing his warm, naked chest.

She didn't know why the dratted man insisted on ruining both their lives because of the commands of one old woman. She'd heard his despair when he'd told her that he would take the vows. His vows meant little to her since they weren't of her church, but judging from Trystan's gloom, they meant a great deal to him.

Not that she had any notion of how to escape while she was starved and half-frozen from her dip in the sea. Apparently gods didn't feel cold, if she was to judge by Trystan's lack of shivering. Of course, normally she didn't feel the sea's cold either. Fear made her icy, perhaps. Or the warmth of that strikingly wide, muscled chest had stolen her stamina. She had never seen a man's naked chest before. If they were all like his, no wonder men kept them covered. Women would not be able to work for wanting to touch and stroke and admire.

She carefully kept her gaze from straying lower. For some reason his trousers were in tatters, revealing far more of his masculine physique than she was prepared to acknowledge.

From the jungle's darkness a warm, masculine voice replied to Trystan's inquiry. "There's a birthing on the other side of the mountain that she had to attend."

The voice seemed to hold all the assurance and compassion of a man of God, and Mariel's hopes rose. Surely even an Aelynn priest would not allow such a travesty of justice. Or at least he wouldn't profane the marriage vows. She relaxed her grip around her waist, and Trystan immediately grasped her wrists together in one strong hand.

Mariel tossed her hair out of her eyes so she could stare into the forest's shadows and find the newcomer. Trystan had returned her to the temple.

Even chilled as she was, her insides knotted in fear and anticipation. He could use all the polite euphemisms he liked about vows and rings, but she'd seen the way he'd looked at her. He had only one thing on his mind, and that involved her near nakedness and the strange cushion that had bound and left her helpless earlier.

She would be ravished by midnight, thrown back home to starve by dawn, and no doubt left to bear a child who would be ostracized by his peers, provided she lived so long.

"My amacara has agreed to share our vows," Trystan said clearly as she struggled to be free of his grasp. "We need the Oracle's blessing."

"I can see that," the rich chocolate voice replied dryly. "You might release her and treat her with a little more respect, if she has willingly agreed to join us."

"Mermaidens are slippery. I would see her safely contained first."

Despite his words, Trystan released his hold on one

of her wrists, although Mariel was certain he'd break the other before he'd let her go. With her free arm she tried to cover the thin wet cloth clinging to her breasts and heard her captor's low curse.

"She needs food and clothing. Is there somewhere safe I can leave her until I gather them?" Trystan asked.

"My mother's sanctuary should suit. She keeps supplies and a bed there."

The speaker's silhouette filled the space between two of the temple stones. Tall and lean, he wore brown robes that concealed all but his bare feet. His hair blended with the darkness, and his face was little more than a blur. She had only his voice on which to judge his character.

She thought it wisest to hold her rash tongue for a change.

"Is there a lock for the door?" Trystan asked wryly.

"She has to agree to the vows," the voiced warned.

"She's agreed, if she can find no means of escape first."

Her captor was not a stupid man. Mariel managed a grin despite her chattering teeth. At least neither of them harbored any illusions.

"Trystan has spent the better part of his life aboard a ship of men," the voice explained. "Will you excuse his uncouth manners until he learns more grace?"

"He's no more or less than I expect of any man," she replied bravely, but her chattering teeth weakened the response.

"Then we understand each other." Without warning, Trystan swept her into his arms, warming her against his chest again. "I repeat, are there locks and bolts? I have never been inside your mother's private quarters."

"The seals work both ways," the figure said, hurrying to keep up as Trystan carried her across the clearing. "My mother likes her privacy."

Her captor smelled of salt water and incense and male musk. His arms cradled her firmly, the ripple of his muscles on her almost bare flesh shooting sharp arrows of awareness through her. She had the urge to slide her hand over the back of his neck, to comb her fingers through his golden mane. Hiding her shocking reaction, Mariel buried her cold nose against his shoulder. She could feel his heart pound beneath all those solid muscles, so perhaps he really was a flesh-and-blood man and not a god. That did not make her fate any easier to accept.

"My name is Iason. My friends call me Ian." The warm voice chuckled from beyond Trystan's shoulder. "Feel free to call for me if our friend is too crude."

Iason lit a taper, and Mariel lifted her head in time to glimpse striking angles and planes and dark eyes that held wells of wisdom and pain before she was carried into a dungeon.

She stared at the smoke-darkened rock walls in disbelief. They'd descended no cliffs. She'd seen no mountain. But this was a cave, nevertheless.

A fire abruptly leapt to life in a small hearth.

"My mother keeps fruit, bread, and spring water here. Please help yourself," Iason said from a cool distance, unlike his earlier warmth. "She will not mind if you borrow her blankets or cloaks. When she returns, she will instruct you in the rituals. I think she will want to hear your vows privately, without Trystan's intimidation."

"He doesn't intimidate me," Mariel muttered as the barbarian lowered her to the ground. But the magical fire did. Had Trystan ignited that? Or Iason? Neither man had gone near the grate. Neither man voiced surprise at the fire's origin. She'd assumed the islanders had special skills like hers, but this was the first obvious and frightening example of them. Lissandra's uncanny knowledge of Mariel's ability to milk goats didn't count as frightening.

"I'd suggest you let Dylys intimidate you into keeping your mouth shut," Trystan growled, bending near her ear to impart his message. "Or she'll feed you to Aelynn without my consent. One does not argue with an Oracle."

"Then I shall hope your Oracle is far wiser than you and says sensible things with which I need not argue," she retorted, hiding her fear by drifting toward the warmth and forcing a distance between them. Her foolish body might enjoy his strength, but she could not rely on a dangerous stranger who had promised to hold her captive until she appeased his wishes.

"You have argued with every sensible thing I've said." With that parting remark, her bridegroom left, slamming a wooden door in the rock wall behind her. A bolt grated across it from the outside.

Iason had already disappeared, she noted with a hint of panic at being locked inside a mountain. She had held some brief hope that the possessor of such a compassionate voice might rescue her, but it seemed none questioned the authority of the old lady.

She'd rested well, so she wasn't tired, just very confused, and growing more than a little worried. Even as a child, defeat was not in her nature, but she was tempted by it now. How had Trystan known to come after her? Unless he could fly, he shouldn't have had time to reach her. Exactly what abilities did he possess?

She studied the fire that had appeared from nowhere and seemed to burn without fuel. If she believed in magic, she'd declare herself bewitched and the whole island ensorcelled.

She'd lived with the superstition of the villagers all her life and believed none of it. They made up stories to explain the inexplicable. She had heard fishermen talk of seeing an enormous green sea monster herding schools of fish beneath their boats to explain a particularly fine catch—one she'd driven into their nets. She'd been so insulted at the description that she'd refrained from helping them again for a long time. Green sea monster, indeed!

She'd quit leaving oysters at the parish door after the priest threw her offering back into the ocean, exhorting the devil who had scratched at his door with the temptations of evil.

Devils and sea monsters didn't exist. They were just her.

Somehow, she must outwit these people and escape.

She studied the bowl on the table and chose the familiar cherries over an exotic unknown fruit. The fire quickly dried her sheer shift, but even in her dazed state she recognized the need for more concealing garments. Locating a long white robe on a wardrobe shelf, she pulled it over her head and belted it with a strip of leather that lay next to it, offering a brief prayer of gratitude to Trystan's gods—just in case.

Warmth and food returned some of her energy. Perhaps the distance from her obstinate captor helped also. Her desire for him muted her need to flee. Physical desire was an earthly form of ensorcellment, and more frightening than magic since it was real. She did not wish to fall victim to either. She had to go home.

She tried the door, but it would neither push nor pull. She opened more cabinets and ran her fingers over shelves in hopes of finding a key or a secret passage.

She lifted a flaming taper from its holder and, munching on the bread and cheese she'd discovered in a cupboard, approached the darkened back wall. A narrow aperture led into a Spartan cell with a single bed and a shelf of books. She was a nobleman's daughter and had had tutors growing up. She could read, but these weren't in a language she recognized.

She began a thorough search of the walls, running her hands over rocks and shelves and hunting for any sign of exit. Excitement danced in Mariel's middle when she slid her hand behind a tapestry and felt a place that was not solid rock. She knew the cliff caves of home well, used them to hide her unorthodox proclivities. Many of them had more than one entrance, if one was daring enough to brave the unknown.

What did she have to lose?

Pulling the tapestry back so she could see the wall, she still couldn't make out the opening that she felt. She ran her hand over the stone until her fingers sank into a substance that seemed thick and resilient, much like a jellyfish. For all their translucence, jellyfish were tough creatures, not easily permeable.

She held up the torch and studied the rock. She could only feel the aperture where there seemed to be an outcropping of rock. Her hand did not want to go through, but when she pushed . . . she could feel fresh air on the other side.

Nothing ventured, nothing gained. She shoved her foot through the invisible aperture. Nothing ate it. The thick jellylike air rippled up her bare leg beneath the robe when she pressed her knee through. She gritted her teeth against terror when she continued forward, and she felt it tingle across the place between her legs that had throbbed with need hours ago. But the substance did not penetrate. She squeezed through the barrier, holding her breath and letting the thick air touch her head last.

In seconds, she had passed through to another

chamber and lifted the taper on a musty storage room full of oddities. Disappointed, she rummaged briefly, having no idea what she sought. It wasn't as if she could wield a sword or wave a magic wand and escape.

She saw odd metal chairs with cushions, and crates of strangely ornamented substances she did not recognize, mixed with dented candlesticks, pots with broken handles, and similar items a careful housekeeper might hope to mend someday. Did anyone even know the chamber existed?

Examining the walls, Mariel glimpsed a pretty blue light winking at her from a cabinet in a shadowy corner. Climbing over the chairs covered in a material similar to leather, she studied the sealed cabinet with puzzlement. It held no blue on the outside.

She ran her fingers over the graven metal door, looking for a handle and finding none. Just when she was about to turn away, the cabinet opened of its own accord.

The blue winked again. This time, she could see the object through a crack in a wooden partition. She pushed aside a moldering scabbard, pressed along the old wood, and finally opened the back of the cupboard to examine a battered pewter vessel that did not seem valuable enough to have been deliberately hidden so much as forgotten.

It possessed the bowl and pedestal of a chalice, but it was not formed like any chalice she had ever seen. The bowl was too wide for easy drinking, and the stem was too stubby for a man's hand, although hers wrapped around it neatly. The foot of the chalice was smaller than the bowl. She couldn't imagine it balanced well when filled.

But the pretty blue stones twinkled merrily in the torchlight, and it seemed a shame to hide them away in this dark hole. Perhaps she could use the bowl as a weapon of sorts. It wasn't heavy enough to bash out a man's brains, but the pewter would leave a nice dent in his head.

With the partition closed up again and the vessel tucked in her belt, Mariel felt invincible. Somehow, she knew there was a door out of here, if she just looked in the right way.

She lifted the torch to shine on the back wall, searching for the exit. She didn't know how much time she had left, but she wouldn't give up hope of escape.

A breeze fluttered an old cloak lying over a chest in the far corner.

There should be no breeze inside a mountain—unless there was an opening to the outside.

Triumphant, Mariel tugged the chest away from the rocky wall. Using the torch, she examined every inch until she found a crack just along the bottom where rocks had shifted, perhaps in an earth tremor. She might very well get stuck in anything so narrow, and rot here until she was naught but bones. Or until she got hungry and cursed Trystan loudly enough to bring someone looking for her.

Her luck had held thus far, and something beyond her normal common sense urged her on. She would question the urge later, when she was safe at home, preparing a hot meal for Francine. Then she might well go mad pondering her peculiar adventure.

Propping the taper in an old lantern holder, she slid her feet through the crack first. A rush of chilly air caressed her toes. Excitement tickled beneath her skin, but she'd learned to be cautious exploring the winding channels carved by sea and wind. This crack could drop into a mile of nothingness. Or straight into the volcano's maw. Trystan thought she didn't know what Aelynn was, but she wasn't a complete nodcock. Volcanoes created islands.

She pulled her feet back, found a rusted mug, and dropped it through the hole. She heard a splash almost instantly.

Water. Perfect. She had reached the sea.

Eager now, she poked her head through—salt air greeted her and she breathed deeply of that blessed scent. *Freedom!*

Within minutes, she was standing knee-deep in salt water in a crevasse jutting into the mountain from the sea. Remembering her borrowed clothing, she set the chalice aside, unfastened the leather belt, and tugged the confining robes over her head.

Now what? Trystan had said the reefs would eat her alive. She'd arrived on the rope hanging from his ship. She couldn't expect the same escape now.

She debated leaving the old chalice behind, but the blue stones sparkled cheerfully, as if begging for the light of day after years of abandonment. Deciding she deserved some reward for being kidnapped, imprisoned, and threatened with death, she knotted the ugly thing into the leather belt and tied the belt to her waist.

The torchlight flared momentarily through the crevasse, as if caught by a wind. In that momentary flare, she saw a small dory.

Perfect. She could row past the coral before swimming home.

"Unless your mermaiden has a skill for invisibility and makes herself known shortly, you are in very deep trouble, young man."

Trystan's heart froze at the tone of Dylys's voice as she entered her sanctuary with the first light of dawn. She'd scolded him enough when he was a bold child who dared climb the peaks to explore Aelynn's eagle nests. She'd punished him for a week when he'd led Iason to do the same. She had never sounded so coldly furious as this. What could he possibly have done to anger the island's leader?

He stepped past her into the room where he'd left Mariel. Last night, Iason had locked the outer door so even Trystan couldn't enter. With the Oracle's arrival, he'd been confident he would find Mariel peeling fruit for her breakfast and aiming murderous glares at him.

He didn't expect to find a chilled and empty room. Even the fire in the hearth had gone out—leaving him cold all over.

He rushed past the table to the back room, where Dylys waited in a bedchamber that was also empty and untouched. Disasters like this did not happen to him! How could one wretched waif destroy all he had worked so hard to accomplish? "How could she leave with none knowing of it?" he shouted.

"That is the purpose of this place," Dylys explained, as if to a dense student. "I come here for privacy from all your passing thoughts and to think my own without intrusion."

"Even if there is some way out, she can't escape the reefs and my shield!" Trystan hated the note of panic in his words. He should be relieved that Mariel had decided her own fate and was no longer his problem.

Except that she would always be his problem, a voice said in the back of his head.

"I assume the gods wish you to find out if she can," Dylys said dryly, responding to both his thoughts and his words. "Only people Aelynn trusts should be able to leave these rooms. Until you know her fate, there is naught you can do here."

Her statement tolled a death knell to his hope.

Reluctant to believe Mariel could escape so easily, Trystan ran his hands over the back wall. If the room was protected as Dylys said, then there might be a force shield. It took him several minutes to locate the opening to the secret storage room, but he found a familiar barrier that allowed him to push through. The abandoned taper and billowing tapestry on the distant wall said it all—although how Mariel could have found a concealed entrance, much less passed Dylys's barrier without a ring, was as mysterious as her survival of *his* shield.

"She should never have been able to access this room," Dylys complained. "She should never have known of its existence."

"Now you know how I feel," Trystan grumbled, glancing around to be certain there was no place she could have hidden. He was certain he would have sensed her if she were here, but he looked anyway. The torch revealed no more than a jumble of dusty junk. No one knew precisely where Dylys kept the island's treasures—the chalice and the sword that were the reason for the island's existence. The Oracle might even transport the sacred objects from place to place. If they were in here, they would be disguised. Mariel wouldn't know what they were. Besides, she wasn't a thief. She hadn't even taken their clothes last time she'd left.

Dropping to his knees, he gazed into the dark crack revealed by the chest.

A white robe waved in the breeze below, held down by a rock so it wouldn't blow away. Again, she'd left behind everything given to her.

Mariel could have been gone for hours.

Trystan felt the cold shock of Aelynn's demands as he realized he was not master of his fate. Mariel's escape was a threat to all he knew and loved, a breach of his duties as Guardian.

"I didn't know your sanctuary led to the sea, or I'd not have left her alone," he said bitterly, rising to his feet and striding toward an entrance more suited to his size. He'd known Mariel was slender, but only a slippery fish could have slid through that crack. Perhaps slippery fish could slide through all their impenetrable barriers. Shouldn't Iason have known of the exit?

If so, why had Iason betrayed him? Pondering the logic of an unfathomable mystic was beyond Trystan's capability at the moment.

"I am sorry, Trystan," Dylys said with grave regret, following him to the entrance of her sanctuary. "I can call a council if you ask it, but we both know what they will say."

They would say no one was allowed to leave Aelynn without a ring of silence. He had to fetch Mariel back, dead or alive.

The empty altar in the temple gleamed in the dawn light, mocking him. There would be no rites or consummation today. The ring he'd fetched from home burned a hole in his pocket.

"If she's alive, she will go straight to her village." At least he knew where to find her. The big "if" was in whether she would survive the journey.

In the twenty-four hours he'd known Mariel, she'd caused him more grief, hope, and frustration than he'd ever experienced. He wanted to strangle her and make love to her, get rid of her and have a child with her. He'd not understood that an amacara could affect more than his body, and he wasn't at all certain that he wanted to spend the rest of his life in this emotional cyclone. Stoic Lissandra was far more his type.

Standing in the dawn's light, fingers clenched into fists of frustration, Trystan tried telling himself that if he found Mariel's body floating in the passage, he would be free to return to Lissandra and the stable future he'd always envisioned.

But when he imagined seagulls pecking clean Mariel's elegant bones, or sharks nibbling her vibrant entrails, his soul groaned in horror. Even without the vows, she had sunk her hooks into him.

With a roar of futility, Trystan flung the ring that matched his own into the temple altar—the altar where he should be taking Mariel now, where he should be creating their child. He had spent this night picturing how he would take her, and how she would respond. That image had been all that had helped him through the night.

The altar spit his ring back out. The band of gold and opal rattled across the stones.

"You cannot come back without her or her body," Dylys reminded him. "You have less than half a moon cycle before you must rebuild the shield or transfer your power to another."

But all Trystan could hear was the wail of a gull overhead and the haunting cry of a lost dolphin below.

Smoke twisted from Aelynn's peak. Rain pattered in the sand, creating ripples at his feet.

"Should you fail at your task, you will be greatly missed," Dylys said sadly. "Your nephew, Kerry, is young yet, but he has potential. We will have to transfer your Guardian powers to him."

Banished, like Murdoch. Forbidden ever to walk the sands of his home again, to argue with his sister, to play with his nieces and nephew, to sail with his friends. Waylan would no doubt eat his goats.

Worse yet, if he could not return with her before the full moon, his shield—all that he was—would be taken from him.

Anguish howled through the emptiness within. The gods had surely turned their backs on him.

Seven

"I'll need a smaller ship that won't be missed if I must stay off Aelynn." Trystan faced his friends with resignation. "I cannot involve anyone else in this journey. Is the sloop repaired? I'll trade whatever you think will make a fair price for her."

Waylan owned the sloop. When he was not aboard a ship, he was mending or building one. His was a restless nature not given to leisure. Unlike most of the island's other bachelors, he lived in the shack his Aelynn foster father had built near the sea.

"Your ship is more than fair recompense," Waylan agreed without inflection. "We'll trade back when you return."

No one wished to estimate the chances of his returning. Those given to living in the Outside World seldom came back. The reasons were as varied as the seas, although death was often the final reason. Aelynners did not survive long in a primitive and violent world where their principles did not allow them to use their uncanny gifts, for good reason—witch hunts were unpleasant and often harmed the innocent, including the families they established there.

"Don't eat my goats," Trystan warned. "They're valuable for their milk and make lousy meat."

"Then come back for them," Waylan growled, incapable of showing his feelings elsewise.

Nevan swung away from the table. "I'll go with you. I've nothing to hold me here, and you might need an extra hand with the sails and navigation."

"I can sail a sloop on my own. Waylan can't sail the *Destiny* without you. But I thank you for the thought."

His friends stood there, clenching their fingers into fists, looking angry and unhappy.

Trystan did not know how to say farewell. He had thought this last was his final journey, and now he might never see his beloved home again. Acting as if he were only going for a short swim, he nodded, and strolled from the tavern, wearing the clothes of the Outside World.

The goats he kept in town ran to butt against his boots in hopes of acquiring the treats he usually carried on him. When he was very young, other boys had taunted him over his softness for animals, but his pets' affection filled an empty place in his life as an orphan. So he'd pounded sense into his friends over the years, and confident in himself, he was no longer discomfited by anything or anyone. Until Mariel had come along.

Pulling a leather bag from the pocket of his tailed frock coat, Trystan fed his pets by hand, scratching their silken heads in farewell. He would have to see Erithea before he left. He had to explain to her children somehow. His fifteen-year-old nephew, Kerry, would have to travel as Translator sooner than his age should allow, if Trystan did not return.

He didn't need to say anything to Lissandra. She already knew, and she did nothing to change her mother's decision. A future Oracle had to learn to be cruel in her objectivity, but he would have liked some sign that she would miss him. He'd lost his parents years ago, and his sister had her own family to keep her occupied. He was just realizing how much he craved a home and a family he could call his own. Lissandra would have fulfilled that dream.

The future of the island was now in his hands in a manner he hadn't expected. If Mariel survived her swim, he had to halt her before she said too much, before the greedy of the world sought the rare treasures here, then overran and destroyed their way of life.

It was a terrifying responsibility, but one he was fully prepared to uphold in whatever manner necessary. He buckled on his sword and rapier and strode from the village.

Swimming to shore in the gray dawn of the fourth day since her departure, Mariel stood when her feet touched sand. Every muscle of her body ached as she lugged the belt with the chalice to the rocks that hid her clothes.

Once dressed, she rubbed the mottled metal of the old cup and pondered the best method of disposing of it. The blue stones twinkled like blue eyes in the dawn's early light, and she smiled. "You would like to live in luxury, would you not?" she asked of it. "You do not belong in a musty old cabinet. You should be polished to a lovely shine for all the world to see."

That's when she thought of her father's distant cousin, the baroness.

The lady was seldom in Pouchay and scarcely acknowledged the existence of her poor country relations, but she had wealth and no one to spend it on but herself. Perhaps she could be persuaded to buy the chalice.

Mariel was exhausted and needed rest, but she could not return to Francine empty-handed. Once she was dressed in her plain black gown and white apron, determination forced her up the cliffs to the vicomte's castle fortress, where the baroness sometimes stayed.

She braided her wet hair and shoved it into her cap on the way up the cliff. She needed to look as modest as possible when she greeted the guards and asked after her cousin. She had avoided the upper echelons of society since her father's death. Eduard's name didn't offer enough protection for women who wandered about without maid or consort, and she disliked drawing attention to herself. But this matter was too important for her to be squeamish.

To Mariel's relief, the guard reported the baroness was currently in residence. Mariel wound her way through the narrow alleys inside the castle walls without incident at this near-dawn hour and prayed that her cousin was an early riser. In her present state, she would fall asleep if she must cool her heels waiting for the lady to awake.

She caught the Baroness Celeste Beloit preparing for bed.

"Mariel St. Just!" the baroness cried as the maid led her into the overperfumed, overdecorated bedchamber. "I thought you married and long gone from here."

"It is my sister who married, my lady." Mariel curtsied as she'd been taught, although balancing with the awkward cup in her arms wasn't easy. "She and her husband are expecting a blessed event shortly."

"Ah, excellent." The lady gazed into her gilded mirror to cream the powder off her face. Widowed young, she'd lived alone for years. Although she appeared almost Mariel's age, she must be close to forty. "And what brings you here so unexpectedly? Surely that is not your father's silver you carry?" She nodded at Mariel's reflection to indicate the chalice.

"No, it is a pewter cup I found half-buried in the

sand," she lied. "It has pretty gems on it and is useless to us." Francine would never forgive her if she begged for food, and the cost of bread was so steep it was frivolity to ask for it. Best to request coins, then choose whatever was fresh in the market. "I would like to buy some presents for the baby," which really wasn't a lie, "and thought perhaps you would know someone who might be interested in purchasing it."

White powder wrinkled in the lady's frown, but she turned on her vanity seat and held out her hands for the object. "One cup has little purpose. One needs a set."

Holding her breath, Mariel handed over the pretty chalice. The blue gems reminded her of the sea and beckoned to her. She almost hated to let it go.

The baroness gasped when she touched the stem. Instead of handling it with disdain, she examined the cup reverently. "It has an interesting vibration," she murmured in admiration.

Vibration? Mariel blinked sleepily at her cousin, wondering which of them had lost her mind, or had she lost track of the conversation? She really needed to get some rest.

"It's winking at me!" the lady cried in delight, cradling the chalice in her arms. "This is exactly the sign I needed. Thank you so much, my dear! I shall accept the chevalier's proposal. The cup will make a lovely wedding gift for a financier of his extraordinary good sense."

"Then you will buy it from me?" Mariel prodded, hoping her cousin did not think this was a generous gift.

"My dear, I will give you anything you like. Name your price." The baroness set the cup on her dressing table and stroked it with the fondness one expends upon a pet.

Staggered by this generosity, Mariel asked for enough wheat to feed a village, a price so obscene she could not believe anyone would pay it.

Still staring at the winking chalice as if she could not turn away, the baroness nodded. "Of course, child. If it is wheat you want, I'll pay the vicomte to open his stores. And give you some coins for yourself and the babe. You must call me Celeste, and ask Francine if she will make some of her lovely lace for my wedding present."

Almost fainting from hunger and fatigue, Mariel bobbed another curtsy and prayed she wasn't dreaming. Could one cup provide plenty for all? Was this how the golden god was meant to save them? It was a miracle, after all.

"Isn't this worth the wait?" Mariel crowed, sitting at the table and watching her sister rip into the soft golden crust fresh from the baker's oven. "I'm sorry I made you fret for so long, but it could not be avoided. The sea does not give up its treasures easily."

She had left the wheat with the baker and gone home to sleep for hours. Not until the first loaf had been delivered to their door had her sister dared to wake her.

"I feared you had drowned," Francine said, tears rushing to her eyes.

"Well, I'd rather drown at sea than starve on land." Mariel pulled off a hunk of yeasty soft bread for herself. "Besides, I'm far more likely to starve than drown. You know that. Have you had word from Eduard yet? Has the Assembly bargained with the king for wheat?"

Mariel knew better. The men gathering in Paris wouldn't do anything so practical as ask for bread when all the country was hungry. They would argue politics until they turned blue, brought out swords, and started killing each other. The best she could hope was that Eduard would have the sense to come home then. The word that the king's mercenary armies were gathering around Paris did not suggest any agreement was near.

Until Eduard came home, she had to distract her sister from fretting. It couldn't be good for the child she carried. Smugly, Mariel caressed the coins in her pocket. She even had enough left from the sale of the chalice to host a banquet for the midwife and all the relatives who would descend upon them when the child was born. The old piece had been worth far more than she'd imagined. The nobility had strange tastes.

"You know Eduard explained that the king must consent to tax his nobles to fill the empty treasury so we can buy grain," Francine chided. "Once the Assembly is agreed on how it should be done, things will right themselves."

"The nobles and the clergy have never in the history of France agreed to be taxed," Mariel said. "It is against human nature to believe those in power will tax themselves."

"We should not be as greedy as the nobility," Francine admonished, ignoring her sister's pessimism. "You should give a portion of your treasure to the church."

"I will. I just wanted to see you eat and smile first." Rising from her chair, Mariel tested her cap pins. She detested the cap and the bodice that squeezed the air from her, but she must look like the landed gentry—however impoverished—that she purported to be. Appearances were the only protection they had in these uncertain times.

"I trust Father Antoine will spend the coins on the

poor and not on wine for himself," Mariel said darkly. "I am tempted to hand out the coins directly to the needy."

"And be murdered for your purse?" Francine asked. "I really am not so blind to the ways of the world as you believe. Purchasing the grain was an excellent idea. We will all have bread for weeks, and no one need know from whence it came. But silver is too rare to hold safely. Take only the coins you mean to give and do not let anyone see you give them."

"I shall be properly humble in my charity," Mariel said with mockery at her baby sister's orders. She handed over the coins intended for the midwife and other necessities before slipping out the door and into the village street.

It felt odd to see familiar surroundings after her strange journey. The ancient stones of buildings worn smooth by the ocean's storms seemed gray and dismal in comparison to the blinding white and vivid colors of Aelynn. The hard green fruit on gnarled old cherry trees could scarcely equal an extraordinary jungle of ripe, exotic produce.

But she was deeply grateful to have returned safely. She'd been knocked unconscious again while leaving the reefs, and it was only the small boat and a band of dolphins that had saved her. There had been times after she'd woke in the dory that she'd wondered if it had all been a dream.

Except for the chalice. The wonderful, marvelous, ugly chalice.

She skipped a light step on the way to the church. She ought to feel like a thief for stealing such a valuable piece, but it had been shoved in a dark corner and forgotten, if the dust covering it was any indication. No one would miss it. Besides, it seemed a sin to hoard wealth when others went hungry. She would steal again to survive if it meant saving lives.

Not that she would harm anyone to survive, she amended as the church came into view. If she and Francine were meant to die of starvation, then they would die. But it did seem as if God had delivered her to the island and provided the ugly bowl to prevent that from happening.

Was that all Maman's prediction had meant? That Trystan would sail her to a magic island where she could acquire the wealth to save the village for another few weeks? How very . . . disappointing.

She halted outside the small church to genuflect and cross herself and pray for a state of grace for fear of being struck down for her theft. She couldn't possibly confess *all* her sins without being thought mad or worse, so she hoped God understood.

When she straightened, her gaze caught an unusual flash of striking gold from the direction of the harbor. She stopped to stare in dismay at a man taller and broader than any person in town striding briskly up the cobbled hillside, without the shuffle of hunger and misery.

A man whose mere presence caused heads to turn and eyes to widen. A milkmaid stumbled and dropped an empty pail while turning to watch the golden god in all his furious glory. Only the clatter of metal against stone woke her sufficiently to send her scurrying down the hill after it.

Mariel's heart sank to her feet at the formidable sight of Trystan's grim presence, but a small part of her, the female part that she'd only just discovered, sang a song of delight.

She could have slipped inside the church and hidden, but everyone knew her. Not even the most rebellious radical could resist the compelling presence of a village legend. Anyone Trystan asked would direct him to Francine, who would be terrified.

Now that Mariel was on her own ground, she trusted that her friends would rescue her should Trystan try his usual feat of carrying her where he wanted her to go. She defiantly remained where she was. She was as unaccustomed to being told what to do as she suspected he was unaccustomed to being defied. An Episode of Unpleasantness loomed.

Hands on hips, she caught Trystan's gaze from halfway down the stony hill. Poppies danced in reds and pinks along a sagging picket fence across the street. The stone wall of the church's cloistered garden and cemetery lined the space between them. Arms filled with a basket of fresh laundry, a laundress stepped from her shop and swiveled in awe to follow Trystan's path up the hill. He strode past without noticing, his narrowed gaze focused entirely on his goal.

Mariel shivered. She'd like to think his attention was because of her great beauty, but she was a tall, gawky black crow in this gown and cap. She was amazed he even recognized her.

The way he made her feel, she hardly recognized herself. She was awestruck, and consumed with improper thoughts that a maiden should not acknowledge.

The golden god seemed even taller and broader in the narrow gray street of her home. In a futile attempt to blend in with her world, he wore an elegant navy silk coat with gold frogging and white lining to match his white breeches. The buckles on his knee-high boots gleamed with gold. A jeweled scabbard hung on his hip. Except for the absence of a powdered wig, he did not lack the accoutrements of an aristocratic gentleman.

But he was too large, too forceful, too mysterious in his golden aspect to fit the role.

Mariel considered running before his wrath, but her feet were frozen to the cobblestones.

"I have not said a word to anyone about your home," she stated when he halted in front of her. "You are asking for trouble returning here. Everyone knows the legend of the golden god."

"I am not a legend," he growled down on her. "I am a man who has been driven beyond his limits by a female with the brains of a tree frog. You could have killed yourself out there!"

She blinked back her astonishment at this strange argument, and continued on the course of attack she had assumed. "Now that you see I am not so foolish, you may go back to where you came from without fear of my spoiling your life. I have taken care of my people without any help from you, thank you very much."

Trystan's smile was most unpleasant. "And how did you perform this miracle? By multiplying loaves and fishes?"

Shocked at his sacrilege, she nervously jiggled the coins in her pocket. "The sea occasionally throws out its treasures," she lied with the defensiveness she'd had to learn from the time she could swim. "I sold an ugly old cup to a lady at the castle who thought it would make an excellent wedding gift."

She talked too much when she was nervous. But she couldn't calm down beneath that icy blue gaze that seemed to pierce her heart and see the truth.

"An ugly old cup isn't likely to feed a village," he said with suspicion. "I've brought the coins I earned during my last voyage. We will leave them with your sister to dispense as necessary. Then we will return to my home and say the vows you promised."

Flee or argue? Neither seemed practical, but she had more experience at arguing than fleeing. "I left so you needn't say that vow! Go back. Tell them I died. I promise never to say a word about that strange dream I had that is already fading from my poor, mad, overexerted female brain."

Dismissing her sarcasm, Trystan caught Mariel's elbow and forced her to follow him down the street toward the harbor or be ignominiously dragged. "You will say the vows that will ensure that silence, and I will return you, just as promised."

She wasn't stupid. She knew marriage vows involved more than saying words. "Return me whole, just as I am?" she asked with irony.

Trystan's piercing glare said she had guessed rightly. A burning in her midsection warned she wasn't entirely averse to his intent to physically claim her. If she listened to her animal nature, she'd agree to her own ruin without a qualm.

"I believe your kind calls it a marriage of convenience," he said dryly. "I support you and yours, and you grace my bed when I ask. Do you have some lover you will disappoint?"

Put that way, in terms she understood, it almost made sense. Except he had already made it clear he was being forced into this, and she saw no advantage to either of them.

"I believe in *my* world," she mocked as he tugged her past the silversmith, "you would be purchasing the prestige of my family with such a marriage. That is not the case here, is it?"

Trystan halted to grab both her elbows and practically rubbed his nose to hers. "I am purchasing my damned life and yours!"

Shaken by his response, Mariel could not immediately find her tongue. Purchasing their lives? Surely the old woman would not really kill them? If so, his home was as violent as hers.

Apparently taking her silence as agreement, Trystan gripped her more gently.

In so doing, he glanced at the window of the silversmith's and his face lost all its color. "How did that get there?" he asked in a voice so thunderous that it should have shaken the last unripe cherries from the trees.

Mariel nearly didn't recognize the ugly chalice in the window. Since this morning when she'd last seen it, the bowl had been polished until it gleamed silver and the blackened glass on its stem and base shone like rare gems.

The blue stones winked at her.

Eight

"*You stole the Chalice of Plenty?*" Trystan roared incredulously, alarms clamoring at all his Guardian instincts. "How could you steal the chalice?"

The chalice was beyond legend—it and the Sword of Justice were the reason the gods watched over Aelynn and its people. Without the chalice . . . It didn't bear thinking. Everything they were derived from those two treasures. His imagination could not stretch far enough to grasp their fates without the silver bowl.

Instead of guarding the treasure, he had singlehandedly brought ruin to his home. *His* mate had stolen the chalice! How could that be?

Mariel continued to look from Trystan to the window in bewilderment. For a brief—very brief—moment, he thought he was mistaken. She looked so beautiful and forlorn. . . .

But then he remembered she'd admitted selling a cup to buy bread for the village.

A sudden ugly thought struck him, and Trystan gripped the arm of his pretty nemesis hard enough to bruise. "Did Murdoch send you? I swear, if you are in league with him, I will carve you into grains of sand."

The possibility that his former friend had been driven mad by his banishment loomed suddenly terrifying in his mind's eye. Murdoch might not be able to speak of the island, but that didn't prevent his remembering everything about it. What might he do in a fit of revenge?

"Murdoch? Is he another like you?" Still looking uncertain, Mariel pressed her slender palm to the window separating her from the blue stones.

Why had the gods cursed him with such a willful woman?

Trystan dragged Mariel, stumbling, into the tiny shop. He had never in his life dared to touch the chalice. He had seen it once, as a child, for some ceremony where it had twinkled merrily at him, just as it was doing now. There was seldom occasion to drag the relic from its hiding place in these days of plenty. Tales of ancient centuries spoke of dire times when the chalice ventured abroad, but not in his lifetime. A drought and a harsh winter seemed insufficient reason for the chalice to leave of its own accord.

It contained the power of the gods, and Mariel had *stolen* it. His scalp was already aching at the thought of the wrath that was about to be meted out on his head.

Unwilling to touch the sacred object, Trystan produced his sack of coins and slammed it on the counter before the startled silversmith. "I want to buy the cup in the window," he said in the Breton tongue.

The smith looked anxiously at Mariel, who appeared more puzzled than shaken now that Trystan hadn't killed her. He'd correct that.

With malice aforethought, he gripped her chastely covered nape, ostensibly in a gesture of affection. "My bride tells me she was forced to sell the heirloom before I could arrive. I would like to buy it back for her wedding gift."

The smith shook his head sorrowfully. "I'm sorry.

Lady Beloit asked me to merely clean it. She wishes to give it to her fiancé. Perhaps if you will talk with her, she will understand. . . ." He gestured helplessly.

He could steal it. He could simply lift the cup from the shelf and walk off. What was the worst that could happen? The smith would cry thief. The local militia would run after him with muskets—people in the line of fire would be killed. He would be interfering in the Outside World and banished for breaking Aelynn law. Still he was tempted. . . .

"Thank you, monsieur." The woman beneath his hand bobbed a curtsy, interrupting his dangerous thoughts. "When the baroness returns, if you will tell her we wish to speak with her about the cup, we would appreciate it."

She broke Trystan's grip on her nape and walked out the door, down an unpaved alley parallel to the harbor, where the sloop waited. Grabbing his purse of coins, Trystan caught up with her in a few strides.

"Do you have any idea what you've done?" he growled through clenched teeth, shaken by how close he had come to doing the forbidden.

"Obviously, I do not. I am not normally a thief. I simply thought I deserved some recompense for the insult offered me. The cup did not seem very valuable. I thought it pewter with pretty paste stones, worth enough to buy bread for Francine. I was shocked when the baroness offered far more. I almost rejected her charity." She turned down another alley leading toward the cliffs.

"Charity?" He bit back any further roar in favor of learning what went on in that strange mind of hers. He certainly had no immediate idea how to undo what she had done. Throttling her swanlike neck and shaking her until her wits rattled were unlikely to solve the problem. "Where are we going?"

"To see the baroness so I might explain that it was a mistake. I can return some of the coins she gave me, but she spent a dreadful amount on grain for the baker. I must think of some way to explain to Francine that I need the rest of the coins back," she added anxiously, worrying at her bottom lip.

Trystan refused to consider that plump lip and what he'd like to do with it. He felt like a whirling top that she kept hitting with a stick to keep him spinning. "How much did you sell the chalice for?" He had brought all the coins he possessed, but Aelynners mostly bartered, so he did not have a great number.

She named a sum that would beggar him.

Stunned, Trystan sat down on an oak bench outside a tavern. "How much of that have you spent?" he demanded, mentally tallying his coins and wondering if he had anything valuable to trade. He should have brought pearls, but they drew too much attention in rural areas.

Mariel collapsed on the seat beside him, her homespun skirt looking threadbare against his silk. Even though she wore her hair demurely pinned beneath a cap, he recognized the mermaid's wildness. The amacara Aelynn had chosen for him was headstrong and would blow him off course if he did not firmly man the ropes. His blood might still be thick with desire from the arresting memory of this maiden aroused and awaiting his possession on the altar, but nonetheless, his head still worked. At least he thought it did.

"I bought a cartload of grain," she murmured. "We have gone hungry for so long, and the price will only go higher before the next harvest. It cost most of my prize."

"Grain costs that much here?" Trystan asked in amazement, turning her words over and applying them to his predicament. Aelynn did not normally trade for grain, so he had small idea of its value. Forbidden to interfere in the Other World, Aelynners had learned long ago not to question the merchants with whom they traded about anything other than the goods they sought. To do so tempted the soft of heart to meddle. Had the chalice decided his world had plenty, and hers not enough? Surely the chalice wouldn't break the law!

"Do you think I lie?" she asked bitterly.

For some odd reason, he did not. A fortune, for humble wheat. No wonder she looked half starved, as did most of the town's inhabitants. Avoiding considering the consequences of this disaster, Trystan let his mind wander to the tempting female beside him.

She didn't wear rings and gloves like the fine ladies he'd met in this and other countries of Europe. She clasped her bare hands in her skirt, and he could see the calluses from hard work on them. On Aelynn, hearth maids used their earthy abilities to clean without need of harsh scrubbing, and nurturers worked the fields with their special aptitude for growing things, so everyone else was free to follow their own interests and talents to the betterment of society.

The gifted woman fated to be his amacara had been abandoned to survive in a primitive world without even the most basic of necessities or education. *That* was what happened when island children were had by Outsiders instead of in the shelter of Aelynn. He could not approve. Even so worthless an ability as swimming with fishes deserved the care and appreciation of her own kind. If he took Mariel home with him, she need never scrub or farm again.

But the task was no longer as simple as he'd once thought. Now, he had to retrieve a stolen treasure and pray Dylys didn't throw both of them into the mountain for the sacrilege of having taken the chalice from its rightful home.

"If the cup is so valuable, why was it neglected like that?" Mariel asked while his mind reeled.

How by all the gods could he explain? Of all the travesties of justice caused by abandoning the Crossbreeds, this lack of education was the greatest. "The chamber you broke into is protected by the gods," he said. "No one except Dylys should have been able to enter, and no one but she should have been able to recognize or find the sacred object."

She darted him a nervous look from beneath lowered lashes. "A *sacred* object? Irreplaceable?"

"Irreplaceable," he agreed grimly. More than irreplaceable, it was dangerous and unpredictable, but he couldn't explain that to someone who didn't wear the ring.

"And your purse is not large enough to cover the wheat's cost if I give you all I have?"

"How much do you have?" he asked in resignation. Nothing had gone the way he'd planned since he'd first met the mermaiden. Why expect better now?

Mariel gave him the coins she'd intended for the church. She was resisting telling him about the money Francine held in hopes his purse could cover them, but if he did not lie . . . She'd stolen a *sacred* object.

She tried to imagine how she'd feel if he'd stolen the rare gilded porcelain statue of the holy mother that adorned their church. She would be appalled and sickened and would miss it immensely, but she still thought feeding the village was worth the sacrifice. The clergy hoarded their wealth at the expense of their people, just as the nobility did.

Then she tried to dismiss Trystan's pagan gods and their profane magic, but she could not. If she had not seen and done things that did not belong to the narrow world she lived in, she might have scorned his religion, but she had talked to dolphins and knew there were wonders beyond the knowledge of a village priest. The chalice could very well be sacred. It had, after all, provided loaves for many. For all she knew, it may have brought back the fish as well.

"What will happen if you cannot buy back the cup?" she asked.

"Over time, I cannot say precisely. The whole purpose of the Mystic Isle is to guard the chalice and the—" He stopped himself. "Let us just say that the island is a temple of the gods, and if we profane it, the gods will not be happy. I cannot predict the actions of deities."

She shouldn't be concerned about some heathen idols she did not worship, but she was concerned about this honorable man who believed she'd stolen a sacred object. A man who could never return home without it. In effect, her deed held him here, away from his family, much as he'd tried to do to her. That was a calamity she could grasp.

Trystan counted her coins and his, and sat with the purse between his big hands, drawing his fearsome brow into a frown that should quake her to her toes. Even if she could persuade him not to kill her, he would never help the village now. A week's worth of bread would not save them from eventual starvation. She'd ruined everything.

"How much more do we need?" she asked in despair. His stoic dismay caused a pain in her heart that she could not easily fix.

"I will need to sell the sloop to raise a sum that large," he said in distraction, kneading the purse until she feared it would burst beneath the pressure. "I brought nothing else with me."

"I left some coins with my sister," she admitted with a sigh. "It is not much. Just enough for a midwife and for the dinner our guests will expect when they arrive to see the new babe. Will that help?"

"Not enough. She may as well keep them. The sloop is made of rare timbers, with a sleek design, built for speed. It's worth a great deal if I can find someone willing to buy it."

That didn't seem probable. Even the fishermen had no coins these days. And if he sold the ship, he would have no way to return home.

Another thought occurred, and Mariel brightened. "Vicomte Rochefort has a man of business who loans money against ships and the like. You can purchase your sloop back again with a little extra for the service. We can borrow what you need, buy back the cup, and if you can look after Francine for me for a week or two, I will go with the dolphins in search of a shipwreck where I might find something of value with which to repay you. And then you can pay off the loan and take the chalice home again!"

"At the rate things are happening, you will no doubt drown in your efforts, leaving me saddled with your sister and no ship," he replied in muffled fury. "I cannot risk your life."

"Do you have a better suggestion?" she demanded, standing and proceeding in the direction of the castle, expecting him to follow. She was incapable of doing nothing. It would only lead to thoughts of the ridiculous—like a god demanding to marry her, one who was more concerned for her safety than his own. If he'd intended to soften her heart with that offer, he'd succeeded.

"It's an improvement over being heaved into Aelynn," he admitted grudgingly, falling in step with her.

And Francine could even keep her money. This was

a *good* plan, Mariel decided with satisfaction. All she had to do was persuade the vicomte's man that he needed a ship, and Francine to accept a stranger as guardian. And pray she found treasure before the babe arrived.

The old stone fortress stood high upon the bluffs overlooking the channel. Mariel tried to concentrate on the sound of the waves crashing on the rocks below while she waited outside the counting house for Trystan to return.

It was very hard to keep her thoughts from straying to the mysterious island beyond these waters and the bed Trystan insisted awaited them. They were a dream beyond her reach. Her reality was cold and hunger and a beloved sister who would bear a child without knowing what had become of her husband in the maelstrom that was Paris these days.

When Trystan emerged with a bulging purse of coins, she gladly set aside her gloomy thoughts. "Is it enough?" she asked anxiously.

"Not nearly as much as the sloop is worth," he grumbled. "We had best find some means of paying it back swiftly or his high interest will cost all the treasures of the sea."

"Such avaricious buzzards have bankrupted France," she said, relieved that one problem was almost solved. "They loan money at usurious rates to a court with empty coffers. And to pay the interest the king taxes the poor, who do not have the power to refuse."

"You have no say in how you are taxed?" he asked, shaking his head in disbelief. "That is scarcely fair or just."

Relieved that they now had the wherewithal to buy back the chalice, she waxed loquacious as they hastened toward the baroness's quarters. "When greed and selfishness rule, fairness suffers. That will change once the Assembly speaks. France is one of the most advanced nations in the world, after all."

"Advanced?" he said in horror. "The moneylender wore rings that would buy kingdoms, yet people starve? And you call this advanced?"

"We are highly educated," she said stiffly. "In Austria, they still keep serfs in slavery. In France, we have free farmers as well as brilliant philosophers and scientists. Montgolfier has flown to the skies in his hot-air balloon. Mesmer produces magic sleep that may someday help the ill and mad. The court of Versailles is one of the wonders of the world and draws the elite of every continent. Our future is very bright, except we have experienced some bad weather and a costly war. Once the Assembly works out a means of paying our debts by taxing the nobility instead of taking it from the pockets of those who have nothing, I am sure all will be well."

"That seems an obvious conclusion," he said dryly. "Why hasn't your Assembly arranged it before now? Taxing the penniless is not a fiscally responsible policy."

Mariel grimaced. How did she explain the workings of government to someone who lived in peace and prosperity without apparent need of such? "The Assembly hasn't been called in a hundred and seventy-five years," she admitted. "The king has been badly influenced by a foreign queen and simply does not realize how we suffer. My brother-in-law has gone to Paris to represent our village, along with hundreds like him. The king will listen to his people."

"It seems you are a hundred and seventy-five years too late," Trystan growled in the same manner she would expect of an angry tiger. "Did your people really think a king was some nice father who would always look after the interests of helpless children he doesn't know and who never speak up? Have men in power ever done such a thing?"

Mariel halted at the entrance to the three-story building containing the apartments inhabited by aristocrats who had no land of their own. She would like to learn a great deal more about the peaceful world Trystan came from. She would like to learn more about a golden god whose intelligent interest in what she had to say made her heart patter too fast. But she had her responsibilities and he had his, and ne'er the twain would meet.

She cast her escort a telling glance to halt his treasonous arguments. "We need to have a word with the Baroness Beloit," she murmured in her best submissive manner to the guard.

"She is not available," he replied woodenly.

Defiance could land her in a dungeon, but she had Trystan at her back. With confidence, she stood as tall as the guard and looked him straight in the eye. "Chevalier de Pouchay's daughter wishes to speak with the baroness. When will she be available?"

The guard shrugged, leaned against his guardhouse, and looked her up and down as if she were a light skirt.

Without warning, Trystan gripped her arms and set her behind him. His hand fell to his sword hilt, his massive shoulders twitched inside his civilized frock coat, and he glowered as if he would crush the insect in his path. The guard cringed in response. Mariel thought she might get used to having a magic genie who did her bidding, if she could fool herself into believing that was all he would do.

Trystan didn't have to say a word. The soldier eyed

his wrathful expression and his sword and hastily admitted, "The baroness has left for Pontivy."

Trystan grabbed Mariel's elbow and squeezed. She could hear all his questions without his speaking them. Her own heart had sunk to her sabots.

Clenching her teeth, she dipped a quick curtsy and hurried away.

"Where is Pontivy?" he demanded the instant they left the castle wall behind.

"Two days' journey toward Paris." With neither horse nor carriage, they could never catch up to ask the lady's permission. "I think we must steal the chalice back."

Nine

"I will leave the purse in exchange for the chalice. It won't be stealing," Trystan declared arrogantly as they hurried down the hill toward the village jeweler's shop.

"You will have to wait until dark. You cannot simply walk in there." Mariel raced after him by lifting her skirts, attracting more attention than she liked, but unwilling to let an angry god stride about, smiting innocents. He moved faster than seemed humanly possible.

She had to remember he was but a man. Except, when enraged like this, he looked as if he could blow down walls. He practically emanated golden rays. She watched a fisherman trip over his net trying to follow their progress as they raced by.

"I am not a thief," Trystan shouted, covering three strides to her one. "The chalice belongs to Aelynn. I am simply retrieving what is ours."

"*Simply retrieving* it will land us both in the dungeon! Does your magic open locks?"

"I don't have magic." He slowed down enough to look at her with disgust. "Is that what you thought I could do? Raise a magic wand and produce food?"

"I had no idea what you could do. My mother predicted you would save us in a time of great trouble. You have wealth. Your island has wheat. Perhaps she meant you would share." She was almost out of breath from running after him, and she was heartily tired of trying to explain herself.

"We don't interfere in the affairs of the Outside World."

She danced ahead of him and stomped his boot with her wooden sabot. Trystan yelped in surprise, then, undeterred, lifted her by her elbows, set her aside, and continued down the street.

"That was unnecessary," he said coldly.

"Perhaps you would have preferred a kick to the shin? You interfere in our world every time you sail a ship into it. You interfere by stealing the baroness's wedding gift." She would like to say, You interfere by tying me up like a dressed pig, but she preferred not to remind him of that episode on the altar. She could still end up like that if the pirate god had his way.

The terrifying part was that she wasn't entirely certain she objected to returning to that curiously magical moment.

"I'll admit, we have become lax in our standards." Obviously indulging in his masculine ability to think only one thing at a time, Trystan halted across the street from the silversmith's.

The chalice was no longer in the window.

"Do you want to ask, or shall I?" she murmured, appalled.

"It could be on his workbench." Setting his square jaw, Trystan flipped back the flaps of his satin coat to reveal his sword hilt, and stalked across the street and into the shop.

Mariel hurried after him. She didn't know how much a foreigner understood of her tumultuous country, or how far his fury would take him. Somehow, Trystan and the chalice had become her responsibility, and she must look after them.

"The baroness has sent us for the chalice," he informed the smith with an intimidating authority that almost had Mariel convinced. "Where is it?"

A slight man with thinning gray hair, Daniel Dupre, the store's owner, looked even more nervous now than he had earlier. Mariel sidled closer and smiled reassuringly at the man whom she knew only slightly.

"I-I'm s-sorry, m-monsieur," Dupre stuttered, crooking his neck backward to meet Trystan's piercing gaze. "A maid picked it up after you left. I told her you wished to speak to the baroness, and she promised to pass on the message."

"Where is this maid who steals my chalice?" Trystan thundered with Olympian rage.

Mariel tugged at his silk-coated sword arm before he did anything rash. He cast her a swift glance, and with an odd shake seemed to lessen his godly superiority until he appeared a normal, slightly irritated, and very large aristocrat.

"With the lady?" the smith answered, as if afraid to make a statement that Trystan might object to. "They left in a carriage for Pontivy. Perhaps you could catch up with them."

Muttering words under his breath that Mariel could not translate, Trystan swung on his heel and marched out. Passersby darted out of his path as he stormed past them.

"Where can I find a carriage?" In his polished boots, with the tail of his coat flapping in accompaniment to his furious strides, he hurried down the street, gazing toward the east as if he could catch a glimpse of the baroness and her entourage. It was just past the summer solstice, and daylight still lingered at this hour.

"A horse would be faster and less expensive." If

her cousin had left only a little while ago, a good horse might have a chance of catching up. Maybe.

"We live on an island. We sail ships, not ride horses," he said grumpily, his powerful legs in their tight breeches finally faltering to a stop as he realized he had no idea where he was going.

"The only carriages are at the castle." Mariel couldn't look at him, fearing steam would rise from his ears much as it did from a volcano. She was afraid to learn what powers the chalice might have. Almost every church in Brittany possessed an object said to heal or defend. What did his do? "We have only farm carts."

"What would I have to do to obtain a carriage at the castle?"

From his tone, she knew he understood the difficulty. "Steal it?" she suggested. Carriages were rare on the coast. Everyone used water for travel, except Pontivy was not on the sea. Horses were the best mode of land transportation, oxen and mules more common.

He heaved a sigh of exasperation and glanced around. "Let's eat and discuss this further."

"I cannot leave Francine alone much longer. Will you come home with me? We still have bread, and I brought a fish. And the garden should have sprouted a few new greens."

"You brought fish?" He reluctantly fell into stride with her. "You do not feel guilty about eating your comrades?"

Mariel cast him a quick glance to see if he laughed at her. His stony face revealed no expression, but she was learning that the stiff god had a slight indentation beside his mouth when he smiled, and his jutting chin dimpled when he was angry. His eyes seemed to change hue with his mood, like hers. Right now they were a flinty gray.

"In our world, God gave us plants and animals so we would not go hungry," she explained. "I have far more in common with whales than fish. A shark wouldn't hesitate to eat me. I don't hesitate to eat a fish. Do you not eat fish?"

"We live on fish. I was just curious."

For a brief moment, a hint of sadness clouded his eyes and tired lines crinkled their corners. And then he shook off the mood as he'd shaken off his earlier rage. With arrogantly questioning eyebrows, he waited when she stopped at Francine's modest stone cottage.

Her sister had planted poppies by the gate and iris beneath the windows. The iris had lost their blooms, but the first of the poppies caught the evening sun in a burst of red. Mariel pushed open the sagging whitewashed gate and entered the tiny yard. A lamp flickered in the window where Francine sat. She was still making lace.

Nervously, Mariel eased open the carved wooden door. "My sister earns coins by making lace," she murmured before entering. "Does everyone in your home dress as plainly as those I saw?"

"We are not inclined to wear lace," he agreed, keeping his voice soft so anyone inside would not hear.

"A shame." Sighing at this potential loss of income to a clientele that might actually have coins to pay, Mariel entered the narrow front room.

Francine was already struggling to her feet, looking anxiously to Mariel and then to the large man who had to bend over to dodge the low lintel.

"I am sorry to be so late, but I ran into a friend." Mariel stepped aside. "Madame Francine Rousseau, Monsieur Trystan . . . d'Aelynn." She did not have a better way of introducing him. The woman called Lissandra had introduced him as *l'Enforcer*, and that did not seem quite . . . appropriate.

"My pleasure, madame." He bowed over Francine's hand as if she were as noble as any court lady. His golden queue of hair fell over his shoulder. "Please do not disturb yourself on my account. Your sister was concerned about you, and I simply escorted her home."

"Oh, you must come in and have a bite to eat," Francine replied breathlessly, staring at Trystan the same way Mariel must have the first time. *Stronger than Hercules . . . more beautiful than a sun-blessed day.* The story was imprinted on their minds. Golden gods were hard to miss—especially when wearing a gentleman's bejeweled sword and rapier.

When it seemed the golden idiot intended to take himself off without eating, Mariel murmured under her breath, "You will not find a carriage without me."

He slanted her a masculine look that could mean he might murder her or humor her. She was too overwrought to care. Francine would be expecting miracles now, when all Mariel had done was bring disaster.

"I'll fry up the salted fish with some of the wild garlic," Mariel told her sister. "Have you eaten? Sit down before you wear me out watching you. Trystan, have a seat at the table. The fare is simple, but we cannot let you go hungry."

"Bring out the wine," Francine called as Mariel crossed the front room to the kitchen. "Eduard would be insulted if we did not provide our guest with wine."

Eduard should be here looking after his wife, but glory, honor, and country came first, Mariel thought, slapping fish into a skillet.

At least the icy winter had not harmed the wine cellar. And they still had many of their parents' cherished possessions, so their plates were hand-painted porcelain and the table a beautifully polished walnut topped with Francine's lace cloth. Normally, Mariel stroked them with pleasure at the memory of sharing happy meals. At the moment, she only hoped Trystan was suitably impressed.

Not that there was any reason she should impress him, she told herself.

The muscular gentleman standing formidably in front of delicate china and lace wasn't a god, admittedly. He might be a prince, but mostly he was a narrow-minded male who believed in duty above all, just like her brother-in-law. Except Trystan's God and country weren't hers, but so foreign as to be unimaginable. Perhaps it would take a foreign prince to save them.

Francine poured wine into crystal glasses before taking her seat at the table. Trystan remained standing until Mariel returned with bread and fish and greens. She used a bit of the wine and a spoon of precious olive oil to create a vinaigrette, then took her seat beside Francine. Trystan finally lowered his large frame onto a sturdy chair.

"I am not accustomed to such fine dining," he admitted after they said grace. "I spend much of my time aboard ship with men who eat off tin at a crude table carved with their initials. This is a luxury, thank you."

Francine beamed as if he'd given her silver and gold. "This is a very meager repast, I fear. Next time, we will be better prepared."

As if there would be a next time. Softened by his generous display of gratitude, Mariel sent their guest a surreptitious look. She appreciated his good manners on Francine's behalf. Impatience ticked his jaw muscle, but she saw no mockery in his expression.

"So, Monsieur d'Aelynn, what brings you to our fair town?" Francine asked.

Mariel willed her hands not to tremble while waiting for his reply. Trystan slanted her a flinty look that spoke volumes, but he answered as a gentleman should.

"Mundane business, I fear. Mademoiselle St. Just has been courteous in introducing me to the right people."

"Do you stay at the castle?" Francine asked with interest.

"My business there is over. I will continue on to Pontivy this evening."

Mariel couldn't tolerate the polite evasions any longer. Reassured that she wasn't in imminent danger of being strangled, she addressed both of them. "He's a stranger and does not know our ways. I have told him I will help him find Pontivy." She gave Francine a meaningful look, hoping her sister understood that she must help their mother's prediction come true.

"Pontivy," Francine murmured, trying to hide her dismay. "That is so *far*."

"If we find a cart tonight, we could be there by sunset tomorrow," Mariel assured her. Providing they didn't sleep, the weather held, the road wasn't mud, and they weren't beset by brigands in the duc's forest. She blessed Francine for mentioning none of those possibilities.

"It is not necessary that you come with me," Trystan said stiffly. "I will be obliged if you will help me find transportation, but you must stay with your sister."

"I will ask the neighbors to look after Francine," Mariel persevered, "but I cannot in all good conscience allow you to travel without a guide."

On the face of it, her argument was without basis.

Trystan's sword and size would terrify brigands into hiding. He might run afoul of a soldier or two should he be forced to steal the chalice, but Francine would not know that. Mariel simply realized she could not leave him to the task that her perfidy had caused. She knew the baroness. He did not.

Francine's pale brow wrinkled in worry as she glanced between them, obviously balancing all the implications of danger versus savior, as well as the impropriety of an unmarried couple traveling together.

With a growl of exasperation, Trystan ended the dilemma. He addressed Francine but pointed his knife in Mariel's direction. "Help your sister pack her belongings. When I return from Pontivy, she sails with me as my bride."

"Over my dead body," Mariel replied sweetly, rising to take her plate to the kitchen.

Francine's startled gaze darted between them.

"That can be arranged," Trystan shouted after her.

So much for politeness. Fighting a frisson of fear, Mariel kicked the door closed at the sound of Francine's faint, "Oh, dear."

Her sister was made of stern stuff. She could deal with the lummox while Mariel let her temper reduce from boil to simmer.

She had no intention of marrying, ever, especially not a man who would take her from home.

That did not mean she wouldn't do whatever was necessary to protect her family. If that included ruining her reputation by following a golden god to Pontivy, then so be it.

Ten

"I will heave you over my shoulder and start walking if you do not quit making up stories and get in that cart," Trystan muttered into the perfect shell of an ear not inches from his lips. Admittedly, he would rather nibble that ear, but now was not the time.

The ear might as well be deaf for all the woman attached to it indicated that she'd heard. Mariel stood tall and lovely beside the borrowed farm cart, like royalty bestowing favors.

"Bless you for looking after Francine," Mariel trilled to the elderly neighbors she'd cajoled into this task. "My beloved is impatient to have Eduard's approval before he must set sail. This is so kind of you."

His *beloved* was an improvisational liar of the highest caliber, although he assumed she was merely protecting her sister from gossip with this bit of stage dressing. His growing impatience sparked a roguish retaliation to her obstinacy. He leaned over and nibbled her seemingly deaf ear, and when she turned in shock, he covered her mouth with his, swallowing the rest of her lies before she could speak them.

Mariel squeaked in surprise. Her eyes widened. Then, to his satisfaction, her lashes swept downward, she balanced her hands on his shoulders, and she kissed him back, with as much enthusiasm as he could possibly desire.

So much enthusiasm that he almost didn't come up for air. Her plump lips tasted of sunshine and sea and promises far beyond any he'd come to expect. . . .

Gasping, he pulled back. She stared back at him with as much astonishment as he felt.

Struggling to regain control of the situation, Trystan wrapped his arm around her shoulder, knowing she had to comply with the loving gesture to verify her story. She shot him a glare from beneath lowered lashes, and with a smug grin, he hugged her tighter.

"It is the least we can do for the generous gentleman who brought us wheat," the old lady assured them, beaming happily at their loverlike behavior. "I hope Jacques's cart will suit."

Trystan didn't know when he'd become the hero of the wheat story, but he was certain it had to have been at Mariel's behest. Odd that she didn't bask in the effusive gratitude the villagers had displayed in their every encounter this evening. His amacara was as modest as she was devious.

The bakery was apparently working overtime. The entire town smelled of yeast. People were literally dancing in the street. He'd never been hugged and kissed so many times in his life. But it was Mariel's kiss that had him rethinking his disdain for emotional displays. His impatience gathered new momentum, and he tugged her toward the cart.

"We will fly on dreams," Mariel promised the couple as he dragged her onward.

Trystan was beginning to understand that quick wits and clever tales were how Crossbreeds concealed their true nature from Outsiders. That was the only reason he hadn't strangled her yet. That, and because the hugs and kisses had mellowed his wrath.

Fear of losing the chalice shredded his innards, but

he refused to let his headstrong partner take the lead any longer.

"Come along. The moon will light our way for a while yet." Trystan bowed to Mariel's sister, who had watched them worriedly throughout the evening. He understood Mariel's concern for her. Francine seemed overly frail in her pregnancy.

"We have plenty of time to reach Pontivy," Mariel murmured, tugging her skirts around her limbs as he practically heaved her into the cart. "I've learned the baroness is determined to wed on Saturday, before her chevalier leaves for his new appointment at Versailles."

He ought to be worrying over returning her to Aelynn. He ought to be horrified imagining what would happen to the chalice in the hands of an infidel. Instead, he was admiring Mariel's trim ankle and wondering how long it would take to reach the next inn. He was surely ensorcelled.

She was his match. Even though he might not understand the reasoning, the gods had decreed it. He might as well enjoy the arduous task he'd been assigned. If he got her with child before they reached the altar, the chance of producing his heir was less, but there would always be next time. The gods had never failed to provide what the island needed.

First, they had to reach an inn. He'd always stayed in seaports during his travels, having no need to journey inland. Trystan glared dubiously at the swinging tail of the pony as he took his seat in the big-wheeled cart. He was a seafarer. He hadn't driven a vehicle since he was a child and had hitched a goat to a garden cart.

"Shake the reins so they hit the pony's sides," she murmured beside him, straightening the lace cap that hid her magnificent hair.

Trystan slapped the leather up and down and winced when the pony broke into a trot, throwing him back against the hard wooden seat. "Walking would be simpler."

"But not faster. Rein him in a little or you'll run over someone."

"Why aren't you driving if you know so much about it?" He pulled back on the leather a little and breathed easier when the pony slowed. The jostling trot would have driven his tailbone into his skull if he'd maintained it much longer.

She eyed him skeptically. "You would let me?"

"Why should I not?" he asked. "Goats are the biggest beasts we have at home. I know nothing of even a small horse like this one."

"Here, men do not let women drive. A widow might be excused for using a pony cart, but no man would allow a woman to take the leather. It would offend their honor."

Trystan snorted. "Your world is ridiculous."

"No more so than one made of powerful gods who refuse to aid those who are different from themselves," she retorted.

The argument was specious, and he refused to take her up on it.

The seaside village of Pouchay had only one main road inland, so Trystan had no difficulty following it. Once they were beyond the last cottage, he handed the reins to her. "Are those gloves thick enough to protect your palms?"

She glanced at her thin black gloves and shrugged. "I have no idea. Brace yourself."

She slapped the reins and sent the pony into a smooth stride. While Trystan might be able to run faster than the cart for a while, Mariel couldn't. And he supposed that her aid created less likelihood that he would have to steal the chalice or otherwise use his special strengths to interfere in her world, so he must accept her company. Reclaiming the chalice was far more important than his pride or frustration.

He kept one hand on his sword and warily watched the passing shrubbery for possible brigands. They carried a fortune in gold from the loan against his ship, and he did not mean to surrender it until he had the chalice in his hands.

"We are not betrothed," she announced, finally taking offense at his kiss now that they were out of sight of the village.

"I agree. That was your tall tale." That didn't mean he wouldn't take her to his bed at the first opportunity. He was already aroused just watching her luscious rosy lips from the corner of his eye and letting his mind drift to the ways she could put them to good use. Now that they were away from the aroma of baking bread, he could smell her spicy scent of lilies and surf.

"I will wave you off at the dock and then announce later that you were lost at sea," she continued, obviously enjoying the tale she now embroidered.

"You will be on the ship when I sail, and we'll exchange vows on Aelynn," he corrected.

"You said yourself that it is the duty of *Crossbreeds* like myself to look after the people off the island."

"You may return to your home after we say our vows. Right now, I am concerned only about finding the chalice."

"Is it like the Holy Grail to you?" she asked. "In my father's books, King Arthur's knights went on quests in search of the Grail, and Pontivy was often mentioned."

"I know nothing of King Arthur or knights, although I have heard of your Holy Grail. I seriously doubt that they are the same."

"I always thought a Holy Grail ought to be able to find its own way to wherever it wanted to be, but the stories were interesting."

"In our legends, the Chalice of Plenty left Aelynn by way of a dragon during the Black Plague. One legend makes it sound as if the chalice caused the plague. Another hints that it cured the disease. Still another claims the chalice was responsible for the repopulation of Europe, however that might be."

Mariel chuckled. "I like the last one. A Chalice of Plenty should provide what is needed, and that would be births after so many deaths."

"I don't think I care to speculate on how that is possible. This is a modern age, and we should leave such superstition behind. But I refuse to be the one responsible for losing an object so valued by my people." He hoped the legends were just superstition. He didn't want to think what would happen to the island if the chalice took away the gifts the gods had granted them.

"Do your legends say how the chalice returned after the dragon stole it?"

"No. For all I know it rolled down the road and up the gangplank of one of our ships. I don't think I wish to wait for that to happen."

"No, there are too many people like me who would see the chalice as a means of putting food on the table." She yawned and tried to hide it behind the back of her hand.

"Have you rested at all since you returned home?" Trystan demanded.

She shrugged. "A few hours. You sail faster than I swim. I'll be fine."

Trystan grabbed the reins from her. "In the back, *now*. Get some sleep. I can keep the animal on the road until we find an inn."

She didn't bother fighting him for the reins, but she didn't climb in back either. "I am not sleeping with you, so you may as well keep going until we reach Pontivy. Unless you haven't had any sleep either?"

He was unlikely to sleep until he had found the chalice and returned home with Mariel in tow, but Trystan didn't think she fully understood his predicament. He had to complete his task and return to Aelynn before the full moon to reinforce the island's shield. He glanced upward. Little more than a week now.

"I will look for an inn," he informed her firmly.

"Not many barns or inns in the forest. We may just have to tether the pony near a stream and sleep in the cart."

"I thought you wouldn't sleep with me."

That shut her up. There was none to see or hear them out in the woods. They could do anything they liked. Perhaps through the physical pleasure of being mated he could persuade her to willingly accompany him home.

Suddenly Trystan wondered if Dylys's decree was her way of saying she didn't approve of his marriage to Lissandra. That was a dismaying thought. The Oracle's late husband had been in favor of their pairing. But Luther had been a Council Leader, not an Oracle. Had Dylys "seen" something unpleasant in his future if he wedded Lissandra?

Mentally cursing the unfathomable minds of women, Trystan slapped the pony's reins and urged it into another bone-jarring trot.

He glanced at Mariel. She had wrapped her unbecoming black dress in an old velvet cloak that even he knew had been out of style for a decade or more. Her eyelids kept drifting closed. The sun had set, but there was enough moonlight to see the shadows of Mariel's long black lashes against her fair cheeks.

When he verbally sparred with her, she challenged him into thinking she was older and more stalwart than she actually was. With her lids closed, she appeared barely more than a weary girl, and too thin at that. Her cheekbones jutted against her pale skin, leaving dark shadows in the hollows beneath.

No wonder she had stolen the chalice. She was wasting away.

Guilt crept under his skin, but he could see no way of remedying the situation. He could not change the laws of Aelynn.

He supposed if he could find the chalice and right his world again, he could return to trading and bring cheap grain to port—but unless he smuggled it past the authorities, the tariffs would put the price well beyond the means of Mariel's family.

Maybe he should become a soldier with Murdoch and interfere in this country's chaotic affairs, although to do so would be a flagrant violation of Aelynn's laws and reason for eternal banishment. Well, he'd be banished and worse if he didn't find the chalice and persuade Mariel to wear his ring. He'd rather not dwell on that.

Sighing in exasperation, Trystan wrapped his arm around her and tugged her against his side. She resisted briefly, but finally nestled into his warmth, nearly purring as she lay her head against his shoulder.

"Sleep. I will let you know if I get lost."

"Don't bother," she murmured. "I don't need to know."

He chuckled and settled her more comfortably against him.

He might thoroughly resent this unexpected upheaval in his carefully planned life, but he could appreciate the altar's choosing an *interesting* amacara for him.

Eleven

Mariel woke when the wheels stopped rolling, but Trystan made reassuring noises as he lifted her to the back of the cart. Once she was snuggled into her cloak, she fell into a deep sleep, feeling incongruously safe for the first time in a very long while.

She woke to the dawn calls of mating birds and Trystan's bulk stretched out beside her, sheltering her from the cool and damp. She'd never slept with anyone before, and it felt strange. She knew she ought to be alarmed, but her companion's hard thighs warming her rump made a cozy bed, and his muscular arm around her waist provided a comforting blanket.

It felt even odder, and definitely shocking, when she stirred, and his hand cupped her breast through her clothes.

"Shall I whistle a mating call like the birds?" he murmured into her hair.

Mariel's stomach knotted in understanding of his intent, but apparently the power of his kiss yesterday had drained her resistance. She could not seem to object to the fascinating sensation of his stroking fingers. Her nipples ached to be caressed. Even his breath against her nape was seductive, and she had the urge to burrow backward into his embrace.

She didn't need to act at all. He moved forward, pressing her backside with the hard male length of him, until it became impossible not to recognize the danger she courted. She might be physically innocent, but she had listened to enough old wives' tales to know what he was about. Men often woke aroused and ready for rutting.

But what he was doing didn't seem quite so unpleasant as she had expected. His explorations had located the ties of her bodice, and his hand slid over her thin chemise to heat her breast. Warmth flowered in her woman's place, and she had the urge to discover more.

She was falling victim to physical sensation without need of the island's mystical altar.

Before she could focus her fuzzy thoughts on escape, Trystan caught her shoulder and urged her back to the cart floor. Then he leaned over and covered her mouth with his.

His kiss produced a powerful drugging sensation that captivated her. With his beard stubble scraping her jaw, Mariel clung to the muscled arms pinning her to the cart and drank in the rich wine of his mouth. She parted her lips to accept the invasion of his tongue and felt the tenderness of his possession all the way down to the place that already rippled with desire.

Trystan whispered foreign words that sounded like endearments while dragging his kisses across her cheek. The loving tone seemed more important than the translation. She greedily inhaled the scent of his stubbled jaw, the male musk of yesterday's sojourn overriding the faint scent of his sandalwood soap. His hand returned to its depredations, opening her chemise and corset completely, so he could fill his palm with her bare flesh.

Her hips rose in expectation, meeting his.

He groaned and pressed greedily into her. "You are an answer to a man's prayer," he said fervently.

His fingers found her aroused nipple and pinched it

in such a way that Mariel nearly rose from the cart on the pure pleasure of it. But common sense intruded. "No," she whispered, finally finding her tongue and putting it to its proper use.

"Yes," he insisted, tugging her skirt upward so that the morning air caressed her stockinged legs, though it did nothing to cool the heat building between them. "The gods have blessed us with this physical bond. This is meant to be."

It *felt* as if it was meant to be, but Mariel knew better than to trust physical sensation. She might revel in the scent of last fall's leaves and the fresh earth of summer, but that did not mean she should wallow in them like an animal.

She struggled against Trystan's greater strength, pushing at his powerful arms and wiggling away from his invading fingers. "No. I will not. I cannot."

He slid his broad hand up her bare thigh, urging her to part her legs, weakening her will. "Why fight it? You are mine, and I take care of what is mine. You have nothing to fear."

Promises like that were double-edged swords. As much as she'd like to believe the temptation of a golden god, he was but a man who would take what he wanted and then do as he pleased. When he raised up to gather more of her skirts, Mariel brought her knee up as quickly as she could. She missed her target as Trystan tumbled sideways to avoid her blow. His big body hit the side of the wooden cart, splintering one of the old boards with his weight.

"I said *no.*" Scrambling to pull her skirt in place and tug her corset closed, she leaped from the back of the cart. "I am not yours, nor will I ever be."

She stalked to the stream and hid behind the bush where he'd hobbled the pony. She was shaking all over. It was all she could do to stick to her morning routine and pretend a golden god hadn't turned her insular world upside down. She wasn't at all certain she knew the woman he made of her. Her insides *ached.* She had wanted—needed—his caress and missed it now that it was gone. This was not at all like her.

Trystan's angry stomps shook the forest floor like an earthquake. She waited until she heard him farther upstream before she emerged from her ablutions. An angry man was a dangerous man, she knew, but at least he hadn't come after her. She could take offense at his insult of thinking her a loose woman, and start walking home, but she was levelheaded enough to know she'd encouraged him with her impulsive actions. Maman and Francine had criticized her more than once for acting without thinking.

But how could one *think* when wrapped in bliss?

Don't consider that. She knew better than to let Trystan touch her now. No more touching. Ever. At all. She would sleep on the ground before sharing a bed with him.

She returned to the cart and produced the basket Francine and the neighbors had packed for them. The bread was still fresh enough and the cheese was delightful. A sip of watered wine, and she was quite restored. If she was very careful, their provisions would last several days. Bodice fastened, cap on tight, she harnessed the pony, then sat primly on the cart seat, waiting for Trystan to quit splashing in the stream.

She tried not to look too closely when he returned from his bathing. Men had been known to beat women for what she had done. Then rape them. She wasn't a complete naïf. She was simply naïve enough to believe Trystan was different from other men.

When he took his seat beside her and accepted the basket without knocking her to the ground or having his way with her, she let out her breath with relief, picked up the reins, and set the cart back on the road. Only then did she dare a surreptitious glance at him.

He was stoically eating his bread and cheese, quaffing the watered wine rather heavily. The muscle over his square jaw jumped, and his languor-inducing mouth was pressed tight as he chewed.

"I do not intend to have children," she told him boldly. She was discovering it was liberating to talk with someone who knew what she was so she need not fabricate or hedge around every topic. "I do not wish to bring another freak like me into the world. I could not help the fishermen if I were in Francine's condition. So it's best for all that we do not repeat this morning's episode."

"Freak." He cast her a glare. "Is that what you are? What I am? What we all are? Freaks?"

She shrugged. "I don't know what you are. You speak my language. You live in a country that is not like mine. That is unusual, but I see nothing freakish about it or you—except for that strange bed," she amended. "And that . . . wall of jelly in a cave. I'm not well versed in geography, so if your island doesn't exist on maps, it doesn't seem odd to me."

He ripped off another hunk of bread and studied blackly on that for a while. "You will understand better when we return to Aelynn. Explaining isn't the same as showing you the differences in our worlds."

"I will help you find the chalice because I stole it, but I will not leave my home again," she insisted. "You live on an island. You know you cannot hold me."

Putting the basket of food behind the seat, he glared at her and took back the reins. "The island is protected by a barrier that *I* control. You were rendered unconscious the first time you went through it. I don't know how you survived the second time."

Mariel had tried not to think about that. She stirred uneasily but she could not comprehend invisible barriers or a man who produced them. That was the stuff of myth. "I left in a dory. I woke up outside the fog. I don't remember the part in between."

"Aelynn or the chalice must protect you," he said grimly. "I cannot imagine any other explanation. The barrier accepts only those who wear the ring of silence or who sail with us."

She cast him a sideways look. "If you are the one who produces the barrier, could this . . . this *bond* you say exists between us affect it?"

He fell silent. The birds had stopped singing at the creak of the cartwheels. The June day was warming rapidly, even beneath the shade of the new green foliage overhead. Mariel removed her cloak and pretended not to notice her awareness of the man who sat so close that his lean hip jostled hers when they hit a rut.

She could not, would not marry, but she would burn forever if she stayed in Trystan's company. They needed to hurry and find the chalice so she could send him off. Perhaps she should have stayed home and scoured the ocean floor for riches so she could buy back his ship while he went to Pontivy, but she felt responsible for this journey and wanted to make it right.

Was that feeling of responsibility also part of the bond between them?

"The gods work in mysterious ways," Trystan muttered, unable to explain better.

"That's always been my thought," she agreed. "You will have to ask your Oracle when you return. I'm certain my speaking with Father Antoine would not be enlightening."

Trystan assumed from her tone that this was an understatement. He mused on their differences and how they could possibly make a match when she did not know his culture or believe in his gods. But the Oracle would never have decreed it if it were not possible, and it did seem as if his language abilities made him more suitable than most.

They stopped at a farmhouse when the sun was high and exchanged one of their small coins for bowls of vegetable soup, a refill of their flask, and oats for the pony.

Mariel fretted over the creature, brushing it down, checking its hooves, and insisting it rest. Trystan wished for his trusty ship, but followed her advice since he knew nothing of horses.

They learned from the farmwife that the baroness's carriage had been seen that morning. Trystan surmised an aristocrat's entourage would have turned off the forest road last evening and found its way to the manor house that owned the farm.

According to Mariel, the forest was a duc's personal hunting preserve. To poach even a rabbit would result in a death sentence, another inanity he did not understand.

"Your country is much too large," he muttered when they started out again. "An island is easier to traverse."

"I suppose that is one reason the tariffs here are high. Transporting goods must be expensive," Mariel said.

"But this should be a wealthy country," he argued. "We pay dearly for your wines. You have trees that can be sold at high prices. I cannot understand why you starve."

Trystan had made certain that his amacara ate more of their provisions than he did, and that her soup bowl had been filled continuously until she pushed it away. She was still paler than he thought healthy, but her cheeks had a hint of color now that she'd eaten. He hoped they reached the city soon so he could find better fare for her. She might be his bitter downfall, but she was also destined to be the mother of his child. The irony did not escape him.

"I do not understand economics," she admitted. "The nobility owns the forests, so we cannot sell the wood. Eduard says that workers pay medieval taxes to duchies that no longer provide any services, but I think the king should put an end to that."

"There is no reason for the nobility to stop taking what it wants if the people allow it." He wasn't a politician so much as a merchant, but he'd been to England and knew about the revolt of the colonies against the British king. As a future leader of his country, he had analyzed the factors involved. A lack of representation for the common man often led to a huge gap between rich and poor, and from there, to revolution. He grimaced, realizing he had to consider the future of Mariel and his children if he took her as amacara. Life had become very complicated.

"How would we fight?" she asked with a shrug, distracting his grim thoughts with the lift of her breasts. "We should stop muskets with our pitchforks? No, Eduard does the best thing by taking our petitions to Paris. Surely the voices of all France cannot be ignored."

Since it was not his fight, Trystan didn't argue. He turned the conversation to Mariel's childhood to learn more about the woman he'd been ordered to take as mate.

"So, you think your mother's father must be the

Aelynner from whom you're descended?" he asked after she'd explained her family history. "Do you know his name?"

"My mother's name before she married was Marie-Jeanne d'Orca. The Marie-Jeanne is from her mother. D'Orca is rather unusual."

"An orca is a killer whale. Our family names are descended from our long-ago ancestors who settled Aelynn. Orca is not one of them, but we seldom use our family names off the island, so it's not unusual. One of our fishermen could have landed here easily enough, but if your mother was a Seer, I would say her father had to have come from one of the great families."

"And had a real wife at home," Mariel agreed wisely. "We always suspected that. But he took good care of my mother and grandmother. It seemed to be an affair of convenience."

"If that is what you wish for us, I will honor it," he agreed, "but because you have seen Aelynn, the vows must be exchanged there."

"Then instead of your Oracle dropping me into a volcano, your *intended* would have to kill me," she said with a shrug. "I don't see a pleasant ending in this any way I look at it."

In horror, Trystan realized she was right. If Lissandra wished to take her position as Oracle immediately and chose him as husband in order to do so, she was quite capable of ordering Mariel's death to avoid competition and conflict. An Oracle had responsibilities to her people that often required unpleasant commands.

They had been taking turns driving the pony, and Mariel had the leathers. Mulling over the horrible prospect she'd presented, Trystan was not paying attention to his surroundings as he should. The journey had been safe thus far, and they appeared to be miles from the middle of nowhere, in a never-ending forest where he occasionally noticed menhirs much like those of his home, a sign that his ancestors may once have inhabited the area.

Perhaps it was the familiarity of his surroundings that lulled him into lowering his guard. He could blame no one but himself for not noticing the pony's restiveness or the silence of the birds, or for his slowness to react when the bandit leaped from the bushes wielding a sword almost as large as he was.

"Your money or your life!" the dwarfish fiend cried, slicing the pony's leathers with one deft stroke and disabling the cart.

Twelve

Mariel barely had time to realize the reins in her hands no longer guided the pony before Trystan sprang from the high seat with the preternatural swiftness of a cat. Bereft of guidance, the pony halted of its own accord.

Before Mariel could register her companion's reaction, the thief's weapon was already spinning end over end into the bushes in a shining silver arc. Trystan stood, feet braced, his own sword at the dwarf's throat. She didn't fully realize what he'd done until the would-be thief stood there empty-handed, wide-eyed in stunned alarm.

Recovering from her shock—more at Trystan's uncanny quickness than at the thief's appearance—Mariel realized their attacker was little more than a boy, albeit one so filthy that the black on his face could be mistaken for a full-grown beard.

Trystan must have realized the same thing since he didn't take the child's head off but tipped the boy's chin up with his weapon. He'd doffed his coat earlier, and his golden queue hung down between broad shoulder blades. "Mariel, tell me what to do with him. I have dispensation to kill thieves in self-defense, but they're seldom this young."

The boy seemed to pale beneath his filth, and his

ice blue eyes widened in terror as he turned from Trystan to the cart. Mariel didn't think she saw pleading in them, but she recognized fear. He was no hardened criminal.

What in the world could they do with a half-grown bandit? Disarming him would almost certainly mean he'd be killed by the real bandits that inhabited the forest, or starve to death without the meat his weapon might provide. "Where did you get the sword?" she asked.

"From the militia who murdered my father," the boy said angrily, replacing some of his fear with defiance. "I can use a knife if I must, but I know how to wield a sword. I can act as your guard, *madame*."

Mariel raised her eyebrows and Trystan snorted, but he lowered his weapon so the boy could stand at ease.

"Why did the soldiers murder your father? Was he a thief, too?" she asked.

"They called him so, but he was just a tariff collector!" the boy protested, near tears. "They tore our house apart, stole everything we owned, then killed him when he came home."

"And the rest of your family?" Trystan asked.

"There was just us." The boy sniffed but refused to wipe his face or show his tears. "Papa was the magistrate until Maman died. I took lessons in fencing so I could be a soldier. *They* were the thieves. Not us."

Fencing lessons were expensive, and magistrates were not chosen from common folk. If he spoke truth, the lad came from wealth.

"Are you from Pontivy?" Mariel reached for the basket with their meager provisions.

"Quimper," he replied sullenly, eyeing the basket.

"You have traveled a long way." Trystan returned his sword to its sheath, then fished the boy's weapon from the bushes.

The child shrugged. "I killed the soldier who killed my papa. I didn't stay for them to arrest me."

A cold feeling cramped Mariel's stomach, a portent of things to come—children killing in cold blood. She shook off the sensation. "Killing in self-defense is one thing, but murder is indefensible. Perhaps we should leave him."

"He stole my sword!" the boy shouted. "He left me there to die without it. I had no choice but to push him down the stairs and retrieve my weapon."

Trystan nodded as if he agreed. "A man does what he must to survive. Up in the cart, lad. We'll take you into Pontivy with us. Perhaps you can make a better living there than stealing from the poor. Have you a name?"

"Nick," he replied grudgingly, easing toward the cart, one eye on the basket and the other on Trystan, who still held his weapon.

"We don't have much," Mariel warned him. "But we will share what we have. Have you no family you can go to?"

"My uncle is from Pontivy," he admitted, climbing into the back of the cart when it became apparent Mariel would withhold the basket until he did. "I was trying to make my way there."

"Excellent. Then we will take you to him, and you won't need to steal." Sliding the boy's weapon under the seat, Trystan took the reins as if he was always in charge of the horse. Not until the pony remained motionless did he realize the problem.

"Do you know a sailor's knot for leather?" Mariel murmured, keeping an eye on Nick as he tore hungrily into their food. Now that she wasn't terrified, she could see the lad was practically gaunt. How long had he been surviving in the woods like this?

And why had the peaceful world she knew suddenly gone mad?

"I'll see what I can do." Trystan climbed down and grabbed both ends of the severed reins as if they were the rigging on his ship.

The man could do almost anything he put his mind to, Mariel suspected. He claimed to mysteriously erect barriers around islands, but she couldn't understand that skill. It wasn't like her ability to swim beneath the waves. But earlier he had moved faster than her eye could follow. She was still stunned by that blur of motion. Perhaps she had been so frightened she'd imagined his uncanny swiftness.

"The knot might hold if we don't have to jerk the reins too hard," he said, climbing back to the seat. He glanced over his shoulder at the boy. "That was a good move, cutting the reins without hurting the pony. Who taught you that?"

With bread crammed in his mouth, Nick only shook his head.

"I think we'd better find somewhere he can bathe before we look for his family or they'll not claim him," Mariel decided, watching the lad over her shoulder. "What is your family's name? Do you know where they live?"

He shrugged and, his hunger somewhat assuaged, drank from the flask before replying. "I've never been to Pontivy. I haven't seen anyone from there since my mother's funeral. They're court nobles who don't like Bretons, my father says. Said."

"Their name?" she asked again.

"De Berrier. I won't go where I'm not wanted," he insisted. "I meant to watch them first."

"Give the lad a little food and he becomes a bull again." Trystan chuckled. "He's had training to wield a sword that large. Surely any decent family won't turn him away."

There wasn't much to be said about that. Mariel's family had been decent, but they couldn't afford to feed a growing boy who ate enough for two people. Unless the de Berriers were wealthy, they'd have to be very decent people to take him in.

"There's a river," Trystan grumbled in disgust as they left the forest and entered open fields late that afternoon. "We could have sailed here instead of taking this forsaken route."

"The river Aulne does not go to Pouchay, and with all the twists and turns, it is probably four times the length of the road," she explained. "Besides, rivers flow to the sea and it takes longer going against the current."

And his oceangoing vessel could not navigate shallow waters, even if he could steal it back. He was just irked at having to rely on anyone except himself.

He cast Mariel a look of concern. The rose color had seeped from her cheeks again. Her once moist lips had dried and cracked, as if she were fevered. She'd not protested when he'd kept the reins. He'd learned enough of her character to recognize this for a sign that she wasn't well.

Much to Trystan's relief, they reached the medieval village of Pontivy before sunset. Hampered by an ill woman, a surly child, and a pony that could not be made to go faster than a bone-jarring trot, he'd felt as if the day had been a week long. The chalice could have gone halfway around the world in such a length of time.

He'd left the island nearly three days ago. He now had seven days before the next full moon in which to find the chalice, buy back his ship, and carry Mariel home.

At home, he could have run into town four times faster than the pony could trot, asked the Finder where the chalice was, grabbed it, and been back at sea by dawn. Here, he had to cloak his abilities, become an Other, and rely on people of lesser skill. It grated on his rapidly fraying patience.

He guided the cart down a narrow, winding street overhung by wooden buildings huddled in the shadow of the castle on the hill. He'd learned to appreciate the wisdom of his ancestors in choosing to limit the size of their houses. It not only saved the island's resources but prevented the intimidation of such flagrant displays of wealth as the castle. How could people hanging out their laundry behind drafty shacks not resent a mighty fortress that blocked even their fair share of the sun?

"There's an inn with a stable," Mariel said, nodding toward a faded sign on the corner. "We could stable the pony and look for a bathhouse, then ask after Nick's family before going on to the castle."

Simmering with resentment and irritation at the implication he could not manage on his own, Trystan steered the pony to the stable. Ignoring Mariel's suggestion, he left the cart with a stableboy and, while Mariel fussed over the pony and the boy, he entered the inn and negotiated for a room for the night, a hot bath for Mariel, and a hearty meal for all three of them.

"We may need every sou to buy back the chalice," Mariel hissed when he took her arm and steered her inside. "We cannot afford this."

"I will bargain hard for the chalice," he told her, disliking the grim set of his voice. He'd never been short of funds in his life.

Or, the way things were looking, maybe he *should* start practicing life as a pauper. If the worst came to pass, could he earn a living as a landless foreigner in this mercurial country? The thought was too dreary to consider.

The room they were assigned was narrow and dark, with a single small cot. Mariel stripped back the cover and, with a gesture of disgust, ordered the innkeeper to take away the sheets and flimsy mattress.

"We would fare better in the barn," she muttered. "I dislike sleeping with bugs."

"I'll fetch hay," Trystan said dryly. "I'm sure your thin skin will delight in it."

Apparently too weary to spar with him, she shrugged. "Give me a moment alone to tidy up, and I will go in search of the baroness," she said, not looking at him. "If you wish to waste coins, you might find some clean clothes for Nick before foisting him on his uncle."

"You are going nowhere tonight. I'll have food sent up to you before I take the boy out. Bathe, rest, and I'll be back for you in the morning."

That wasn't what he'd intended to say. He'd wanted to get rid of the boy and come back to sleep with her. He'd almost had her where he wanted her this morning, and every considerable inch of his body longed to find that happy place again. Maybe this time she'd recognize that they couldn't fight the desire between them.

But she looked too ill to enjoy what he had in mind, and he'd been reared to respect those weaker than he. It would be far less frustrating to sleep away from temptation. He gave Nick a shove toward the door.

"I'll be down to join you," she answered stubbornly.

"This isn't Pouchay. You're not the mayor's daughter here. Unless you carry a sword and know how to use it, you will stay until I come back for you." Trystan followed Nick out and slammed the door.

"You don't know a thing about women, do you?" he boy asked in disgust as they traversed the dark all.

"And you do?" Disregarding a child who had neiher sister nor mother as models of female behavior, 'rystan clattered down the narrow staircase and out o the street.

"My father did," Nick argued, following on his eels. "He said you never tell women what to do beause they'll always do the opposite."

"Mariel is not that stupid." Trystan didn't know vhy he'd said that. She'd certainly done some highly uestionable things in their brief acquaintance. Of ourse, he wasn't at all certain that he wouldn't have lone the same had he been in her place.

He was an analytical man, but the boy was right; e didn't know women.

"Is she with child? She does not look well." Undeerred by Trystan's curtness, Nick trailed after him.

That was knowing a little *too* much about women. 'How old are you anyway?" Scanning the signs and hops they passed, Trystan located the baths first.

"Fifteen. I'm slight for my age."

"Slight. Hmpf." He would have guessed the boy to e twelve, at best, but then, he came from a land of ig men. Flipping still another coin to the attendant, e shoved Nick toward the steamy public bath. "I'll e back by the time the bells ring the half hour. Scrub ntil you shine."

Now that he'd disposed of the anchors weighing him lown, Trystan hurried toward another sign he'd noted arther down the street. They didn't have shops as uch on Aelynn. When a ship arrived with cargo from he Outside World, everyone gathered to admire the oods and bid on them. They bartered among themelves for wool or wheat or goat's milk. If someone

wanted anything in particular, they placed an orde
with the captain of the next ship to sail.

But Trystan had strolled the streets of London an
other ports. He knew what to look for, even if th
village was meager in comparison—as was the selec
tion in the secondhand shop.

Beggars couldn't be choosers for good reason, h
decided. Making his selections, he slapped a generou
coin on the counter and ordered the goods sent bac
to the inn. With garments for Nick under his arm, h
hurried back to the baths.

Trystan heard the furious shouts before he reache
the door. He grabbed his sword hilt with his righ
hand and shouldered open the swinging panel.

Naked, Nick swung a long wooden pole at a pair c
robed clerics in priest's collars, holding them off whil
other bathers in various states of undress urged hi
on.

Trystan didn't miss the look of relief in the lad
eyes at his arrival.

"Tell the buggers I'm no woman they can haul o
for their perverted games," Nick shouted in a fury s
great it almost sounded like tears.

Flinging clean clothes at the boy, then placing hin
self between Nick and the priests, Trystan substitute
the tip of his sword for Nick's pole. "Gentlemen,
suggest you move on. As far as I understand it, thi
is a free country where *no* still means no."

Undeterred, the taller of the two clergymen glare
balefully at him. "A child of that age does not belon
in a public bath with grown men. We sought only t
provide shelter. You are not old enough to be hi
father. It is our duty to God to save children from th
likes of you."

Struggling into his clothes, Nick yelled, "Don't be
lieve that! I know what I know."

Trystan understood what the boy meant. Celibates did not generally linger around bathhouses. Priests belonged in churches. Unless they were looking for Nick in particular, they had no business interfering.

"My brother is older than you think." Trystan mentally rolled his eyes. Now he was lying like Mariel. "We'll be leaving now, gentlemen," he said politely, holding his sword up until Nick had time to reach the door.

Apparently summoned by some concerned citizen, a burly soldier darkened the doorway before they could escape. "What is the meaning of this, Père Joseph?"

"Take the boy to the church," the taller priest commanded. "We will deal with his molester."

The soldier grabbed for Nick, who dodged, ducked beneath his arm, and darted out the door, still pulling on his new shirt.

Wondering what sin he'd committed for the gods to test his patience like this, Trystan used his rapier to neatly slice the buttons from the priest's cassock, forcing Père Joseph to grab his robe closed while Trystan turned on the soldier raising his rusty musket. After years of practice in undressing his fellow Aelynners with his sword, Trystan considered Other Worlders much too slow to be fun.

Flashing his rapier for distraction, Trystan nicked the soldier's musket hand before the man had fully raised the gun. Then Trystan shoved the yelping soldier aside and raced after Nick.

He had a hunch that he had just committed the cardinal sin of using his supernatural abilities to interfere in the Other World.

Thirteen

Mariel hadn't intended to fall asleep, but th downy mattress and quilt that had arrived afte her bath had been too tempting to resist. She didn' know where Trystan had found them, and she ough to return them and get his coins back, but she was s very tired. . . .

The next thing she knew, Nick and Trystan crashe through the bedroom door, jarring her awake. Whil Mariel stumbled to her feet, Nick slid under the be at the golden pirate's urging. Garbed only in he threadbare corset and chemise, Mariel wrapped her self in her old cloak for modesty while Trystan shu the door.

Still wearing gentleman's silks and polished boots hair neatly clubbed, looking for all the world as if h owned the ground he walked on, Trystan slammed th bolt home. Arrogantly unhurried, he crossed the roon to press a kiss to her forehead. "Lie," he murmured before sitting on the windowsill and swinging out.

She checked to see that the quilt concealed Nic but didn't dare glance out the window. She could hea heavy feet racing up the stairs, and from the pantin and gasping, the new arrivals had been led on a merr chase. They would not be in a good humor.

It would have been nice if she knew what this wa all about. But there were only four doors up here, an theirs was the first. With a loud kick, the panel slammed against the bar and splintered.

Without missing a beat, Mariel started screaming.

A shabby soldier and a skeletal priest with a badly buttoned cassock froze in the act of removing the bar with an ancient musket. She shrieked hysterically, wrapping her cloak tighter, backing toward the window as the door fell open.

"Thieves! Murderers! Help me!" she wailed, staring at the intruders in what she hoped was wide-eyed horror. "Shame, shame on you! May you roast in hell for masquerading as men of honor!"

"A thousand pardons, madame," the priest muttered, covering his eyes so as not to see her dishabille. "We but seek a boy—"

"Out!" Mariel screamed. "You cannot break in on a woman alone without causing shame! Oh, help me, someone," she shouted to anyone within hearing. If naught else, she'd gather an audience and embarrass the men to death.

With hastily muttered apologies, the priest tugged the soldier's arm, and the men backed out, gently closing the remains of the door after them.

From beneath the bed, Nick snickered.

Trystan swung his large frame back through the window, blocking the sunlight. "That won't fool them for long. Hurry," he ordered, without expression. "Get dressed."

Mariel arched an eyebrow.

"I'll not look, madame," Nick whispered from under the bed. "I'm sorry to be so much trouble."

Mariel continued to stare pointedly at Trystan, who didn't seem to grasp her meaning, even after Nick's polite apology. Boots clattered up and down the hall, accompanied by much shouting. If the sea god thought she would panic and leap to his bidding because of those laughable clowns, he needed to learn a thing or two more about her. He might be tall and forbidding and accustomed to people jumping when he ordered, but he didn't frighten her.

She gestured with her fingers, indicating that Trystan turn around. Finally enlightened, he scowled and obeyed.

"How do you propose we leave?" she asked, hurriedly stepping into the gown that had arrived with the mattress. Trystan had obviously had a busy evening. She would be grateful for his thoughtfulness if she wasn't so worried over what trouble he'd raised now. They'd only just arrived, and he already had the authorities after him. He should have listened when she said he needed her aid. *Men!* They were too cocksure of themselves.

"I sense the river is nearby. I wish I had the Weathermaker here," he said in frustration, gripping the sill with both hands. "I cannot do much without Aelynn's heat."

Since this made no sense to her, Mariel continued tying the tapes of the splendid lavender silk he'd bought for her. She'd not had anything so fine since Papa had died. Unfortunately, the fashionable skirt required a host of loops, tapes, and underpinnings to tie up the acres of frail finery or it would drag on the ground.

Lacking time to loop and tape, she hurriedly slid her arms into the elbow-length sleeves of the bodice and hooked the front. The lacing in back wasn't tight enough, and the waist sagged. Her heavy stockings and wooden sabots looked ridiculous with the delicate garment, and she had no embroidered petticoat to add the layers of bounce the fashion required. She was tall. She would simply leave the skirt to trail on the floor like a train.

"What have you done to anger both church and state?" she asked as she struggled with the last of the hooks.

"Didn't give them what they wanted," Trystan suggested. "Are they accustomed to taking whatever they see?"

Mariel thought about that. "Depends on their level of honesty. Mostly, people don't question authority."

"That explains this rash of petty despots," he muttered.

The noise in the hall had become that of muttered curses. She didn't know how dire the problem was nor how soon they would dare her screams again. She fought the last loose hook with shaking hands.

"What now?" she asked, lifting her coarse cloak and wincing at the contrast to the silk.

"Give me the cloak. Nick, out from there." Coattails pulled back to reveal narrow hips and muscular thighs in tight breeches—and the hilts of his rapier and sword—Trystan examined the dim light of the window that had just displayed the rays of a clear sunset.

Oddly, the sunny day had turned dark and foggy while Mariel had dressed.

When Trystan turned to face her again, she basked in the admiring gaze he finally bestowed upon her. Of course, he'd seen her with next to nothing on, but she preferred the protection of silk and flounces under these circumstances. The lace covering her bosom was so sheer that it daringly revealed the shadow between her breasts. The gossamer fabric didn't prevent heat from rising at his prolonged stare.

"Can you pin your hair up the way ladies do?" he asked, his eyes focused on her bosom. "I like your curls the way they are, but we need you to distract our pursuers."

"Ladies wear their hair powdered," she pointed out, reaching for the pins she'd discarded before her bath. The angry stomps in the hall echoed closer.

"No matter. There isn't time. I apologize for this, but you will fare better with us gone. I'll find Nick's family and return in the morning."

He pressed a hard kiss to her forehead. Then, resolutely, he flung the shabby cloak around his broad shoulders and grabbed the back of Nick's shirt to point at some feature outside the window. Before she could protest, Trystan had thrown his powerful leg over the sill, and the pair disappeared from sight.

It was impossible for a man that large not to be noticed, even in the back alley of an inn. Branded by the too-brief kiss, Mariel fumed as she circled the bed to look outside, fearing she'd see them being marched off at gunpoint.

A mist shrouded the alley and swirled up the side of the building, masking all sight of the pair.

Lost in amazement that a pea soup so thick could have risen so quickly on a warm summer evening, she jumped, startled, at the pounding on the door, even though she'd been expecting it. Giving another puzzled glance out the window, she dallied before answering the knock. Ladies never hurried.

She gave her hair a last pat, brushed down her elegant skirt before laying the train gently over her arm, then donned a vapid smile and cracked open the broken door. Peering through the gap, she raised her eyebrows in mock surprise and dismay at seeing the earlier intruders returned. "This is most unseemly, messieurs. Must I call the innkeeper?"

"Begging your pardon, madame, but we have been slandered and attacked by rogues who may be threatening you, for all we know," the soldier said stiffly.

"We must search your room. Please to stand in the hall where you will be safe."

"Threatening me?" She strived for the querulous tone of the Vicomtess Rochefort. "I cannot imagine such a thing. Were you not in uniform, I would not allow this insult. I am awaiting my maid's return. This is truly invasive. I would speak to the baroness of this as soon as I see her, but I detest ruining her nuptials with such chicanery."

She rattled on, delaying them by adjusting her skirts and patting her hair before stepping into the hall and standing in their way until she was certain they would like nothing better than to throw her down the stairs. "What is the meaning of this, precisely?" she continued. "I should think a soldier ought to be able to stop spineless thieves. And does the church now assist in apprehending lawbreakers? I know my husband insists that travel widens one's mind, but I say people in these parts are barely more than heathens, if this is how they treat visitors."

Finally shoving past her, the soldier hurried into the room and opened the window to peer into the fog. The priest merely glanced under the bed and behind the door. Both looked puzzled and irritated, but not bright enough to question a lady they'd insulted and harassed.

With many apologies and bows, they backed out. She shut the door and listened as they clattered back down the stairs.

She'd dealt with officious men all her life, so she wasn't particularly surprised that she'd driven these off, but she was absolutely dying of curiosity, and her wretched companion didn't intend to return to satisfy her interest until morning. What was she supposed to do in the meantime? Twiddle her thumbs? Flap her eyelashes?

She'd eaten the meal the innkeeper had sent up. She'd rested. She was garbed in this lovely gown. As much as she'd like to fling off the silk and climb between the covers and sleep for a week, she wouldn't let a little weakness stop her from her purpose.

She'd come to get the chalice. And so she would. The sooner she could send Trystan out of her life, the faster she would return to normal.

A part of her wondered if she really wanted to return to her dull, restricted life, but she ignored the thought. Francine and her babe were her reality, not silk dresses and adventures with enigmatic sea gods.

"We probably shouldn't be seen together," Trystan said, not looking at the boy following him. The fog he'd created had begun to dissipate, unable to sustain itself for long without the aid of Aelynn or the Weathermaker. Shadowy figures could already be discerned through the lifting mist. "This isn't a large town. I can ask after your family in the tavern if you can find a safe place to hide."

"You don't like working with others, do you?" Nick asked, pretending to linger at a shop window a pace behind him. "I'll meet you here when the bell rings nine."

He and Waylan and Nevan worked together, Trystan thought righteously, striding off. Well, they each had their own tasks and did them in conjunction, at least. He was the diplomat who dealt with port authorities and merchants and so forth.

He just happened to like doing things his own way. As a future leader, he'd learned early that people preferred to be told what to do. Since he enjoyed telling them, it worked out well.

Beneath the cloak, he tugged off his silks and donned the leather jerkin of a working man that he'd bought in the secondhand shop. He stuffed his expensive garments into a canvas shoulder bag he'd also purchased there. Covering his hair with a cap, he entered a smoky, ill-lit tavern, pointed at a tankard of what everyone else seemed to be drinking, and prepared to locate Nick's family.

"It is taxation without representation, just like in the Americas," he overheard his neighbor say to a group gathered around him.

"We elected Pierre to go to Paris," a frock-coated gentleman at a table on the other side of the speaker said. "Save your lawyer's sedition for the courtroom."

So much for thinking he was entering a rural tavern of phlegmatic farmers. Trystan considered donning his coat again but decided against it. There were enough men in shirtsleeves that he did not stand out.

"Pierre is a nobleman's son, just like you, Chevalier," a farmer in manure-encrusted boots argued. "He may agree to accept taxation if the Assembly does, but he will never agree to change the way things are and make us equal."

Despite what the American colonists claimed, all men weren't created equal, Trystan mused. He couldn't raise a thunderstorm as Waylan could. Waylan couldn't practice diplomacy if his life depended upon it.

On the other side of the lawyer, the scholarly gentleman who'd been addressed as Chevalier finished his drink and pushed back from the table. "People are rioting for bread that cannot be had. Soldiers are raising arms against women and children. The Assembly has illegally declared itself above the king's command. The natural order is being disturbed by these wayward notions. You cannot change the way things have always been done. The nobility have wealth and education and are better able to govern than a chicken farmer and a cabbage picker. God gave us the tasks we were meant to do."

Trystan started to nod in agreement, but the worrisome mention of riots and the chevalier's pompous tone forced him to stop and reconsider. If he believed the gods had given him his talent for languages and protecting Aelynn, then why would they take away the task for which he was destined and banish him? Might mankind not mistake the intention of the gods?

And if soldiers were raising arms against protesting women and children in Paris, did that mean the militia he'd seen might turn their muskets against the villagers arguing in the streets of Mariel's home? Should people be *killed* for speaking their differing opinions?

"Oh, heaven forbid that we change the way things have always been done," the lawyer said mockingly, interrupting Trystan's struggle to grasp the country's politics. "The Africans have always been slaves, so thus they must stay into eternity. Kings have always murdered their brothers, and so they must continue. The Queen of France eats cake while her citizens starve. Let us introduce no innovation!"

"De Berrier will not have it any other way," the chicken farmer echoed, gesturing toward the chevalier.

Uh-oh. Trystan watched the man in the frock coat—*de Berrier*—shrug dismissively.

"The problem is that no one understands economics or heeds the lessons of history. That must be corrected." Without waiting for disagreement, the chevalier walked out.

Draining his cup, Trystan was about to follow the scholarly de Berrier when the argument picked up again.

"Did you not hear, you stupid peasant?" the lawyer asked without anger. "De Berrier is to marry a wealthy baroness and inherit the guardianship of a rich little boy. He has high connections and the court listens when he speaks. He has been called to Versailles to give advice on financial matters there, where he can earn a better title and lands than the duc can provide."

The farmer growled threateningly. "We will see about that on the morrow. If we are as strong as our comrades in Paris who march against the king's injustice, we will show the chevalier and the duc that they cannot feast while we starve."

Trystan rolled his eyes heavenward. *Why me?* he inquired of any gods listening. *All I want is your chalice back. I'm not the revolutionary sort.*

But if Mariel and young Nick were caught in an uprising, it would be his fault. And he could not hand the boy over to a man who might use Nick's inheritance to gain a king's favor. He needed to find out more.

Trystan lifted his finger and ordered another round.

It would be easy enough to find de Berrier later, when the rebels stuffed the arrogant scholar down a privy. For now, he'd listen and learn.

Fourteen

After leaving the tavern, Trystan still had no idea what to do about Nick, but he did know he had to find the chalice and escape before they were caught up in a protest that could easily lead to riot and violence. He was incapable of running away from a fight, particularly in defense of the helpless, and he would most certainly end up breaking Aelynn law. The noose kept tightening around his neck, and he squirmed inside the confounded neckcloth this society required that he wear.

Local gossip confirmed Nick's story of de Berrier being his relation. There seemed to be a warrant on the boy's head, but like everything else in this country, politics decided whether anyone believed the murder was justified or not.

As the church bells chimed nine, Trystan hurried to the store where Nick should be waiting. The boy wasn't there.

Alarmed, he paced back and forth for another five minutes, cursing himself for leaving a thief alone. Nick had no reason to trust Trystan, or vice versa. He should be relieved that he had one less obstacle to his goal. Instead, he worried.

Trystan disliked feeling as if he was shirking his duty by walking away, but he did no one any good standing on a street corner. He had to find the chalice.

Mariel would look after the boy if he'd returned to the inn.

As he made his way to the castle and the baroness, once again wearing his silk, he was uncomfortably aware of the unusual number of armed soldiers in the streets. He fought the urge to keep his hand on his sword hilt. People stared enough at him as it was.

To avoid notice once he was inside the stone fortress, Trystan turned his back on a priest and smiled at a pretty maid. Bowing, he inquired the direction to the baroness's quarters.

The corridors were chilly and lit only by sparsely spaced torches. His boot heels echoed against cold stone, and the tails of his frock coat rustled in the gloomy silence. He was a man of sea and sunlight. Dark figures lurking in shadows aroused suspicion in him. The words of rebellion he'd heard earlier echoed in his ears. The urge to remove Mariel from such dangerous environs escalated.

And the chalice. Imagining the ancient artifact loose in a land on the verge of chaos made Trystan hurry faster.

And almost run straight into Nick.

The boy grabbed his coat with an expression of relief, and contrary to expectation, began tugging him deeper into the bowels of the castle. "Hurry, hurry! I am sorry I was late, but I followed Madame Mariel."

They had not given the boy their full names, so he had none to call them by, Trystan observed as they raced down the stone corridor. An odd thing to think upon while his heart was about to leap from his chest in terror. Although why he should be terrified over a hellion like Mariel, who could get herself into and out of trouble faster than she could breathe, was beyond his capacity to reason at the moment. What the *devil* was she doing here?

He heard her shouts before he saw her. Never had

he been so eager to wring someone's neck as he was now. Better that *he* do it than whoever menaced her at the moment.

He slowed to a clipped gait as Nick raced around a corner and added his voice to the melee. Trystan's first glimpse of Mariel produced the impression of a mighty warrior about to smite de Berrier with her invisible sword. With her ebony hair piled high, she was as tall as the gentleman, and she wielded her slender hand with dramatic energy.

He discarded his first impression when she swayed like a willow while reaching to hug Nick's shoulders. It appeared as if she was using the boy for support.

When she glanced up and gave Trystan a blazing smile of welcome, he nearly tripped over his own feet at the surprising warmth spreading through him. He could not remember anyone ever greeting him with such joy. He'd like to frame this moment to admire on lonely days in the future.

Which was another insane thought, given that he had just wanted wring her neck for disobeying orders. But Mariel seemed to inspire insanity. Gripping the sword beneath his coat, Trystan nodded in her direction, then turned a cold gaze on de Berrier.

"Your arrival is opportune, my dear," she called, with only a slight quaver of—fear? Anger? "This gentleman seems to be under some misapprehension that Nick belongs to him. It is all very puzzling, and I fear my head goes weak with dizziness working it out."

Misapprehension? Trystan thought the point was to deliver Nick to his family, not keep him away. But given his doubts about the man earlier, he played ignorant. "You weren't supposed to leave your bed for the rest of the day, my dear," he said in his best doting husband manner, adapting to the situation as Mariel did.

Turning to the irate gentleman, he added, "She

takes on too much. In her condition, it is best not to argue. What seems to be the problem, Chevalier?"

"As you have apparently ascertained, I am Marc Cassell, the Chevalier de Berrier. That is my disreputable nephew." De Berrier reached for Nick, who dodged behind Mariel's skirts. "The authorities have been searching for him this past week or more. His father was murdered, and he is both witness and suspect. It seems he has also been haunting the duc's forest as a bandit. I must take him into my custody."

"And we know that is nonsense, don't we, dear?" Mariel simpered. "He has been with you on your ship, so he cannot possibly have done any of these things."

"I don't know this person," Nick growled, jerking his head in de Berrier's direction. The boy's head barely came to Mariel's shoulders but he sounded man enough.

"This isn't your uncle?" Trystan asked in mock surprise. "You told me he was a wealthy man in Pontivy and would reimburse me for your fare. You would not lie to me, would you?"

"No, monsieur, I would not lie, but I have never seen this man in my life," Nick asserted. "My uncle would not tell terrible stories about me. I think he is like those men in the baths today. You warned me not to talk to them."

The chevalier scowled. "Père Joseph was merely doing his duty by apprehending you so he might bring you safely to me, you ungrateful wretch." He turned a steely gaze to Trystan. "I shall be forced to call the authorities if you do not hand him over at once."

Trystan was tempted to do so, and be rid of the lying, thieving brat, but Mariel's eyes reflected the sea green of trust, and to his amazement he couldn't disappoint her any more than he could abandon the boy to a questionable fate.

"You must understand that I am responsible for the child since he was placed in my care. Until the proper authorities prove your relationship, I must ask you to leave him with us." Trystan clasped Nick on the shoulder and offered his arm to Mariel. "Come along, dear, we must return you to your room. You look positively faint."

She appeared to be a ghost of the woman she'd been on Aelynn, but Trystan refrained from saying so. Anxiety was starting to pound rhythmically in his head, and he wanted no more than to be out of here. Except they still had to find the chalice.

"But the baroness, dear . . ." Mariel leaned on his arm for support rather than merely resting her hand there, and another shiver of unease rippled through him. "We really must see her this evening or we will have no chance on the morrow."

"Guards!" de Berrier shouted, waving to a pair of liveried servants at the other end of the corridor.

Trystan debated throwing Mariel over his shoulder and running.

"The Baroness Beloit will be most displeased," she argued, refusing to give ground as the men hurried in their direction. "We have traveled a long way to be with her on this occasion. If you will send word to her," she addressed the arriving servants, "all will be well. This gentleman is mistaken."

"For your information, madame, my *fiancée*," the chevalier said coldly, "has expressed no interest in the arrival of any cousin. Take these impostors out of here, and leave my nephew with me," he ordered.

Rolling his eyes, Trystan reached for his sword.

Again.

Fifteen

Mariel hadn't been lying earlier when she'd said her head was spinning, and de Berrier's announcement that he was the man her cousin was marrying didn't help. She should have remembered the lady had called him a chevalier. She clutched Trystan's arm and struggled to stay upright.

Amazingly, Trystan was already wielding his sword, forcing de Berrier and the servants to stand back. She hadn't seen him unsheathe the weapon. Had she briefly lost consciousness?

"You touch my wife at peril of your lives," Trystan said in a tone that would strike cold in the hearts of the most stalwart of men.

The liveried servants didn't seem to be that stout of heart. In fact, they appeared to be looking at the chevalier as if he were the worm who'd turned. She grabbed the advantage Trystan offered.

"Come along, Nick. We will settle this matter in the morning. I really must lie down." She smiled weakly at the servants. "Please, tell the baroness that I was not well enough to correct her betrothed."

She held her gown over her arm to keep from falling on her face, and teetered down the corridor as if she were wearing heels. She had to hope the train still covered her ugly shoes. Trystan prodded Nick into going ahead of them, and when the servants offered no argument, he sheathed his sword to escort her back the way he'd come.

De Berrier's deep voice boomed in fury behind them.

"To the right," she whispered.

Nick darted down the side hall first, and Mariel followed. Trystan checked over his shoulder, and apparently deciding they weren't being pursued, hurried after them.

"What in the name of the gods did you think you were doing?" Trystan muttered near her ear as they raced after Nick.

"Helping." Her train slipped, and she tripped over the hem. Trystan held her steady. It was most unusual for her to feel unwell. She didn't have time for illness. "But then the chevalier saw Nick, and there was a lot of shouting, and I didn't get to see the baroness."

"We can no longer wait until morning. Is there somewhere I can leave you and Nick while I search for the chalice?"

He sounded gruff. With Trystan, it was difficult to tell if that meant he was angry or worried. She simply knew she had seen no one so welcome as the sea god wielding his sword in her defense. "Why isn't there time? What is happening?"

"There are a lot of unhappy people out there who don't think it fair that the wedding participants will be feasting while they're starving. I want to be gone before the two sides come together."

Mariel nodded, understanding his concern about the unrest seething through the heart of France. "If the rich would simply invite the poor to dinner, there wouldn't be riots," she replied.

Nick halted at the entrance to a grand hall. "Where are we going?"

"That is the baroness's suite." She nodded at an

ornate set of doors to one side of the hall. "But if de Berrier is returning there, we cannot visit. We must draw her out."

Trystan narrowed his eyes at their young companion. "Nick, is that man your uncle?"

The boy shrugged and stared at the floor. "Could be. I was little when I saw him last, but my father thought he was a miserly snob with no soul," he finished. "Although he is said to be a brilliant financier. He will no doubt beat me and hand me over to the authorities."

Trystan pressed harder. "Your father did not call the chevalier a thief or worse? Would he trust de Berrier as your guardian?"

Nick glowered. "My mother's family is of the finest. They are not thieves."

"Then you are the first of the sort?" Trystan asked dryly. Before the boy could object, he continued, "Have you no other relatives?"

"None, monsieur. I will go with you as your cabin boy," he said eagerly. "You did say you had a ship, did you not?"

"That is out of the question. Can the chevalier be trusted with the guardianship of you and your inheritance?"

"At best, he will send me off to school and make my life a misery!" Furious now, Nick took off at a run.

Trystan reacted so quickly that he had the boy's coat in his fist before Nick had gone two steps. "You have a choice. You may return to the inn, remove our bags to the cart, and take the cart to the woods to wait for us."

Nick's eyes widened, and he glanced back and forth between the two of them. "You would let me go with you?"

"Do you wish to stay here?" Trystan asked, arching an eyebrow.

Nick shook his head. "Most certainly not."

"Even knowing the chevalier will have your inheritance if you do not claim it?"

Nick looked a little less certain. "He threatened to turn me over to the authorities."

"True," Trystan agreed, releasing the boy's coat. "He may simply not understand children. I cannot tell you whom to trust. If you wish to make your decision from a distance, you may go with us."

"Yes, sir." Nick suddenly looked as young as he was. "How long should I wait?"

"We should be back before dawn. If we have not arrived when the clock strikes noon, you will have to make your own decision as to how you should go on. It is a great responsibility I place on you, I know."

Nick straightened, visibly growing two inches. "I will guard your possessions with my life, monsieur."

"They're hardly worth that," Mariel said with a laugh, deciding the poor boy had enough of a burden on him. "But the pony and cart belong to a neighbor, and I would hate to lose them. If we do not return in a timely manner, I'd recommend taking them back to Pouchay. My sister will find you a place there. Just ask for Francine Rousseau."

"I will not leave you," Nick said in horror. "I will come find you."

"No," Trystan replied curtly, cutting off Mariel's softer reply. "I do not want to have to come looking for you. If you and the cart are not at the edge of the woods when we arrive, we will assume you have gone on to Pouchay. If only the cart awaits us, we will assume you have decided to stay here and claim your inheritance. It will be much easier for me to persuade my lady to leave if she believes you are safe."

Nick bit his lip and uncertainty wavered in his eyes. Mariel quit leaning on Trystan to brush her fingers over the boy's smooth jaw. "We will find another way home if necessary, but I'm certain we will be joining you in a few hours."

Nick held out his hand to Trystan. "Thank you, monsieur. You may rely on me."

They shook, and with worry wrinkling her brow, Mariel watched the boy run off. "A boy like that should be in school and playing in the street. I do not like the way the world is headed."

"It is just your world that is unsafe," Trystan said imperiously. "Mine is secure and normal. You will see that you are far better off with me."

She shot him an exasperated look. "And you will take my sister and all of Pouchay with you to this sane world of yours?"

Not expecting an answer, she swept up her skirt, looped her hand around his elbow, and started for the stairs.

She hated letting Nick go off on his own. She disliked sneaking about as if she didn't belong here. She desperately wanted to go home. But circumstances being what they were, subterfuge seemed the safest and fastest way to retrieve the chalice and return everything to the way it should be.

"Behave as if we are a couple on an assignation and watch for a maid or footman," she commanded him as arrogantly as he did her.

"An assignation is what I wish more than anything in the world," Trystan murmured silkily in her ear, leaning over and brushing his lips against her hair, behaving just as she'd ordered him to do.

His playacting sent warm shivers down her spine. "No, the *chalice* is what you wish more than anything in the world," she replied sweetly, smiling as if they were exchanging flatteries, for the benefit of a guard hurrying past.

"The chalice exists. Retrieving it is a task I must accomplish," he argued. "That is not the same thing as wanting it for myself. Have you never felt a need to hold someone, to cherish them, to be closer to them than anyone else in the world? Share your secrets, your lives, your dreams?"

She had dreamed such things ever since she was a small child and realized she was not like anyone she knew. After her mother died, she'd spent many adolescent nights weeping with loneliness, longing for someone to whom she could speak honestly. If Trystan were truly such a man, it would be the answer to her prayers.

But menial prayers like hers didn't deserve an answer, and Trystan was merely a man who wanted his own way. She'd lived in the real world long enough to know these things.

"Share their bodies and their beds, you mean?" she said mockingly. Before he could answer, she saw two maids enter a room down the corridor, and she hurried toward them, forcing Trystan to increase his stride to keep up with her.

"Mesdemoiselles," she whispered loudly to the two maids folding linen in the closet. When they curtsied hastily, she put a finger to her lips. "My . . . *friend* . . . has only just arrived. We have but a few hours together, and the baroness's rooms . . . How should I say it? They are very busy. Is there an empty chamber where we might go undisturbed for just a little while?"

She giggled with the maids and hid behind Trystan's muscled arm while he gallantly looked stoic with his hand on his sword, prepared for anything. Golden gods need not say much. They must only *exist*, she observed. The maids were awed by his presence.

One of them pointed to the ceiling. "Above. The

rooms have not been opened there." She offered a stack of clean linen, which Mariel accepted.

Taking charge now that the situation was clear, Trystan handed out silver coins and thanked them gallantly, then placed his hand at Mariel's waist and hurried her toward the stairs.

She was gasping for breath and scarcely able to hold the linen by the time they reached the next floor and located a narrow unused chamber overlooking the courtyard. Mariel did her best to hide her weakness by releasing Trystan's arm to examine their hiding place. From the moon's light they could detect the silhouettes of a tester bed draped in satin hangings and a dresser with a tall gilded mirror.

"Excellent," Trystan said with satisfaction. "There is even a bar on the door. You may rest here while I fetch the chalice."

As much as the idea appealed, she could not let him barge about, running his sword through people. "Don't be ridiculous," she replied more sharply than she had intended. "The lady does not know you, but de Berrier does. He will never let you near her. Here, I think I've found a lamp. Have you a flint?"

Once he took the lamp, Mariel perched on the edge of the naked mattress for fear of falling over. The lamp flared to life without her even noticing the spark of a flint. She glanced up nervously to see Trystan hovering too close, his bronzed face all harsh angles in the shadows flung by the flame, his large frame so much more—physical—than hers. Her heart pounded a little faster as she realized they were alone, and his intentions toward her were plain. He might be a man of mystery, but he had no subtlety. She was in no condition to either fight him or give him what he wanted. Distraction was her only hope.

She gestured toward the ornate writing desk at the window. "See if there is any notepaper in the drawers. If there are no pen and ink there, we may find them in the library."

He slid a thin accounting ledger from his inside coat pocket. "I have paper. What do you intend to do?"

"Send a note to the baroness. I can't use accounting sheets." She knew she sounded petulant, but she was having some difficulty concentrating. Resting in bed was mightily tempting, but she did not dare suggest it with Trystan in the room.

He carefully removed the gilt-edged flyleaf. "Will this suit?"

"Excellent, yes." Rising slowly, she carried the lamp over to examine the desk's contents. "There is ink here, but it may be too dry. Can you sharpen the pen nib?"

He produced a small knife from his sword belt and took the quill. Mariel refrained from raising her eyebrows at the assortment of weaponry he carried on his person. These were perilous times, and Trystan was no fool. He carried a pouch of gold worth more than everything her family had ever possessed. He wouldn't carry it so confidently if he couldn't protect it.

She moistened the tip of her finger with her tongue and rubbed it on the sharpened quill, then dipped it into the dry ink and swirled it about. The note would have to be brief.

It is most urgent that I speak with you about the chalice. Follow the footman to my room. Mariel.

It was not at all the type of thing she would have written had she time and ink, or if her brain wasn't so weary. But perhaps her words would raise enough curiosity to do the trick.

"Now, we need find a footman to deliver the note

and direct her here." Just the thought of hunting down a footman exhausted her.

Trystan took the note and tucked it into his pocket. "I will find a footman. You will stay here. It might be best if the baroness sees you alone. There is a niche just down the hall where I can wait, unobserved. You may call for me after you've explained."

This sounded such an excellent plan that she returned to perch on the edge of the bed and agreed with a nod. It was marvelous having someone with whom to share the burden of duty. She could almost weep with the relief, but then she'd know she was delirious. "You will let me know if she is delayed?"

"If I can. I will impress the urgency upon the servant, though." He hesitated, then took a long stride across the narrow room, bringing him within arm's reach. He pressed a finger under her chin and lifted it. "I will be back," he promised.

Before Mariel could say a word, or even think one, Trystan leaned over and covered her mouth with his.

His lips tasted of honey and wine and the faint tingle of salt. Weak already, Mariel did not even attempt to fight the flaring need that sprang through her midsection, seared her heart, and caused her to clasp the silk of his coat as he parted her lips. She took him in and drank deeply of all he offered, finding strength in the desire flowing through his lips, evident in his urgency. The possession of his tongue spoke of darker needs and desires, and filled her with longing.

Reluctantly, he pulled back, running his fingers over her cheek. "Soon. We will be together soon."

His rough vow spoke to the emptiness inside her, and she nearly cried when he walked out the door.

She truly must be ill to weep over a man who could never be more than a passing stranger.

Sixteen

Trystan tipped a footman to carry the message to the baroness, then lingered in a doorway to watch her suite. At the rate he was handing out coins, he would be fortunate to have enough left to pay the chalice's original purchase price, much less any extra that might be demanded.

He hated leaving Mariel upstairs alone. She seemed to have become a shadow of herself over these last days. A woman who could swim to Aelynn shouldn't be so weak from a slight journey in a pony cart.

A warning niggled at the back of Trystan's mind, but he didn't have time to fret over what he could not change. In due time, he would be able to take care of Mariel in the manner any mistress of his deserved. He was actually considering ways of introducing her to the pleasures of his home so that she would be convinced to stay.

But right now, all his concentration rested on the door of the suite. He had no way of knowing if the chevalier was inside.

To his immense relief, the bewigged and liveried footman he'd sent emerged from the suite with a lady on his arm. Trystan had to assume it was the baroness. She wasn't overly tall, but her powdered and puffed headdress towered higher than the servant's head. Unlike Mariel's, her skirts billowed out and swung gracefully about her ankles. Trystan realized his mistake in purchasing the pretty gown—he hadn't bought the proper undergarments or shoes to go with it. He had much to learn of women's clothing.

He'd told the footman what room to go to. He hoped he'd been understood.

"My little cousin is here? In the castle? How very amazing," the baroness chattered as she passed Trystan on the way to the stairs.

So, Mariel was truly the lady's cousin? He'd thought it another of her lies.

"Mariel *never* leaves Pouchay." The baroness's voice carried down the stairs.

Trystan lingered in the shadows at the bottom until she turned down the corridor; then he dashed up the marble steps to stop again in an unlit niche of the hall.

"I cannot imagine her leaving her sister. I hope nothing is wrong at home."

Trystan rolled his eyes and thanked the gods that Mariel was not such a chatterbox. Lady Beloit would drive him mad within minutes.

And Mariel would drive him mad with just her existence if he did not bed her soon. He was a cautious man not given to impulse. He was able to contain his physical urges for long periods of time, and he never gave in to them with the wrong women. But Mariel . . . That moment at the temple, learning he had a physical match in this world, had altered his brain until his every thought was reduced to getting her into his bed. He hadn't walked around in a constant state of arousal since adolescence, and he didn't appreciate it now. He adjusted his tight breeches and hoped the gods were having a good laugh over his predicament.

The footman knocked at the correct door. The baroness chattered meaninglessly, waiting for a response from inside.

None came.

Trystan straightened, his hand instinctively resting on his sword hilt.

The footman knocked again. The baroness called a greeting.

No one answered.

The footman tried the latch. The door hit against the bar.

Still, no one inside spoke.

"Oh, dear," the baroness murmured. "She said it was most urgent. Do you think anything could be wrong?"

The footman stood stoically, waiting for orders instead of dithering.

"Mariel, Mariel, dear," the baroness called a little louder. When there was still no reply, she turned back to the footman. "Could you, umm, try to break open the door?"

Praying Mariel had just fallen into a sound sleep—although the lady's chattering ought to have wakened the dead—Trystan slipped from his niche with the noise of the footman ramming his shoulder against the heavy door. He'd break down the damned door himself if Mariel didn't open it soon. If the door was barred, she had to be inside. Pretending he'd just run up the stairs, he strode briskly down the hall.

"May I be of assistance, my lady?"

The baroness eyed him with interest. "Yes, I believe you may."

Since he was twice the footman's size, Trystan assumed she was thinking in terms of a battering ram. But he didn't intend to cause damage if he could avoid it.

"My cousin must have fallen asleep in this room, and we cannot open the door. Could you help us?"

"I am Trystan d'Aelynn, Mariel's betrothed. I left

her sleeping there just a short time ago. If I may?" Removing his knife from its sheath, he slid it through the crack in the door and forced the bar upward.

"Mariel's betrothed? She did not mention you to me," the lady was saying as the bar clattered to the floor.

"We had not yet told her sister." Trystan shoved the door open, praying for Mariel's welcoming smile. If she had not heard the noise he'd just made—

In the dying light of the lantern he'd lit, he could see the lavender silk of her skirt falling motionless down the side of the curtained bed, and his throat closed in fear. Mariel was never so still, even in sleep.

He crossed the room in a stride and tossed back the curtain. On the linen sheets of the newly made-up bed, Mariel lay as pale and unmoving as one dead.

Had he killed her? If so, he did not know how, but Trystan didn't doubt that he was to blame. This was twice now that he'd caused her grief.

"She looks so pale. Is she ill?" the baroness whispered, jarring him back to the present.

Praying frantically, Trystan covered her brow with his cold hand. "She's not felt well since we set out on this journey." Watching her chest rise slightly, he realized she breathed, but relief did not come to him while she lay so still. "She does not seem feverish."

He should never have let the potential mother of his heir escape Aelynn. He should never have let her come with him to this place. Guilt crawled into his belly and gnawed.

"Tell my maid to bring my smelling salts," the baroness commanded the footman, suddenly assuming the authority of her title.

Ignoring the lady, Trystan sat down beside Mariel and lifted her into his arms. To his relief, her eyelids fluttered.

"I don't believe the child has ever left home." Lady Beloit rubbed Mariel's wrist. "Perhaps the travel has exhausted her."

"Mariel," he murmured, lifting her head so it rested like a doll's upon his shoulder. "Mariel, your sister needs you."

That got a response. Her head jerked, and her lashes lifted. Seeing him, she produced a smile so heartbreaking that he might have wept. Her eyes were the bright green of spring leaves before her lids closed over them again, and she lay limp as death in his arms. Terror ripped through him.

A young girl in a maid's apron hurried in with a silver cylinder. The baroness flourished it under Mariel's nose.

Mariel inhaled sharply, then coughed. She convulsed so harshly that Trystan waved the cylinder away. Her cough grew weaker, but she didn't regain consciousness.

Lady Beloit gestured the servants into the hall and closed the door. "What was the urgent matter that brought you here?" she demanded. "She looks as if she's half starved, yet I know she bought every grain of wheat in the entire region."

"I have kept her fed. She is not starved. She was fine when we left Pouchay." Trystan caressed her face and kissed her brow, praying for some response. He desperately missed the vibrant female who alternately annoyed and attracted him. Her kiss earlier had inspired dreams beyond any he deserved.

"Then what was so urgent that she must see me on the eve of my marriage? Marc is not a patient man. At my age, I cannot risk losing him over some frivolous notion."

Trystan glanced at the lady. He'd not bothered

studying her earlier, since the baroness looked like every other aristocratic female in France, covered in useless powder and silk and frills. He saw the lines around her eyes now, the sharpness of her nose, the thin stripe of her rouged lips. Despite the cosmetics, there was intelligence in her sharp gaze and crispness in her command.

"Mariel did not know that the chalice she sold you was a holy vessel stolen from a church. I have come to buy it back from you, with a little extra for your troubles. She was extremely upset that she had done such a thing and refused to stay home when I said I would come after you."

"Stolen? From a church?" The lady looked shocked. "How *dreadful*. Who would commit such a sacrilege?"

Trystan invented the first explanation that came to mind. "Radicals, I fear. Those who would tear down the church and the aristocracy."

He was proving to be as adept at lying as Mariel.

The lady gasped in horror. "I did not believe the insurgents would go so far! That is beyond *monstrous*. Of course, you must have it back. I thought only to give Mariel coins so she might feed her friends, but once the jeweler cleaned it up, I could see it was of great value. Marc loves it, but I'm sure he'll agree that it must be returned."

Trystan silently praised the heavens that Mariel's relation was more sensible than she looked. The triumph and relief he'd expected at attaining his goal did not follow, though.

He had once thought that reclaiming the Chalice of Plenty would be worth any price, but no more. He bowed his head in acceptance that he could no longer wish Mariel out of his life. He had lied and broken laws, not for the chalice, but for Mariel. She brightened a corner of the vast wasteland that was his heart, and he could not bear to lose all that she promised.

She might be impulsive and disobedient, but she had a generosity larger than the sea. He'd never met a woman so sympathetic that she was willing to sacrifice all she was for her sister and her neighbors. She was quick-witted enough to meet him as an equal without being foolish enough to compete with him. Instead, she smiled and made him feel welcome, then flipped him head over heels when he was off balance. A woman who could spin him around like that could teach him much and was worth her weight in pearls.

And he was in danger of losing this mate the gods had chosen for him. He ground his teeth and tried to be pragmatic rather than shake his fist at the fates. "I think we must send for a physician."

"I'll have the footman look for one, and my maid will fetch water to bathe her forehead." Briskly, the baroness opened the chamber door and sent her servants on their errands.

"Water," Mariel murmured, as if echoing her cousin's words.

Trystan froze, some instinctive part of his brain waking under the pressure of panic. "We will bring water," he assured her, cradling her like a child in his arms. He nodded at the silver cylinder the lady held. "Is that really salt?"

Lady Beloit looked at the smelling salts as if she'd forgotten she held them. "No, I don't think so. It smells like ammonia."

Knowing he sounded as if he'd taken leave of his mind, Trystan asked, "Could we find a cellar of salt?"

"I'm sure we can." She looked at Mariel uncertainly. "But salt cannot be good for her if she is thirsty already."

"We will try just water first," he assured her. "But Mariel loves the sea. I have taken her far from her home. I know it sounds implausible . . ."

The baroness looked at him shrewdly, then nodded without argument. "I will send someone with salt."

Within minutes, servants carried in pitchers of water and cellars of salt.

"Drink, *mi ama*, we have found water for you." Trystan pressed a glass to her mouth.

Her lips moved. Lady Beloit shooed the servants from the room while Trystan patiently trickled water past Mariel's parted lips.

She moaned and stirred slightly, but still, she did not wake.

"They've not found a physician yet," the baroness murmured. "Not a sober one, at least." She hesitated, then offered, "You cannot get much water into her like this. I can send for a bath. Perhaps she can soak it up through her skin. Would that help?"

Trystan looked up in relief. "It can't hurt."

She rustled to the door and gave more orders while Trystan shook salt into the glass he was holding. He sprinkled a few drops of salty water between her lips, and Mariel's tongue licked eagerly at them.

Hope rising, he held her head up and tipped the crystal more, so that a steady dribble seeped between her lips. She swallowed eagerly and drank more.

"Amazing," the baroness whispered. "You must be a genius."

No, merely a man who knew the limitations of his kind. Every strength had a weakness, but his ring of silence prevented him from saying as much to Mariel's Other World cousin. "It is an old home remedy," he assured her. "I think she will be fine by morning."

He had wanted to grab the chalice and go, but he could not take Mariel into the cold night while she was so weak. His ability to act independently had been severed, even without the ritual of binding.

"If you are staying, you must join the wedding party," Lady Beloit said as footmen carried in a small tub and maids brought pitchers of water. "It will be a very festive occasion."

Trystan didn't wish to say anything of the rebel plans for the morrow in front of servants. Gossip ran loose even in Aelynn. He could imagine what the whispers must be like in a place torn by strife. He dribbled water into Mariel, more aware than ever of the cushion of her breasts pressed into his chest, the slightness of her waist in his arms. Perhaps the gods meant for him to learn the value of the precious gift they'd given him.

Perhaps they intended for him to share his strength with her. *Immediately*. The bonding ceremony would do that, but he was not on Aelynn, and he was no priest. Would it work here?

He would have to take her as his amacara and find out.

"Should I have my maid bathe her?" the lady asked when all the servants had departed.

Troubled, and needing time to think, Trystan shook his head. "She is too weak to sit. I must hold her. We are married in my church. Do not concern yourself with the proprieties."

With the servants gone, he offered his gratitude. "I am in your debt for your promise to return the chalice. I cannot repay you easily except in coin."

He sought the diplomatic means of telling the lady what he knew. "But I would warn you about the morrow. There are . . . radicals . . . in town who would protest your festivities. I do not know what they have planned, but they have weapons, and the alehouse has promised cheap liquor. I don't know your guests, but if they are drunk—"

"And they will be." The baroness nodded curtly. "It will be a horrendous brawl and people could be harmed, even killed. I take your point. Marc wanted to show his joy by giving me a party, but perhaps this was not the best time. I thank you for the warning, but I don't know how we can stop the festivities."

Trystan recalled Mariel's wise words of earlier and offered them now. "Perhaps riots could be prevented should the poor eat as well as the rich." He glanced down and thought Mariel's cheeks might be gaining more color. He needed to immerse her in the bath.

The lady hummed with interest. "If I have aught to say about it, I will have no fighting at *my* wedding. I'll leave Adele outside should you need anything else. I have some new arrangements to make. Have Adele come to me if my cousin awakes."

The lady strode out like a soldier off to war. Although there was no physical resemblance between Mariel and her cousin, Trystan thought he saw the family resemblance in their attitude. The St. Justs were not to be taken lightly.

And neither were Aelynners. He accepted the gods' decision. They'd given him an amacara to carry the child that would be the island's future Guardian. As much as he'd hoped Lissandra would be both wife and mate, it seemed unimportant now. He could not sacrifice Mariel or the island's future for his own desires. He *would* not!

Gazing determinedly at the bath into which the salt had been emptied, Trystan surrendered his freedom and began murmuring the prayers that would bind him permanently to Mariel St. Just.

Seventeen

Mariel floated on a submerged log, her hair drifting behind her. Bubbles murmured in her ears, filling her with contentment. Confusion nagged at the back of her mind, but she lost all sense of self in the sea. She became one with all living things, just another creature in a primordial soup surviving on instinct.

The log moved, and she reached back to grab it, enjoying the floating sensation.

Instead of sliding through water, her knuckles hit a metal boundary, jarring her from her unconscious state.

The log jerked beneath her fingers, and before she could quite grasp what was happening, she was abruptly hauled from the water, choking and spluttering.

"Aelynn be praised," a male voice whispered above her head. "You're alive!"

And naked, Mariel realized. Not that it mattered in the sea, except she had the distinct impression that she wasn't riding a submerged log but a man's sinewy arm.

An instant later, she was clasped against a broad, furred chest and lifted from her watery world into the chilly air. Water ran in rivulets from her hair down the hard bare arms holding her. Cold air chilled her backside, but her front rested against heated, muscular flesh. She closed her eyes so she didn't have to ponder these complexities, but that only heightened her awareness.

Had she been captured and pulled from the sea? The hands held her tenderly, and the whispering voice seemed familiar. She tried to fight recognition, preferring to hide her embarrassment in ignorance, but her breasts were aching and aroused from contact with firm muscle, and the familiar scent of male musk woke her to what her body already knew.

She was naked, and Trystan held her.

He lay her gently on linen sheets so fine they felt like silk. She vaguely remembered smoothing them across a mattress, reveling in their luxury. She almost protested parting from the heat of him, but Trystan climbed in beside her to keep her warm.

He was as naked as she was.

He was so broad, his size overwhelmed her. And reassured her. He was an extraordinary man unafraid of her unusual skill, patient with her impulsiveness, willing to listen to her ideas even when he didn't want to. She'd never met a man quite like him, and that didn't count his strange swiftness and the fascinating world from which he came. It seemed very odd to appreciate a man's mind and character while confronted with his blatant physicality.

"I know you're awake. Your fingers are digging into my arms." He chuckled from somewhere above her head since she'd buried her face against his shoulder rather than release him. "Are you feeling better?"

"What happened? Why aren't we wearing clothes?" She hastily released her grip and lay back against the pillows so that he could turn to his side and tug the covers up.

She was definitely awake now, and feeling more than better when Trystan's big hand came to rest on her belly, and his heat warmed her side. Parts of her, whose existence she'd ignored for years, were protesting loudly for an action she'd never thought to desire. Tentatively, she turned sideways to face him, and her knee rubbed against his leg. She thrilled at feeling the light hairs and taut muscle of a masculine limb, but was glad the darkness hid her discomfiture.

He slid his hand downward to the curve of her hip. "You were unconscious when I brought your cousin to you. Have you never been far from the sea before?"

She wasn't certain what one had to do with the other, and his touch wasn't helping her think clearly. She clung to the question foremost in her mind. "You saw my cousin? Did you buy back the chalice?"

"She will bring it to us in the morning."

"We can have the chalice?" With this wondrous news, Mariel forgot her nakedness. She pushed up from her comfortable position to study his face in the glow of a lantern outside the bed-curtains. "Then we must hurry and leave."

He shook his head. "We were most concerned about you. You were very ill. I had to make a salt-water bath to bring you back to me."

To him? Mariel pulled the sheet up to cover herself when his gaze dropped to her breasts. Rather than recognize the ache his words created, she looked over his shoulder to the tub she could see through the partially open curtains, and her cheeks flushed. He'd given her a *bath*?

"It is after midnight," he replied, tugging the sheet until she dropped down beside him again.

She was aware of his size and heat, although the only place they touched was through his hand on her hip. When she lay still, the hand began to slowly stroke her, gentling her fears.

"I don't think the baroness would appreciate having her beauty sleep interrupted," he continued. "And I wish to be certain you are well enough to travel. We can wait until morning—unless you need the sea more than a saltwater bath."

Attempting to ignore the way Trystan's hand roamed, Mariel absorbed what he said. She lived by the sea and had never thought of it as necessary to her life, but she supposed, in some way, it was. Even in winter, she often felt compelled to dip in her toes and splash her face. Mostly, she breathed the salt air and was invigorated by the sun.

She tested her toes and fingers, but the strange lethargy had left her. "I am fine." She didn't try to leave the bed while Trystan's hand roamed to her breasts. She still wasn't thinking straight, because she did not retreat, but basked in the sensations he created. "I think we should go."

"No, tonight, if you are well, we have better things to do." His wide hand slid upward to cup the back of her head and draw her toward him, so their mouths met and her breasts pressed into his chest.

The heat of his breath surprised her. She hadn't realized how cold she was, inside and out, until Trystan warmed her. Her fingers skimmed across the wide expanse of his chest, curling in the fine hairs there, clinging while his tongue swept past her lips and teeth and set her on fire. Her nipples became hard points demanding satisfaction.

The realization popped into her head: *She'd almost died.* Deprived of the sea she craved as others craved water, she'd weakened and become ill. Trystan had bathed her in the liquid of life. And now she burned with sensation, hungered for new experiences, desired the touch of the man who had saved her. A man who understood the needs of her soul as well as her body.

And Trystan obliged. As if he knew what she required, he lay flat against the bed and hauled her upward so he could more easily suckle her breasts. Delight mixed with driving need. Unable to bear the torment any longer, Mariel swung her leg over his, settling across his thighs and rubbing to satisfy the itch that demanded attention.

She discovered the appendage that made him male and daringly ran her hand from his chest downward to satisfy her curiosity. Trystan groaned at her stroke, and captured her fingers.

"Not this time," he whispered. "I want you too much, and this first time must be perfect. For the rest of our lives, you will remember this bonding. Let us take it slowly."

For the rest of their lives sounded permanent and terrifying. She ought to think twice about what they did. She knew he was right. If they continued on this path, it would bind them in ways that could be eternal. She was doing something so reckless she ought to be horrified. But she had a desperate desire to celebrate life, and learning what it meant to be a woman seemed the perfect means. She didn't want to die ignorant of one of life's few pleasures.

And somehow, she knew that it would be pleasurable with this man.

Mariel let Trystan maneuver her back to the mattress. He leaned over her, and his kiss deepened, intensified, until her body sang with need. She dug her fingers into his biceps on either side of her head and raised her hips, indicating her desire. Only this time there was no intoxicating perfume other than his male scent; no erotic shackles to hold her captive beyond their own needs. She did this of her own accord. She wanted to be mated to this intriguing man who had returned her to life.

She had not realized how alone she was in the world until Trystan worshipped her with his hands and mouth, making her believe there was just the two of them in this enchanting cocoon. She cried out her longing when his kisses captured her breasts. And she gasped in surprise when his hand slid between her thighs to stroke her there.

She did not pull away.

"I worship thee with my body," Trystan murmured, lowering his knee between hers to spread her legs wider. *"I take thee for amacara, keeper of my future. With these vows, I do promise to cherish you in sickness and health, from now until Aelynn calls."*

Trystan knew she did not understand. His opal ring glowed in acceptance of the vows, but he could not place his ring on Mariel's finger until she gave her promise. Mating for life, creating a new generation to shield Aelynn, was not a process as easily accomplished as taking a wife in a simple civil ceremony. Even he had his doubts that he was doing it properly.

But his faith was strong. If this woman had been chosen as his amacara, mother of future Guardians, there must be a reason, even if he couldn't see it.

His vow would allow her to safely enter his world. Once he brought her there, she would have to repeat the words for Dylys to let her live. That was taking away Mariel's choices, he understood. He trusted in her intelligence to accept the inevitable.

As if to concur, she circled his neck and tugged at his hair, urging him on. Trystan smiled at her haste. Many women had pursued him. Not all were so honest in their demands. The women of his home desired his wealth and position. The women of her world simply wanted base physical release, without understanding who or what he was. None of them knew him in both his worlds. Mariel did.

"This is forever," he told her, trying to explain the commitment they were making. "Once we are mated, we share a bond, and there can be no denying each other. When I call, you will come. And when you call, I will come." Or so he'd heard.

Mariel laughed heedlessly. "Even if a sea separates us?" She ran her hands up his arms and raised her hips tauntingly to brush against his sex.

"I do not know the distance involved. I just know that I will have you now and tomorrow and whenever I wish." Out of fairness, he had to remind her of what she'd said she didn't want, before he committed her to a connection she did not understand. He'd sworn never to be involved with an Outsider, never to do what he was about to do, but circumstances changed. Only she could stop him now.

Trystan captured Mariel's wrists and held them pinned above her head so she must listen to his warning. "Ultimately, there will be children of our coupling. Without the approval of Aelynn, they may not be gifted, which would be a sin. We would make talented, strong children together. But whichever your choice, I will take care of them and you for as long as I live."

The panicked "no" had barely passed her lips before he leaned over and suckled her breast.

That was unfair of him, he knew, since she had yet to take the vow and lacked his knowledge. Her hips rose of their own volition, while her head tossed in dissent. She might attempt to fight him, but the knot binding them was too strong. He could feel it deep in his gut, a hook and thread that tightened and drew them together.

She writhed her protest beneath his grasp, and he held her still with the weight of his thigh across hers. With one hand holding her to the bed, he penetrated her sex with his finger. Still shaking her head in denial,

Mariel cried out in renewed anger, frustration, and hungry desire at his physical command. Ignoring her objection, he rubbed her swollen sex, and she rose to admit him, even while she twisted away in rejection.

"I need the words, Mariel. Tell me you accept this. I cannot enter you until you give me permission."

Trystan wished the altar was available now. Its shackles had more than one purpose. For a loving couple, they were symbolic of the bonds they willingly tied. For a couple long mated and desiring children, the binding was erotic. But sometimes, when the gods decreed that a couple unite, the bonds forced submission. The reluctant one writhed in an agony of desire while the willing one waited for acceptance. He needed the altar's persuasive powers now.

"There can't be children," she cried, unable to wrench from his hold. "There are ways to prevent children."

"There are. I have used them. I will not use them with you. That is what this union means. With this act, we agree to share responsibility for the new life that comes of it. Just as your grandfather provided your mother's support, I will look after you and our children. Because I know this is not what you would choose right now, I offer you the choice of whether we raise them here or on Aelynn." He introduced a second finger, stretching her, sliding rhythmically back and forth until her hips danced with the need pounding through him. "Let me hear the words, Mariel."

"Never." Her hair whipped back and forth, and she strained upward, as if that would break his hold.

Mostly, it brought her ripe breasts closer to his mouth. She was slender, too slender. He could see her ribs beneath skin taut with muscle from her swimming. But her breasts were soft plump fruits that tempted with their sweetness. With the need to mate thrumming primitively through his blood, Trystan could not stop had his life depended on it.

His flesh swelled strong and ready, and somehow, he had to persuade her to his will or burst from the effort. He was not a man to use force, but he now had an understanding of the desperation that could drive a man to do what he shouldn't.

He was a prince of his country, and he was reduced to begging. They tortured each other equally, for no good reason other than her stubbornness.

Leaning on one elbow, Trystan bent over and licked an aroused nipple. Mariel screamed her outrage and twisted away. He could not hold her legs imprisoned, just her wrists, but he kneeled over her, blocking her escape.

"We are both ready now. There is no sense in denying the pleasure we can derive from our bodies. Tell me yes, Mariel. Give me permission."

"No children," she said furiously. "Let me go."

"Too late." He didn't say it with sorrow. He knew this was for the best, even if she did not. They'd spent a week fighting the inevitable, and he, for one, was tired of wasting his energy. It would be simpler to persuade her once they were mated. "Your body wants what I have to offer. The gods have decreed it. I have said an irrevocable vow. We must hasten back to the sea to keep you well. So let's not quibble over what is done and unchangeable. With me as mate, you need not take care of the village all on your own. Children are no longer an argument."

"No children," she whispered again, but he could tell that even she knew it was too late. In the light of the lamp, she watched in wide-eyed alarm as he loosened the sheet and used it to tie her wrists together over her head.

"We must leave soon. I don't want you ill again. So I will agree. This one time, I will prevent children. Do not ask it of me again." He knotted the sheet through the carved headboard, freeing his hands to reach over the side to retrieve his coat and pull a sheath from an inner pocket.

Following his every movement, Mariel gulped nervously as he kneeled over her and sheathed himself.

"I await your permission, my dear," he murmured in her ear, lowering himself to cover her entirely with his body.

Eighteen

Mariel feared she would be consumed by Trystan's heat as his bulk pressed her into the soft mattress, and the hot iron of his sex seared her flesh. Hands bound to the bed, she couldn't fight him, but she no longer had a will to do so. The sensual lethargy she'd experienced in his temple was overtaking her again.

Leisurely, Trystan aroused her traitorous body with his wicked kisses.

She cried out in surprise when Trystan circled her waist with his big hands and held her hips still. He moved lower, trailing his lips between her breasts and down her belly, taking away the dangerous sword of his manhood, replacing it with the seductive softness of his mouth. He had both his knees between her thighs, opening her, before she realized it. The vulnerability of this position aroused as much as terrified her. He'd rendered her helpless to push him away.

Before she could protest in fear, his tongue swept her sex, and she was lost.

"Ohhh," she cried.

His tongue dipped deeper.

"Please," she called in surrender, desperate to tangle her hands in his hair but unable to touch him. She writhed, tossing her head back and forth, lifting her

hips to take his tongue still deeper. "Please," she whimpered.

He obliged, stroking and teasing until a knot coiled and tightened inside her, and she felt as if she would fly to pieces if he did not release it. She would accept anything he wished, if only he would save her from this pleasurable torture.

She wept with the wonder of the sensations to which he introduced her. Her womb cried with emptiness, and she opened wider to accept the coupling that would fill it. She wanted what a man—this man—could do so much that she willingly rose so Trystan could lift her to his mouth and drink of the elixir there. His knowing fingers cupped her bottom and spread her cheeks at the same time he dipped his tongue.

The knot almost came unraveled then, but he pulled back, waiting, and Mariel screamed her frustration. "Now," she cried. "Make it happen. Make it stop. Please!"

"Say the words, Mariel," he insisted in a voice raw with need. "Tell me you are mine forever. Tell me I may take you."

His, forever. She could not think. Or speak. Need consumed her, her sole instinct to couple with this golden god who claimed her.

The lamp cast flickering light and shadow across the tangled gold of his hair and the bronzed planes of his chest. Pirate or god, he was magnificent. And he could be hers.

He lowered her hips to the bed when the words froze on her tongue. He rose, kneeling between her legs to look down on her with eyes misty gray in disappointment. She was tied to the bed. He could take her easily. She *wanted* him to take her, to accept all responsibility for this act that seemed so important to him and so dangerous to her.

She wanted him to relieve the ache, dissolve the knot that tightened just looking at him, watching his sex grow in impatience to have her.

Her mother had not warned her about the price she must pay for the services of a god.

The lamplight silhouetted Trystan's breadth, the tight muscles of his abdomen, and illuminated the dark hair leading down to the maleness that sooner or later would impregnate her.

And her womb cried for his child. She understood the knot now. Somehow, he'd already possessed her, and the craving for release became something more, a need to surrender to her natural self and become one with this man. The altar had induced some magic that took away their individual wills, replacing them with desperate desire. He was as chained to her as she was to him. Her hips rose of their own accord, begging with words her voice refused to speak. That a man of his stature and character didn't seem to resent the connection—that he actually *wanted* this union with someone as freakish as her—added another layer of exhilaration.

His searing gaze drifted from her breasts downward to the sexual solace she offered, and Mariel could feel her entrance swell to take him.

He'd saved her life. She must give him hers.

It was as if she'd been struck with a branch of the tree of knowledge. He was right. This union was inevitable.

The fire inside her melted her will. "I am yours forever," she whispered. "Take me, please."

Mariel did not understand his reply in the Aelynn tongue, but his voice was thick with gratitude as he propped his hands on either side of her head and leaned over to kiss her. She tasted herself on his lips, drank greedily of the saltiness as he angled his hips between her legs.

The knotted sheet fell loose from the headboard, and she grabbed his arms just as this stranger she scarcely knew thrust inside her, violating the sanctity of her body. A mournful cry broke past her lips as Trystan shattered her virginity in a single stroke, taking possession and laying claim to what had once been hers alone. Despite her cry of protest, her inner muscles stretched and rippled with pleasure at the intrusion, as if they would never let go.

With a rough laugh of relief, Trystan rubbed his stubbled cheek against her tears. "Our first time, Mariel. Remember it well."

She throbbed with need, felt liquid with desire and taut with hunger. She wasn't likely to ever forget the moment he withdrew that first shallow invasion to plunge deeper. Tension undulated through her muscles to her womb as his masculine hardness seared soft tissues. At her cry, he drove higher, repeatedly, stretching her, until her body finally understood and succumbed to his rhythm. Until at last, he struck the internal knot that held them bound.

"Let go, Mariel. Trust me. Let me take you higher," he murmured, licking her breasts until they peaked into aching buds.

Closing her eyes, she let sensation replace thought and terror. If she could be as one with the sea, she could become one with the man who claimed her. Sensing her capitulation, Trystan eased his rhythm, driving slower and deeper, until he seemed to reach her heart.

Releasing her fears, Mariel clung to his arms and surrendered her body into his custody—and miraculously, that surrender released the shackles of denial.

The knot came unbound, and she soared free with this man who'd known what she needed more than she had.

And as he promised, he flew her to a peak far beyond her imagination, one that invoked the towering volcano of his home. And once there, their bodies erupted with such forceful pleasure that they merged in a vapor of fire and water, joined as one, settling gently back to earth as the tremors ceased.

"Pax," Trystan whispered against her ear, cuddling her in the arms that had sheltered her through the tempest.

"I don't believe *peace* is the word for what we just did," she replied, and wished again she didn't hear the echo of her mother's prophecies while her body still vibrated with joy.

Trystan woke the next morning to the notes of a woodwind drifting from the courtyard. A stringed instrument followed. He seldom had a chance to enjoy music, and he would have liked to lie in the cozy draped bed with the warm woman at his side and make leisurely love.

That he'd completed his half of the vow that bound him physically for life to the woman beside him caused him to break out in a cold sweat, but glancing at Mariel's peaceful features as she slept beside him reassured him that his decision was the right one.

Trystan kissed her awake, then covered her warm, lithe body, fully prepared to service her again. Once would never be enough with a woman as responsive and as perfect for his needs as this mermaid who was maid no longer, but his for all time.

He would endure no passive mating with Mariel. She had participated last evening with such wild abandon that just recalling it had his seed pounding for instant release.

He smiled wickedly when her eyes grew round at the sight of him mounted and ready. Her thighs slackened beneath him, eager to part, and he felt the tie tightening between them.

"This time, there will be no sheath," he warned her, separating her knees with his.

"No," she whispered in sudden alarm, staring at his erection. "No children. We have settled nothing. We must hurry and buy back the chalice. Nick is waiting."

Primed to dive into deep waters, Trystan cursed this delay. He should never have agreed to the sheath. Remaining where he was, he met her gaze defiantly, then stroked her sex. She was moist and ready for him.

"I could take you now," he asserted, "and there would be no repercussions. You gave your consent. You are my mermaiden now, to do with as I please." He'd explained that. Imperfectly, perhaps, but she'd seemed to comprehend.

For his kind, the anticipation of children meant even more than the physical joining. Children were crucial to their existence. He would not use the sheath again. That was for whores, and she was his amacara, mother of his children. "This is our future," he reminded her.

Even more alarmed, she attempted to scoot out from under him, backing up against the headboard. "Forever," she repeated in a voice of terror. "I agreed to forever, didn't I?"

"Not one of your better impulses, I assume?" he asked mockingly.

She looked so upset that he hid his disappointment and swung from the bed. He would not force an unwilling woman. Besides, if they waited until they returned to Aelynn, she could confirm her vow and the gods would grant him a child who would be heir to his abilities. Another day or two of waiting was worth the reward and would not kill him. Quite.

"This isn't a marriage," she protested, tugging the sheet to her chin and wrapping it around her as she sat up. "We weren't in church. We merely suffered the heat of passion. And we can't indulge ourselves now."

"The gods forbid that we enjoy what they have given us," he said bitterly. Gritting his teeth, he strode to the tub and stepped into the cold bathwater to douse his ardor. "I waited all my life for a woman who would enjoy my attentions, and I gain one who prefers suffering. What is it you want of me?" he asked. "I have no wealth without my ship or my home."

"I don't want anything of you," she said proudly, dipping a cloth into the water to wash from her body the evidence of what they had done. "Perhaps the pleasure," she reluctantly admitted, "but I'm not ready yet for the results of pleasure. I want our task done first."

Trystan rose dripping from the water, and reached for a sheet to dry himself. "Fine. We will fetch the chalice and meet Nick. I cannot take you into Paris if you sicken without the sea, so I cannot obtain your brother-in-law's permission for a wedding. What is the protocol under such circumstances?"

"Protocol?" She had donned her undergarments and was staring in dismay at the bodice laces he'd undone last night. The garment laced in back, where she could not reach, but the hooks in front allowed her to fasten it without aid. Her complicated clothing was a nuisance.

"For taking vows in your church, so you will feel comfortable with what is between us," he explained.

Her church meant nothing on Aelynn, but if her

ceremony made her happy and willing to take his vows, then he could say hers.

He grabbed the bodice and held it up so she could place her arms in the sleeves. He would prefer to see her in the simple togas and saris of his home, clothing that opened easily when he wished to make love to her. But if she meant to make him wait, perhaps burying her in acres of cloth was wise. "I made promises last night. You do not really think I will forget them, do you?"

"Men usually do," she said without anger. "I wanted to experience what we did last night, but I don't really expect you to return once you have your chalice."

Trystan tugged her laces for her and stifled the impulse to strangle her. "I did not realize that vows were so easily forsworn in your world, or I would have been more cautious. Our cultures differ in ways that will cause us trouble if we don't learn from our mistakes. I assume you did not understand that our pledge was serious, or you might have been less impulsive about taking it."

"We made a mistake," she agreed. "We rushed into something neither of us is prepared for. We scarcely know each other."

"It is too late to regret what we did. Under Aelynn's laws, a verbal promise is binding. I cannot take another as amacara." Knotting the lace, Trystan whirled her around and glared down at her.

"You are sore from last night," he decided, "and that reduces desire, giving you strength to deny me. But it is not likely to happen again. The bond tightens even as I speak. Your breasts swell with need. I can feel it here, inside me." He punched his midsection, where the hunger burned.

Her eyes reflected the molten gold of lust, so he

knew she felt it, too, no matter how much she shook her lovely curls in brave denial.

She was afraid of the joining between them. No one had ever explained to her what it meant to bear the blood of Aelynn.

Softening toward her as he would a child who does not comprehend, Trystan placed his hand on Mariel's delicate jaw and pressed a kiss to her wide brow. "This is all new to you. I will try to be patient, if you will be patient with me. I have waited a long time to have an amacara, and it is hard for me to accept that you do not want the same."

"I want it," she whispered with all honesty, "I just cannot have it. Your world is not mine, and it never will be."

A cold chill shot down his spine as he recognized the kernel of truth in her declaration. As the Guardian, he could not abandon Aelynn. He was key to the island's survival. His children must inherit his abilities.

Without children, the island would die. What disaster was this if she would not have his children?

Nineteen

Trystan had tied her laces so tight that Mariel felt as if her bodice pushed all her flesh to spill out the top. Without an apron for modesty, she was almost grateful for her ratty old cloak. She was much too aware of the plumpness of her breasts now that Trystan had taught her how a touch could lead to mind-consuming pleasure. Just the lace caressing her nipples produced a liquid fire between her legs. She could barely concentrate on facing her cousin's door.

She'd tied up the tapes on her billowing skirt to create fashionable puffs so she didn't trip, but without the proper hip pads the silk still sagged and trailed behind her. Trystan had bought her embroidered shoes so she need not clump about in sabots, but the heels did not raise her high enough to eliminate the need for petticoats. Then again, perhaps she was not missing much by being unable to afford court finery. She didn't lead a life suited to frivolity.

In his knee boots, Trystan stood tall and elegant beside her, comfortable as any duc or prince in his tight silk breeches, linen cravat, and dark frock coat, even though she knew now that these were not his normal attire. He wore his golden hair neatly bound by a black satin ribbon, but he had not adopted the side curls of fashion, for which she was grateful. His was a hard face of angles and planes that should not be softened with curls.

He carried a duc's air of authority even though he had no such power here.

He knocked peremptorily on the door of the baroness's suite. Mariel's stomach rumbled, since they'd had no time for breakfast. It was late, and a crowd had already gathered in the hall. A troop of musicians was playing, and if the wedding ceremony was not conducted soon, the party would start without the bride and groom.

A frazzled maid answered the knock. Over her shoulder, Mariel could see Lady Beloit in a far room, gowned in what appeared to be her chemise, except it had blue ribbons tying the waist and gauzy puffed sleeves. She'd heard the aristocracy had adopted the simple dress of rural milkmaids, but this seemed highly informal for a wedding.

"How could you do this, Marc?" Lady Beloit cried while the servant hesitated about allowing them in. "It was a *gift*!"

"Precisely, madame, and one can do as one wishes with a gift. I did not realize there were strings attached," de Berrier replied in stiff tones.

"You said it was splendid, that you would always treasure it. Do your words mean so little then?"

Mariel had a very bad feeling about this argument. She dug her fingers into Trystan's coat sleeve and nodded toward the empty front parlor. Understanding, he stepped inside, pushing past the maid.

"Your gift was beyond priceless, madame. I did not dare keep such a treasure in my humble home. Versailles is a far safer place for it. All the world converges there. Perhaps the king will be grateful for the admiration the vessel brings and be more receptive to my suggestions for restoring balance to the budget. Avoiding national bankruptcy is of higher importance than selfish pride."

While Mariel could only applaud the chevalier's reasoning, she despaired at his method of achieving it.

"Celeste?" Mariel called, trying to keep desperation from her voice. She could not stand the suspense any longer. The mention of a "vessel" sounded too much like a chalice. "We are ready to leave for Pouchay and have come to give our regards." Reluctant to ask about the chalice in the chevalier's presence, she paused, unsure of what to do next.

The baroness swung around to acknowledge them. Sapphires to match her ribbons adorned her throat and ears, and jewels were entwined in her powdered hair. Her gown might be simple, but there was no questioning her wealth.

"You cannot go so soon!" she cried. "There is room for you in the chapel, and there will be grand celebrations afterward. I would have family with me at this time." Anger stained her rouged cheeks, and her lips tightened over words left unsaid.

The chevalier appeared in the doorway. A vein on his forehead began to bulge at the sight of the parlor's occupants. "You! Where is my nephew? I will call the guards if you do not produce him at once."

"He claims he is not your nephew," Trystan said with a shrug. "He ran off last night without paying me for my efforts. One tries to do good deeds, but they are seldom rewarded."

Mariel nearly winced at his caustic tone. She suspected that statement was a subtle arrow meant for her. It was possible he'd saved her from her reckless actions by rescuing her from his precious Oracle, and again last night, with the salt bath. And not once had he chastised her for the trouble she caused him. He was a man above all men, and she had rejected him. It was a wonder his gods did not smite her dead.

It had never occurred to her that she might need the sea to live, and that she should not journey far—probably because she'd never before thought to leave Pouchay. She felt much stronger today, but she had a day and night of travel ahead of her—in the company of a man who expected something she would not give. How long would she have the strength to resist him?

"Francine awaits me, my lady," she said into the stony silence. "We must return immediately to Pouchay. I wish you well of your new marriage. We will have the lace cloth for your wedding gift ready by the time you return."

Concealing her anger behind a trill of laughter, the baroness tapped Mariel's cheek with her fan. "Come along. It won't hurt to tarry another hour so you may attend the ceremony. Your sister's lace is famous. You must be able to tell her about the wedding in return. We have brought in lilies from Paris."

She took Mariel's arm and forcibly steered her toward the exit.

Convinced the baroness was delaying them for a purpose, Mariel threw an uncertain look over her shoulder to Trystan. He shook his head slightly to indicate that she should not protest even though impatience tightened his jaw.

This was all her fault. She had taken the sacred chalice. And the baroness was her relation. She would have to be the one to find out what had happened to it. Her stomach gripped at the thought of what might befall Trystan and his world if the treasure was lost.

The groom had merely growled at Trystan's earlier reply, apparently unwilling to say more in front of his bride—as his bride was reluctant to say more about the chalice in front of him. That did not seem the best manner of starting a marriage, Mariel thought, but both bride and groom were older and set in their ways. They would need to learn compromise. "I thought it was ill luck to see the groom before the wedding," Mariel said as the four of them entered the corridor.

"That is the superstition of rural peasants," de Berrier scoffed from behind them. "We are more sophisticated than that."

In the castle hall, Lady Beloit halted to admire the bedecked trestle tables heaped with delicacies. Servants scurried to and fro carrying monumental platters heaped with meats, cakes, and fruit. Mariel's stomach rumbled in appreciation, and she wished she was close enough to snatch even a small cake from a laden tray.

"Why did you decide to marry the chevalier?" she asked, easing her curiosity since she could not reach the table where marzipan glistened temptingly. "You decided so abruptly."

"Marriage suddenly made sense," the lady replied. "And that afternoon, Marc dropped down on one knee and begged me again to marry him. This time, he said he could not bear to return to his lonely home without me. I had thought he only wanted my money, but I finally understood that he *needed* me."

The day the lady had acquired the chalice, both nobles had waxed romantic, against their practical natures. Had the chalice made them realize they were suited?

Odd that two couples had been brought together because of a piece of silver. Would her cousin have accepted the chevalier's proposal without it? Had the chalice affected her and Trystan in a similar manner?

Trystan intruded upon this odd notion by claiming two raisin buns and handing one to Mariel. "You have not yet eaten," he said without apology. "I will not have you fainting again."

"Oh, my dear, I had no idea! Please, help yourself. Shall I call for some champagne to toast our upcoming nuptials?"

The lady signaled a servant, but the chevalier stepped beside her and shook his head to send the man away. "Afterward, my sweet. The priest is waiting, and the crowd grows restless." His tone was more doting than annoyed as he caught the lady's elbow and steered her toward the chapel.

Grabbing chicken legs from another platter, Trystan handed one to Mariel and fell in step behind the bride and groom.

"He is marrying her for the damned chalice," Trystan grumbled.

"No," Mariel said after swallowing a bite of bun. "He did not know of the chalice when he offered." Licking her fingers, she stared after the couple ahead of them. "I don't know how the chalice is involved, if it is at all. De Berrier has land and Celeste has wealth. Together, they will have land, money, and title, which gives them a position of power."

"Politics and power, just like at home," Trystan said with a shrug. "It makes sense."

Mariel watched as the chevalier gently guided his bride over the chapel threshold. The loving look they exchanged caused an ache in her heart. "Despite first appearances, I really think they are in love."

At her tone, Trystan gave her an odd look but did not question her idea of love. "Then perhaps the chalice has no part in this. Do you think he truly sent it to the king?"

Mariel didn't want to accept that appalling possibility. She couldn't go to Versailles unless she could be certain there would be tubs of salt water along the way. And unleashing a man with Trystan's uncanny abilities into the increasingly anarchic environs of the royal court could be wildly dangerous.

They entered the chapel, where towering white lilies scented the air. White lace and satin ribbons adorned the pews. Heads turned at their entrance, and Trystan hastily tugged Mariel into a seat while the couple proceeded up the aisle to the waiting priest.

"There is not much ceremony involved, is there?" he asked with interest as the couple kneeled before the altar.

"This one has more than most," she admitted. "At home, the couple would speak privately with the priest in the days before the ceremony to be certain they understood the solemnity of their vows. Close family might attend to witness the words being said. But the food and the gift giving afterward are the big entertainment."

"There is not so much difference between us then." He studied the ornate carvings of the wooden chapel. "We prefer the outdoors, but then, our weather is better. An ama match is a religious ceremony similar to what you describe. The Oracle speaks with the participants in advance, explaining the meaning of the vows; then when she is certain the couple is prepared, she purifies them with oils and takes them to the altar bed, where the mating is consummated."

Mariel looked at him with horror. "In public?"

He shrugged. "An ama match is usually private. The gods act as witnesses. And a child born exactly nine months later is proof that the vows were made. The families give their gifts at the birth."

"What if a child isn't conceived? It takes longer than once for most people."

"Not for couples united at the altar. That is the purpose of the temple, to hold the spirits and power of our ancestors to be passed on to the next generation. Is that not what your cousin is asking now? For the gods to grant her children?"

Mariel was still struggling with the idea of instant children. If she and Trystan had *mated* in his temple, would she be with child now? His child. One carrying his strength. Why did the idea suddenly appeal when it went against everything she had ever feared?

She tried to concentrate on explaining her dislike for what the baroness was doing. "She is giving up her right as an independent woman and agreeing to be de Berrier's chattel. He is promising to care for her until they die. In a love match, this might happen, but in actuality, it seldom does. The man acquires the woman's worldly goods, and she acquires his name. She becomes a childbearing nonentity, and her husband makes all the decisions. Marriage is not an institution that interests me greatly since only I know what is best for me."

"Ah, marriage, not bonding," he said with a knowing nod. "That is entirely different. The civil marriage ceremonies of our more powerful families are conducted in the Council courtyard, so that all on the island know two families have joined legally and financially. Mostly it determines what seat the couple may take in the Council."

"What *seat*?"

Mariel didn't think he intended to explain. He looked uncomfortable and studied the ceremony taking place instead of replying. But when the groom leaned over to kiss the bride, Trystan looked resigned.

"Although you and I are bonded, I still have the right to marry Lissandra, and I intend to do so. Our joint family positions will qualify us for the highest seat on the Council. We will be acknowledged as the chief legal authority in the land. If I marry an Outsider with no Aelynn abilities, I would lose the family seat to which I'm entitled and could not vote on island matters. If I marry a Crossbreed with powers but no property, my seat would be decided on the value of what I own and our joint abilities. We could hope that our value to the island would eventually increase our holdings and thus raise our position in the Council, but it would take time."

Mariel looked at him blankly. "The vows you say we made last night? They were not marriage vows?"

"No," he said curtly, without a change in his stern features. "They were bonding vows, which are much stronger since they are made under the authority of the gods instead of the courts. I have agreed to take care of you for life, and to make you the mother of my heirs."

"But not to forsake all others," Mariel said.

"I can still legally marry another," he said with a shrug. "But the gods promise only one amacara at a time. I could take a wife and a dozen mistresses, but those couplings provide no guarantee of children or assurance of progeny who will carry my abilities. Amacara matches are rare and much treasured. Aelynn has arranged it so that an amacara match produces the offspring with the characteristics the island needs."

The sugary bun Mariel had just eaten churned in her stomach. "And if I die without producing a child?" she whispered.

"Only then may Aelynn find another amacara for me."

He spoke with such finality that Mariel believed him.

Another thought struck. "What happens if I do not go back with you?"

He pressed his lips together and stared ahead.

"Tell me. It involves me. I have a right to know."

He explained in terse, brief sentences, his voice tight.

"You would be banished," she whispered, stunned. "You will lose everything?" She absorbed the truth of it as he continued to hold his head high, saying nothing. "Your world is as cruel as mine," she said, finally understanding that they could find no compromise.

Twenty

"Come, join the dancing." The bride tugged on Trystan's arm.

Outside the chapel after the ceremony, de Berrier had stopped to converse with a uniformed guard. They had only this one chance to speak privately with the lady.

"The chalice, my lady?" Trystan inquired. "We really must return it to the church so Mariel may go home to her sister."

The baroness waved a dismissive hand. "There has been a minor delay. I have sent a servant after it. Enjoy the food and wine and music. You and my cousin are much too solemn."

"This is a serious matter," he warned. "We cannot enjoy the frivolity until we are assured the sacred vessel has been returned where it belongs."

"I have taken care of the matter. I regret the delay, but you will have the chalice in your hands by evening," she said.

The lady's ruby lips parted in greeting as the chevalier hastened their way, and her hand released its grip on Trystan's arm. "Hurry, darling, our guests grow impatient."

Trystan was so angry, he had to suppress an urge to reach for his sword and cut someone's throat. Instead he stepped back and grabbed Mariel's hand.

Hard. "She's sent someone to fetch it," he muttered for her ears only.

Mariel looked worried as they joined the other guests trailing after the couple toward the great hall. "I do not know if she will be true to her word. Should we find out more?"

"We can try, but it won't be easy. If he's sent it to Versailles, you cannot follow," Trystan said, thinking ahead to what could happen now.

The last he'd seen of Murdoch, the other man had been acting as a mercenary in the king's army near Versailles. Should the chalice cross Murdoch's path—Trystan fought a shiver of horror. He prayed that Dylys had been as successful as she claimed in suppressing Murdoch's varied abilities, or he would know by now that the chalice was within his reach.

When he focused his gifts properly, Murdoch had visionary sight to rival Lissandra's, a gift for finding things that was almost as strong as Kiernan's, and a strength and swordsmanship to match Trystan's. With even a fraction of those powers, he could find the chalice and hold it for ransom—at the very least. What other uses he might make of the sacred vessel were beyond Trystan's knowledge. Trystan had gained his experience and education at sea, while Murdoch had been personally trained by Dylys in an attempt to harness his wild energies.

It seemed an ominous coincidence that the vessel should escape into the world at the same time an Aelynner of such exceptional strength as Murdoch was banished from the island. Trystan wished he could consult with the Oracle. And Lissandra. Maybe even Iason—although, after having allowed Mariel to escape, the Oracle's son seemed less than trustworthy.

But Trystan couldn't let the chalice slip away without making every effort to reclaim it, just in case it was simple chance that had loosed it.

"You can't go to Versailles on your own," Mariel was protesting in a heated undertone as they proceeded down the corridor. "You may be strong as an ox, but you are only one man. You would need an army to steal the chalice from a king."

He'd encountered very few obstacles in his privileged life, he was starting to realize. He had vastly *over*estimated his ability to reclaim a cunning lump of silver. And he had *under*estimated the power of the chalice. He had the dread fear now that the legends were all true—the chalice came and went as it willed.

"If the chalice gets too far ahead of me, I may need help in locating it." He could admit that much to Mariel. "Let us speak with the servants and see if we can find out who is taking it to Versailles."

"First, we have to know who the servants are," she said dryly, gazing at the throng gathering around the feast.

"This is where Lissandra would be useful. Most days, her ability to read minds is frightening."

"The lady is frightening without any such abilities," Mariel grumbled. "She has the soul of a shark."

"And you should know about the souls of sharks?" he inquired, trusting it was simple jealousy that made her speak so. He hoped it meant his amacara was feeling possessive. That would be a good sign. When she merely glowered at his question, he offered a more sensible, if equally volatile, argument. "If we cannot locate the servants, I think it will be best if I take you to the cart. It will be noon soon. Young Nick can see you home."

She shot him a scathing glare that almost made him smile. Children of a Guardian needed a strong mother, and Mariel was certainly no vaporish maiden. Of course, that reckless strength of hers could be an onerous burden when she defied his orders.

"I cannot go home until I know your chalice is safe. I will speak with my cousin's maids and you will speak with the chevalier's footmen, and we will discover who took the chalice, and where and who my cousin sent to fetch it back." Without waiting for his response, she swung around and marched into the crowd.

Trystan swore under his breath and contemplated the satisfaction he'd derive in dunking Mariel in another salt bath.

Then again, it was possible neither of them would survive the mob that intended to storm the castle's gates.

Were they out there yet? He could hear no shouts over the noise of the musicians and crowd. He prayed his warning had given the baroness time to divert the rebels' plans.

The church bells chimed noon as Mariel circled the hall in search of more servants whose information might add to the small store she'd garnered so far. If he was following their plans, Nick would be heading to Pouchay to return the cart. She wished him a safe journey.

The musicians played loudly and enthusiastically, if not perfectly, in the balcony above the grandiose hall. Replete with wine and food, the aristocratic guests had reached a high state of jollity that had them dancing reels like simple peasants. Watching men and women in powdered wigs and richly embroidered satins bobbing and dipping like a bunch of drunken farmers was most amusing.

Toe tapping, Mariel glanced around in search of Trystan. She was quite capable of continuing her search alone, but she had an odd need to be close to him, to share with him what little she had discovered. And perhaps to dance with him. One ought to have danced with the man one had made love to.

Just thinking of what they had done last night caused a tightening in her womb that she was starting to recognize. They must not do *that* again. But try as she might to resent him for introducing her to such dangerous desires, she still wanted to make love again.

Unconsciously, she traversed the edge of the crowd, searching for the man who made her crave cool sheets and heated flesh. Her lips tingled with the need for Trystan's kiss. Her breasts ached for the press of his palm. A simple dance might suffice, though she wanted far more.

A hand reached from behind a column to grasp her arm and drag her into the shadows beneath the balcony.

She almost screamed, but she knew his touch, his smell, and she fell into his arms without a sound, standing on her toes and seeking his lips. As Trystan sought hers.

His tongue took possession of her mouth, quieting any protest. His hand dipped smoothly into her gown, lifting her breast free of encumbrance. "I had a sudden craving for this," he muttered. He rotated his thumb over her aroused nipple, and she nearly wept with pleasure.

He steered her into a curtained niche in the shadows beneath the overhang. "You came," he said with what sounded like surprise. "Even though you have not said the vows, you came when I called."

She might have questioned his statement, but Trystan's golden head dipped and his mouth took her breast.

Even as desire flooded her senses, and she gripped

his arms and offered herself to him, Mariel realized what he meant—as he'd warned, she'd come when he'd called, not with a shout, but with the tug of the mental and emotional bond between them. Alarm washed through her at the strength of their mystical union.

Except, instead of fighting him as her mind screamed to do, she sought his mouth when he raised his head, and returned his passionate kiss while he lifted her skirts.

She stiffened in response when his clever fingers slid along her cleft and found the swollen, sensitive bud there. She wasn't at all certain whether her reaction was in protest or from frustration because she did not know how to reach that part of him that would satisfy her craving.

"I have decided to wait until we are at the temple before finishing this," he whispered, lifting his head to study her as he spoke. His eyes burned with the amber of lust, and a strand of his silken hair had escaped its binding. "If you are the one woman bound to carry my heir, I would see that child conceived properly before you slip away again."

She could only use the wall as brace for her shoulders and whimper in need and writhe beneath his questing fingers. Trystan smiled wickedly at her predicament while he continued to play a merry dance between her thighs. "Do you sing a different tune today? Are you ready to return to Aelynn with me?"

Mariel wanted to scream her frustration. "Don't toy with me, curse you!" she forced from between clenched teeth while her body's needs climbed higher, demanding immediate satisfaction. Trapped against the wall by Trystan's greater size, she retaliated by lifting her leg and wrapping it around his knee, forcing him to press his arousal into her midsection.

"I'm merely proving a point, *mi ama*." He brushed kisses across her cheek but did not remove his hand from its depredations, although she'd seriously restricted his movements. "I have verified with the lady's servants that she has sent a footman after the chevalier's courier, and I have a description of both. If I set out now, the chalice should be in our hands by nightfall. I have been assured a barge can be found at the river tonight. If all goes well, we'll be on Aelynn in three days' time. I want you willing and ready when we reach the temple."

Shifting his position, he introduced a second finger, and to prevent crying out, Mariel leaned into his shoulder and bit into his coat. The relief of knowing the chalice could be recovered scarcely registered beneath her burgeoning desire. She dug her fingers into the soft silk of his sleeves while Trystan's fingers worked their magic.

He had far too much advantage over her with his greater experience. He brought her to the brink of release and gently pushed her over. As the tremors exploded within her, her bones turned to jelly, and she almost slid down the wall before he caught her.

Trystan wrapped her tightly in his embrace as if he would never let her go, and she felt the bulge of his arousal against her belly. She had done that to him. The knot that tied her to him worked as tightly in the other direction. Knowing the suffering of unrequited desire, she reached to take him in her hands. He let her caress his length through his tight breeches, but pushed back when she fumbled with the buttons.

"The sheath is for whores. I threw it away, *mi ama*. We will wait." Proving his character was stronger than hers, Trystan caught her firmly by the waist and swung her out into the crowd, letting her full skirts hide what she had done to him.

He meant to take no more whores. The confidence of his claim thundered between them.

"You must be made of stone," she whispered roughly as he twirled her about the floor in the decadent dance the Austrian queen had introduced at court. She would trip over her feet except her slippers scarcely touched the floor. In his heeled boots, Trystan towered over her. She was vaguely aware of the stares they attracted, but she could not take her eyes from her golden partner.

"I am likely to petrify like this if we don't reach Aelynn soon," he agreed with muffled mirth. "But the result will be worth it. Is there privacy on barges? If so, I will teach you how to relieve my dilemma."

Mariel felt as if she had imbibed a flask of wine, so heady was the music and the dancing and Trystan's arms about her. She was still light-headed from what he'd done to her. He could do *that* without using his masculine weapon on her? Why had she not known?

What could she do for him in return? His words had her head spinning with curiosity. It was almost enough to drive the chalice out of her mind. Almost. "How can you take this . . . this *thing* between us so lightly?"

"Our joining?" He shrugged his broad shoulders and whisked her in faster, more seductive circles as the tempo increased. "I do not take it lightly. I am terrified, if you must know. But I put my trust in Aelynn. It is a pity you have no similar custom. It is both reassuring and humbling to know that between us we have the capacity to produce progeny who will duplicate our traits."

"That is so insanely arrogant as to be almost laughable." And the very last thing she wished to do—produce another misfit like herself. What a cruel thing to do to her own child!

Gasping for breath, Mariel said no more until the dance ended, and Trystan set her on her feet again. Clinging to his shoulder, his arm supporting her waist, she let him lead her away from the throng around the tables. "I did not inherit my mother's traits," she argued with his proud conviction. "I cannot imagine she was anything like her father or she would have said so. Are you an exact replica of your father?"

He set her on a velvet bench along the wall so she could catch her breath. "I doubt that your grandmother shared vows with your grandfather, and she certainly didn't visit Aelynn and the altar or I would have heard. It is possible that she was a Crossbreed herself. That increases the chances of children having some of Aelynn's traits, although not necessarily desired ones. There are Crossbreeds scattered across seven continents, but it is unlikely for an amacara match like ours to be formed anywhere outside Aelynn's borders."

Trystan snatched a glass of champagne from a passing servant and handed it to her. "Drink this, and I will be on my way."

She didn't want him to go without her, but he had to go inland, and she couldn't. She sipped carefully to delay while she considered the problem. "Why have you not made a match on your precious island?"

"Amacara matches are infrequent," he explained. "And because of my gift with language, I traveled far and was seldom home, so I never discovered if any maid there was destined for me."

"I thought Lissandra was your destiny," Mariel said with a hint of bitterness. She'd had only a sip of the champagne, but her tongue was already loose.

He didn't want her for *wife*, Mariel thought. Just breeding stock for his children. She really should slap his face, but the tie between them was too physical to pretend it didn't exist. His test to call her to him had proven that beyond any doubt. She ought to be terrified, but the connection with this awesome man was far too exhilarating.

She would simply have to hope the bond did not work over the distance of the sea or she would exhaust herself going to him, or waiting for him to return to her.

Her breath stalled in her throat. Had she really accepted the bond between them?

"Sometimes it happens that a wife is also made an *ama*," Trystan said with a casual shrug, diverting her thoughts. "It might have happened had I not met you. Lissandra and I both possess powerful traits that Aelynn must pass on. But it cannot happen now. Lissandra will have only half a mate, assuming she still wants to be Oracle enough to marry me at all." He seemed quite stoic about that fact.

"You could always kill me," Mariel reminded him, still staggered by all the implications of their bond. He probably should. Then he could return home and pick up his life as if she had not unwittingly interrupted it.

Laughter crinkled the corners of Trystan's eyes. "Aye, there is that. But it's much more fun to make you come, in all senses of the word."

He was doing it again. He appeared so charming and affable when he laughed like that. . . . She could almost adore a man who looked at her with understanding and affection. She simply had to remember the ruthless swordsman and arrogant— What did one call the nobility of Aelynn? No matter. He still thought he was better than she. He probably thought he did her a favor by mating with her.

Yet *still* she tingled with need when he wanted her. Even now, his desire poured like molten honey through her, heating her as much as the golden look of lust he bestowed upon her. At least she knew she didn't suffer alone, or she'd feel like a whore. Or a slave. She threw back a large swallow of the wine.

"It is too close to Francine's time," she protested in an effort to keep her feet on the ground. "I cannot leave her again until Eduard returns. Unless you find some way to turn off this"—she gestured—"whatever this is between us, we will both endure many a sleepless night."

"Too late," he said, swallowing a lusty gulp of his own wine. "It is done. We will find some way of dealing with it. I am not averse to having a beautiful woman at my beck and call."

She narrowed her eyes at his rudeness. "Your goats may come when called, but not I."

Chuckling, Trystan set aside the empty glass. "Nick must be gone by now. Shall I find somewhere private with a large tub where you can wait for my return?"

She would suffer the torment of the damned no matter what she did, Mariel reflected as he drew her from the bench.

A loud pounding erupted at the door, followed by shouts that vibrated the old wood.

The musicians halted, startled by the racket. Mariel grasped Trystan's hand tighter, although she could not say if it was to tug him to safety or keep from being parted from him.

The drunken crowd stumbled in their dancing and glanced about in bewilderment.

"There's a mob forming at the gates!" a voice shouted.

Into the fearful silence, the baroness called, "Those are my guests! The guards have been ordered to let them in."

Muttering a foreign curse, Trystan grabbed his

sword with one hand and Mariel's elbow with the other.

"You will await the chalice's return somewhere less . . . volatile," he said, dragging her backward toward the nearest doorway.

Desire replaced by anger, Mariel jerked her arm away and lifted her skirts. "You may go, if you wish, but there are people outside starving. If my cousin wishes to feed them, then I shall help her do so."

Without a single look back, she hurried to join the baroness.

Twenty-one

The resplendently garbed guards rushed toward the front of the hall at the threat of rabble entering, but Lady de Berrier née Beloit had already ordered several servants to slide open the bar on the towering oak doors that led to the courtyard.

Apparently having already passed the outside gates, the mob surged into the interior, led by the radicals from the tavern. At her cousin's side, Mariel was lost to Trystan in the swirl of humanity.

Trystan was under no illusion that this situation could turn out well. Cursing the gods, headstrong women, and rebellious peasants, he sought the best course for protecting his mate.

In two steps he leapt from a chair to the buffet table, heedless of the marzipan he crushed beneath his boots. Tumbling ice sculptures into soup tureens, he took the open path of the tabletop to reach Mariel before guards could engage the surging mob. Sliding through jellified vegetables and sending a basket of hard rolls tumbling, he grabbed the knot of her lovely hair and yanked her still.

He bounded from table to chair to the floor before she could rip the hair out of her head trying to escape. He refused to let her look of shock distract his purpose. "Stay here," he ordered, "or more than you will be hurt." He shoved her under the floor-length tablecloth.

He didn't know if she understood his admonition. There wasn't time to explain how the bond between them could cause him to react instinctively to any threat to her. Or to repeat that he was not her golden savior but sworn by Aelynn's law against swinging his swift sword in the Outside World for any reason except the defense of his mate or fellow countrymen.

The baroness's cries of outrage indicated that her benevolent plans had gone awry.

Trystan wrapped his hand around his sword hilt as he returned to his preferred path of the tabletop. Despite the laws of Aelynn, he could not let the baroness come to harm for many and varied reasons—the chalice not being the least of them.

Around the great hall, women screamed in excitement and men argued among themselves, but few of the aristocrats seemed to take the mob seriously enough to lift a hand to defend the hall from the intruders. After all, the guards had weapons and uniforms and were thus superior to the motley rabble.

As they shoved past the doors, the mob outnumbered not only the guards but also the noble guests. Trystan feared the imminent clash would not be pretty.

While the baroness used a broken fan to swat the overwhelmed guardsman attempting to protect her from her guests, men with shabby frock coats over neatly pressed if threadbare linen, and women in stiff starched aprons over their faded homespun skirts paraded through the doors, bobbing their courtesies to the baroness before heading hungrily for the immense banquet tables.

"They're my guests," the baroness shouted over the commotion as several of the aristocratic company fi nally reached for swords to hold off the newcomers crowding around them, crushing silks and laces in their eagerness to reach the tables. "I invited them!"

Trystan almost sympathized with the chevalier, who watched in resignation while men in leather jerkins lifted bottles of champagne and drank as if it were water. Two shabbily dressed women reached for the remains of the same chicken carcass and started squabbling, while others stuffed their apron pockets with sweets. The radical bourgeois leaders from the tavern shook the chevalier's hand, apparently congratulating him on his nuptials.

The baroness had meant well with her invitation. Most of the mob had come politely garbed in their best finery, intending no harm, but wealth and poverty combined in one place unleashed the whirlwind of resentment and bitterness, even when not goaded by the rabble-rousers certain to be found in every crowd. Trystan was starting to believe that was the purpose of the chalice after all, to cause mayhem and anarchy when set free upon the unsuspecting world.

The guards slammed the doors closed and held them with brute force in order to lock out the remaining "guests." Nearly blinding her lone captor with her broken fan, the baroness escaped and joined several of the radicals in attempting to open the doors again.

Unable to resist the temptation to command as he'd been taught to do since birth, Trystan strode down the table, rapier in hand. While the captain of the guard struggled to regain control of the furious bride, Trystan tapped the man on his shoulder with his blade, perhaps a little harder than was absolutely necessary, just to assure his attention.

As the mustached captain scowled in his direction, Trystan jabbed his rapier tip on the man's nose. "Release the lady," he said pleasantly. "You serve no purpose in holding her back."

"This is the home of a duc," the man protested. "We do not open the gates for peasants!"

"The lady invited friends to her nuptials," Trystan replied, restraining himself quite admirably, in his opinion. Some of the *guests* were thin as rails and more ragged than scarecrows. "What will you charge her with? Obstructing starvation?"

Finding Trystan to be a target they could fight, more guards closed in. Muskets waved ominously. Trystan continued holding his rapier point to the captain's bulbous nose.

"Madame Mariel! Monsieur Trystan! There are soldiers coming!"

Nick burst through the crowd still pushing and shoving at the doors. He jumped up and down to be seen and shouted at the top of his lungs. "King's soldiers!"

Trystan cursed. Could nothing in this bedeviled world go as he planned? The boy should be safely on his way to the coast by now.

He didn't care to examine what disaster Nick's arrival portended, but Trystan's duty was clear. He had to remove Mariel to safety before violence broke out. While the captain's attention was diverted by Nick's shouts, Trystan pricked the arm holding the baroness. As expected, the man shook his sleeve with annoyance, and the lady broke free.

"Most gallant of you, monsieur," she called, dancing toward her husband. "A riot on our wedding day would have been such a bad omen, wouldn't it, dear?" she called. "Isn't this much more entertaining?"

Trystan rolled his eyes as the besotted groom nodded his agreement. If Mariel's theory was correct, and the chalice was responsible for turning this sensible man into a sentimental fool, it had much to account for.

The impoverished crowd made room for Nick to shove through. Most continued to devour the buffet. Trystan parried the angry captain's sword, then flipped the weapon from the guard's hand without effort.

But tempers were rapidly fraying. Frustrated by the guards' inability to control the ragtag crowd, the drunken nobility was congregating in one corner. Equally irritated, the guards were torn between keeping more people from entering the hall and preventing the ones who were already there from slipping off to explore the castle corridors.

Preferring not to set himself up as a large target for all that simmering anger, Trystan jumped down from the table just in time to see Mariel emerge almost beneath his boots. He glared at her show of defiance.

"Do you ever listen?" he growled, catching her arm and dragging her toward Nick. As long as they were both this close to the front gates, he saw no purpose in lingering. He'd done what he could for the baroness. She was on her own now.

"I listen," Mariel replied pertly, hurrying to keep up with him. "I just choose whether or not to obey. And I am not in an obedient mood."

"Are you ever?" He jerked her faster, nearly carrying her toward the door.

"I doubt you'll have time to find out."

She swore as the chevalier shouted for the guards. He'd spotted Nick.

Trystan wrestled with the exasperating knowledge that Mariel still thought she could escape the bonds between them, but there was little he could do to correct her now. He could reach Nick faster without Mariel holding him back, but he could not leave her in this dangerous crush. Circling her waist as if they were dancing, he lifted her from her feet and pushed forward, past a farmer sucking a chicken bone clean and an old lady shoving an entire chocolate petit four into her mouth, looking as if she'd died and gone to heaven.

Mariel gasped at her abrupt flight but didn't have time to form a protest before they reached Nick. Unfortunately, in his attempt to meet them, the boy darted straight into a guardsman's grip. Lifting Nick by the back of his coat, the soldier held him at arm's length to avoid the boy's flailing feet and signaled for his companions to open a path through the melee.

Weapon in hand, Trystan pushed Mariel behind him. He lunged forward to slice off the guardsman's pretty gold buttons, sending them spinning into the mob. Instantly, half a dozen ragged people dropped to their knees to search for the valuables, preventing Nick's captor from going anywhere. "Unhand the boy," Trystan shouted over the tumult.

"Not likely. We're paid well to catch poachers," the guard scoffed, his confidence roused by his fellow guards rushing to shove the scavengers away.

"Oh, for heaven's sake, he's just a scared little boy." Unfazed by either mob or uniformed guards, Mariel slipped around Trystan to come between him and his target. "Put him down," she ordered. "You're terrifying the lad."

Trystan sighed in resignation. He might not understand a great deal about women, but he knew enough by now to respect Mariel's choices. He stepped back, giving his mate the freedom to act as she saw fit.

Undeterred by musket or authority, Mariel smacked the sneer from the guard's face with enough strength to startle him into dropping Nick. The boy ducked into the crowd and disappeared. In frustration, the man lifted his newly empty arm in a threat.

Whether the guard intended to hit Mariel or reach for his weapon, Trystan didn't take time to discern. He shoved the point of his rapier against the man's waistcoat, forcing him backward so Mariel could race after Nick, who dodged toward the door.

Finding Trystan a larger target for their frustration, the duc's men closed in.

Acknowledging the fruitlessness of attempting to escape while avoiding violence, Trystan grudgingly released the captain from his blade point. With regret, he watched Mariel flee his protection and dive into the crowd.

Donning his best bored expression, he twirled his foil menacingly while he waited for events to unfold. He could have outleaped, outrun, and outdodged an entire bevy of armed soldiers, but he had yet to decide whether Nick's earlier warning of approaching soldiers was a cause for concern. Until he understood the boy's admonition, he preferred to keep his interference minimal and his abilities hidden.

Whistling tunelessly, Trystan arced his rapier in the direction of the captain who dared attempt to grab his arm. Startled by his speed, the captain stepped back and gestured for his men to seize their prisoner. Insouciantly, Trystan unsheathed his sword with his left hand and circled both weapons in broad sweeps, forcing the guards farther back.

"I suggest you ask the bride and groom to come forward before you take a step closer, gentlemen. I do not go anywhere I do not wish to go, and we will mar their lovely wedding with bloodshed should you attempt to force me to do otherwise."

"This is the duc's home, and we are under his command," the captain replied roughly, gesturing for his men to do their duty.

Such feudal loyalty did not bode well for national affairs, but unconcerned with French tribulations, Trystan amused himself by switching sword and rapier from hand to hand, nicking at buttons and cuffs, the lacings of breeches, and any object that dared intrude upon his defined limits, swinging about as necessary to prevent them from coming up behind him.

The bachelor melees on Aelynn made this clash of wills a picnic. He chuckled as one of the guards tripped over his overlarge breeches when they fell about his ankles.

Slicing elaborate figure eights in the air with his steel, Trystan maneuvered the soldiers into a position of his choosing, with his back to the table. Satisfied his exit route was in place, he sat on the table's edge wielding his weapons, carelessly crossed his legs, and swung his foot. "Sorry, gentlemen, but I do not bow to the orders of any man," he explained.

A shout from the door, followed by Mariel's shriek of disagreement, pumped alarm through Trystan's blood, shattering his unruffled demeanor. In a single swift bound, he reached the tabletop to investigate the disturbance.

The guards had caught his amacara and Nick at the gate.

His blood boiled at the sight of one of the men daring to grab Mariel's waist, hauling her from her feet. But the addlepated soldier failed to secure his prisoner's arms. In a movement almost as swift as Trystan's own, Mariel reached behind her and grabbed her captor's testicles, twisting hard enough that even Trystan winced at the guard's scream of agony.

His mate was no weak woman, and he grinned with foolish pride as she escaped her captor. Trystan saluted her with his sword as she stalked in his direction, angrily swishing her silk skirts, unencumbered by any man's hand. Nick didn't fare quite so well, but he swung fists and feet as the guard holding him hurried after Mariel.

Although he might seriously consider throttling her later, Trystan smiled in satisfaction at Mariel's approach. She had finally recognized that she was safer with him.

When the baroness and the chevalier emerged from the mob to join them, Trystan returned to the floor. Still holding both his weapons at an angle that defied anyone's approach, he shoved his way to Mariel's side. He raised his eyebrows at his host and hostess while Mariel smacked the hand of the man holding Nick. The man dropped the boy, and with a look of shock that a mere woman could and would use such force, he cradled his injured hand against his coat.

"Now, we will sort this out, will we not?" Trystan asked casually, hiding his pleasure at Mariel's protective instincts. "I have decided to shelter the lad until I have been given good reason to do otherwise. Anyone who dares lay another hand on him will have it sliced off. And if anyone"—he glared at the offensive creature who had dared touch Mariel—"if *anyone* dares to so much as touch a finger to my wife, I shall remove his balls. Are we understood?"

Still shivering at being so basely manhandled, Mariel snorted at Trystan's audacity. *He* was the one surrounded by armed and uniformed guards, outnumbered twenty to one, and *he* was giving orders? She'd consider him quite mad, except she hadn't missed his swordsmanship. She had never seen such a skilled display in her life.

Watching from afar, she'd seen Trystan amid the mob's chaos, appearing as nonchalant as if he were taking a pleasant walk. Not a lace or hair out of place, he'd casually wielded his deadly weapons and held off an army. Even now, he seemed no more than a languid aristocrat, playing at fencing, until one looked in his eyes and saw the glint of steel reflected there.

She'd think him a pirate or one of the old king's musketeers did she not know better, and foolishly, she thrilled at his unyielding strength. She didn't care to see the bloody mess he'd leave behind should anyone be dim-witted enough to defy him. She stood quietly, clasping Nick's shoulder, allowing Trystan to handle their captors.

Belatedly, she was recognizing her companion as far more than a sailor but less than a god—he was a dangerous man whose formidable weapons could cause serious bloodshed should his implacable reserve be breached. She might have an argument to pick with the arrogant princeling, but she'd prefer to keep his strength and nobility on her side.

"That's my ward," de Berrier argued. "I demand that he be turned over to me at once."

The new Lady de Berrier brightened as she studied Nick. "Your ward? Why did you not say so? I had no idea, Marc. What's your name, child?"

"I'm not a child," Nick protested. "I'm fifteen. And I'm not his ward."

Mariel hugged his thin shoulders. He squirmed but did not pull away. "His father was killed by militia. He has a right to suspect anyone in uniform."

"Killed?" Lady de Berrier looked around her, much as a bird blinks and turns its head to study its surroundings. "Has someone found the murderers?"

"It was a mob, madame. I did not wish to concern you over such matters," de Berrier replied. "It is just such a mob I wished to prevent by ordering the gates barred." He gestured at the drunken throng now dancing awkwardly to a tune the musicians had struck up. "The times are unsettled and events can escalate rapidly."

Both Mariel and Lady de Berrier followed his gesture, nodding attentively at the sight of satiated women sitting on the floor, leaning against the tables, and blissfully stuffing grapes and nuts into their mouths. Shabbily dressed men roared and pounded each other on the back, jovially quaffing wine from bottles and punch from bowls.

The elegant nobles who had once adorned the hall had for the most part slipped away. A few of the younger ones had joined the party and were as merrily lifting bottles as their impoverished counterparts.

"Yes, I can see where feeding a mob is a messy thing," the lady agreed, blithely misunderstanding her new husband. "We shall have to reimburse the duc for the cleaning. How very silly of me."

Mariel elbowed Trystan to reprimand his grin of appreciation at the lady's quick wit, but the mischievous amusement in his expression revealed something of the boy he must have been before duty and responsibility carved his face into stone. Her heart nearly knotted at seeing this side of him that he so closely guarded.

"The boy is wanted for poaching," the captain of the guard reported, ignoring the family squabble. "Poachers are hung to discourage others from committing the offense."

Mariel wrapped her hand over Nick's mouth and pulled him back into her skirts before he could shout his protests. Dropping his pretense of disinterest, Trystan straightened and raised his rapier to the captain's throat.

"The boy was with me. Find another poor poacher attempting to feed his starving family. Take yourself off and do something useful, like preventing those fools from raiding the cellars." He nodded toward a few inebriated young men who were slipping down a corridor into the castle, and lowered his rapier as the captain's gaze followed his nod.

Alarmed first by the threat of Trystan's weapon and then by the sight of the vandals, the captain shouted, sending half his command racing across prone bodies and around dancing bacchanalians. Then, relieved of the blade point at his throat, he swung back to Trystan and drew his sword with renewed authority. "I will present the boy's case to the duc when he returns. Until then, he is remanded into my custody."

"It would be amusing to see you try to take him from me," Trystan replied with a wicked smile that did not hide the deftness with which the point of his rapier instantly pressed into the wrist of the captain's sword hand.

"King's soldiers are coming. Up river from Quimper," Nick muttered so only Mariel and Trystan could hear. "We must leave."

If the king's soldiers had killed Nick's father, Mariel didn't think it wise to await their arrival. Praying she had assessed Celeste's character rightly, as well as her influence over her new husband, she turned to the new Lady de Berrier. "My lady, Nick is heir to a fortune, and there are those who would see him parted from it. We do not have the means to know friend from foe. We would rather take him with us than leave him to fend for himself."

"Nonsense. If he is Marc's ward, he will go with us. I have always wanted a son. Come along, dear, let's find you a nice new suit of clothes." Celeste marched between raised swords, took Nick's shoulders, and steered him past the astonished guards. "A bath, first thing," she stated, wrinkling her nose. "Do not concern yourselves. He will be safe with me."

No one questioned her ability to take care of the boy. The steel in her voice rivaled that of Trystan's sword.

Unable to contradict a baroness, the captain stood with jaw dropped, letting them go.

Nick sent a panicky look back to Trystan and Mariel, but a disturbance at the front of the hall drew all eyes in a new direction.

Twenty-two

Did she imagine it, or had Trystan just snarled at the sight he could see above the heads of the crowd? Mariel thought she could sense a dangerous energy pulsating around him, as if he would begin to glow any minute. Mostly, he kept his strengths hidden by playing the part of languid aristocrat or merchant, but she knew him for what he was, and the menace in that disquieting growl did not bode well for someone.

Distracted from Nick's plight, she followed Trystan's narrowed gaze to a ripple in the crowd nearest the doors. She heard no tramp of soldiers' boots. No phalanx of uniformed men entered. But *someone* was cutting through the crowd like a shark through the sea—one man, commanding attention with his aura of danger.

Peering around Trystan's broad frame and bristling menace, Mariel stared at the second most striking man she'd ever encountered.

The stranger couldn't be called conventionally handsome. He carried himself like a man who knew his worth and reveled in it, but he was not as tall, broad, or muscular as Trystan. He was dark and lean as a lone wolf, with a blade-thin nose, hollowed cheeks beneath high cheekbones, and thick mink-colored hair that he had clubbed at his nape without bothering with powder or pomade. Although he wore the royal blue of a king's soldier with only a cloak pin for adornment, he had the air of a man sporting silk and diamonds.

Mariel caught her breath as he came closer. *He had Trystan's eyes*, except black-lashed rather than golden brown. She watched the uncanny change of color from grim gray to mocking blue as he caught her stare—and saw *her* eyes, changing hue just as his did.

Body tensed, Trystan blocked her with his brawny arm, then placed himself between her and his adversary. Mariel was almost relieved to be released from the soldier's formidable study.

"What do you here?" Trystan demanded, or Mariel thought he demanded. The words weren't ones she knew, but she seemed to understand them. The advantage to having unique abilities herself was that very little of what others did surprised her, so she concentrated on the conversation and not the anomaly.

"I could ask the same, old friend," the newcomer replied with dark amusement. "I thought my senses fooled me when I felt you here. Did you come to tell me I have been found innocent?"

He'd *felt* Trystan's presence? That did not make sense in any language Mariel knew.

"Not likely," Trystan said gruffly. "Dylys did not suppress you entirely then."

Mariel heard the underlying relief in Trystan's comment, although on the surface he was caustic. Was that disappointment flashing through the other man's expressive eyes? The atmosphere seemed taut with emotion, but she could not discern why.

Before she could feel sympathy for his obvious pain, the soldier's gaze became hard, menacing, and he responded with an obscene gesture. "We will not talk of that or we must talk of why you are interfering in the events of Others. I believe only I am allowed that sin."

Following this conversation from behind Trystan's right shoulder, Mariel saw the dark soldier nod toward Nick and the baroness. "He might have died had you not interfered. There is no telling what will come of his survival."

"What did you intend his death to achieve?" Trystan asked acerbically.

The question drew the soldier's attention back to them. "It was not my men who murdered the boy's father. My squad was there to stop the hotheaded radicals who are up in arms everywhere. They blamed his father for their taxes, held a tribunal, and called for his death as justice. The killers have been incarcerated."

"You came from Quimper to tell the boy that?"

Mariel knew from Trystan's voice that he didn't believe that for a minute. She wished she understood the currents of the conversation as well as she did the words.

"The woman. She understands." The dark man nodded in Mariel's direction. "Dylys will banish you, too, if she finds out you've sworn vows with a ringless Crossbreed."

"Leave Mariel out of this. Why are you here, Murdoch?"

For a moment, the soldier looked uncertain. Without the mask of hauteur, he seemed almost human, but he hid the weakness swiftly with a sardonic expression and curt bow.

"I thought perhaps you had a message for me. Forgive my foolishness. I haven't quite got the knack of forgetting my friends." He nodded at Mariel and spoke in court French. "A pleasure to meet you, mademoiselle. Be assured, your young comrade will be safe with his guardian. Your cousin is a far stronger woman than she appears."

Shocked that he addressed her with such familiarity, and that a stranger could know her enigmatic cousin better than she, Mariel could not hope to reply. She spoke Breton, not the language of the court. Not well, at least. Even though she'd understood the words he and Trystan had exchanged, she could not possibly reply in either tongue.

The man called Murdoch did not seem to require an answer. With a sharp bark of command, he set the guards scurrying to protect the corridors from vandals and thieves.

Then he turned to Trystan with a dark, foreboding look. "The future I predicted is coming to pass. The chalice is out in the world where it is destined to be. It will not return to your hands tonight. Or ever. You were my friend in the past, so I will warn you this once. Go home while you still can. From now on, we work toward different purposes."

Spinning on his heels, Murdoch strode out as swiftly as he'd entered, leaving Mariel to wonder if she'd imagined the whole episode.

Except the concerned man who had fascinated her these last days had suddenly reverted to the rigid board she'd first met on the island, a grim authority with a nasty duty to perform.

"I must leave you with your cousin," Trystan said stiffly. His blank gray eyes concealed his considerable restraint, but his mighty fists and tensed muscles projected danger without need of the connection throbbing between them. "I cannot let the chalice fall into Murdoch's hands. If it is already on its way back here, then it should not take me long to intercept it."

"How could he know about the chalice?" she asked in an undertone when Trystan grasped her elbow to steer her after the baroness and Nick. Her head danced with questions.

"He *shouldn't* know," Trystan said through clenched teeth. "Once, he had the Sight, but Dylys suppressed his powers. When gifted, Murdoch had the combined abilities of all of us, but he is irrationally unpredictable. He should know *nothing*."

"He seems to know everything," Mariel pointed out, resisting his tug. "And I need to return to Francine. As you said, I will only be a hindrance if I accompany you inland."

Far better than before, Mariel could sense Trystan's grief at losing the precious object, and his fear that it would be lost forever. She hated that the chalice might be gone, and she could not help him, but already she was feeling the weakening she'd experienced yesterday. Why had her mother never told her of her limitations?

Because her mother hadn't known. Mariel would have to learn on her own. For that, alone, she should resent the arrogant Aelynners.

And yet, she could have *died* had Trystan not realized what was wrong with her.

What if Francine's baby was born with some special ability? It might die if Mariel didn't know to watch for its limitations and weaknesses.

Panicking, Mariel grabbed Trystan's arm and dragged him to a halt. "Your people? Do they have midwives? Can I bring one to Francine?"

He looked at her as if she were crazed. "What are you talking about?"

"My sister! Our mother was of your kind, so Francine's child might be also, right?"

He hesitated briefly, his wooden expression softening with thought. Then he froze up again. "It's no matter. Crossbreeds survive if it is meant to be. Treat the child as any other. Now, let go so I might ask your cousin to look after you while I'm gone."

Her temper flared, and Mariel swung her fist into his massive upper arm. Trystan didn't flinch, which made her even more furious. "My cousin is newly *married*. She has just taken on *Nick*. And I am going home." She assumed Nick had left the pony and cart where they'd hidden them. She hadn't had a chance to ask before the newlyweds hastened him off.

"It is too dangerous for you to traverse the forest alone!" her self-appointed guardian roared.

She shot him an arched look and patted his arm to alleviate his fury. Then she stepped back, the better to hurl his words in his face. "I will be fine. After all, Crossbreeds survive if it's meant to be."

Then she lost herself in the crowd, leaving Trystan staring after her, torn right down the middle between two conflicting responsibilities.

For a man who had never veered from the one constant goal in his life, the conflict was akin to an earthquake shattering and cracking his foundation. Aelynn was all to him. He was the island's shield against the Outside World. His life was devoted to his home's protection.

The chalice was a sacred part of the island, his home. He had to retrieve it.

But Mariel was his future, and he hated to part from her for even a minute. How could he protect both Mariel and Aelynn?

This was why he should never have taken a Crossbreed amacara. He didn't know what madness had inspired him to believe he could do what others could not. *Arrogance*, she'd said. *Stupidity*, more like. And now he must pay the price.

He had to retrieve the sacred chalice first and rely on Aelynn for the rest. His own personal needs did not enter the equation.

He had to trust that Mariel would be safe.

With despair ripping out his insides, he strode for the castle gates and the nearest horse or carriage he could steal. He might seriously dislike riding, but he couldn't run through crowded streets without drawing undue attention, and even his stamina wouldn't last until Versailles. Perhaps if he moved swiftly enough, he could meet the messenger and be back before nightfall.

An irritating voice in his head kept repeating—*Mariel will not be waiting.*

He disliked abandoning young Nick as well, but for whatever reason, Murdoch had given the boy an opportunity for freedom and a home. Trystan hoped the baroness was as strong-minded as Mariel and would defend the boy as fiercely as Mariel guarded her sister.

The image of babies appearing in the world without the wisdom of an Aelynn midwife haunted the back of Trystan's mind as he raced down the castle steps. He had promised Mariel she could remain in her home. He had really not thought that through at all. His child had to be cared for by women who understood the needs of an Aelynner.

His child. He was losing his mind. The child had yet to be conceived, might never be, if Mariel had anything to say about it. He might pass on to the next world without leaving an heir. Except that if he died, there would be none ready to take his place.

And if he died while not on Aelynn, his soul and his power would be lost.

He'd have to arrange it so he didn't die, then.

Locating a horse saddled and ready as if waiting for him, Trystan awkwardly grasped the leather and gained the seat. He despised being inept, but he nudged the huge beast into motion and hung on for dear life as it broke through the crowd of people in the market and headed down the road toward Versailles.

From the shadow of the castle stairs, Mariel watched Trystan go. A piece of her heart must have splintered and lodged in her lungs, so sharp was the pain of watching his departure. He looked the part of grand gentleman riding off on the expensive steed, even though he had little training on how to ride the animal. He would learn through sheer strength of will, she was certain. Never had she met such a complex, intriguing man, and now he was going away. She clenched her hand in a fist and held it between her breasts, taking short breaths to keep from crying out. Tears filled her eyes.

She had hoped he would stay for her.

She should have known better. He'd done what every man did, pursued his duty and his ambition, leaving behind family to muddle through as best they could. She understood the inevitability. In this case, she even accepted the necessity.

Trystan was as much a part of his dratted island as the rocks and trees. Her heart broke knowing he could never be completely hers. Better that she learn this now.

She needed to reassure Nick. Then she must find the pony cart and head home. She knew better than to believe in golden gods. And she'd learned a few things about herself, so all was not hopelessly lost.

She wasn't a virgin any longer, but she had never expected to marry, so that was no concern. She was better for the experience, and she would not mourn the loss of a man she'd learned to trust and respect.

It wasn't as if he were the love of her life, even if tears foolishly dripped down her cheeks.

Rather than fight the mob and guards and the dank cold of the castle corridors, she sent a footman to her cousin and remained outside in the sun. Perhaps part of her weakening had to do with lack of sunlight. She was always less healthy in winter.

She eventually recovered some of her composure, enough to realize she would need food for her journey. She returned to the hall and wrapped any remains from the banquet she could find in a tablecloth. The musicians and most of the guests had gone home.

The tables had been fairly well stripped, but a smashed cake here, an orange rolling about there, and a few other scraps found their way into her pack. She had eaten well these last days. She would save as much food as she could for Francine.

Nick finally arrived looking appropriately wealthy in a new satin suit with bright white linen. His hair had been trimmed and tied back in a satin sacque, and he even wore shiny silver buckles on his shoes. How Celeste had performed this miracle of transformation was beyond Mariel's ability to comprehend. The wealthy lived in another world entirely.

Which started her thinking about other worlds, even though she preferred to forget such things.

She hauled Nick into her arms and hugged him until his ears turned red, then she let him go. "You look very lordly, young man. My cousin is a good woman, but her husband courts dangerous politicians. If you wish to come with me, the offer is still open. But I cannot afford what my cousin can."

He stared at the tips of his shoes. "She has promised to send me to school in Paris. I would very much like to be a great swordsman, like Monsieur Trystan."

Trystan was a frighteningly amazing swordsman.

Mariel had not missed the extent of his skill or the fact that he'd restrained himself. He had far too many exciting facets that she didn't understand and wished she could have explored. But for the sake of her future, she had to believe that he was a man like any other, and he was gone from her life. He would soon realize he was better off without her.

On a deep breath of determination, she smiled at Nick. "Then you shall be a wonderful swordsman. Just try not to get yourself killed in the process," she warned. "Your guardian might enjoy that too much."

Nick grinned. "The baroness has already assigned her lawyers to tie up my inheritance so it cannot be used for anything except my schooling until I am twenty-five. I think I have met a whirlwind." He lifted the basket he carried on his arm. "She sends you this and wishes you safety on your journey."

"Good. I think she means well, and the rich carry their own shield of invulnerability that will serve you well. But you are to come to Pouchay should you ever have need of anything. Is the pony where we left it?"

He nodded vigorously. "I gave him more feed and there is water. But he could eat his way through the bushes and be seen if he is not rescued soon." He looked about with curiosity. "I would say farewell to the monsieur. Where is he?"

"He has gone after a chalice. He will be back, no doubt, bellowing and shouting. Tell him I have gone home. I cannot wait."

Nick looked doubtful. "On your own, madame? Is that wise? There are villains all through the forest."

"I think they have all come to the wedding and are now lying blissfully under the tables. If I hurry, I will be fine," she assured him, although she was not nearly so sure herself.

It didn't matter. She must go. She kissed the boy's head, waved him off, and made her way back through Pontivy to her cart. This might be the last time she strayed outside her own village, but she did not have time to admire the sights any longer. She was going home, where she belonged.

Twenty-three

Market day was the worst possible time to ride a distractible horse, Trystan discovered, tugging the reins of the animal as it tried to eat the hat of a peasant trundling hens into town.

He'd fare better walking, except that in this region a man on horseback received far more deference than a man on foot. And he needed all the help he could find to track down the lady's messenger.

He'd been told the messenger wore red, white, and blue, but then, so did half the gentlemen on the road. He could overlook the farmers in their homespun browns, and the soldiers in their epaulets and hats, which narrowed the search somewhat. He knew the messenger traveled by horse, so he eliminated anyone in a carriage.

But there were still far too many people to be certain he hadn't overlooked anyone. The servant had half a day's start over him. Trystan prayed that meant by now the man was returning from his task of recovering the chalice, so he studied all men carrying sacks as well.

By late afternoon the horde of travelers had thinned out, and Trystan was doubting his wisdom in chasing after the impossible. Had Murdoch thrown down the challenge of the chalice to distract him from some other scheme?

Once upon a time, they'd been friends. Admittedly, Trystan had been at sea and not home often enough to experience his friend's unpredictable behavior as others had, but he'd seen no meanness in him.

According to all who had witnessed the event, Murdoch had killed the Oracle's husband by causing a platform to fall on him after calling down lightning to ignite fireworks. A trained Weathermaker would never have made the mistake of drawing lightning into a crowd, much less near a platform loaded with gunpowder. As the ill-bred descendant of a hearthwitch and a farmer, Murdoch should have no weathermaking abilities, but from youth he'd possessed wild powers that rivaled Trystan's strength. Perhaps he hadn't even meant to call the lightning.

But Murdoch had said he'd *seen* the future. A cold chill of dread washed through Trystan. Only the Oracle and her progeny should have the power to deliberately call up the future. Had Murdoch stolen powers from the gods, or was he simply lying about his visions?

For years, Murdoch had been Trystan's greatest rival for Lissandra's hand. Despite his unreliable behavior, Murdoch was the smartest man on the island, perhaps the only one who could understand Lissandra's visions.

Trystan didn't feel competent enough to sort out whether the all-knowing Oracle had been wrong to banish Murdoch, or if she'd been right. He simply knew all Aelynners had been taught from birth that their gifts were to be used in service to the island, and not for their own selfish purposes.

Murdoch's warning aginst seeking the sacred chalice did not sound as if he had the island's best interest in mind—unless the warning was a diversion. Had Murdoch somehow "seen" what had happened on Aelynn with Mariel? How much could the outcast possibly know? Did Murdoch plan to win back the Oracle's favor by killing Mariel once he had Trystan out of the way?

Murdoch had known Mariel could understand their language.

How had that happened anyway? Trystan knew amacaras shared their strengths, but Mariel hadn't agreed to the vows. Could she really understand all languages as he did?

Alarm knifing through him, Trystan pulled his horse under the shade of a beech tree, ignoring the mare's dancing and prancing.

He had to protect Mariel. Somehow, she had become as important to him as Aelynn, and the two were irrevocably tied in his mind, and in his heart. Terror slid just beneath his skin.

Before he could rush after Mariel, he had to care for the horse. He knew nothing of the animals, except that Mariel had insisted the pony be fed and watered and rested regularly. Unlike ships, animals could not sail on indefinitely.

With the care he gave to his own pets, Trystan turned the creature back toward an inn he'd passed earlier. Abandoning his search for the chalice went against every precept ingrained in him, but he saw no alternative.

He didn't know when Mariel had become more important to him than duty. He'd blame it on the vows he'd taken last night when she'd nearly died, but the need to keep her safe had been there even before then. Perhaps from the first moment he'd laid eyes on her. She complicated every damned thing.

And still, he had the urgent need to see that she was safe. He wanted to discuss this new development with her and hear her insights.

While a groom fed and watered the horse, Trystan stalked into the inn for some liquid refreshment and to ease his confused anger. Considering the long ride ahead, he ordered bread and cheese and a flask of wine. He knew Mariel wouldn't be waiting. She was in that cursed pony cart, heading back to her sister, alone.

Someone should have warned him of the dangers of amacara bonds. He'd simply thought in terms of sex any time he liked and a child to carry on his inheritance. He'd not understood that it also meant he gave his heart and soul to a woman who did not want them.

Mariel had to be even more confused and torn than he, with more questions than answers. Morosely, he took a seat in a corner of the tavern and tipped the chair back on two legs as he sipped his ale and studied the room's occupants. Most were farmers and tradesmen apparently intent on drinking up their profits. . . .

The front legs of his chair slammed back to the floor. With an accelerating heartbeat, Trystan blindly slid his tankard onto the table.

In a far corner, a frivolous fellow in a blue satin coat with a red embroidered waistcoat and finicky white linen glanced at his pocket watch. Apparently deciding it was time to leave, he arranged a fringed blue tricorne on his powdered hair and rose from the table.

Not until the fribble lifted a black velvet sack from his seat did Trystan rise, his chair banging against the wall. Perhaps Aelynn had blessed him after all.

Striding quickly toward the door, he intercepted the gentleman before he could depart. "Are you from Lady Beloit—de Berrier?"

The messenger was hardly more than a boy, one

who grew pale beneath his powdered curls at being confronted. His gloved hand curled around the hilt of his sword.

"No cause for that, boy." Trystan held both his hands away from his weapons. "The lady asked me to catch up with her servant, if that is you."

The boy nodded warily, and his tricorne slipped askew.

It was all Trystan could do to keep from rolling his eyes. He was stuck with a lad probably in his first post, wearing his first livery, and anxious to please. At least he'd reached the servant before Murdoch had.

"The lady is in a hurry to return the chalice to Pouchay. I am to speed it on its way." He reached for the sack.

The boy backed away.

"May I see the chalice and verify that you have it?"

Warily, the lad held the sack open for inspection. From the shadows of the interior, the glitter of silver and blue winked reassuringly, and Trystan breathed in relief. Perhaps all would be well after all.

Before he could savor relief or triumph, a familiar twinge twisted in Trystan's gut. He winced and almost bent double as a rush of heat surged to his groin. *Mariel.*

Lust clouded his mind and crippled his thinking. He could scarcely stand straight for the need surging through him. With only one part of his anatomy working, Trystan yanked the pouch of gold from his inside pocket and shoved it at the startled lad. "See that the baroness receives this." Grabbing the velvet sack, he yanked it free of the boy's grip, and ran for the horse.

The boy's panicked shouts couldn't begin to deter him.

With the sun dipping into the western horizon,

Trystan caught the reins of his stolen horse, swung into the saddle, and raced toward the forest and Mariel.

Knowing the late June sun was close to setting, Mariel led the pony off the path toward a stream she sensed in the distance. She wasn't certain why or how she knew the stream was there, but she was much too weary to question her intuition.

She unharnessed the pony and hobbled him near new grass and the burbling brook. The baroness's basket included a large cellar of salt, for which Mariel was grateful.

Filling her cup with water and adding the condiment, she drank of it as if it were a nourishing broth. While she nibbled her cheese and bread, she tried to clear her mind of regrets and wishes and all things she was powerless to direct.

But she could not deny the river of desire flowing strongly through her, flooding her with needs she'd never known or wanted.

Damn the man, she did not even have to be with him to desire him.

Which, admittedly, he'd warned her about, but she had not heeded the warning. Mariel wondered what Trystan would do if she attempted to summon *him* as he had her? Would he drop the chalice or whatever maid he might be entertaining now and rush to her side?

At some future time would he drop Lissandra and sail the Channel to reach her?

Not likely, Mariel thought sourly. He would lose his precious *seat* on the Council.

It shouldn't matter. She had no intention of marrying any man, so she had no right to be jealous of

Trystan's future. She was tired and being petty. She was awash with lust and needed satisfaction.

She had sinned, and now she was paying the price. She consoled herself; at least the village had bread and Francine did not go hungry. They would live to see another day.

She lingered over her supper, then stripped and washed in the stream. But water flowing over her naked breasts only evoked the glide of Trystan's fingers over her skin.

She was exhausted and ought to be able to sleep. Perhaps if she were warm . . .

She dressed and wrapped in her cloak, then lay down in the back of the cart and tried hard to be responsible and not call Trystan to ease her needs. But she longed for the comfort of his big body beside her, even wished she could hear his sarcasm as he joined her. She trusted his mockery more than his flattery.

Closing her eyes, Mariel recognized her real sacrifice—her independence. She was no longer content to be alone.

This wasn't just lust churning her insides. This was a need to dance with Trystan, to laugh and talk and hold hands. To exchange ideas and worries with a companion who shared her concerns. To amend her plans for the future just as he must. She not only wanted to know if he'd found the chalice, but she desperately cared about the answer. She wanted to know more about his world. About him. She had so many questions. . . .

This yearning would pass, she hoped. Once she was in her own home, with the fishermen needing her aid, and Francine holding the baby, the bond between her and Trystan would fray and break. She would be back to normal. She'd experienced a lot in a few days. It was natural that she was not quite herself.

Biting her lip, she pressed her hand over her skirt where her legs met and wondered if she could ease the longing on her own.

She eased her skirt up, feeling ashamed for doing so but unable to sleep without relief. Trystan had told her he would not take her again unless she went to the island with him. He had said there were other means to ease their needs. She simply needed to teach herself.

Her fingers slid along the cleft that he had taught to ache for him. Desire rippled and intensified with the touch, but she did not feel the liquid flow of surrender or the driving urge to spread her legs. Perhaps she was not doing it properly.

She experimented with her fingers until she heard the snap of a twig beneath a heavy boot, shoved hastily at her skirts, and sat up.

"For Aelynn's sake, woman, do not call me like that again," a rough voice said from the darkness. "I almost made a eunuch of myself falling from the damned horse."

Not certain she was entirely awake, Mariel stared in amazement as Trystan strode toward her, stripping off coat and shirt and unfastening his breeches. His gloriously bare, bronzed chest rendered her speechless, breathless, and without any thought except that he was here. With her.

"Trystan?" She thought she said his name aloud and not in a dream.

He glanced up, and he was close enough that she could see him in the moonlight. Annoyance fled his expression, replaced by concern and a hint of laughter.

"You look as if I've already tumbled you." He sat down on the back of the cart to tug off his boots. "I wish my father had lived long enough to explain these things to me. My mother wasn't his amacara, so perhaps even he did not understand."

"I . . . I *called* you?" She shoved her hair from her face and watched with fascination the movement of powerful muscles in his bare back.

"I am so hard I could not fit the saddle," he said. "But we are not doing this until we reach Aelynn. As punishment for crippling me like this, I'll teach you how to satisfy me first."

That did not sound like punishment to Mariel as she watched him strip off his breeches and tower over her—much as he had that day at the temple. Except now, he was the one who was naked and fully aroused.

And she was ready for him.

Twenty-four

"Behold what you have wrought," Trystan said wryly as Mariel stared at his extremely aroused nudity with a bewildering array of emotions in her eyes. "I feel like a rutting bull, and I'm regretting this amacara responsibility right now. I don't like having a woman control me."

Heaving the sack containing the chalice onto the seat of the cart, he climbed into the back and on top of her, closing her long, lovely legs and pinning her skirt to the cart bed. She seemed too stunned to reply, which suited his purposes. Propping himself up on his hands, he leaned down and kissed her until both their heads spun.

Not until she was gasping for air and clinging to his arms did he relent.

"I didn't mean to call you," she whispered, lifting her hips closer.

"Yes, you did. You just didn't know for certain that you could," he said with a laugh, covering her face with kisses.

"It *is* only fair," she declared, capturing his mouth with hers and plying him with her tongue until he almost lost control.

Straining to complete an act he'd fully intended to avoid tonight, Trystan cursed under his breath in his own language. When she frowned at his obscenities, he bent his forehead to touch hers and attempted to leash his raging lust.

"I apologize, *mi ama.* I'd forgotten that you seem to understand my words now. This is as new to me as it is to you, so we must blunder through it together."

Her hands released his arms and fluttered across his chest, stroking, nipping, reducing his strength to dust. He nibbled her ear, then ripped open her bodice hooks so he could find her breasts. They would be too mindless to desist if he wasn't careful. Perhaps he already was.

"I ached," she murmured. "I tried to seek relief, but I did not know how. Will it be like this for the rest of our lives?"

Forever whispered through the leaves. Accepting the inevitable, he closed his hand over a warm, yielding curve with a pointed peak. "I can't say for certain. I know no other amacaras well enough to ask. This is something Dylys would teach us. Until then . . ." He sighed in relief as he nuzzled between her breasts. "We must practice thinking of anything *except* this."

She laughed breathily above his head as he swept her nipples with his tongue. "One and one are two. Two and two are four. Four and four are—" She gasped and writhed beneath him as he took the ripe fruit of her breast between his teeth. "I doubt thought has anything to do with this," she said between whimpers of passion that tortured his lust even more.

"At this rate, we will be multiplying, not just adding." He groaned as her hand stroked downward to reach his sex, and her fingers closed around him. "If you don't want children, you had best stop what you're doing now."

"Then show me what to do instead," she demanded.

"By all the gods, you are the most demanding, immodest, stubborn, unnatural female I've ever had the pleasure to meet, and I'll be delighted to grant your request," he grumbled to her laughter, rolling to his side so he could divest her of her clothing.

"Did you think your precious Lissandra would come when called and murmur sweet nothings in your ear and stroke your masculine arrogance without complaint?" she mocked, eagerly helping him to push off her skirt.

She sat naked in the moonlight, her ebony hair curling down her back and over swollen pink buds accenting her ivory breasts. Her waist nipped in to fit his hands, then swelled out in glorious hips and tight buttocks unlike any he'd ever beheld. Her years of swimming the ocean's currents had carved her legs into supple muscles that he could imagine wrapping around him. Trystan was almost too stunned by Mariel's moonkissed beauty to reply to her taunt. Almost.

"No, I expected nothing of the kind from Lissandra," he admitted. "We were bred to keep Aelynn strong. I had hoped that we might find this softness. . . ." He used his hands to indicate the way their bodies gravitated together. Her nipples puckered under his caress, and she swayed toward him without persuasion. "But I see now that it was unlikely. I do not understand the logic of the gods, unless you wish to murmur sweet nothings in my ear?" he added hopefully.

"Right now, I will do anything you ask, if only you will keep me from going up in flames," she replied, and this time, there was no mockery in her tone.

He nodded, matching her seriousness. "You understand that I still intend to take you to Aelynn and plant my seed in your womb, and this is how the gods aid me in persuading you to do my bidding?"

Sorrow haunted her expression. "If you understand that you cannot keep me there."

Trystan closed his eyes and fought the anguish of fearing his son would be deprived of the rough-and-tumble learning with other boys who had his skills and strengths and speed. "I understand," he agreed. "That does not mean I accept it."

He changed his mind about teaching her how to pleasure him first. He had a strong urge to prove her need for him. Before she could argue, he took her breast into his mouth and rocked the heel of his hand against the swollen bud between her legs. To his satisfaction, she cried out her desire and did not protest when he laid her down on the cart bed beneath him.

He used his tongue to pleasure her, and to teach her that he could offer far, far more once she agreed to take her vows.

In retaliation, she used her hands on him, and with his guidance, showed him the cruelty of release without true joining.

Hollow and unsatisfied, they rolled into each other's arms and slept restlessly for the remaining hours until dawn.

"Stop thinking," Mariel said crossly, feeling desire ripple through her womb as the cart rattled down the rutted road toward home. She had yet to unravel the thrill that he had actually come for her from her fear for their future.

She ought to be reassured by the sight of the man beside her. He had doffed his silk coat in deference to the increasing warmth of the day and looked as unrumpled and unruffled as a golden god should be. He was every inch the lofty aristocrat, despite the decidedly earthy intimacy they had shared.

Trystan cast her a wry glance that almost stopped her heart. "It's hard not to think of you when my arm rubs your breast every time I rein this animal around another hole. I should not have sent the horse back to its owner."

"Horses are too valuable to steal. I hope it returns safely," she said, frowning with worry.

"I would have left him in his stable if you hadn't called," Trystan replied. "Would you prefer walking?"

She rubbed her hands over the hollow in her middle and wished for the welcoming depths of the sea to wash away this urge for his arms around her again. "No, thank you. We must hurry. Francine could have her babe any day. It is a good thing Father Antoine is still on sabbatical or I would be missing mass right now."

"First, we need to return the chalice to Aelynn. And you must take your vows. You promised." His voice sounded sterner than she thought necessary.

"I know, and I will. But Francine comes first." It wasn't as if she could think of anything else except his damned island and that strange bed and what he would do to her there.

And the results thereof. He seemed confident a child would come of it. And curse him, she actually *wanted* the child. And yet, the thought of growing big and round like Francine terrified her. What would she do with herself if she couldn't swim?

How would she explain to a child why their father couldn't live with them? Why they were different? Her heart broke over a child that had yet to be born!

She wanted to weep with unhappiness, but she had called this down upon herself. Bargaining with gods was always a risky business.

"I will see that Francine is provided for while you're away," Trystan said. "It's imperative that we return the chalice before it has a chance to escape again."

"And to satisfy your need to perpetuate the species," she retorted. "I am not at all certain that I like the idea of being your breeding cow."

"And I'm positive I don't like the idea of being your rutting bull. But you reduce us to this by refusing to stay with me so we could learn to be true mates."

"This whole thing is too confusing for reason." Even as she said it, Mariel wished he would stop the pony and kiss her until she forgot their argument. Conflicting desires would tear her in two. "I wish I'd never heard of Aelynn or your people or you. I think I would be better off starving."

"I could wish you'd never heard of us either, but it's done. And your sister and your neighbors are better off for it."

Unexpectedly, Trystan halted the pony, and Mariel's heart flipped in excitement at the prospect of his kisses, but he merely shot her a burning amber look and resisted. Instead, he stood on the cart seat, and with the point of his rapier cut down a branch of ripening cherries. His broad shoulders strained at the seams of his linen shirt, and without his coat, his trim, muscled waist and buttocks showed to advantage. She almost expired from lust just watching him move.

"You've done your civic duty; now I must do mine," he continued, returning to his seat and handing her the branch. "I suppose a life without sacrifice is not a life lived."

Heart melting at his generous action, Mariel plucked the ripest fruit from the branch and placed it between Trystan's lips, before tasting one herself. Caught by surprise, he accepted her offering, then bent to lick and kiss her cherry-sweetened lips.

This wasn't a kiss of lust, but one of appreciation, and Mariel melted further. How could anyone deny a man who so evidently meant to cherish and protect?

Before she could forget their differences, she reached for their food pack and tore off a piece of bread to satisfy a craving that couldn't really be satisfied with food. "I will remind your son of the importance of duty and sacrifice on some snowy Christmas Eve when he asks about you."

His eyes flared with anger before he picked up the reins and sent the cart rolling again. Mariel moved to the far edge of the seat and attempted to dodge his arm when he lifted the reins, but just avoiding his touch induced images of what he'd done to her last night. And what she had done to him.

Trystan stiffened, sighed, and adjusted his tight breeches. Unable to stay angry with this ridiculous situation, Mariel giggled.

"How do your amacaras ever get out of bed?" she asked, genuinely curious.

"I daresay, with time and satiation the craving diminishes." In thoughtful mode, his chiseled face lost some of its hardness, and intelligence lit his expression. "In England, they give newlyweds a week alone, or longer, and call it a honeymoon. After that, they are expected to act like normal married people. I'm not certain if this applies to amacaras, but I should think it would be much alike."

"A week?" Mariel tried to imagine a week in a room with a bed and Trystan. "I think we'd starve."

He chuckled. "I've not heard of anyone starving from lust. Dylys will be able to tell us more. And I suppose pregnancy would decrease the cravings. You don't see your sister pining away from desire."

"With Francine, it would be hard to tell." Mariel thought of her complacent sister, rocking in her chair, constantly twisting delicate threads into intricate patterns. "Perhaps I should take up rocking and lace making. It must dull the senses."

"Admittedly, you are more physical than most women. Even on Aelynn, the women are usually Healers and nurturers and Seers, which do not require much athleticism. You, on the other hand, live inside your body as much as in your head."

"Is that a good thing?" she asked suspiciously.

Trystan shot her a wicked grin. "For my intentions, assuredly."

If this were a game of chess, she would send all the pieces flying in a fit of frustration. No matter what she did, he had her in check.

"We cannot return to Aelynn immediately," she reminded him. "Unless you wish to steal back your ship as you stole the chevalier's horse?"

"Was it de Berrier's?"

"He'd had it saddled and ready to ride after the chalice at his bride's behest."

"Well, I saved him the trouble, so he cannot complain." Trystan urged the pony into a faster trot when it tried to snack on a particularly sweet clump of grass.

"You mean you did not buy back the chalice?"

"I exchanged the chalice for gold with the lady's servant. I am down to my last silver coin. I assume the lady will have already bought a ruby ring for her bridegroom from some impoverished noble about to lose his land. Your country's finances are very peculiar."

"Eduard says the economy is a house of cards about to collapse. That is why Francine and I were left with almost nothing when Father died. It all went to pay his debts. And the price of everything is so dear, we cannot live on the little we earn."

Trystan frowned. "I knew there was poverty and corruption here, but if the debt you describe is so pervasive, that is a very dangerous situation. If your brother-in-law is correct, it will take a radical change in your laws and many years to fix it."

Mariel nodded wearily and closed her eyes. "A revolution," she whispered. "That is what Eduard says. They all think they can be Americans."

"Not without a war," Trystan agreed. "And you want me to leave you in the midst of such strife?" he asked in astonishment.

She leaned her elbows on the back of the cart seat and absorbed the rays of the sun as they reached the edge of the orchard. "I have friends in low places," she said with an unease she tried to hide with a jest. At his inquiring expression, she explained, "I have only to go to the sea, and no one can follow. You need not worry about me."

The sun was nearly in their eyes as they rode west. They'd made good time. Mariel felt stronger already as she sought the first familiar glimpse of fields and farms. "You never answered my question," she reminded him.

"What question?"

"Do you intend to steal back your ship?"

He shook the reins to speed the pony's progress. "I must return by the full of the moon, and that is but two days away. I don't think it would be difficult to steal the ship. I could gather the funds to pay for it when we reached Aelynn."

If she could learn to communicate better with dolphins, they could probably help her find riches, but how did one say "treasure" to an animal with no comprehension of currency?

"I hate for people to think my husband is a thief. It will be bad enough explaining your absence if I must grow fat with child."

"I said I would marry you in your church. I don't wish to bring shame on you."

"Only give me children to whom I must explain why they are different," she said crossly.

Trystan slanted her a lazy look, and prickles of desire crawled across Mariel's breasts and inside her belly. She balled up her fist and punched Trystan's hard upper arm. "Stop that."

He laughed, obviously pleased with her reaction. "It's torment, but I am learning how to use it. Given time, we should never have another argument."

Mary, Mother of Jesus, help her! He would have her rolling beneath him every time she wanted to hit him for his thickheadedness.

She would have to pray for pregnancy just to end these cravings that put her under his spell.

Twenty-five

As the cart rolled into Pouchay, Trystan scanned the horizon for the sloop, but the cliffs were too high. Instinct called for him to head straight for the ship, heave Mariel and the chalice aboard, and abscond with his prizes before anything else could keep him from the island.

But honor required that he return Mariel to her sister and marry Mariel in her church so his child would not be scorned in her world.

With the power he'd been granted, it wasn't easy to abide by her laws. Perhaps Murdoch had the right of it: Do as one must and to hell with all else. France was obviously ripe for anarchy—the perfect country for a man like Murdoch who didn't recognize any law but his own.

But unlike Murdoch, Trystan was a patient man who recognized the need for boundaries.

With reluctance, he guided the pony back to Francine's cottage rather than to the sea. At least now he knew a bit about horses. They were not so difficult to control as he'd assumed.

"Francine is usually by that window," Mariel said worriedly, biting her lip as he halted the pony in the street outside her gate.

"She cannot always be by the window." Climbing down, Trystan waved to the neighbor who had loaned them the cart. He had no right to become friendly with Outsiders, but Mariel would have to rely on these people when he was gone. "She could be napping or preparing a meal or any number of things. You are overanxious."

He was overanxious. He started nervously when Mariel leaped down without his aid and raced toward the house. He didn't want her out of his sight. But the neighbor was coming to fetch the pony, and he had to remove the chalice and their baggage so he might return the cart. He could not rudely abandon all to follow his impetuous mate.

Mariel had become like an extra limb he had to learn to cope with. Once she fit into his life the way his goats or his ship did, he'd undoubtedly function better. Until then, he felt as if he listed to one side like a ship with half a mainsail.

He'd obviously been enjoying Mariel's company too much. She added colorful insights to his black-and-white world. In his years of trading, he'd learned a little about Other World laws and money, but through Mariel he'd grasped the thoughts and emotions that drove them.

Still feeling slightly off balance now that they had returned to his new reality, Trystan finally escaped the elderly neighbor to follow Mariel into the house.

A cold sweat broke upon his brow at a low moan of pain from a back room. "Mariel?" he called, crossing the dark front room and trying not to panic.

"Here," she called. "Bring the hot water from the stove, will you?"

Moans of agony permeated the suffocating air of the cottage, and he writhed internally. Mariel hadn't sounded as if she were in pain, but Aelynn had Healers who knew how to relieve pain. Suffering wasn't part of his world. This was one of the many reasons they were not to interfere in the Outside World. The inhabitants of one tiny island could do nothing for the primitive conditions in which millions of Others existed, especially when the superstitious and ignorant insisted on burning valuable Healers at the stake as witches.

He carried the pot of steaming water toward a room off the side of the kitchen from which the groans emanated. He could hear the murmur of feminine voices and really didn't want to intervene. But the anxiety in Mariel's voice as a louder cry erupted forced him to hurry.

With the window shuttered, the scents of sweat and blood mixed with heat and humidity into a nightmare of confusion and human suffering. He staggered at the unexpectedness of it.

He didn't know the older woman who directed him to set the water upon a washstand, but he recognized a haggard Francine lying upon the sagging bed. Mariel sat at her side, holding her sister's hand and looking terrified. He didn't want Mariel to fear anything, but he was helpless to make this scene go away.

The expectant mother looked pale and feverish. Her hair straggled limply on the pillow, and her bloated belly seemed to fill the room as she struggled to sit up, then cried out again.

Even as Trystan set the water where indicated, Francine screamed as if she'd been ripped open. He'd never heard a sound so wrenching. He instinctively reached for his sword, even while understanding that his weapon would not solve the problem.

In mute appeal, he turned to Mariel for direction, but she was frozen still, letting her sister crush her hand, no more able to halt the agonized screams than he was. She lifted her gaze to him, and Trystan read her terror.

The old woman noticed him standing there helpless and snorted scornfully. "Aye, this is what you men do to your women with your rutting. Take a good look, young fellow, and remember the result of your pleasure, so you'll think twice about putting your poker between a woman's legs. Then go. You have no use here."

Mariel nodded agreement and turned back to her sister. Staggered by the immensity of this scene that held both life and death, reluctant to leave Mariel but powerless against suffering, he stumbled back to the kitchen.

By all the gods, *this* was what Mariel must suffer to bring his heir into the world?

It was a marvel she did not threaten to sever his . . . *poker* . . . and shove it down his throat.

Trystan rubbed anxiously at the maligned appendage for reassurance.

From the other room, Mariel shouted, "Stop that, this instant!"

Biting back a painful chuckle, he jerked his hand from his groin, and wiped moisture from his eye. The shrieking from the other room ended abruptly, and into the silence crept the weak cry of a babe.

Trystan sat down heavily on a dining chair in the front room. He'd seen injury and pain before. One couldn't sail a ship without it. But his schooner always carried a Healer, and his men were up and smiling within hours of their mishaps. So he'd skimmed along the surface of the real world as a ship skims over the water, never truly knowing the dangerous depths beneath.

Mariel *lived* in those murky waters. She could suffer agony without relief, as her sister had. She could *die* in childbirth, or from some accident her primitive world could not heal. And so could his child, should he be so fortunate as to have one. *If* Mariel still agreed after this. If he could bring himself to torture her in such a manner.

He stared longingly at the front window, where the first star of the evening appeared. He could leave while the women were busy, walk to the bay, slip onto his ship with none to notice. He'd be gone before anyone knew, back to the mystic world that was invisible to Others, never to be seen again.

Not without Mariel. He would not, could not, leave her to struggle with the hardships of her world. About that, he was adamant.

Trystan rested his elbows on his knees, bowed his head, and dug his fingers into his hair. She had entwined her way around his heart, flowed through his blood, and crept into every crevice of his mind. He could not force her out if he tried. And the knowledge that he was no longer alone terrified him.

Was this what Others called love? If so, it was maddening and more like *possession*.

He was two people now, not just himself. He could never act on his own again without thinking of how it would affect Mariel.

He looked up in response to a light step in the kitchen. He knew how she walked, sensed her presence even when he couldn't see her. Desired her when he should not. And he was beginning to anticipate the sensation. This possession might drive him mad, but recognizing that he would never be alone again suddenly filled him with pleasure.

Mariel appeared in the doorway holding a bundle of blankets, wiping out his anxiety with a beatific smile. "Come see," she whispered. "She's so beautiful."

The kitchen fire glowed behind her. Ebony ringlets spilled from beneath her cap, caressing her long slender throat. Holding the child like that, she looked like a Madonna from the icons he'd studied in churches on his journeys. And she was his.

The pain in his chest broke free beneath a flood of emotion he could not name. Rising, Trystan peered into the bundle of blankets at a sleeping red-faced babe. But it was Mariel who held his attention. He felt her as surely as if they were lying naked in each other's arms. She soothed his rattled nerves with her presence, awakened his hopes with her warm voice, vibrated his senses until he felt more alive than he'd ever been.

"She is incredible," he murmured in reply, but he wasn't talking about the babe.

At the sensual timbre of Trystan's voice, Mariel hastily looked up. What she saw in his eyes robbed her of breath and swept away what remained of her doubt. The bond between them throbbed with more than lust. It tugged at the hollow place in her chest where her heart had been until he'd usurped it.

"How is your sister?" His deep voice rumbled in the semidarkness of the unlit room, and she felt the tremor of his fears along with it.

"She is sleeping. I am so glad we arrived in time." Balancing the newborn in the curve of her arm, she stroked Trystan's beard-stubbled cheek. "I've been told that we forget the pain once we hold the babe in our arms. Would you like to hold her?"

He looked as if he'd rather fly off a cliff, but bravely he held out his big palms so she could place her niece in them. Once he held the child, he instinctively brought the bundle to his wide chest and pressed a butterfly kiss to her downy hair.

"You're a natural at this," she said with a smile.

"It is not much different from holding a kid that must be hand-fed. They're very tiny when they're first born." The light of laughter lit Trystan's eyes as he glanced from the child to her. "Perhaps we should stick to raising goats."

"I'm inclined to agree," she said tartly, but she didn't mean it. Not after holding the babe. She craved one of her own, one with Trystan's studious frown and golden hair.

She ought to be terrified after what Francine had gone through, but watching her sister give birth had made her look at life from a different perspective. If her calm, modest sister could risk such travail to bring a child into the world, Mariel could do it as well. And as Trystan had reminded her, she would not have to fear losing her ability to navigate the sea if he provided for them while she carried the child. Perhaps she could swim the same as a pregnant dolphin.

"I am out of my depth here," he said honestly, handing the child back. "You will have to tell me what to do next. Do I find the priest to marry us? To bless the child?"

"For now, you will have to eat the food we brought with us. Francine has been in labor all day, and there is nothing prepared. I will start a broth for when she wakes. I don't know if Father Antoine has returned yet. You could go to the church and ask, I suppose, but the christening must come first, and it will be some days before we're ready for that. We'll have to prepare a feast and send invitations."

His brows drew together. "Could that other woman with your sister not make those preparations? It's imperative that we return before the last day of the full moon. We could sail to Aelynn and be back in days."

We. Not he. With that one word, Mariel knew the chalice and the moon weren't all he had on his mind. Her silence still had to be ensured by taking his strange vows. If she did not go back with him, he would be banished, lose his home, his world, his future.

If she went with him, she would come back a different woman. The idea had had time to grow and become a part of her, in the same way Trystan had infused her soul.

She was ready.

Shivering at the immensity of the decision she'd just made, Mariel cuddled her niece to her shoulder and took a deep breath to steady her voice. "There are still coins remaining from those we left with Francine. They will pay Helene to stay with her for a few more days. With Helene's help, Francine can begin the preparations for a feast. I will have to wait until my sister wakes, though, to tell her that I'm leaving again."

Trystan's golden eyes darkened to a deep indigo she could not read, but the color took her breath away just the same. She could stare into his eyes for the rest of her days, fall into them as into the deep blue of the sea and never come up again.

"Tell her," he urged, "and we'll sail with the tide before dawn. And when we come back, I will take the vows of your church for all to see that you are mine."

In that moment, Mariel could almost believe that they would be a couple in the eyes of God and church. He meant to return with her. For how long?

She had never prepared for this, but she discovered she wanted it more than she had ever imagined. To wake beside him every day . . .

But that would still not be. He would return home to take Lissandra as wife and assume his proper place in his proper society, leaving her to cope alone.

If her grandmother could do it, so could she.

She studied hard on the man who watched her so hopefully. Even in shirtsleeves, with his cravat loosened to reveal glimpses of golden curls, Trystan looked imposing and all-powerful. A stray strand of hair fell from his queue, emphasizing the stubborn strength of his jaw. She could never hope to find a man like him again if she should live forever.

She bowed her head in acceptance and hugged the babe. She wouldn't be totally alone if he gave her a child.

She nodded her agreement to his wishes.

Twenty-six

Hating that they must sneak about like common thieves, Trystan shifted the burden of the sack containing the chalice to his shoulder and placed a proprietary hand at Mariel's back to steer her past a raucous tavern in an alley near the cliffs.

"What are all these people doing in a tavern at this hour?" he asked grimly. He meant the question to be rhetorical. He knew what sailors did in taverns.

"Talking politics," was her unexpected reply.

"Your country is mad," he muttered. "If it has not learned to govern itself after so many centuries, how does anyone expect to correct that fault now?"

"It's my home," she replied simply. "Would you leave your home for mine?"

"I can't. I am the island's Guardian." He had been relieved when she'd finally agreed to exchange vows with him, but now he had to undertake the burden of educating her about what their bonding meant. "I know you do not understand how our society works, but without me, my home would be overrun and destroyed by invaders."

"And how does it fare now, without you?" She hurried to keep up with his pace.

Trystan could tell from her tone that she asked simply to hear his voice and hide her nervousness while they hurried down darkened streets toward the harbor. There were an unusual number of soldiers lounging about for a port so small. He had the uneasy feeling that the country was gearing up for war, and he didn't wish to be caught in the middle of it. He tucked the chalice beneath his arm to hide its bulk.

"If I am not there to draw on Aelynn's power, the fog shield will begin to crumble when the moon grows full and the tide rises. That is why I must return home shortly." He glanced at the sky out of habit. One more day.

"And you must be on the island to do this?" she asked, following his gaze.

"I have not done it any other way," he admitted. "We draw our strength from Aelynn."

"The island, or the god?"

"I will let Dylys explain," he grumbled. "I am no priest."

"This way," she murmured when they reached a street overlooking the sea. "There are ways down to the shore without taking the main road."

Within minutes they had reached a wall of tumbled boulders that looked impassable. Mariel scrambled onto them as if she were half seal, disappearing over the far side into the inky shadows beyond.

Trystan tied the sack to his waist so he might find hand- and footholds in the rocks and follow his slippery mate. With any other woman he might plot to hold her on Aelynn once they arrived, but he could never imprison Mariel. How the gods must be laughing at this trick they played to show he was not master of all he surveyed.

On the other side of the boulder, she slipped from a crevasse to catch his hand and guide him down a cliff path that only she could see. Lifting his head, Trystan could just distinguish his sloop anchored in the inlet where he'd left it, and he let relief carry him swiftly forward. He'd feared the moneylender might have sold it or sent it fishing, but it was obvious the man had no idea what to do with so valuable an item as an Aelynn ship.

"How do you produce your shield?" she asked. "Can you not try it from here if you must?"

"I cannot feel Aelynn's life force from here. I must connect with her and the waters surrounding her. How do you feel when you swim beneath the sea? Is there not some . . . connection . . . between you and the water that allows you to breathe?"

"I can feel the sea now, feel the tide changing, the waves breaking as if they're in my blood." Reaching the sand, she threw back her cloak and lifted her arms to the sky, letting the salty breeze plaster her garments against her as she exulted in the force of the ocean's power. "I understand what you say," she called over the noise of the breaking waves. "I could not feel this in Pontivy, but the closer we came to the sea, the stronger the . . . *connection* . . . as you call it."

He could feel it, too, a sensual roll of waves rhythmically building to a greater tide, drawing him to Mariel like iron to lodestone. With the chalice bouncing against his thigh, Trystan caught her slender waist and hurried her along the sand, unable to separate the pounding of his blood from the pounding waves, and reveling in both.

"The sooner we return to the island, the sooner we can connect on all levels." He stated fact, but the words emerged as an erotic promise.

She flung him a look that said she knew and understood and accepted, and his spirits soared with the wind that would take him home.

He'd found his mate, and the primitive animal inside him roared in victory.

* * *

The perpetual fog around the island crept into the nooks and crannies of the rocky shoals, dancing upon the warm waters in misty whirlwinds of sunlight and shadow as the sloop approached the island in the early twilight of the next day. From here, the island was invisible to human eyes, but Trystan felt its power and sensed the shimmering shield that prevented unauthorized entry.

He glanced at Mariel leaning against the mast, and wondered if she sensed the protective force he wielded, just as he experienced the sea through her.

Her light muslin gown, wet from the mist, clung to her curves like a second skin. She'd left her cap behind, and her hair streamed in the wind as she sang a tune filled with longing and hope, although even he could not translate the words.

Over this past day, he'd taught her how to set the sails and heel and tack in the wind, and she was keeping an expert eye on the canvas.

As aware of him as she was of the sail, she turned to meet his gaze, and her song changed to one of homecoming—the Siren tune they'd heard when last he'd sailed home.

He knew then that it had been Mariel singing, not imaginary Sirens. He didn't have the answer to all his questions, but he had the answer to an older fable. Mermaids and Sirens were descendants of Aelynn, left behind in the Other World and longing for home.

The straits were too narrow for him to leave the sloop unguided, so he could not ask her if there were others like her beneath the waves, luring men from Aelynn. He wished they had many nights ahead to discuss the differences between their two worlds.

Instead of questioning, he turned his attention to the force swelling inside him. He needed to vent it now by drawing power from Aelynn to heat the sea.

"Take the wheel," he ordered, startling Mariel from her song.

Eyes growing wide, she hurried to do so, holding the wheel steady so he could strip off his shirt, revealing his armbands. They were there to protect his body from the full brunt of Aelynn's strength, allowing the power to pour into the shield rather than him.

Trystan spread his arms above his head to take the full impact of Aelynn's force. Lightning crackled through his blood and radiated from his pores. The bands on his upper arms caught the energy and multiplied it, feeding and fortifying the invisible force that would guard the island for another moon cycle. The rush of power reinvigorated him, set the hairs of his arms on end, and produced the golden glow of sunlight like an aurora around him. Once again, he rejoiced in his ability to perform his duty.

Throwing his head back, boots firmly planted on the deck, he parted the shield in front of the sloop, allowing Mariel to pass through without harm. No loud boom permeated the air this time. Aelynn accepted his amacara.

With a sweep of his hands, he closed the barrier behind them again, and gave thanks to Aelynn for her help and guidance.

Then he reclaimed the wheel, brushing a kiss of thanks across Mariel's brow. The golden aura surrounding him would fade within minutes, but he basked in her awe and appreciation now. Mariel's earlier song had seemed to add speed and potency to his task, and he smiled at her, nodding for her to look behind them.

Aelynn's fog now shimmered with the rainbow colors of happiness. She gave an excited cry of surprise that warmed his blood as much as the tropical air flowing around them. He'd always thrilled in his duty, but Mariel's admiration added an extra spice that made all his sacrifices worthwhile. She touched his bare chest as if to test the glowing energy, and he sucked in his breath at the electricity of the contact. She jerked her hand back, then daringly kissed him where her hand had stroked.

Trystan thought he would surely go up in flames. To his relief, she laughingly darted back to her post to help guide the sloop through the final strait.

Iason and Lissandra, the Oracle's son and daughter, waited at the dock as the sloop sailed into the calm, turquoise waters of the bay.

Lissandra wore her golden hair clipped with tortoiseshell combs, but the breeze still tugged at loose curls. She looked like a goddess, but Trystan didn't experience the same warmth of desire for her that he did just thinking about his amacara. The Oracle's daughter possessed greater powers than anyone on the island except her mother. Since leadership was bestowed based on the mutual ability of a couple, Trystan could expect to claim the highest seat on the Council when he married her. But the power he'd thought would fulfill him did not equal the deep-seated pleasure he found with Mariel.

Mariel, he wanted to explore. With Lissandra, he would always be at odds. There were infinitely more advantages to an amacara.

Mariel would bring him joy and terror, as she had these past days, but there would also be this deep, abiding affection. With Mariel, he had found the gift Aelynn would bestow upon him above and beyond the call of duty.

But Lissandra was the island's future, and so she must be part of his future as well.

The Oracle's daughter crossed her bare arms over her tunic in a gesture that conveyed both defiance and disapproval, and Trystan's heart sank. Wooing her for his wife had just multiplied in difficulty—she had "seen" why he'd returned with a live mermaid.

Iason walked out on the dock to help Mariel make the leap from the sloop. Both tall, slender, and dark-haired, the Oracle's son and Mariel made a picture-perfect couple, and Trystan felt the cold bite of jealousy—until Mariel turned a laughing smile in his direction. In that moment he realized she had not looked at another man since he'd met her—despite the many eligible males she'd encountered.

A fierce pride of possession welled inside him at knowing that Mariel had no need to look at any other. It was not a noble sentiment, but he could not deny his satisfaction.

Stepping up to the dock, Trystan clasped Mariel's waist and calmly handed the sack bearing the chalice to Iason. "You may have missed this by now."

To Trystan's surprise, Iason gave the sack little notice. "Not so much as you might have thought," he murmured, eyeing the two of them with interest.

Shocked by Iason's nonchalance toward the sacred object, wondering if Iason even knew the chalice had gone missing, Trystan changed the subject to one of most importance to him. "We are returned and ready to say our vows."

The Oracle's son lifted his dark eyebrows. "That is a change of heart since last we saw the two of you. Does the mermaiden agree and promise not to steal away again?"

Mariel's smile could have blinded the sun. "I am ready, but I shall always come and go as I please."

"I think not," Lissandra murmured silkily, crossing the sand to join them. "You misunderstand the forces here if you believe you have any choice in the matter."

In another time and place, Mariel might have been

intimidated by the golden goddess who apparently wielded powers that awed even men. But she'd just seen Trystan's full powers, seen how he'd drawn energy from the land he guarded and applied it to the crystalline sea around them, seen the marvelously strong man that he was, and understood his responsibilities more fully. She admired a man of his greatness for accepting her as she was, even after enduring all the trouble that she'd brought down upon his head.

And she knew he would never allow harm to come to her.

She nodded acknowledgment of the other woman's declaration. "Admittedly, there is much I do not understand yet," she agreed. "And I regret any trouble I may have caused you. But I cannot regret what I did if it means my friends and family will not starve. Do I owe you an apology for being what you are not?"

Trystan coughed and Iason chuckled. Lissandra granted them haughty glares.

"Aelynn does not bestow miracles without a price, as you have already discovered. You would do well to anticipate what additional cost you must pay. I am needed elsewhere this evening, so I will bid you good fortune on your mating and blessings on the child to be conceived. Good day." She nodded regally, and without waiting for their reaction, glided into the long jungle shadows.

Lissandra knows we have returned as mates. Mariel glanced at Trystan to see if he regretted his decision, but he wasn't even watching his intended. He was smiling down on her, and she basked in his admiration.

"Forgive my sister," Iason said stiffly, shifting the sack holding the chalice to his shoulder. "She lives with the pain of too much knowledge and does not always know how to hold it back."

"Nor does she care to learn how," Trystan replied

with a shrug. "You do not need to make excuses for Lissandra. She is what she is. I never meant to add to her pain."

Mariel wrapped her fingers around Trystan's arm. "I think she brings the pain upon herself," she said softly, feeling for the right words. "Holding herself aloof is how she has learned to deal with what she sees, but it hurts."

Iason looked upon her with a glint of admiration. "You understand more than you think if you know that much. Lissandra could never have bonded with Trystan as you have. She would not have allowed it."

He looked at Trystan. "But my sister is right. You have made a choice for which you must pay. You will want to see your friends and family before you make this commitment. I will take Mariel to the temple."

With his free hand, he gently tugged Mariel from Trystan's arm. She threw a look of panic over her shoulder as Trystan stepped away, effectively abandoning her to this stranger.

In the fading sunlight, her bold, brave, giant of a *mate* looked grave, and sadness colored his eyes. Or was that regret? She could not tell. The distance and the shadows between them were too great as Iason hurried her toward the jungle path.

Lush leaves shut out the last rays of twilight, but Iason led the way without hesitation. Fireflies flitted among the vegetation, flashing against the luminous reds and yellows and whites of the flowers she could smell more than see. Exotic aromas filled her senses, and perhaps she remembered that most of all. They reminded her of the musky scents of sex and perfumed soap and instantly aroused her despite her fear.

"You need not be afraid," Iason said, as if reading her mind. "You will see Trystan again tomorrow at moonrise, if my mother approves the match."

"Tomorrow? Why not tonight? I must return home as quickly as possible," she argued, in a panic. She had been imprisoned here once. Had she misplaced her trust in Trystan and was to be imprisoned again? Was that what his eyes had been telling her?

"You both need rest," said Iason reasonably enough. "The ceremony is not brief, and we must give the gods time to choose your child. We are not so very different from your people. Trystan's friends will wish to ply him with strong drink and help him say farewell to his bachelor ways."

He halted to regard her with a worried frown. "You do understand that this is not a casual union? If Trystan had wanted a mistress, he could have taken you as your grandfather took your grandmother. Or he could have returned you here and handed you to the Oracle to do with as she pleased. The bond you will make tomorrow is permanent. It cannot be cast off, even in his absence."

Mariel sniffed in disparagement. "You have not suffered this amacara bond, have you? If you had, you would know you are telling me nothing new."

She could feel Trystan under her skin even as they spoke. She'd felt him in the fog that guarded the island. He was a constant warmth in her chest and womb.

Just watching him sail his sloop had been an erotic experience beyond any she could possibly dream. She knew the lean golden flesh and muscle concealed beneath his clothes. When he'd fastened his heated gaze on her over those long hours, it had been easy to imagine him steering his will directly toward her. It was like watching two ships on a collision course. Soon, they would both be in pieces.

"The gods grant strength to those they tear asunder," Iason said, shifting the chalice and once again half dragging her down the path. "You will find you are stronger as one whole than as separate halves."

"Are you reading my mind?" she demanded, too agitated to be polite.

"You are practically screaming your thoughts. I cannot help it," he apologized. "I am usually good at shutting out other people, but admittedly, I do not often come in contact with Others. Your mind is more open and accessible than ours."

"I do not thank you for that knowledge," she grumbled. "That will assuredly drive off any intimate thoughts I might have."

He chuckled. "By the time you see Trystan again, you will have forgotten my existence. My mother has been Oracle for forty years and grows weary of the burden, but she still enjoys the anointing ceremony that brings new life to our old world. She will prepare you."

"You're all very certain about this ceremony, aren't you? I have known couples who have been married a lifetime and never conceived a child. I do not believe in magic or your gods, and I cannot believe that one night in your temple will ensure any such thing."

"It will for amacaras, whose bodies are meant to be mated. You do not have to believe. It will happen. You must simply prepare yourself and be ready. Trystan is a wealthy man. Afterward, he can take you into town and let you choose a house you may furnish as you desire. The child will need many things when it enters this world."

Another statement bound to cause her panic. Mariel wanted to dig in her heels and halt this rush toward destiny, but Iason's pull was too strong. *Trystan's* pull was too strong. She could not turn back.

"I will not be staying here," she asserted, to prove she was still herself and not a broodmare for these people.

Iason halted so quickly she almost smashed into him.

"I was afraid Lissandra was right." His dark eyes glowed in the moonlight filtering through the fern trees. "Her visions are prophetic but seldom clear. She says the children in our future will be born on the edges of hell. I knew she did not mean here."

"*Here* is a beautiful prison," Mariel retorted, the words coming to her tongue without thought. "The real world, the one we must make better, lies beyond your waters."

That was not a thought she'd ever had reason to think in her life, but as soon as it was spoken, she could see that it was true.

Even Iason nodded thoughtfully in acknowledgment. "You are possibly right. Trystan thinks that Lissandra shares his vision of the future, but secretly she views the world beyond the Guardian's shield as hell, because she does not understand it."

"Then it's time she learned. Education and experience are the first steps toward understanding." Deciding she'd had enough of this weirdness, Mariel pulled her arm free of his grip and marched on ahead of him, to the shining stone temple.

Iason cautiously kept the chalice in his possession when he turned Mariel over to his mother.

Twenty-seven

The usual noisy arguments, drunken songs, and clattering of mugs in Teutor's Tavern ground to a halt when Trystan entered. Evidently, word of his arrival and his predicament had already spread throughout the bachelor village.

"Did I sprout horns while I was gone?" he asked dryly of his audience, signaling Teutor's wife for a tankard of the island's ale.

"Lissandra has bedded no other man, if that is what you ask," Waylan answered, breaking the silence and allowing the murmur of gossip and clink of glasses to begin again. "But methinks we see a golden chain wrapped around your John Peter. Do we say farewell to another of our merry band of bachelors?"

Trystan tried not to wince at the image as he accepted his tankard and shoved his way to the bar beside his friend. But his *John Peter* twitched and his thoughts instantly traveled to Mariel. Golden chains didn't begin to explain the bond between them.

"Marriage to Mariel isn't in the plans," he said coolly, but even as he denied marriage with Mariel, he couldn't find the words to explain why. He phrased his mating in ways they could grasp. "But Aelynn may have another l'Enforcer in the spring."

Shouts of "l'Enforcer!" and "Amacara!" rang through the room, along with the crashing of tankard against tankard. Waylan clanked his mug to Trystan's, and Nevan slapped his back so hard Trystan nearly spewed his ale.

"Congratulations. She's a beauty. You are fortunate to find such a one in the Other World. May the two of you breed a multitude of talented l'Enforcers to shield Aelynn into the future." Nevan signaled for another round. "Keep them coming, Trudy! We must give Trystan strength for the coming night."

"An aching head won't give me strength," Trystan commented, but he accepted the second round after throwing back the first. The next twenty-four hours would be long, and he wasn't feeling patient.

He dismissed Lissandra's vague warning about the price he would have to pay. She would do better to keep her obscure predictions to herself if she couldn't interpret what she saw, and to Hades with her if she merely meant to play with his mind.

"It's not your *head* that's needed when the moon rises," Kiernan, the Finder, jested, echoing Trystan's thoughts. "The part with the golden chain attached works fine without thinking."

Laughter erupted and the jests turned blue—as if Trystan needed encouragement to think of the night ahead when he could have Mariel in any way his imagination conjured. His loins would burst with need before then.

Oddly, lusty thoughts did not fill the hollow ache left by Mariel's absence. His friends no longer provided sufficient companionship. The pastimes that had once made him yearn for home now seemed juvenile and lacking in ways he could not quite identify.

Perhaps a *real* round of swordsmanship, instead of that tepid encounter with the duc's guard, would let off some steam and keep him from thinking too much about what Mariel was doing now. . . .

"Mayhap you'd have a woman, too, if you thought with your head instead of your balls," Trystan countered, releasing his rapier and stepping back.

"I have more brains in my nose than you have in your balls," Kiernan returned with the senseless boast of too much ale, reaching for his own weapon. "And I'll prove it."

"To arms! To arms!" Waylan shouted as Kiernan and Trystan squared off, rapiers reflecting lamplight.

With shouts and laughter, the all-male crowd spilled into the street.

"I'm relieved to find you still here," the Oracle said dryly, entering the chamber as Mariel blinked awake.

The cave admitted no light, but somehow Mariel knew it was dawn. She'd slept away her first hours in Trystan's mystical home.

The tall lady in brown robes held out a pewter goblet. She wore her thick silver hair stacked loosely on top of her regal head, as if she ought to be wearing a crown instead of acting as servant. "This should refresh you. You needed rest before we could begin."

Mariel rubbed her eyes, brushed hair from her face, and tried to adjust to this new and strange environment. "How do I know it's dawn?" she asked sleepily, reaching for the goblet.

"Aelynn tells you. This is good. It means you are truly connected to us, and bodes well for your bond with Trystan."

Dylys sensibly said nothing further while Mariel sipped juice that tasted as she imagined ambrosia would taste. She glanced at the milky orange liquid in surprise. "What is this?"

"Unobtainable anywhere else in the world," Dylys said. "Mostly it is oranges, lemons, and coconut juice. But I must teach you a lifetime of lessons in a day, so I have added ingredients granted to us by the Ancients."

"The Ancients?" Mariel sipped the drink more carefully. After this past exhausting week, her strength ought to be flagging by now. But the juice flowed through her blood with swifter effect than strong wine.

The Oracle arranged a tray of hot rolls and honey at a cupboard on the rocky wall. "The Ones Who Came Before Us. We do not have time for lengthy explanations, but the chalice is one of the many artifacts they have given us to guard and use wisely. You see their work in the standing stones of your own home. Have you never wondered how such immense stones could have been carried from so far away?"

"I had not realized they came from anywhere else but some poor farmer's field, although I did wonder why anyone would waste so much energy standing them on end. They make a poor foundation for a house." Mariel tore into the roll offered and let the exquisite bread melt in her mouth. She would be tempted to stay in Trystan's home for the bread alone. She wished she could bring Francine and the babe here.

"You are a practical person. That is good. Not everyone is, and you were not raised among us, so I feared otherwise."

Mariel wasn't quite accustomed to the leaps in topic that came so easily to the Oracle and her children. "Thinking of house foundations is practical?" she asked warily, trying to follow the path of her logic.

"Yes. Others see the stones and have fanciful notions of faeries and witches and giants. You think of houses. And of your sister. She cannot come here, but I'm sure you realize that."

In some manner, Mariel understood why Francine would be forbidden these pleasant shores. That did not mean she'd accepted it. The finality in the Oracle's comment forced her to admit that Francine would never see this land—especially since the woman guarding it seemed to have the power to read minds.

"The legends of the Ancient Ones have been garbled over time," Dylys said, "interpreted to suit people and society, much as has been done with your Bible. I think our legends and your holy books have much in common, as most religions do. It's my belief that they come from the same source but have been interpreted differently as cultures grew apart."

She waited again, giving Mariel's thoughts time to catch up. Since realizing the church would most likely condemn her to death should her unusual abilities be discovered, Mariel had been wary of the religion into which she'd been born. She knew there was a God, because she could not imagine the myriad creatures of land and sea and all the wonders of nature could exist without a Supreme Creator. But she questioned Father Antoine's narrow teachings far more than she ought.

"You are saying your God is the same as mine?" Mariel asked.

"Quite possibly. I am not so arrogant as to believe we on this small island worship the only true God. At the same time, I fully believe in my God and His apostles and cannot envision the heavens populated with different gods looking over all the diverse people on this earth, or a pantheon of unruly giants as the Greeks and Romans believed. I believe there is only one God. The difference in our religions is simply in how we choose to worship Him."

"I thought you worshipped Aelynn, the volcano?" Mariel asked tentatively, before biting into the last roll.

Dylys placed a plate of fruits on the tray. "The

mountain is a symbol and has become part of our society, just as your statues of Mother Mary. It is simpler to assume one's God lives inside a mountain when this island is all one knows. The more well traveled of us have wider perspectives, but sometimes we use the simpler references of our childhood. And since we believe that God is everywhere, it is not unreasonable to believe He is in the mountain."

"Trystan believes in Aelynn," Mariel argued.

"Of course he does. He feels her force just as you do. He has seen the world and knows our people are blessed as most others are not. That does not mean he can't understand that Aelynn is a physical representation of the same God you worship, and that our minor gods are similar to your saints."

Mariel sighed and shook her head. "It would take a lifetime to ask all the questions necessary to understand you."

"Precisely. All you need to know now is that you and Trystan worship the same God, just in different ways. Just as we interpret the will of God in different ways. The two of you must work out these differences between you for the sake of your children."

"Any children I have must be raised in the church," Mariel protested. "To do elsewise would make them outcasts."

Opening the cupboard, the Oracle reached into the hidden depths of the highest shelf and brought down a vial. She assembled an assortment of jars and tins on the table. "I have not learned of any other amacara living off the island in recent times. The earlier ones have all been disastrous. You may wish to seriously reconsider your decision to return to your village."

No judgment tinted her voice. She continued mixing

her powders as if she'd merely stated a mathematical theory rather than asking Mariel to give up her life.

"I cannot," Mariel whispered, no longer hungry for the delicious fruit. "I have agreed to come here only because Trystan insisted that it was necessary. I knew it would create difficulty. If you think I should, I will leave now. I promise not to tell anyone of this place."

In saying this, she broke her heart and handed it to Dylys. She would love nothing more than to live in this ideal world, making love and babies with Trystan. But she may as well say she'd like to die and go to heaven. Heaven didn't need her. Francine did.

"Don't be foolish, child," Dylys scoffed. "Finish your breakfast. From what I can see, you would be swimming here or Trystan would be sailing to your world on a daily basis if we did not go through with this ceremony. The bond is forged. It needs only approval of the Ones Who Came Before Us. After that, the two of you will have to find your own path."

"You will not force me to stay here?" Mariel asked, still wary of imprisonment.

"No. Once your vows are made and you wear the ring of silence, you are as free as the rest of us to come and go. It would be preferable if you returned here for the birth of your children so they can be official Aelynners and granted their rings without any ceremony. But if that is not possible, then they must return before they reach puberty so they may be initiated without need of a spouse or amacara."

Mariel sucked on a sweet orange and pondered this complication. She truly had not thought this through, but there had scarcely been time to discuss all the elements of courtship, much less the problems of children. "It will seem strange to my family for me to leave home to give birth, but I would like any child we might have to know his father. Trystan must teach our offspring of Aelynn and the things I never learned. Perhaps that would make our child more confident than I was while growing up."

"Excellent, and very wise. The two of you will need wisdom to reconcile your upbringings. You would not marry a prince or a Russian without considering these things."

Given the disparity of their homes, she may as well have been marrying Russian royalty. Mariel shivered, feeling more like a broodmare or a mistress than ever. She and Trystan truly had only one thing in common.

"Not true." Dylys matter-of-factly threw a mixture of herbs into a steaming cauldron over the fire. "You have acknowledged in your heart that Trystan is not like other men. You converse together, and he listens, honors you by giving you choices and respecting the ones you make . . . and you really must learn to curb your thoughts when you visit here. They can be quite painful to those of us who are sensitive to them."

Mariel contemplated crawling under the covers, then deliberately attempted to blank out that thought.

Dylys chuckled. "You might have difficulty thinking nothing. Your mind is much too active. For now, it will be easier if you try to remain composed. Emotions shout more loudly and are harder for us to screen out."

"It is a little difficult to avoid hysteria under the circumstances," Mariel said carefully, practicing serenity. "You truly believe that Trystan and I have more in common than a bed?"

The Oracle laughed, a pleasant chime that warred with her ascetic features. "Well done. You learn quickly. I only felt your rebellious desire to scream at me this time. If you were of the hysterical sort, Trystan would have drowned you before now. He is not normally a sentimental man. He lost his parents when young. His sister raised him until he was fifteen. He's been sailing the seas since then. His pets are the main recipient of his affections."

Rather than stamp her feet in frustration at never receiving a direct answer, Mariel sought the screened chamber pot she had used the prior night. She took advantage of the break to assimilate all the information the Oracle had doled out in chunks as large as she could consume.

When she returned, the bed was gone and a tub of aromatic water stood in its place.

The older woman gestured at the bath. "We will begin with the cleansing ritual. This is usually performed by the bride's friends."

"You raise more questions than you answer," Mariel complained, examining the enormous tub with suspicion. "Where is this place? How did you fill the tub so swiftly? Do you mean to boil me alive?"

"We are in a limestone cavern beneath the forest floor, and the hot springs provided by Aelynn are piped in to fill the bath. We could use the grotto, but I prefer to contain the full effect of my herbs in the tub. Vows of silence are not magic. They happen for reasons not easily explained. I believe you have a man of science called Mesmer who might shed light on some of the powers of the mind, although he doesn't possess my herbs and can't do what I do."

Dylys gestured at the nightgown Mariel had been given the night before. "If you feel better wearing the gown into the bath, please do."

Feeling like a fool submerging in a bath wearing linen, Mariel clung to this last measure of modesty in a place where even her thoughts were exposed. She caught her breath as she climbed the step and dipped her toe into the scalding water.

"You won't burn, I promise." Dylys had already crossed the room to light tapers, whose incense filled the air with the fragrance Mariel remembered from her first visit.

This was really happening then. She was preparing for her wedding night. Of a sort.

Lifting the hem, she dipped her leg deeper. The water welcomed her like smooth silk. "Tell me what Trystan and I have in common," she asked again, to keep hysteria at bay. For all she knew, Trystan's people were cannibals.

At the Oracle's chuckle, Mariel flushed and lowered herself into the tub. For whatever reason, Dylys reminded her of her own mother, and she trusted the older woman to teach her what she must know to make this joining with Trystan work, for his sake as well as her own. He was sacrificing a great deal for her and perhaps harming his beloved island in the process. She hoped Dylys could show her how to prevent that.

A man who had never known family ought to have a woman's love, but she could not fathom how to give it to him from a distance.

The heat relaxed Mariel's muscles until she felt like seaweed floating on the ocean's edge, and the Oracle's voice came to her from beyond the gentle lap of waves.

"You are both intelligent, independent, headstrong, and care for others above yourselves. You lead with your heart and Trystan leads with his head, but together you possess the best traits of Guardians to pass on to your children."

Children. Dreamily, Mariel lay back against the tub rim and let the water touch where Trystan would plant his seed. She was finding it amazingly easy not to think while snuggled in the luxury of steam and the scents of exotic flowers. Dylys set a brace of candles on a table beside the tub, and incense wafted around her, adding to her disorientation.

"I cannot help but think the gods have chosen a mermaid for a l'Enforcer's mate for a reason. My powers begin to fade with age. There are times of trouble ahead for which I am not adequately prepared." The Oracle's voice twisted languorously into the smoke and steam, while Mariel floated in pleasure.

"I see your children protecting us from underwater. I see some things poorly and cannot always understand," the Oracle continued. "Perhaps they carry the force shield beneath the sea."

Mariel could not respond. The high-pitched, haunting quality of the Oracle's singsong voice held her captive with its resemblance to her mother's. Somehow, she understood the prophet was drifting into the same trance that held her enthralled.

"But just as Lissandra does, I see your children growing up elsewhere than on the black sands of Aelynn," Dylys continued dreamily. "They do not belong here, with us. They are like seals who warm themselves on our shores and then swim away. You cannot take the easy road and let Trystan rule their future by keeping them here. It will be your duty to open their eyes to a wider world. As it will be your duty to guard your shores from the terrors of fire and blood to come."

Terrors? Mariel had drifted on a cloud until a suddenly unruly wind arose with her fear. In her mindless state, she tried to grasp the mist and only wafted deeper into shadow.

The Oracle's predictions murmured like leaves on a tree, spinning on the breeze raised by the smoke of bonfires, swirling Mariel farther away.

"Your life will be a long one. Do not fear when

danger lies ahead. The gods have appointed you for a purpose. Heed them, and your future will be safe. Heed them not, and you will die as selfishly as you lived."

Mariel lost consciousness as the Oracle whispered, "Beware of Murdoch until he repents and the chalice returns. . . ."

Twenty-eight

"The Guardian succumbs," Iason said dryly as Waylan and Kiernan lugged Trystan into the grotto.

Awakening to the clatter of sandals on rocks, Trystan grimaced in pain. He didn't attempt to unwrap his swollen tongue from his gritty teeth for fear one or the other would fall out of his head. *What in Hades had happened?* He never got drunk.

"Took a dozen of us to bring him down as you requested," Waylan said bluntly. "We thought we'd have to slam an iron skillet into his skull before he'd give in. I don't suppose you can explain why he had to be rendered unconscious?"

"All will become clear in time," Iason intoned. "Although alcohol is preferable to mashing his brains with a skillet."

Trystan's head felt as if they'd used that skillet. Or two. He never lost melees. He didn't remember going down. But now that he was awake again, he was beginning to feel the sharp sting of cuts and bruises, and he remembered the mugs of ale with which they'd rewarded his wins. The dastards. They'd provoked him deliberately. Why had they needed him unconscious?

"He must be ready to accept Aelynn's will, but turning his skull to mush wasn't what I had in mind. Couldn't you have at least had a Healer look at him before you brought him here?" Iason asked, poking at a particularly agonizing slice in Trystan's shoulder.

"If anyone so much as said a word within a hundred feet of him, he went for his sword. Lust and frustration and the strength of ten men form a lethal combination."

Kiernan's voice. His friends had tried to kill him.

Trystan wrinkled his brow. No, he'd tried to kill *them*. The memory of the battle swirled away on alcohol fumes.

Iason growled something contentious, but Trystan lost the gist of it when he was unceremoniously tipped into the steaming waters of the grotto. Water closed over his head. Gasping and thrashing, he fought his way up through the bubbles.

By the time he reached the surface, his friends were gone, and Iason alone remained.

The tall mystic looked down with amusement from his lofty perch on the edge of the waterhole. "My father once told me he was relieved that your father did not take an amacara but chose to use the altar with his wife. It seems all l'Enforcers have hard heads. It is not easy to soften them with mere herbs. An amacara ceremony requires surrendering independence, and men of power have difficulty accepting that."

Treading water, Trystan rubbed his eyes and tried to wipe away the grogginess of alcohol and the saltiness of the mineral water dripping down his brow. Aelynn's hot springs mixed with the sea's currents in the cavern. The grotto was the birthplace of Trystan's talents and of the fog that shrouded the island's secrets—the ideal setting for a ritual cleansing. But Ian was more friend than priest.

"I don't think further softening is required in my

case," Trystan said with a hint of irony, squeezing his eyelids closed against the agony of his pounding head. "I have agreed to this without coercion." He shouldn't need to confirm his willingness to take Mariel as his amacara. All she had to do was think, and he rose to the occasion, literally.

"That's a matter of opinion. If my mother had not told you to either kill Mariel or bond with her, would you have gone after her?"

He didn't know. He wasn't the same man he'd been a week and a half ago. "I accept the fate the gods assign me," he replied, recalling his near blinding panic every time Mariel was endangered. He'd been somehow bound to her from the first moment he laid eyes on her.

"You haven't accepted as much as you ought. I am a poor Seer who refuses to predict the future as my mother and sister do, but I am not blind, either. You're too damned stubborn and proud to follow anyone's orders unless they suit your own desires." The last words sounded closer to Trystan.

He started to open his eyes, but Ian shoved his head under the water before he could speak.

Spluttering, Trystan fought his way back up and glared at the Oracle's son. "Are you trying to get even for every time I bested you in swordplay?"

"My father isn't here to act as priest, and my mother is busy anointing your intended for the ceremony, so the duty of teaching you Aelynn's will becomes mine," Ian said with a gleam in his eyes. "Remember who I am, if you please."

"You're an arrogant piece of—"

Ian shoved him under again.

Diving down, Trystan yanked his nemesis's legs from under him, pulling Ian into the water with him.

With their clothes tugging them down, they could do no more than tussle and emerge coughing to glower at each other.

"That's why a priest needs to be old," Trystan pointed out. "It's hard to take a man seriously when you've seen him in filthy breechclouts."

"You'll take me seriously before this is over," Ian warned, swimming out of reach and melting into the deeper shadows. "You're still fighting Aelynn's will."

"How do you know Aelynn's will?" Trystan yelled after him.

"How do you know how to shield the island?" Ian called back. "It is who I am, what I must be, and you will have to learn to respect that. I know Aelynn expects more of you than you have yet admitted." Water rippled and splashed as Iason climbed out. "Bathe, and I will send a Healer to tend your wounds."

Trystan closed his eyes and let the steam bathe his bruises. He might survive if Ian left him alone.

"Push aside your material desires and let Aelynn show you your true needs." The words echoed hauntingly from the cavern's interior. "There are three hours until moonrise," a final whisper reminded him.

Until moonrise, when he could finally have Mariel.

Picturing her as he'd seen her that first day, pinned to the altar, raising her hips in invitation, ripe for the taking, Trystan quit treading water and submerged his own head.

Three more hours as a single man. Three more hours before he planted the seed that would make him a father and burden him forever with duties on two shores.

Picturing Mariel at the prow of his ship, black curls flying like a banner in the wind, siren song haunting his heart, Trystan realized Iason was right. He was fighting Aelynn's will and the future assigned to him.

He didn't want to take Lissandra as his wife.

When the Healer arrived with her sleep-inducing potions, Trystan gladly lost consciousness again.

When Trystan awoke, it wasn't to the steam and gloom of the grotto but to a million blinking fairy lights in the night sky, a cool wind on his skin, and a glimpse of the clouds at Aelynn's peak through a hole in the tree canopy. He lay still, not daring to move while his skull cleared of whatever magic brew had been fed to him.

A rustle of shrubbery warned of someone's approach, but he was not yet ready to wake fully. He was home and did not expect treachery, so he relaxed into the moment. The Healer had soothed the wounds he'd gained in fighting. His limbs felt supple and strong. The stink of ale had been replaced with the exotic scents of unguents and lotion. He was lying on his back and gazing at the stars and awaiting a beautiful woman. What more could a man want?

A slight feminine gasp drew his gaze back from the leaves to search the surrounding shrubbery. He made several shocking discoveries at once.

He was in the temple—which meant he was lying on the altar.

It was nearly moonrise.

And the altar held his wrists and ankles firmly clasped so that he could not move.

Damn Iason was his first enraged thought. And then Mariel appeared at his feet, and he could think no further.

She was beyond lovely, ethereal in gossamer cloth like some moon goddess. He could see the rosy color of her skin through the wispy fabric, but she wore her hair over her breasts so he could not see their darker aureoles. Still, his flesh rose at the sight of high, rounded curves and slender waist.

"I do not understand," she whispered, staring unabashedly at his nakedness. She traced his toe with an outstretched finger, as if to test his reality.

Just the touch of her finger caused blood to rush to his groin, and Trystan bit back a groan of desire so as not to frighten her. "It seems I am the one who must be forced into submission," he ground out through clenched teeth.

He'd anticipated this moment for what seemed like his entire life, but not this way, not helpless to claim his elusive mate. Frustration boiled through his blood. Tied up like this, he was hardly the god and savior she'd once thought him.

He *wanted* to be her hero, he realized with a pang.

"Submission?" She eyed him warily.

As well she ought. He was rapidly becoming rock hard and straight as a flagpole. And somehow, he had to persuade a wary almost-maiden to accept him while he lay here like a damned sacrificial virgin.

Rather than explain what little he knew of Aelynn's archaic ceremonies of submission, Trystan took the more appealing route. "You must choose me as your mate for the ceremony to take effect. I have already chosen you and said my vows the first time we made love. Now, it is your turn to make your promises to me and to Aelynn."

Mariel's eyes widened into golden orbs that fed his hunger even more. But she did not seem any closer to climbing up on the altar with him.

"I don't know what to do," she said uncertainly, seemingly unaware that her fingers stroked his foot, his calf, driving him mad. But her touch, and stare of fascination, returned some measure of his self-esteem, even if his ability to think clearly still faltered.

"Anything," he muttered. "*Everything.*"

As Mariel continued to hesitate, Iason's counsel in

the grotto slowly penetrated the fog of Trystan's desire. He was *still* fighting Aelynn's will and the future assigned to him, just as Iason said. He had yet to accept Mariel as his equal.

Mariel had trusted and accepted all Trystan had told her, even though this was not her world. She was willingly sacrificing herself and her future, for him. Somehow, he had to show that he deserved her trust. He must meet her halfway, as equals in both their worlds.

If he could not . . . Fear gripped him—fear that she would change her mind. That she would leave him here like this. Alone.

He couldn't bear that. He summoned all the words available to him to woo and win her, words he should have said much earlier. In doing so, he knew he did what was best for both of them, and for the child they would share. Fighting his aggressive need to take and possess, he sought a part of him long buried.

"Push back your hair," he said gently. "If you will not take off your gown, I wish to see as much of your beautiful breasts as you will allow."

She was still innocent of her effect on him, unaware of her sexuality. She appeared puzzled as she shook back her hair, then looked down at the high, firm curves barely covered by the gauzy gown to see what held his interest. The naïveté of the gesture nearly raised him off his spongy bed, making him understand just how much she offered.

He needed to touch her, to kiss her, to pull her under him and persuade her back to the intimacy they'd explored in France. And all he could do was watch and pray. Trystan twisted at the unrelenting straps and refrained from bellowing his frustration to the heavens.

"Lift your breasts higher so I can see them," he commanded softly.

She did so without self-consciousness, placing a hand beneath each round breast and holding them up for his inspection. Glimpsing her rosy nipples through the gauze, he thought he might expire of lust right then.

"Is there some way I can free you?" she asked in bewilderment.

She still cupped the undersides of her breasts and unconsciously caressed them as he would have done had he been free. Desire throbbed through him as if his hands stroked her. He had not realized that the bond between them could be used to such good effect.

"What is it I am supposed to do?" she asked.

"Climb up here with me," he requested.

"How?" She studied the way his big naked body filled the giving softness of the altar. "There is no room for me."

"Place your legs on either side of mine," he instructed, trying hard not to imagine further for fear he'd spew his seed just thinking of it.

Intelligent eyes shot him another suspicious look, and he almost had heart failure fearing she would decide to walk off and swim home, and he would have to chase her all over again.

And he would do just that . . . as often as necessary until she was his, he realized with the loss of breath as if from an unexpected blow.

"Wouldn't it be easier if I unfastened the . . ." She studied the manacles on his ankles, apparently not possessing a word to describe the altar's peculiar tendency to entrap its user.

"You can't," he admitted. "The bed is a living being that reacts only to Aelynn's will. There is a place by my foot that you can press if you do not wish the ceremony to continue, but that is all."

He held his breath while his stubbornly independent

mate pondered his admission. He was helpless to stop her. And now she knew it. Her eyes grew round with realization.

"This is really my choice?" she whispered.

He nodded again, too stricken by panic to speak.

She tilted her head in consideration. "I must be the one to . . ." She gestured to indicate him.

His patience fractured. "By Aelynn, woman, if you do not climb up here soon, I will expire, petrified like this for all time. Seduce me or gut me—I care not which," he commanded.

She smiled, and he wondered if he imagined a hint of a smirk in her expression.

With relief, he realized she wasn't afraid, and she wouldn't run away.

To his sigh of exaltation, Mariel located the step at the base and climbed up, lifting her hem and placing one rounded knee on either side of his legs. He hadn't realized he'd been holding his breath until he gulped air into his lungs, and she admired the way his chest heaved.

Mariel was choosing *him*, and the knowledge moved him profoundly. He swelled with pride at her acceptance of their bond. Aelynn had found a magnificent amacara for him.

In the back of his mind, an insistent notion pierced his shield of resistance. Mariel would make an even better wife. But he could not . . . Duty required . . .

Distracted as Mariel crawled up his length, Trystan looked down the opening of her gown, but he could not touch the sweet fruit he saw there, not even when her knees pressed into his thighs, and she was within hands' reach.

"Take off the gown," he nearly begged as she came just short of where he needed her.

His member jutted between them, and she stroked

it lightly, sending paroxysms of desire shooting through him until his hips rose of their own accord. She stared admiringly, then stroked his balls rather than obey his command. The damned woman dared toy with him!

Trystan groaned aloud and thrust upward. "Unless you want our first child spilled on the ground, let me ready you as I am ready."

"You think I am not ready?" she asked in amusement, grasping the hem of her gown and twisting the gossamer over her head, exposing her slim nakedness just as the moon rose into the opening of the foliage to illuminate the fine ivory of her skin.

Trystan devoured the sight of Mariel kneeling above him. Shadows and light played along distinct curves and sculpted limbs. His gaze dropped to her belly, then lower, to the dark moist hair hiding the pink folds he needed to kiss and caress and make his—forever and always.

"Not ready enough," he said hungrily. "Come here. Let me kiss you."

She slid her hands along his chest, teased his nipples, and tugged his hair, until he bucked and sent her sprawling across him. She wiggled upward until his erection stroked the juncture of her thighs; then she propped her elbows on his chest so she could kiss him. The she-devil was in his blood, as much a part of him as the shield surrounding Aelynn.

Heat flared as their breath and tongues mingled. Trystan felt a tugging at his soul, at a desire so deeply rooted that he feared being pulled inside out by the need. He wanted to grab and ravish and possess, and he could do no more than bruise her mouth with demands and strain against his bonds. Helpless . . . vulnerable. *Hers*.

As if she heard his thoughts, Mariel lifted herself

so her breasts brushed against his lips, and he eagerly licked, then suckled a nipple as brutally as the passion tugging at him. He nibbled at her with his teeth until she cried out and writhed against his hips.

"Mine," he growled when she pulled back, speaking from his heart and bypassing his mind. "You are mine, for now and into all eternity. Did Dylys give you the vows to say?"

"I worship thee with my body," she whispered, scooting back down his chest until their sex touched again. "I take thee for father of my child. With this vow, I do promise to take you to my bed, from now until Aelynn calls."

And with that promise, she kneeled above him, held his gaze, and sank slowly down upon his lust-crazed loins until Trystan howled his joy.

Twenty-nine

Giddy with desire, heated to boiling by Trystan's amorous commands, and still reeling from the hypnotic effects of Dylys's ministrations, Mariel surrendered her freedom with relief.

Having Trystan's body filling her hollowness completed her, and she threw back her head, letting her hair fall past her waist to caress his powerful thighs. The moonlight illuminated her breasts as she exulted in the pressure piercing her womb. Lust bubbled up through the bond between them.

"By Aelynn's will, I cannot take another," Trystan gasped, surging upward, attempting to push higher inside her. "I take thee for amacara, keeper of my children, and as *wife*, keeper of my body and soul. Free me, Aelynn, for I accept your will."

Astounded, Mariel stared at him. She watched as Trystan grew still and his eyes widened, as if he'd surprised himself as much as he'd stunned her.

Wife. He'd used the vows for wife and not just amacara.

Dylys had drilled a good deal into her head in the hours she'd drifted on the mystical cloud of incense and herbs. She understood Trystan did not just offer a marriage of convenience or a mating for children. He asked for a mating of souls for eternity, a true *marriage*, and her insides quivered at the enormity of his request. He would give up the Oracle's daughter and his leadership of the island for her? A Cross-breed?

Until now, she hadn't realized how desperately she wanted the right to claim this man as hers. Still she was afraid to believe him, until he spoke.

"I gave up the wrong dream when I found the right one," he declared with the urgency of truth. "You are my heart, my soul, my family. I want no other. I'll do all within my power to see that you never regret it, if you'll say the same."

Mariel's mind reeled at what he'd done, at what he'd given her, and her heart swelled in love.

As if his words had appeased the gods, the altar released the manacles.

Mariel gasped when the powerful male under her suddenly grasped her hips and surged upward. She felt him deep in her soul, and impaled, she could not move.

"Tell me the same," he asked again. "Take me as husband, under the laws of Aelynn. Make our children true heirs to all I possess."

Lost in sensation, she only vaguely remembered why he had resisted this final step. In the power of their joining, the reasons no longer seemed relevant. "I take thee for *husband*, keeper of my body and soul," she repeated, accepting the possession of his body and the ultimate tie that would bind them. "And amacara, father of my children, from now until the heavens decree."

The bond between them melded them into one whole, joined in spirit as well as body. Mariel sighed with the rightness of it.

Trystan wrapped her tightly in his arms and nearly crushed her in gratitude. "Thank Aelynn," he whispered. Softening his grip, he ran his hand along the altar until he'd produced a ring with a sparkling moonstone inset among pearls.

He slid the ring onto her finger. Mariel looked at him in surprise as she felt the ring's binding inside of her.

Trystan smiled. "You belong to Aelynn now. Your body is mine, as mine is yours. We are one. Did Dylys not explain?"

She had, but not in ways that made sense until now. Instead of just feeling the power of his sex, she felt the foggy shield shrouding the island's coastline as he must sense it, felt the beating of his heart inside his chest.

"I can feel the pull of the sea," he whispered, acknowledging her impressions and reciprocating. "The tide is coming in. I can smell it even now."

"Will you be able to swim with me?" she asked, almost forgetting the joining of their bodies in the wonder of being inside of him in this other miraculous way.

"I suppose we shall see."

Abruptly, her new husband rolled her under him until his broad muscled chest loomed over her, and she was looking up into the golden excitement shining through Trystan's eyes. His long legs held her pinned against the giving altar. His hair spilled loose over his shoulders, and whiskers darkened his jaw. He was pure male animal, and he was hers. He was inside of her in body, mind, and being.

"Give me your child," she whispered back, feeling her womb soften and open beneath the approval of the one God. She was ready, in both mind and body.

Her hips rose to Trystan's thrusts, but their gazes never parted. Her breasts ached, her breath came in short pants, and her legs wrapped around him to take him deeper. The tightening in her lower belly threatened to explode as he swelled to fill her. And holding her shoulders pinned to the altar, Trystan thrust with the force and power of a pagan god.

The clouds parted from the mountain, hot sparks shot from Aelynn, and the sky exploded in fiery stars. With wild, shouting abandon, Trystan pumped once more, then released his seed deep inside her.

The sensation stung like sparks inside Mariel's womb, even as her muscles spasmed in ecstasy, bringing her hips higher, forcing the seed deeper, until it found its destination and multiplied in a fertile sea, and she cried out her joy.

Joined and shuddering and overawed by the miracle, Mariel wrapped her arms around her golden god and let tears of happiness seep from the corners of her eyes as they returned to earth.

She knew beyond a shadow of a doubt that she had just conceived an Aelynn child—and oddly enough, she knew her mother's promise had come true.

"One more time before dawn," Trystan insisted with a teasing smile, fingering Mariel's nipples into tight points and releasing the liquid between her thighs that eased his way inside her. "We will make love as man and wife, not as creators of Aelynn's spawn."

They'd slept their wedding night away, cradled in the softness of the altar, watched over by the temple and the mountain—giving his heir time to take firm root.

"I can feel the child growing inside me," Mariel said in awe. "How is that possible?"

"You feel the spirit who entered you," he explained, swelling with pride. "The spirits of the Ancient Ones do not leave this island but linger in the temple, waiting for the creation of new life. I suppose spirits may wait elsewhere for the moment of conception, but in the temple, it is a certainty, if Aelynn approves."

And Aelynn had approved with glowing showers of fire. Lying sprawled on top of him, where he'd returned her, Mariel touched her forehead to his in acknowledgment of his God as hers. They were one and the same now.

He kissed her with warmth and understanding as he stroked her into readiness.

She rose to her knees, and he groaned in pleasure as she willingly sank down upon his arousal. With natural grace, she moved with him, riding him as she rode the ocean's waves. He closed his eyes and fed on the sensation she projected, feeling her joyous uplifting as he thrust, and all thought ceased.

At the moment of their release, Trystan gripped Mariel's buttocks and pushed, pumping deep inside until sparks flared inside his head as they had burst above Aelynn earlier. He felt her muscles contract and expand, felt her release spiraling higher, and then felt the explosion as his seed collided with the waiting life inside her.

A silver shadow slid between them, and Mariel cried out her surprise when it entered through him. Trystan felt the ripple along his still engorged sex, felt the sliding sigh as the spirit slipped inside the new life they'd formed, and he shivered in amazement.

Instead of collapsing in his arms, Mariel pushed up on her hands to stare down at him. Their gazes locked, and wordlessly, Trystan wrapped his hands around her waist and pressed his thumbs into her flat belly.

"We created two," he murmured in astonishment. "There are two lives in there." Children of his own, to cherish and care for. The wonder of it astounded him.

His new bride began to shake, and he pulled her

slender body into his arms and held her close. What had he done to her?

"Let us leave before we create a litter," he whispered against her ear, before either of them could regret or fear the night they'd spent together.

She choked on a sob of laughter and nodded.

"I want you to see what Aelynn has to offer," Trystan insisted, dragging Mariel through ripe vegetation and explosions of flowers. He was already making mental lists. They needed to legalize their marriage vows publicly in front of the Council and in her church. He needed to provide for *two* children. He was still staggering under that knowledge.

But most of all, he wanted Mariel to stay here, where he could take care of her and the two lively l'Enforcers they'd just created. His heart was beating so fast in anticipation that he could scarcely contain it.

He had a family. His narrow world suddenly widened and gleamed brand-new again. He wanted to jump with joy like a lad of ten, and he couldn't wipe the foolish grin from his face.

Mariel seemed somewhat shaken and silent at the enormity of what they had done. She had a right to fear the changes ahead. But Trystan was confident that he and Aelynn could take care of her.

After washing in the spring water of the temple's basin, they'd donned the matching wedding raiment Dylys had left outside the temple. Trystan's tunic fell loosely over white trousers, trimmed in the same Roman border pattern as Mariel's sleeveless gown. Fine white linen embroidered in gold braid flowed loosely over her breasts and down to her bare feet.

Her hand kept creeping to her belly, as if she was half-convinced the prior night had been one of the Oracle's incense-enhanced dreams. But the morning's conception was clear in both their minds. Aelynn hadn't erupted, but the ground had moved. Trystan had no idea what that meant. He'd have to ask Iason.

The smocked gathering at Mariel's waist molded the cloth enticingly to her curves before flowing down over her hips. Her ring sparkled in harmony with his, and he smiled as she kept pushing at it in wonder. His fit perfectly and comfortably, but like hers, it could not be pulled beyond the knuckle. He could *feel* her ring, as he felt the bond between them. She was tied to Aelynn just as he was.

And between them, they had created two tiny miracles. His children were mere specks, no bigger than the sparks Aelynn had showered into the sky. He sensed they were as ephemeral as those sparks and might blink out if not tended with care.

She needed food. And he was aware of her hunger. Trystan laughed and halted, reaching into the tree above his head to produce a long yellow fruit. He held it upright for her to admire. "Is it not a large and naughty specimen?"

At sight of the thick, long fruit, Mariel blushed. From his warm gaze, she knew her new husband was remembering how she'd stared at his arousal the night before. It had been most impolite of her to stare, but she hadn't been able to help it. He was a magnificent male, and she loved looking at him.

Unbalanced by all the strange sensations she'd experienced at his hands, she accepted the fruit and tried to determine if she could bite into it or must peel it. "Not so large as my husband," she admitted, acknowledging his jest. "But this is a much prettier color."

He coughed on laughter and outrage, grabbing the fruit back and peeling the sides to reveal the ivory flesh. "The island natives where this comes from call it a banana. But it is too soft for any use but this." He set the fruit between her lips and let her nibble.

She savored the sweetness and decided it was safe to eat.

"Your lips are a pleasure that can be used for better purpose once we reach the house," he murmured seductively, capturing her waist and tracing a finger down her breast.

Instantly, she saw the image he had in mind, and she nearly choked on the banana. She could do *that*? She stared at the fruit in wonder and tried to imagine it.

"Perhaps you might start with licking it," he prompted teasingly, guiding her into a clearing dominated by a low, sprawling house and a yard full of goats.

"Stop that," she replied, striving for outrage but still too in awe of what was happening to manage it.

He'd taken her for *wife*. The immensity of Trystan's sacrifice was overwhelming, and she did not fully understand his capitulation. She supposed there would be time to comprehend it in the years to come.

Their sexual bond had not diminished with lovemaking, but Mariel realized she could resist it a little easier now that the first hunger had been assuaged. She knew precisely what he had in mind and was eager to experiment, but she didn't have to do it right this minute. Maybe in the next half hour, after she'd had time to explore their surroundings. And eat.

"We really must try lovemaking without baby making," Trystan insisted cheerfully. "We are free to try it anywhere." Glancing toward some shrubbery, he rolled his eyes and murmured, "Excuse me a minute."

Startled, Mariel halted where she was while Trystan strode—or leapt, his steps were so high—over an overgrown thicket of brambles. An instant later, he returned carrying a small bleating goat under one muscular arm. He briskly checked the animal for harm, tugged its silky ears, then returned it to the grassy turf. "Bitsy thinks the grass is sweeter if she has to work for it. We'll never be able to use her hair for weaving if it's full of brambles."

Finishing the fruit, Mariel held out her hand to the brown-and-white kid, who sniffed tentatively and then tried to taste her. "She's adorable. Is she yours?"

He gestured at the small herd nibbling the shrubs around the house. "They're the largest animal we grow on Aelynn. Lissandra accuses me of making pets of them, and I suppose she's right. We don't have dogs, and they keep me company when I'm home."

"You don't eat them, then?" she asked as the animals began bounding toward them. She had a hard time imagining a man who commanded ships sitting at home alone with none but his goats for companionship. Her heart grew softer at this side of her new mate, and she took his arm and leaned her head against it. His muscles tightened beneath her touch, and he pressed a kiss against her hair, proving that he would be a loving, thoughtful husband.

"We breed them for milk and for their fine pelts," he said, easing her concern for his pets. "We buy most of our cloth from your markets, but we have women who can spin magic with goat hair."

He gestured toward the low, sprawling house they approached. "This was my parents' home, and now it is mine. I have a chair inside that you might enjoy. A quick lunch and a little practice session, perhaps?" he asked with a leer.

"You are trying to seduce me into thinking I belong here, aren't you?" And it was almost working. Her own home, plentiful food for her babes, and a man vho would make everything easy for her. "But I'm ike Bitsy and must work for my sweets. I must go iome. I promised."

She had an obligation not only to Francine but also o the Oracle. Dylys had been fretful when she'd come out of her trance, brushing off questions with clipped nstructions. Mariel had been inclined to dismiss the predictions that had come to her through a haze of ncense, but after the miracles of last night . . .

She thought perhaps her husband's people were a ittle more in touch with what heaven wanted than she iad realized, and she had better listen to their priestess.

Dylys had told her she must go home and guard the shores and the people of both Aelynn and Brittany against some unnamed *terror*. Not to do so would be fatal.

Obviously Trystan had not been given a glimpse of their fate. He still belonged here. Sadness tinted everything that passed between them now.

"I can take you to visit Francine and her child anytime you like," he was saying, hoping to override her fears as he led her through the yard to the handcarved door. No glass filled the windows, although the shutters would keep out rain and sun.

Mariel stepped inside to cool tile beneath her bare feet and sun spilling over an open room bigger than Francine's entire cottage. "It is lovely!" she cried in surprise.

The trunks of tall, straight trees provided posts for the thatch of the roof high above their heads. Benches adorned with tile and painted designs circled the columns. A large trestle table covered in a mosaic of bright red, yellow, and blue flowers gleamed in the light coming from the long oblong window at the rear of the house. A cone-shaped terra-cotta fireplace was centered on the far right wall with a pipe running up through the thatch to release the smoke.

Chairs and lounges, padded so thickly that they appeared to be pillows, were covered in a sturdy fabric of a natural oatmeal color. She knew exactly which inviting chair Trystan had in mind for their lovemaking, and she had to tear her gaze away to explore the rest of the house.

He slid back a rattan screen to reveal a wide bed covered in the same oatmeal fabric and piled high in colorful pillows. Bamboo tables were littered with books and writing utensils, as if he spent many nights here at his studies.

"I thought you lived in the village," she said rather than admire his home too overtly.

He lived simply, but in a house more beautiful than even the one her father had once lived in. Sunshine and warmth filled every cranny.

"I prefer the space here for my pets, and our children." Standing behind her, he wrapped his arms around her waist. "I can bring you silks from the Orient, flowers from the tropics, all that your heart desires."

"You will have to stay a trader merchant because you married me," she said sadly. "You have lost your chance to lead the Council because of me."

He cupped her breast and brushed kisses into her hair. He was taller and broader, and Mariel could lean against him and feel secure in his embrace. All should be right in her world. New life grew in her belly. A beautiful home lay before her. She had a husband who had given up duty for her and promised her the stars.

But if she believed his God and priestess, she had to leave this heaven.

"I have what I want right here," Trystan said, rubbing his hand down her belly. "You and our children are more than enough for any man."

And even more sadly, she knew he lied.

She turned and patted Trystan's whiskered jaw and gazed into his silvery eyes. Storms of uncertainty roiled there. "We are bonded now, husband. I will soon know you as well as you know yourself. You were made to lead men and run countries. You are a defender of justice. You are not a merchant trader. Come, let us eat, and then you will take me home. I don't know how to rescue you from the life of a merchant, but I do know I must go home."

Trystan's arms tightened around her. "You are being foolish. How can you give up all this for that chaotic place?"

She shoved away from his hold and crossed to a kitchen cupboard. "In the same way you cannot give up what is yours to follow me. The Oracle said we have much in common. She was right in that."

"You are mine," he said stubbornly, setting his hands at his waist and not moving from where she'd left him.

Mariel flashed him a sunny smile. "As you are mine. And when I swim away from here, you are free to follow any time you like."

She prayed he would. But men like Trystan didn't like being thwarted.

Thirty

A hearth maid appeared to wield her special brand of magic in the kitchen, then departed as silently as she'd arrived, leaving steaming bowls of scrumptious mussel stew and loaves of hot bread to fill their empty stomachs.

"I wish I could take her home with me," Mariel said wistfully, savoring the stew and inhaling the yeasty aroma of bread. "I would never have to cook again."

"You would never have to cook again if you stayed here," Trystan grumbled.

She did not deign to answer that since he already knew her reply.

"If you insist on returning to your home, I will build you a house and dock by the shore where I can come to you more easily," he said, stirring his stew while making mental lists.

"My father's house is empty. If you can afford to build a house, you could afford to buy it back from the vicomte," she suggested. The idea of living in that gloomy old house without family—or Trystan—to fill it with laughter did not interest her, but the easy climb to the beach did. She tried hard not to panic at the idea of living without him. When had she become so dependent on him? It was not like her at all, and she wasn't certain she appreciated being left so vulnerable to heartbreak. She would spend the rest of her life wondering how her husband was doing, what he was doing. She lost her appetite just thinking of it.

He nodded grimly. "If that is your wish. We will sail my schooner back, so your people know that I am not a poor man. I will reimburse the moneylender for the sloop, buy the house, and we will marry according to your customs."

"You will have to tell the priest you are Catholic," she pointed out. "You do not fear frying in hell for lying?"

"I am Catholic. I am all things. And I do not believe in any hell except on earth."

Given the suffering she'd seen these last winters, Mariel was almost inclined to agree. "And after we're married in my church?" she asked.

His eyes looked bleak. "My crew can still use my talent for translation. I am still needed here once a month to replenish the shield and to sit on the Council. Since I cannot interfere in your world, I cannot see that I will have much to offer there."

"Except to me," she said softly. "Could you promise to see me once a month as well?"

"I want to see you every damned night." He angrily scraped his chair back and stalked outdoors to greet a messenger who had just whistled his arrival.

The two men spoke while standing in the neglected gardens that surrounded the house.

Mariel could feel his love for his home and for his pets. She could feel his longing for a stable life, one where his intelligence, knowledge, and strong sense of justice could lead his people wisely.

But if she truly had been touched by his vision of God, she had to believe that her place was in Brittany.

Would it make a difference if she told him what Dylys had predicted? Or would it make him angrier and more unhappy? Was it preferable to have him angry with her or with his God?

After feeding his animals, Trystan strode back to the house with a determined gleam in his eye. She met him at the door, threw her arms around his neck, and let him carry her to the big bed, where they made love instead of babies for the first time as a married couple.

The first rays of dawn tinted the distant horizon and lit the high peak of the main mast. Not needing to look to know that the tide was rolling into the shores of Mariel's home, Trystan leaned his back against the schooner's rail while Waylan steered toward the harbor.

Now that the island's shield was reinforced, the ship was loaded and prepared to return to its trading. Trystan contemplated signaling Waylan to sail for England and their first port rather than stop here to leave Mariel behind, but it would be a fruitless command. His mermaid wife would simply leap overboard and swim ashore.

As if his thoughts had woken her, Mariel appeared in the hatchway. She clambered out easily enough, but not before Trystan recognized the difficulty she would experience in a few months with the unwieldiness of pregnancy.

Twins. They weren't unheard of on Aelynn, but they were rare. He wanted to shout the news to the world, but superstitiously, he preferred not to tempt the fates.

He could scarcely contain the chaotic emotions overwhelming him at this moment—pride, terror, sorrow, and this deep abiding connection with the beautiful woman gliding toward him, gleaming more brightly than the morning sun. He could endure the chaos, for her.

Beyond his momentary shock at the altar, he had no doubt that Aelynn had helped him choose the right path in taking Mariel for wife. He had felt complete from the moment the vow had left his lips.

Mariel stopped to study the shoreline. She wore a sari he'd given her, one of midnight blue with silver stars woven into the edges. Perhaps after a few weeks in her company he would take for granted the lithe grace with which she moved, the way she tilted her head in delight when she looked at him—but he doubted it. The mating bond coiled tighter around his innards.

"We are almost there," she murmured, coming to stand so close that the wind blew her skirt around his bare legs.

He'd donned the shirt and breeches of her home but had not yet encumbered himself with boots and stockings.

"I will understand if you tell me to jump off so you might be on your way," she continued at his silence.

Trystan snorted. "You'll not be rid of me so easily, Madame l'Enforcer. I intend to come ashore and rip your life asunder as neatly as you have mine. Fair is fair."

Her laughter tumbled like music in his ears. She was his soul mate in truth if she understood his irascible humor.

"My life could use a good upheaval," she said cheerfully. "Could you start by throwing the tariff collectors into the bay so we can bring in wheat without paying a fortune for it?"

That gave him something to ponder while his crew hauled sail and weighed anchor in Pouchay's natural harbor. A few fishing boats stirred farther up the coast, but dawn had not reached the darkened town. How would he provide for Mariel and her family without interfering with the workings of her supremely illogical home? It was one thing to take a mistress in the Other World and leave a pearl beside her bed when he sailed on—but he would have to behave while waiting for their marriage, and every time he visited her.

He would have to visit often. He could not live long as half a being.

"I hope your sister has arranged our wedding for tomorrow," he said grimly, "or I might be forced to slay dragons."

She nodded solemnly in sympathy. "I wish I understood the wisdom of your Ancients in forbidding interference in the world. It seems to me your strengths almost *require* that you interfere."

"Power is a temptation even for us. And with our abilities we would all soon be dictators," he said dryly.

Brawny Waylan approached, his rolling gait adjusting to the dip and sway of the ship with a sailor's ease. "The dinghy is ready any time you are. We'll wait out here until you signal that you want to come back."

His crew had been pragmatic about his decision to return Mariel. Aelynners seldom brought Crossbreeds to live on the island. Of course, the crew had not yet realized Trystan had both bonded with Mariel and married her.

Taking his wife's elbow, Trystan guided her toward the small boat that would take them ashore.

Mariel scanned the cliffs. "I think there are soldiers up there."

He'd seen the flicker of a campfire and the shadows of movement against the night sky, but he had no fear of soldiers. "They have no interest in us. We're not smuggling contraband."

"Still, I prefer my beach rather than the harbor, if you don't mind."

He'd have to climb like a goat again, in the dark, but it was a reasonable request. He had no desire to deal with obnoxious soldiers before the crack of dawn, either.

Trystan helped Mariel scramble over the ship's side and down into the dinghy, then began the silent row to shore. The sun was still a faint orange streak that disappeared behind the towering cliff as they approached the beach.

"I can't wait to see Francine's baby," Mariel said nervously. "I need to learn about diapering and feeding. Do you really think I am carrying two, or was I dreaming?"

Trystan tried to imagine his impulsive, generous wife burdened with the mundane tasks of bathing and diapering two screaming infants and could summon no more than a growl in reply. "There are two. I felt them as clearly as you did. I hope one of them has the gentle spirit of a Healer or hearth maid. Two Enforcers would require an army of nannies."

"I'm sure that could be arranged if we acquired the debt of a duc," she said with a dismissive wave. "Were you a troublesome lad?"

"I nearly pushed Iason into Aelynn's maw once. I needed the constant guard of all the island's inhabitants to keep up with me." He checked their position from over his shoulder. "Do you see someone by that pile of rocks over there?"

Mariel glanced toward where she had once hid her clothing on nights like this. "If so, he's but a boy or a midget. There, I think he's coming forward to greet us."

"Nick!" Trystan said in exasperation, recognizing the boy's rigid stance at the same time Mariel did. "Has he run away again?"

"I told him he must seek us out if he should need us. Do you think the chevalier has turned into the beast we feared?"

They were already moving with more speed than any normal man could achieve, but Trystan rowed harder. Hiding her husband's skills in the village—as she had done her own—would be impossible. Men were not inclined toward subtlety.

The shadow darted into the surf and gestured frantically, but his shouts were lost in the pounding waves.

The oar hit sand. Mariel lifted her hem and clambered out, letting the tide slap against her bare legs as she rushed toward shore. Behind her, she knew Trystan more sensibly pulled the dinghy to safety. She liked knowing she had a man at her back who handled the practicalities and protected her while allowing her to act on her impulses. It added a layer of freedom she enjoyed.

"Nick, is that you? What is wrong?" she called.

The boy rushed to grab her, nearly knocking her over in his haste. Whether he meant to help her from the water or hug her, she couldn't tell. The wind tore at her hair, and she wrapped an arm around his shoulders, allowing him to lead her into the lee of the tall rocks.

"What is it? What brings you here?" As her toes reveled in the cold sands of home, frantic questions raced through her mind.

"The king's soldiers," she thought he said into the clamor of wind and waves.

Trystan strode bare-legged up the shore, wearing the breeches he'd donned while she'd slept. He grabbed her by the shoulders and hauled her into the shelter provided by the rocks.

"The chalice," Nick gasped, almost weeping. "They are calling me thief and murderer and say the chevalier is harboring me and that we have stolen the king's chalice. They mean to execute all of us!"

"All?" Mariel inquired, her hand flying to her throat. "Trystan? Francine?"

Nick shook his head. "No, no. Me, and the baroness, and my guardian. There are posters everywhere calling us thieves and traitors." His breath caught on a sob before he continued. "The king's troops are surrounding the Assembly in Paris, calling their demands treasonous," he cried. "And the soldiers here say they are defending the country by executing those who conspire against the king."

The Assembly—where Francine's husband had gathered with all the other elected officials hoping to solve the country's weighty problems. Did the king mean to imprison his own government? Alarm whispered along her skin. Was this the beginning of the violence the Oracle had predicted?

"It isn't the king's chalice," Trystan protested. "It's mine. I paid the chevalier for it before it ever reached Paris. This makes no sense."

Trystan was right. None of it made sense. But in a country rapidly descending into anarchy, logic had little to do with the unfolding events. Mariel clung to her husband's arm and waited for his assessment. Nick wiped his eyes and did the same.

"Murdoch," Trystan said. "The king knows nothing of the chalice. Murdoch has learned it has escaped him. Where are your guardians?"

"Celeste has friends," Nick replied. "We hide with them, but we cannot stay there much longer."

"How did you know to find us here?" Mariel asked, fearful others also knew of her hiding place.

"Your sister," he told her. "Here, I am just a boy no one notices, so I slipped away. She told me to watch with the incoming tide. I have been here for hours."

Mariel turned to her husband, to the tall golden god who had once before refused to help her. She understood his reasons now. He'd been forbidden to aid people who were not his own. He had come ashore now merely to complete the legal transfer of his sloop and to marry her according to the customs of her church. He had fought for the chalice because it was his duty to guard it. It wasn't his duty to guard Celeste and her patchwork family.

Mariel held her breath as Trystan scanned the campfires on the cliffs, then stared down at her. She couldn't identify the color of his eyes in the darkness.

"Aelynn does not have soldiers," he told her. "She has Guardians."

Mariel waited, understanding the torment writhing in his heart, feeling it in her own.

"My duty is to guard our own, and you are mine," he continued.

"What is mine is yours," she whispered, grasping his dilemma.

"I must believe Aelynn bound us for a reason." Trystan straightened his shoulders, then briskly returned to the dinghy and removed their belongings. He threw his coat over his shoulder and buckled on his sword before striding back to them.

His hand curled around her nape. "By taking back the chalice, I have caused this conflict. I will undo it. Nicholas, return to your guardians. Have them gather what they wish to bring with them and meet me here this evening, after dark. I will take them to safety in

England." He nodded at his vessel bobbing in the harbor. "Quickly. I have work to do."

Nick darted glances at both of them, then tore off at a run down the beach.

Not daring to question, Mariel donned the cloak Trystan handed her, then lifted the hem of her sari and followed him up the rocky path to town.

Thirty-one

"I did not think to see *you* again," the moneylender said, rubbing his sleep-encrusted eyes. His night-cap dangled over one shoulder as he blearily regarded the newcomer who'd woken him with his hasty pounding on the door.

"Circumstances made it necessary to take the ship so I could pay my debt," Trystan said. "I apologize, but here is the amount we agreed upon." He placed the bag of pearls on the man's desk. He'd taken time to don boots and stockings so he did not appear a complete pirate.

"France is beset by thieves who do not pay their debts." The moneylender's eyes gleamed avariciously as he sorted the pearls by size. "The rich prefer to spend without labor, and they borrow against to-morrow."

Trystan shrugged, eager to be gone. "People who do not work are leeches upon society, unless they are spreading their largesse to the community in other ways."

"That was how it worked in the olden days." The moneylender nodded in approval. "But now we have no enemies for knights to fight, and the ladies use their wealth for jewels instead of charity."

Trystan thought of Mariel and her sister, starving while their breadwinner had gone to Paris to fight this injustice. Where would the villagers go for food and physicians? He could provide money for Mariel and her family, but no one should have to live as her neighbors did.

It was not his place to interfere, he reminded himself sharply.

"Perhaps there will be a good crop this summer," he said, heading for the door.

"It's too late for that." The old man slid the pearls into his lockbox. "There is no money for seeds, there are few crops in the field, and the king has hired mercenaries to protect him against his own people. Paris is on the brink of an uprising. I am taking my family from here, as are others with the wealth to do so. I'd advise you to do the same."

Trystan hurried through shadowed streets with the old man's prophetic words gnawing at his insides. He had learned leadership from the perspective of a life of comfort and security, but he had a crude understanding of the politics in the countries to which he sailed. He understood that France had gone heavily into debt fighting wars against their old enemy, England. Bad weather had devastated what remained of the poor laborers' ability to pay increasing tariffs. Without income from taxes, the country had no means to repay its debt.

If the nobles of Mariel's country allowed this situation to continue, then they were bankrupt indeed, morally and fiscally, and revolution was inevitable.

With a heavy heart, he slipped down the alleyways to Francine's cottage.

Mariel greeted him at the door with a babe in her arms and a smile that warmed his heart. Despite her earlier protests that she did not want children, she seemed to take to them with ease and joy.

"I think Aelynn is looking after us," she whispered

to his astonishment, catching his arm and dragging him inside the parlor. "Father Antoine did not return from his sabbatical, and the bishop has sent a replacement. Come meet our new priest."

A priest. They could be married. With his promises fulfilled, he could persuade Mariel to sail with him. Hope rose.

The tiny cottage was filled to overflowing with white-capped women bearing trays of food, toddlers racing to and fro, and solemn men eating their way through the repast spread upon the table. Trystan gazed about him in bewilderment. Surely he had not been at the moneylender's long enough for news of their return to have spread so far.

Only then did he realize the guests hadn't gathered for his nuptials. They were here for the baptism. Unlike on Aelynn, her world did not center around him.

As Mariel shoved him into the throng, Trystan called upon his rusty social skills. He was not accustomed either to anonymity or domestic hospitality. Council meetings were solemn occasions that did not involve food and children. His bachelor village was more inclined to swordplay and drinking than neighborly gossip. He did not have a large family that might gather on holidays. Now, he wasn't entirely certain of the appropriate behavior.

Once he was married in her church, he would become one of these people. He tried to think of any other Aelynner who might provide some guidance, but he could not.

Before Trystan could panic and balk, Mariel introduced him to a tall, gaunt man in priest's cassock and collar. A gnarled brown hand gripped his when Trystan extended it. Taking a deep breath, he schooled his mercurial eyes to a neutral gray and lifted them to acknowledge the introduction.

Blue, gray, and aqua twinkled back at him.

"Father Gaston, this is my fiancé, Trystan d'Aelynn. Trystan, Father Gaston is from Quimper. He tells me he was once a fisherman."

"A fisherman who was called to the priesthood?" Trystan asked, not daring to believe what the priest's eyes were telling him. A *Crossbreed* as a priest?

What abilties might the man have? Would he understand Mariel and their children better than his narrow-minded predecessor? Of course, unless he'd been born on the island, the priest knew nothing of his Aelynn heritage.

"I could not ignore the miracles that saved my life on many occasions," the priest replied, not seeming to notice anything abnormal about Trystan, even though his eyes had probably changed to the brown of surprise or relief.

Of course the man didn't notice. Only Mariel understood about the eyes. The priest was accustomed to seeing changing eye color in his mirror.

The *miracles* of which he spoke . . .

Sometime, Trystan would have to have a long talk with the priest and try to discern what special ability had inspired the miracles. Not now, though, with all Mariel's family around them. But the priest raised wellsprings of hope. Mariel's excitement fed his.

"God works wonders," Trystan replied reverently, and he meant it.

"I understand from Mademoiselle St. Just that there is some desire to hasten this marriage?" the priest inquired with a hint of disapproval.

"Madame d'Aelynn," Trystan corrected. "We exchanged vows in my home, but she wishes to have our marriage blessed in front of her friends and family. We would not be in such a hurry except my ship sails with the tide this evening, and we thought that with everyone already gathered for the baptism this would be an opportune moment."

The priest nodded his understanding. "In these times, it is difficult to provide a wedding feast as well as a baptismal feast. With such a crowd as this, you are wise. It is a pity the child's father cannot be here. You will stand in for him?"

Stand in for a man he did not know? Trystan had no idea what was being asked of him, but Mariel's eager expression reassured him. Odd how less than two weeks ago he would have rebelled against her requests, but now he trusted her decisions.

Mariel placed the sleeping infant in his arms, kissed his cheek, and, whispering her excuses, hurried to help the other women at the stove.

Trystan stared down at the helpless girl child wrapped in lace. Her eyelids were so fragile that he could see the blue of her blood through them. Tiny rosebud lips worked in the first signs of hunger. Fingers scarcely bigger than Trystan's nails bunched into fists that might someday swim the sea with Mariel's strength.

The child was the granddaughter of a Seer. Francine's child might need guidance as much as his own children. This is what Mariel had been trying to tell him. If he could not take her sister and family to Aelynn, she must stay here to raise and protect them.

She was right, damn the devil and all below.

Reluctantly surrendering to her wisdom, Trystan cuddled the infant and accepted the introductions and well wishes of the people crowding around him.

These people would look after Mariel when he was gone. He would do his best to make a good impression so he would be welcome whenever he came. They could be his family now.

He was thinking he'd have to be here far more frequently than he'd originally planned.

Standing beside Trystan at the baptismal font, Mariel scanned the crowded church with pride and joy.

Francine held the newly christened Marie-Jeanne Rousseau for Father Gaston's blessing while all their friends and family looked on. She'd even seen Celeste and the chevalier sneak in with Nick earlier. Apparently, they had slipped away without the notice of the soldiers. She hoped they'd hidden their belongings on the beach.

For now, she was glad the chalice had brought them all together, forging new bonds with her father's family. She wished there was some way of bringing Trystan's family into their celebration, but they had not even been present at the occasion of their marriage on Aelynn. He'd said they would celebrate at the birth of their children, so she would look forward to that. Nervously, she covered her belly with her hand, still in awe of the miracle concealed there.

Francine stepped back, and Father Gaston gestured for Mariel and Trystan to step up to the altar. This was not the formal ceremony that had blessed Francine's marriage to Eduard. The new priest had simply questioned Trystan about his faith and agreed to sanctify the marriage in Mariel's church, so formalities weren't necessary.

Still, Mariel had let her sister fashion one of their mother's silk dresses into a lovely silver gown trimmed in Francine's best lace, and as a mantle over her hair she was using the exquisite blue sari Trystan had given her. She couldn't have been more elegantly attired.

Trystan stood beside her in the formal blue silk frock coat and breeches of a gentleman. He had calves well shaped for stockings, but she preferred his legs bare, Mariel thought mischievously, admiring her husband as he shot her a look warning her to curb her thoughts lest he embarrass himself in front of God and man. She concentrated on the lace-trimmed cravat Francine had given him as a wedding gift. He wore it proudly over his gold waistcoat.

He took Mariel's hand on his arm and led her to the altar as if he did this every day.

They exchanged the vows of her church and kneeled for a proper blessing. It seemed perfect that the priest who joined them in her world should be a descendant of Trystan's people.

Behind them, women wept. The newly christened Marie-Jeanne began to whimper. Children squirmed.

Father Gaston raised them to their feet again while announcing, "I pronounce you man and wife. You may kiss the bride."

Mariel had never thought she could be so happy as when her golden god's lips claimed hers in a kiss for all her world to see. She'd always thought herself a bit of a rebel. She hadn't realized how much she'd wanted children, or how much she'd wanted Trystan to publicly declare her as the only woman in his life.

But she didn't have even a moment to celebrate and savor being the bride of a golden god.

The church's heavy, ornate doors slammed open, and the stomp of soldiers' boots echoed upon the marble entrance.

"There's the thief! Seize him!" a familiar voice shouted.

Thirty-two

Spreading his massive arms, Trystan swept Mariel, the priest, and Francine past the altar and into the sacristy, with the force of his will more than his strength. They retreated to the sound of screams and shouts from the outraged citizens of Pouchay.

"Bar the door," Trystan commanded before turning on his heel and storming off to confront the intruder and his men.

While Francine cuddled her crying daughter in the closet of musty wool and starched linen, Father Gaston lifted the heavy bolt barring the door into the church and slammed it home.

Unwilling to idle in a closet, Mariel waited for her eyes to adjust, then fought her way past the robes to an exterior door that led to the cemetery. The rectory could be reached by a small path from this door, but she wasn't interested in the priest's house. She simply needed to be outside.

"Mariel!" Francine whispered. "What are you doing?"

"Helping Trystan. If there's a lock for this door, use it when I leave." She was certain the soldiers had no interest in her sister or the priest, but it was best to keep them safe until the rioting was over.

She was less certain about whom the soldiers *did* pursue. She had recognized the voice—Murdoch, who had told them they would never retrieve the chalice. She did not fully understand why he and Trystan were at odds, but she did know Murdoch was dangerous.

For whatever reason, the baroness and her family were in peril because of the chalice that Mariel had stolen.

She breathed a sigh of relief when she discovered no soldiers in the cemetery. Perhaps Murdoch did not realize churches—even very small ones—often had more than one entrance. Or else he was so confident in his abilities that he did not think anyone could escape him.

Outside the high, mossy wall, angry shouts rang out as the crowd from the church spilled into the street. Feelings against the king ran high in Brittany, which had historically been a region independent from France. Small villages like Pouchay were so ignored by the distant court that their inhabitants resented all foreign authority. And Murdoch was very foreign.

Heart in throat, Mariel hesitated at the cemetery gate. Hiding behind the entrance pillar, she searched the scene beyond the bars for any sign of Trystan. It did not take long to identify his golden head above the crowd as he engaged in swordplay with his fellow Aelynner. She swallowed a cry of fear as sharp silver slashed, circled, and clashed at lightning speed.

All around them, soldiers and villagers fought. The soldiers were better armed, but they were mercenaries who did not speak Breton, and they were on unfamiliar ground. The villagers had them surrounded, shouting commands to each other the soldiers could not interpret, wielding rocks and hoes and any other weapon they could scavenge from nearby houses and gardens.

Neighbors bearing more arms rushed out to join the wedding party. Daniel from the jewelry store emerged carrying the rusty dagger he used to protect his inventory. Children raced down alleys to gather reinforcements, and even as Mariel watched, fishermen rushed up the street from the harbor, swinging oars and wielding anchor pins.

She wept at the mayhem, but the king could not send mercenaries to a rebellious, impoverished village without expecting a fight. Her goal was to rescue her relatives and see them to safety, and hope order could be restored.

Although Nick was shorter than most of the adults in this melee, Mariel easily spotted him. He'd stolen a sword and was brandishing it valiantly from the recessed doorway of the rectory. Praying her cousin and her husband had sensibly retreated to the interior of that sturdy stone structure, Mariel fled down the cemetery path to the back door of the priest's home. She had spent many nights slipping unseen through town and had long since learned all the less-traveled paths.

Celeste had already made her way to the rectory's back door by the time Mariel opened it. "Thank goodness," the lady cried. "You are safe!"

Mariel hugged her shorter cousin in relief. "And you! I am so sorry we have brought all this down on you."

De Berrier stepped forward with sword drawn, his once autocratic sneer reduced to anxiety for his wife and ward. "It is not all your fault. I sent a message to the king with my advice that the country could not sustain itself unless he taxed the church and nobility. I had hoped my gift of the chalice would ease the sting. But the messenger continued on without it."

"And I am the one who ordered my servant to take back the chalice without telling my husband's messenger to return also, so the letter went to Versailles without the softening of a bribe," the baroness explained.

"The court is in such turmoil these days that anyone who does not support the king's policies is seen as his enemy."

The chevalier threw a glance at the front door. "Fortunately, I am always prepared for any event. Our funds are invested throughout Europe, and my cousin has papers placing my land in a trust. I simply did not foresee affairs disintegrating so rapidly."

"Trystan's enemy is outside," Mariel explained. "He is most likely the one responsible for this travesty of justice, not your very wise advice to the king. We must get you out of here. I will grab Nick, but the two of you must run ahead and not wait for us."

The baroness wore the billowing skirts and hoops of an aristocrat, but there was no time for her to change. Hand on sword hilt, de Berrier listened gravely.

Relieved, Mariel continued, "Go through the cemetery to the back gate. There is an alley there. Turn right and head for the harbor. We will be with you directly."

She didn't linger to see if they obeyed her orders. Racing past the chevalier, she slid back the locks on the rectory door, cracked it open, and grabbed Nick by the coat. Yanking him inside, she slammed the bolts again.

Nick looked relieved. "Monsieur Trystan is surrounded. I cannot reach him."

"Follow your guardians to the ship. You will have to help row the dinghy, but I don't think the soldiers can follow. It will take time for them to commandeer fishing boats."

He looked uncertain, and Mariel hugged him. "Trystan is special. He will join you shortly. Don't ask him to come back to rescue you, please. It will give me failure of the heart."

The boy nodded reluctantly and raced out the back to follow his new parents. Mariel brushed away a tear and turned to a window. She would weep over the loss of her newly acquired family another time, once she knew they were safe. For now, she had to let Trystan know he was needed elsewhere.

Did Murdoch have any of Trystan's powers to understand other languages? He apparently knew court French, but what about rural Breton, with a dash of dolphin thrown in? If Trystan did not understand, she would try something else, but the bond between them was strong. She'd even understood Murdoch when he'd spoken Aelynn and French. Perhaps . . .

Easing open the casement window and standing on a stool so she could throw her voice above the crowd, Mariel began to sing in a mixture of sea language and Breton. "They are safe, to the sea, to the sea, through the gates of death, my love, I will meet you there."

Visible above the crowd, Trystan's head jerked at the first notes, but his concentration remained on his enemy. Murdoch was a formidable opponent, and the two inhumanly swift men were too enrapt in their private combat to regard their surroundings. Already, their clothes were in tatters, and blood spilled from nicks on hands and shoulders.

Frantically, she sang louder, but a rattle of wine barrels tumbling down the cobbled street from the inn up the hill drowned any further attempt to communicate.

But with the arrival of the first barrel, Trystan proved he'd heard her. Employing the nimbleness of one of his goats, he leaped upon the oak staves, guiding the barrel in a daring form of locomotion to bear down on Murdoch with both rapier and sword.

He was heading downhill, toward the main harbor, aiming for Murdoch and the phalanx of soldiers behind him. A raft of loose barrels ricocheted off stones and walls along the street, forcing soldiers and mob to dodge and leap. Mariel frantically repeated her sea-song refrain. In a minute, he would be past the church and the cemetery wall—

She gaped in astonishment as her gifted husband leaped from his barrel to the top of the wall, seemingly with springs on his feet. The barrel continued without him, parting the soldiers, who dived to either side of the narrow street to escape the cask's gathering momentum. Mariel almost lost sight of Trystan when the staves smashed into a corner house, flooding the street with last year's wine and the scent of grape. Even Murdoch, who had rushed to follow Trystan, had to duck and fall back into a doorway to avoid the tidal wave inundating the street as barrel after barrel smashed into the corner.

Catching sight of golden hair disappearing over the cemetery wall, Mariel raced to the back of the rectory and joined Trystan on the pathway.

Not slowing down, he grabbed her hair, and pressed a kiss to her forehead. "Lead on," he shouted, apparently jubilant at his success.

Rolling her eyes at this indication of his male thrill for fighting, Mariel raced down the maze of alleys she knew by heart. Trystan could run faster without her, but her knowledge would bring them safely to her private harbor.

Reaching the rocky sea path, she could hear the yells as the mob grew and spread through the village. Below the cliff, she could see Nick, loaded down with boxes, rushing for the dinghy while the baroness flung her high-heeled shoes into the sand and grabbed portmanteaus hidden among the rocks.

The chevalier guarded his small family from the rear, sword in hand. He was the first to spot Trystan and Mariel scrambling over the cliff and down the path. Throwing them a salute from a distance, he grabbed the rest of their luggage and raced to follow Nick to the small boat.

"With all those bags, the dinghy's not big enough for more than the three of them," Mariel said, scanning the horizon to see the ship beyond the breakers. "I trust you can swim against the tide back to your ship."

"I'll discover if I have as much of your talent as you have of mine," Trystan said with a triumphant laugh. "You are the most brilliant of wives. I do not even know what language that was you used, but the song was beautiful."

"Breton and dolphin," she called back to him, but the wind may have swept away the words. There wasn't time to explain.

Nick and the chevalier struggled to keep the dinghy moving forward against the powerful current, but weighed down as the vessel was, Mariel feared it was a losing battle. Glancing down the beach toward the village's normal harbor access, she saw that some of the soldiers had fought their way through to the harbor path. She assumed Murdoch must be one of them.

"Can Murdoch sail?" she asked, discarding her shoes as they reached the beach, then ripping at the ties of her lovely wedding gown.

"Can fish swim?" Trystan asked dryly, taking his knife to her laces and splitting them so her bodice fell open, then quickly divesting himself of coat and shoes.

Of course Murdoch could sail. Glancing desperately at the small boat fighting the waves, Mariel dropped her gown and petticoats. "Go on. You must signal your ship to come closer to meet the dinghy."

She knew the incoming tide would make it more difficult for the *Sword of Destiny* to depart, but in the meantime she had weapons to use against Murdock that he would not expect.

If she was very, very careful, no one else would suspect either. She must still live in the village when all was said and done.

Trystan studied her worriedly. "It goes against all I am to leave your side."

This was the parting they had both dreaded. Once he had her family safely on his ship, he would sail away, and she must stay behind. They both knew the transitory nature of life. Mariel tried not to cry as she memorized every line of Trystan's frown, the way gold and brown played in his eyes, the way his desire and fear replicated inside her. She caressed his jaw, and his muscles clenched.

"I would not be separated from you if there were any choice, my love," she said, "but you must trust me now as I trusted you earlier." When he still looked harsh, she speared him with a glare. "Trust me as you would Lissandra."

Face hardening, he grabbed her waist and held her close for a kiss that burned straight through her middle. "More than Lissandra," he growled. Setting her back on the sand, he grimly studied her expression. "That is to make certain you will wait for me."

Holding fingers to her bruised lips, she smiled at his arrogance. "That ought to do it. We have a wedding night to share. Hurry, and come back safely."

She tried not to let tears blur her eyes as Trystan raced out past the breakers and dived in. She knew far better than he that they would not have another wedding night soon. He had to sail the baroness and her family safely to England, and she must remain behind.

May he swim like a fish, she prayed as Trystan stroked out to his ship.

An instant later, she also lunged into the gray waves, but instead of bobbing back to the surface, she dived deeper and swam toward where the porpoises and dolphins played.

Trystan knew he wouldn't see Mariel once she plunged beneath the waves, but he tried anyway. Soon he was past the struggling dinghy and could turn over to watch as Mariel slid out of sight. He didn't think the dinghy's occupants noticed her disappearance, or they would be frantically scouring the horizon for her dark head.

Sensing Mariel's comfort with the currents she swam, Trystan returned to swimming toward his ship with a pain in his heart. He despised leaving her.

He yanked his thoughts back to what must be done. If the *Destiny* could sail closer to shore, he could carry a towrope to the dinghy and the ship could tug it to safety.

Apparently spotting the small craft, the *Destiny*'s crew was already raising sail and maneuvering into the wind by the time Trystan reached them. He clambered aboard, breathless and grateful for the sun after the chilly waters.

"Passengers," he said, before his crew could pelt him with questions. "Murdoch." He pointed toward the harbor and a small vessel raising sail farther up the beach.

"Mariel?" Nevan asked in the same cryptic tone while Waylan shouted orders.

Trystan scanned the outcropping of rocks that formed the harbor, but saw no sign of his bride. "Safe with her fishy friends," he replied, knowing he spoke the truth, although their bond spread thin with distance. What the devil was she up to?

As if in answer to Trystan's question, the man in

the crow's nest shouted, "Whale, to starboard!" as the sails caught the breeze and the ship weighed anchor.

Uttering an expletive, Nevan brought his glass to his eye and with his instinctive knowledge of current and wind, started to call commands to avert disaster—until Trystan smacked his shoulder.

"Mariel," he reminded him. "We are not leaving until our passengers are on board."

Nevan shot him a disbelieving look. "You would prefer we run afoul of a sea beast?"

"I think you underestimate my mermaid," Trystan scolded, hiding a smile as he followed the whale's direction without need of a glass. "When have you seen a whale so close to shore?"

Nevan turned back to watch, as did everyone else not otherwise occupied with guiding the ship toward the dinghy—which bobbed directly in the path of the oncoming whale. The ship, too, was on a collision course with the enormous beast.

"It's a baby," Trystan said reassuringly. "It's all alone and looking for guidance."

"Whose guidance?" Nevan asked skeptically. "Your mermaid steers whales like horses?"

"I have no idea what Mariel can do," Trystan acknowledged, "but can you think of any other reason for a whale to swim into these shallow waters?" Pride suffused him as the blunt-nosed mammal gently bumped the back of the dinghy, propelling it forward and almost out of the water. He knew Mariel was somehow responsible. He wished he could ask her how.

"I think the lady in the dinghy has fainted," Nevan said, following the action through his glass.

"Did that keep the chevalier from beating the whale with an oar?" Trystan asked with interest, leaning against the bow and not following the little boat so much as keeping an eye out for black curls.

"It did." Nevan glanced at him in suspicion. "He's been forced to abandon the oar to hold her. The poor lad is paddling as best he can to keep them on course."

Trystan nodded knowingly. "The lady is a relation to Mariel. She knows far more than she lets on, I believe."

"She knows the whale is pushing them toward us?"

Trystan pounded his friend on the back. "Women are mysterious creatures. You should learn more about them than merely how to seduce them."

With that friendly advice, Trystan tore off his wet shirt, climbed upon the rail, and, glorying in his wife's audacity, dived back into the sea to carry the towrope out to the dinghy.

As much as he trusted Mariel, Trystan didn't trust a whale beneath his ship.

Thirty-three

Mariel watched from a distance as the crew helped the baroness up the rope ladder to the *Destiny*'s deck, followed by Nick and the chevalier. When Trystan turned in Mariel's direction, she waved merrily, hoping he could see her. He lifted his hand, although whether it was in greeting or just to shade his eyes and follow the whale's progress, she could not discern.

She dived back beneath the waters, swimming away from shore.

It was just as natural for her to kick her feet and glide through the sea as it was for her to run down the street. She could spin and dance with the current, or push water aside and speed silently from one end of the harbor to the other in minutes.

Murdoch's small fishing sloop could navigate the incoming tide more easily than Trystan's large schooner, but not faster than she could. She knew nothing of naval battles, but she hoped to give the *Destiny* time to escape Murdoch. Trystan might relish warfare, but she preferred to frustrate warriors with peace, especially near her home.

If Trystan was the god of her mother's prophecy, then this was certainly a time of great danger, and Trystan's sword had wreaked justice by saving Nick and his guardians. She didn't want the danger to engulf the entire village—along with her sister and the baby.

The small, shy dolphins who swam beside her were more honor guard than soldiers, useless for warfare but convenient for underwater communication and safety. Whistling, Mariel directed the larger porpoises and the orphaned whale toward the keel of Murdoch's sloop from the Channel side, where he would not expect attack.

She meant only to interfere a little—until the whale abruptly whistled in alarm and dived downward, taking her small army with him.

Startled, Mariel glanced up to Murdoch's small boat.

Over her head, a hose shot streams of appallingly smelly liquid, which caught fire the instant it hit the water. And kept burning.

Fire, the one element she feared with all her heart and soul, burned a barrier between her and Trystan. A wall of flame licked across the water to the *Destiny*, carried on the tide toward her home, cutting her off from land.

"By Zeus and Hades!" Waylan cursed in horror as the small fishing boat approaching their bow spewed liquid fire, turning the sparkling water into an oily cloud of smoke and flame. Racing for the helm, he began shouting orders even before he reached the wheel.

"Greek fire," Nevan said in shock. "He's using the devil's weapon to stop us!"

Every sinew in Trystan's body froze as he watched the sloop draw near to spew another murderous wall of flame. Mariel had been swimming on that spot just moments ago. Mariel, his mermaiden, who lived for water and wasted away without it. She had every reason to fear fire.

The appalling spectacle raced toward them with the first shots. The wind and tide caught the flames and blew them faster and higher, spreading the danger past them, toward the shore. Every boat in Pouchay would go up in flames, and from there, the fire would spread to the tavern. Once it reached shingles and thatch, it would travel up the hill to devastate the village and everyone in it.

Including Mariel. Trystan searched the harbor for any sign of his wife. He'd seen the whale swimming for Murdoch and assumed Mariel was guiding it, as she had earlier. He saw no sign of either now. All he saw was a wall of flame racing across the water toward his ship.

Waylan shouted commands to the men in the rigging. Nevan grabbed the wheel.

Trusting his friends to the sails, Trystan touched his ring for reassurance, but he could not feel Mariel's presence as he had before. Panic closed his lungs.

Every child on Aelynn had been taught the lesson of the ancient fire. The world had thought the formula long lost, but it had been held secret on Aelynn for centuries, just as the Sword of Justice and Chalice of Plenty were kept hidden except on ceremonial occasions. In the case of the formula, it was because it was far too dangerous to be unleashed in the world again. Once, Turkish emperors had used Greek fire as a means of defense, but the weapon was so destructive the gods had decreed that the secret be lost for fear it would fall into offensive hands—like Murdoch's. How had he stolen the formula?

Watching the wall of flame, Trystan realized the tales hadn't explained just how dangerous fire on water could be. For all he knew, it might suffocate all life below it. And this nightmare had been unleashed by an *Aelynner*.

He had to save as many innocent people as possible. Shoving the screaming panic for Mariel inside his heart and locking it in, Trystan swallowed and debated the only two courses open to him.

He could have Waylan blow up the wind at an angle that would take the *Destiny* past the fire and out to sea, letting the fire travel on to the shore where it would undoubtedly consume the village and perhaps all life in the harbor. His men and passengers would be safe, and he would be obeying the laws of Aelynn by not interfering except in defense of his men, as was allowed.

The alternative was to order his crew to fight and protect the village, using their abilities as they'd been forbidden to do.

May the gods banish him, but he could not sail away. He must intervene, with no assurance of the outcome, and become as criminal as Murdoch.

As much as he would prefer to return to the rational Guardian he'd once been, Trystan could not. Fury with Murdoch, fear for his new family, and a screaming agony in his heart overruled logic. Stripped bare to the waist, his hair blowing in the wind, he gestured toward the fire. "Rain aloft," he cried in a command Waylan would grasp instantly.

He prayed his friends would be willing to risk banishment and obey.

Intent only on trapping the *Destiny*, apparently unaware—or uncaring—of the direction in which the waves carried the flames, Murdoch shot another fiery river across their bow. Sparks leaped to the deck and lines. Murdoch was counting on Trystan's not interfering and ordering the ship to surrender.

"All hands on deck. Cannon to the starboard, fire!" Trystan shouted as heavy clouds scudded into place overhead. Thank the gods!—Waylan had followed Trystan's command and worked the weather magic to call up the rain that always lingered over the Channel.

Functioning at the extraordinary speed for which they'd been trained, his crew pumped water and doused flames. Fire on board was deadly. He had to save his ship and crew first, so that he could save the village next.

He had no means of saving Mariel. The fuel would have to burn itself out. He did not want to imagine what the suffocating fumes were doing to the sea life below. The thought of his beautiful wife choking on oil and fumes would cripple him, so he quit thinking and simply acted.

While Waylan worked his magic on the skies, Trystan commanded the cannon fire, driving Murdoch's ship back before his mercenaries could tackle and board the *Destiny*. The other ship was so close, he could see the shock on the soldiers' faces as they gradually realized that flames were sweeping toward land instead of forming an orderly line of fire to ensnare their prey. If Murdoch had thought to control his dastardly weapon, he'd failed.

Once upon a time, before Dylys had suppressed his abilities, Murdoch could have commanded the flames, Trystan realized. It was highly possible that his former friend had planned for years to use this weapon, knowing his ability to direct the blaze. What had he intended to accomplish with the knowledge? A weapon of such destructive power unleashed in the defenseless Other World could level kingdoms.

Any remaining sympathy Trystan harbored for his childhood playmate died with the fire. He located

Waylan near the main mast, his potent gaze focused on the amassing storm.

"Lightning, Tempestium, strike the bastard down!" he shouted.

Waylan cast him a look that spoke aloud what went unsaid. Trystan was not only asking him to disobey Aelynn's commandments—displaying his terrible ability for all humankind—but he was also ordering the death of a man they'd both once called friend.

Trystan met Waylan's frank stare without flinching. Without another word, Waylan lifted his long-fingered hand to the sky and swirled it as if directing an orchestra. The darkening clouds overhead roiled and thickened with the energy gathering around the powerful man commanding it. Drops of rain formed a thick mist, and lightning flickered back and forth. With a bolt and roll of thunder in the distance, rain gushed from the clouds in a sudden burst.

Waylan had yet to call forth a gale, for fear the wind would only drive the flames faster. Beneath the downpour, the small sloop foundered, its sails fluttering haplessly while their enemy ordered the sheets redirected.

Trystan regretted any loss of life among soldiers who'd simply followed Murdoch's orders, but a man who would call down the wrath of gods and inflict it upon the innocent was not a man who could be left loose in the world. Trystan didn't have to look at Waylan or repeat his order of destruction. He could feel the electricity gathering in the air.

As the enemy crew aligned their sails to catch the tide and sail out of reach of fire and the *Destiny*'s cannon, Waylan pointed the fingers of his other hand at the tall man standing in the sloop's bow. Lightning shot from the sky and struck the deck.

With Waylan controlling Murdoch's fate, Trystan finally gave in to the urge to lift Nevan's glass and scan the water for any sign of Mariel. His breath caught in his lungs at the emptiness of the harbor. His ring still lay dead upon his finger. *Let it just be distance disconnecting us,* he prayed. But the shore was not so very distant.

Bucket brigades were forming down the village street, dousing sparks as they landed and fighting the fire in the tavern. The dock had been destroyed by the flames, but the rocky beach and high cliffs acted as a barrier against the worst of the destruction. With the rain beating steadily upon the water, the leaping flames were dying back to smoldering embers among breakers and whitecaps. Each wave toward shore carried less of the fuel. Pockets of fire formed in the shallows at the cliff base, destroying Mariel's wedding dress and the rest of their abandoned clothing.

And still there was no sign of Mariel.

Trystan willed her to climb out upon the rocks and rush up the hill to aid her friends, but only an oily smoke washed across the water.

"They're escaping." His face and hands blackened by the extinguished fire, Kiernan came to stand shoulder to shoulder with Trystan. A frown creased his forehead as he watched the other ship limp away between bolts of lightning. "Shall I direct Nevan to follow?"

Like a hound, Kiernan would follow Murdoch into hell if he were so ordered.

Watching the crippled sloop drift toward an outcropping of rocks in the distance, Trystan shook his head. He would not risk the island's only Finder in his desire for revenge.

As they watched, another lightning bolt struck the

mainmast of the fleeing sloop. It was a sign of Waylan's fury that he could direct the energy so precisely.

"We've interfered enough," Trystan said with a sigh. "We'll wait for the Oracle's orders to go after him." After the uncanny battle that had been fought here today, the villagers would have far too many questions than his ring would allow him to answer. Even if the tide permitted, they must not return to shore. Better to let time blur memories and hope that people had been too busy saving themselves to notice anything peculiar.

The wind picked up, blowing the last flames away from land—filling the *Destiny*'s sails and driving her out of the harbor, into the Channel. Away from Mariel.

Every fiber of his being urged Trystan to leap in the water and look for his wife, to swim closer, to find the bond that distance had severed. Distance, or death.

What little logic Trystan still retained told him he couldn't search the entire sea for her body. If she was alive, she would surface. His heart cracked and bled as he searched for any sign of her while the ship picked up speed. Understanding what he sought, Kiernan gazed steadily into the current, also watching. And with his job done, Waylan soon joined them, squeezing Trystan's shoulder for lack of words.

Nick emerged from the cabin below where the passengers had been ordered to stay. Trystan had promised to take them to England. He owed Mariel that.

He turned back to watch the smoking oil-filled harbor, decimated dock, and the tiny figures that were Mariel's friends and family.

Heavy tears wet his cheeks as his gaze scoured the cliffs where he'd first seen his wife flying down that rocky path to berate him.

He'd give all the world and all its treasures to see her there now, flinging curses.

Finally, he understood that the bond between them was the power that Others called love. For the first time he knew what it meant to long for a single voice, a particular wave, a familiar smile. His heart sinking, he feared he would never share such a powerful force again.

Trystan wrapped his hands around the rail to keep his knees from buckling, and bowed his head against the burden of grief.

The Other World contained fascinating challenges he'd only glimpsed, but he'd lost the one who could have steered him through its treacherous waters with her love and wisdom.

With the cessation of cannon fire and no further need of shouted commands, the ship fell silent. The flapping of canvas overhead played a mournful dirge in his ears as the schooner slipped into the Channel.

The world would be an empty, hollow place without Mariel's siren song to fill it.

Rain pattered on deck, but Trystan didn't notice it running off his bare shoulders. Not a single fish leaped or gull flew over the barren waters.

A sob formed so deep in Trystan's chest that he nearly suffocated.

Waylan clung to the rail and uttered curses. Kiernan awkwardly patted Trystan's back. Running up from the companionway, Nick wedged himself between the men, although he studied the Channel's choppy waves ahead rather than the disappearing horizon.

"Aren't we waiting for Madame Mariel?" he asked.

Trystan's eyes were too blurred with tears to look down at the boy. He couldn't even see land any longer. He felt the waiting depths pressing down on him, breathed salt into his lungs as she must have done. She must have gone down too deep for him to sense her, and still, the fire had consumed her.

Waylan caught Nick's shoulder and tried to turn the boy away. "She'll swim home," he lied in a voice thick with tears.

Nick fought off his big hand and pointed. "I think she's coming this way. Is that a porpoise she's riding? How is that possible? Do you think she'd teach me?"

Waylan swung around to follow Nick's direction, then shouted for the sails to be lowered. Kiernan hooted in disbelief.

Trystan rubbed his eyes and stared at the gray swells through the mist of rain.

In the distance, the sleek backs of a school of dolphins arched and dived through the breakers, their tails flinging spray on their downward plunges. At the head of the pack a larger porpoise swam more steadily. Upon his shiny back, a small figure waved.

Mariel.

Without a second thought, Trystan climbed the rail and dived in after her.

Thirty-four

The porpoise flicked his tail and swam off when Mariel fell into her husband's arms, and they sank beneath the waves, clinging to each other.

He was swimming with her.

She closed her eyes and praised the heavens as Trystan's muscled arms held her safely, and they bobbed below the surface, lips meeting in relief and love. She knew what he had done, for her. But right now, all she could absorb was that he wanted her enough to come for her, even after she'd revealed her uncanny abilities to the world, effectively banishing both of them from the homes they loved.

But as much as she might crave it, they couldn't live in the sea forever. With Trystan's arms around her, her head against his shoulder, they eventually bobbed to the surface. Mariel didn't wish to ever let go, but it could be a trifle difficult scrambling up the side of the ship while wrapped in each other's arms.

"I love you," she murmured in his language and hers. "I worship and adore you."

Trystan's grip tightened and his chest heaved, but no words emerged. He leaned his bronzed cheek against her head, and she understood. Her multilingual husband had lost all the words available to him and was mute from the terror they'd just experienced.

She had no desire to relive those petrifying minutes

under the sea with the fire raging overhead while her husband fought for life and death. She'd done all she could to direct her ocean-faring companions out of the harbor and away from the smothering oil. But she had been helpless to save her home. Trystan had done that for her, just as her mother had predicted.

To the triumphant shouts and cheers of the sailors above them, she clung to Trystan's shoulders and kissed him until they nearly drowned within sight of the ship. Then, once she had him weak and willing, she shoved at his great shoulders, grabbed for the rope ladder, and raced up, with him hot on her heels.

Nick and his family and Trystan's crew were throwing the fish intended for their supper at her merry band of dolphins. Her cheerful friends leaped and cavorted, catching their meal in the air, diving headfirst into the water, and flapping their tails to send sprays of water up the side of the ship in their idea of celebration, to the delight of all those watching.

Aware that she wore next to nothing, that she'd just revealed her deepest secret to Celeste and the chevalier, who had watched it all, Mariel felt exposed in so many ways, she preferred not to think. She gratefully plunged her arms into Waylan's enormous damp coat. Wrapping it around her, she sought Trystan's embrace after he clambered on board. She refused to lift her head from his shoulder once he cradled her against his chest.

Near death made all other concerns irrelevant.

They remained speechless too long for Nick's impatient eagerness.

"Can you ride whales, too?" he demanded. "Why don't you drown?"

There was the problem in a nutshell. After all these years of concealing her secret, she had now revealed the freak she was.

And she was relieved.

"Mariel can swim like a fish," Waylan growled, but Nick wasn't so easily satisfied. He waited expectantly.

Lifting her head to Trystan, Mariel smiled. "We'll have to cast him overboard."

He chuckled deep in his throat. "I'm in enough trouble already without drowning a chatterbox."

"You interfered," she said sadly, her smile disappearing.

"By letting Murdoch and his dangerous knowledge loose upon the world, Aelynn has interfered. I could do no less."

"I am eternally grateful that you saved my home. But what happens now?"

Nick looked from one to the other in puzzlement. The tall Aelynn men backed away to give them privacy.

Trystan tugged Mariel's hair free of the coat and smoothed it over her shoulders. "I am not a Seer. I can take only one day at a time. For now, we sail the de Berriers to England."

The baroness rushed up to hug them. "The two of you were marvelous. We'll never forget what you have done."

The chevalier stepped forward, hat in hand, and bowed formally. "I do not think I wish to have the events of this day explained to me. I am merely grateful that we came away with our lives. With bankruptcy looming, I foresee the need for others to move their investments out of France, and I will be in a position to help them, thanks to you. Our home will be yours."

"Do you think we can buy a christening gift for Marie-Jeanne in England?" Mariel asked.

Reminded of the twins that Mariel carried, Trystan pushed her toward the cabin. "We will buy everything her heart desires. For now, I need to lie down and return my heart to beating. I think I am paralyzed."

His crew laughed knowingly and parted to their separate tasks. The chevalier and the baroness steered their ward to the bridge to watch the dolphins.

And Mariel clambered below to celebrate the wedding night she hadn't expected to have, with the husband who accepted her as she was, who had forfeited his world for hers.

"I love you so much, I think I may burst of it," she told him quietly as he led her inside his cabin. "I don't know what lies ahead, but tell me we never must part again. I thought I would expire of regret the moment I saw you sailing away."

Trystan grabbed fists full of her hair and drew her toward him. "I hope you will never know what I felt when you did not appear after that fire. I think I'll wring your neck for scaring me like that."

Instead, he covered her face with kisses, captured her mouth with his, and drank the breath from her lungs.

Fortunately for both of them, she didn't need much air to breathe.

Which meant he had to come up for breath first. Laughing, they fell into the bed, stripping off their soaked clothing as they did so.

Kneeling over her, Trystan ran kisses across every inch of her exposed skin. "I love you, mermaiden," he declared while she gasped in pleasure. "It is not a word I comprehended until today. Love is not about possession. This is not a manacle that binds us unwillingly. It is a force within our hearts that holds us together, *mi amacara.*"

"You are quite possibly right, husband." Mariel reached up to tug Trystan's head to her mouth, where she could brand him with her kisses. When he gasped for air again, she concluded, "We must dedicate the rest of our time to testing your theory."

Placing his big hand over the place where their children grew, he looked solemn for a moment. "I have learned my lesson. I cannot bear to be parted from you again. If you will not stay in the safety of my home, then I must go with you. Your world is too dangerous without my protection. Are you prepared to return and rebuild your village, to live there as we are?"

With people thinking them freaks, talking of witches and magic, making the sign of the evil eye against them? As opposed to his home, where all was peace and calm?

Mariel finally understood the Oracle's ambiguous prediction. Looking him in the eye, she tried to convey what she understood in her heart. "I am prepared to live where I am needed," she said quietly. And she meant it.

"I love you even more for that," he agreed, nuzzling her ear. "It is time we recognized that what affects the Outside will ultimately affect Aelynn. I am needed more off Aelynn's shores than within them. If Murdoch lives, we must guard against him and his kind."

Thinking of the devastating weapon the banished Aelynner had unleashed, Mariel shuddered. "Your peaceful world is lovely," she said in regret. "I hate that you might have to give it up. I see now why your people have been forbidden to interfere."

"But we've done it and must live with the consequences. Our peace is derived from selfishness. Dylys will have my head for saying so, so let us not impart our discovery to her. For now, I much prefer the role of besotted newlywed."

With that, he turned his attention to a more important subject, pleasuring his wife.

Epilogue

Dylys stood before the Council and raised her arms for silence. The island leaders, both male and female, grew quiet. She bowed her head in brief prayer, and her humble silver braid fell forward before she flung it back again and gazed defiantly upon the audience.

"I have prayed for guidance before coming to you today. In the waters, I have seen fire and war, but I cannot see beyond them. Perhaps the gods are telling me it is time that I step down and let my children rule."

The audience burst into shocked argument until Iason and Lissandra stepped up to the podium with her.

Dylys spoke again. "I know my offspring have not chosen their mates to replace the leader we lost in my husband. I have ordered them both to search outside as well as within our boundaries for their equals. It is a dreadful burden I place upon them, and I regret that I must be the one to bestow it, but the day has arrived when we must acknowledge the world beyond ours. I will leave it to the Council to decide how this must be done, but I request this final act of you before I step down." She nodded at the couple waiting to one side.

Clinging to Trystan's hand, Mariel stepped up with him. They wore matching blue, hers a sari, his a tunic that clung to his shoulders and enhanced his authority in the heavy embroidery and wide belt indicating his position. She still thrilled when she looked at him, even though they'd spent every moment of these last weeks together.

She knew he had wielded his significant powers of persuasion and authority to bring them to this moment. She did not know what had been decided. She did not yet know his world well enough to understand their laws. They still had much to learn of each other's homes.

Standing beside her, Trystan waited for Dylys to continue.

"I cannot ask you to forgive me for unleashing Murdoch LeDroit upon an innocent world, and for my inability to fully suppress his powers," Dylys announced. "But I ask that you forgive Mariel and Trystan l'Enforcer for attempting to right my wrong, and acknowledge their marriage here this day, as they take their rightful seats upon the Council."

Mariel inhaled sharply at the Oracle's request. Trystan's hand tightened on hers, but his stoic expression gave no other indication of his surprise.

Murmurs whipped through the room as all eyes turned to them, but Dylys was not yet ready to cede her position. "The Council must decide how to proceed in an uncertain future, but Trystan has made us all aware that to continue isolating ourselves from the affairs of the Other World in a time of increased travel and naval warfare will only speed our demise."

More gasps. Flares of outrage. Mariel cringed, but she could feel Trystan's confidence. He knew these people as she did not. She took courage from him.

"Since he is our Guardian and shield, I ask that we channel more of Aelynn's strength to give him the power to protect us while he is far distant in his wife's world."

"But that will reduce the power that others command," someone in the audience shouted.

Dylys bowed her head in acceptance. "We are safe here, but those of us who venture afar are not. As we send our young men into the Other World to seek what we do not possess, we must ensure their safety. The Finder will search for other Crossbreeds who can speak with the creatures beneath the sea. They can be l'Enforcer's messengers, sending warnings through his wife against dangers we may not foresee."

Mariel glanced up at Trystan in surprise. His mouth bent slightly upward, but still, he did not look at her. He'd known what Dylys intended to ask of her. How had he thought of that?

Iason spoke into the stunned silence. "If the Finder is to go into the Outside World to seek more mermaidens, he must also seek mates for Lissandra and me. This means we may have more Crossbreeds on our island, people like us who have homes and families they must leave behind. We cannot ask them to help us while we offer nothing in return."

Shocked silence fell across the chamber as all Aelynn considered the future.

Lissandra's clear, high voice rose over the first murmurs. "We cannot change all the laws that protect us, but we can change the one that prevents us from correcting our mistakes, the one that says we cannot use our strengths to interfere outside this island. Let us right our wrongs, the ones we've created in the past and those we might create in the future. And in so doing, let us welcome Trystan and Mariel to our Council as a wedded couple, allow them to move freely from shore to shore, and bless their children as true Aelynners."

A cheer started in the back of the room where Trystan's bachelor friends stood tall and stalwart in his favor. Applause broke out in front of them where others of their age sat in the lower seats of the Council. Gradually, the wave of approval spread from the back to the foremost seats of the elders. As one, the audience rose to its feet and clapped its agreement.

Mariel nearly fainted in awe and shock—and from the sudden movement of the infants in her womb. Trystan caught her, grasping her waist to keep her from falling. Concern lined his bronzed face as she clung to him.

"Are you ill? Do you need to sit down?" he asked.

As the applause continued, Mariel bestowed a smile of joy upon her husband. "I think your children are expressing their approval."

"Let us not hinder their festivity." In front of family and friends, the normally stoic Guardian grinned hugely and kissed his bride. And did not complain in the least when Mariel threw her arms around his neck and returned his affection with great enthusiasm for all to see.

Later, standing beside the steaming waters of the grotto with only his mother and sister to observe, Iason opened the velvet bag Trystan had returned weeks earlier. "Perhaps now is the time to show you this?" he asked, revealing the glittering silver chalice.

Lissandra and the Oracle lifted the vessel from the pouch and studied it in horror.

"This is not the sacred vessel," Dylys exclaimed.

"I know." He shrugged a brown shoulder. "But would you tell our newlyweds that? The honorable Trystan would immediately head to Versailles to confront Murdoch. And you've seen for yourself that he is needed to guard the coast."

Dylys seemed to shrink inside herself and gazed bleakly into the pool. "I have lost the chalice, half the purpose of our existence. I pray the gods punish me and not the island for my failure. The two of you are our future now. You must find mates, and soon, then locate the chalice and return it."

"Perhaps it is time we all explored what lies beyond these shores," Iason agreed.

"One at a time," Lissandra said, surprising him. "One of us must remain safe behind while the other explores. I foresee too much violence in the time ahead."

"You are both adults, well able to make your own decisions. Do as you see fit." Dylys bowed her graying head. "I had once hoped Trystan's strength and sense would lead us into the next century."

"He and I are like brother and sister, Mother," Lissandra objected. "In our own ways, we would both be dictators. It would never have worked. But I agree, now that he has learned to listen to his heart and to work with others, he is a true leader."

Iason glanced at his sister with respect and nodded his approval. "Mariel has only just learned to embrace her talents and accept that her differences are strengths rather than handicaps. She will grow wiser with time."

Lissandra added reassuringly, "The Finder has never failed. He will find the chalice."

"I daresay it will take a wealth of pearls to pry it loose from the king, if that is where it has gone," Dylys responded with a sigh. "With Murdoch still out there, you had best send a fighting man who carries a stronger sword than Kiernan's pen and paper."

Accepting his new responsibility, Iason considered his choices. "Nevan will go with the Finder," he decided. "He can charm a bird from a tree, and strike a crow from the sky."

Dylys harrumphed. "That works if the court is a

flock of birds. Let us hope the chalice has chosen a different path."

"It found Mariel and made twins," he replied. "Perhaps the plenty it promises is more children with great abilities."

"That should give our Guardian a task worthy of his strength," Dylys agreed. "It is a good thing we sent one of us to act as priest in the Other World. If we continue on this path, we will have to send more to guard our children, so they need not hide their secrets."

Watching the rippling images of the future in the water, Iason envied the newlyweds their happiness. Aelynn had blessed the lovers. Despite the black clouds gathering on the horizon, they would live in sunshine, and provide the aid both their kinds would need during the upheaval ahead.

He wished he could see the same for himself.

Author's Note

This is—obviously—a work of fiction. The island of Aelynn, the village of Pouchay, and the characters are all figments of my imagination.

But I have set them against a very real historical background. The era leading up to England's Regency and Napoleon's reign was an exciting, demanding time, a period of great scientific discovery as well as a period of class warfare and revolution. I have used real incidents, settings, and actual quotes from people of that era to reflect the atmosphere. The Castle de Rohan in Pontivy exists, but since most of its improvements were made in Napoleon's time, I have taken liberties with my version, and the events there all belong to my imaginary characters.

With regard to language, it is always difficult to choose between historical accuracy and ease of understanding for the contemporary reader. In this case, since the two languages my characters speak are Breton, which almost no one speaks today, and the language of Aelynn, which I completely made up, I have taken creative license to translate my imaginary dialogue into modern English.

Don't miss Patricia Rice's next exciting romance in the Mystic Isle series,

Mystic Rider

Available from Signet Eclipse in summer 2008.

Also from *New York Times* Bestselling Author

PATRICIA RICE

MAGIC MAN

The finale to the Magic series—

A man of mysterious allure to others, Aidan Dougal is, in fact, isolated in every way—alienated from a family he can never call his own and convinced he brings literal destruction wherever he goes. For such a man, intimacy is impossible and marriage out of the question. Even asking for help is beyond him...until a wily enemy forces him to accept assistance from a gentle young woman whose delicate beauty and strange enchantments turn his cool composure into red-hot passion.

"Rice has a magical touch for creating fascinating plots, delicious romance, and delightful characters." —*Booklist*

Available wherever books are sold or at penguin.com